SHORELINE

ALSO BY CAROLYN BAUGH

Quicksand

The View from Garden City

SHORELINE

A NORA KHALIL NOVEL

CAROLYN BAUGH

A TOM DOHERTY ASSOCIATES BOOK | NEW YORK

SHORELINE

A Forge Book
Published by Tom Doherty Associates
175 Fifth Avenue
New York, NY 10010

www.tor-forge.com

Forge® is a registered trademark of Macmillan Publishing Group, LLC.

The Library of Congress Cataloging-in-Publication Data is available upon request.

ISBN 978-0-7653-7984-9 (hardcover)
ISBN 978-1-4668-7051-2 (ebook)

Our books may be purchased in bulk for promotional, educational, or business use. Please contact your local bookseller or the Macmillan Corporate and Premium Sales Department at 1-800-221-7945, extension 5442, or by email at MacmillanSpecialMarkets@macmillan.com.

First Edition: July 2017

Printed in the United States of America

0 9 8 7 6 5 4 3 2 1

For Layla

PROLOGUE

Nora brushed a few sweat-soaked strands of hair from her eyes in order to better regard her father. In each of Ragab Khalil's hands he clutched the neck of an industrial-sized trash bag containing all of the least-frayed towels, Nora's polka-dotted comforter, three heavy blankets, and six feather pillows. Baba's shirt was dark with perspiration, and the walk down the steep stairs from the family apartment over their restaurant had left him winded. Meeting Nora's eyes, he lifted the bags in a small gesture, and looked with flared nostrils from her to the back end of Ben's SUV. Nora gave a small nod. Frowning fiercely, Baba plopped the bags next to a heavily taped cardboard box.

He was getting better at all this, Nora decided. In the past year she had moved from their apartment to a tiny flat of her own in Chinatown and from there to her twenty weeks of training at Quantico. During her first move, he had confined himself in the restaurant's kitchen, pretending to be immersed in work, and banging pots and pans with such intensity that the din resounded out onto Arch Street. He had not met her eyes for nearly a month after that. When she had announced the second move, which meant her first stint away from Philadelphia, he had sworn most foully in Arabic and gone off to pace at the playground behind the restaurant, muttering darkly.

This time he was making eye contact, talking to her, and ignoring Ben with as little open hostility as possible. When not schlepping what she'd assigned him, he would try to thrust on her as many pots, pans, and ladles on her as the restaurant could spare.

"You might need it, just take it," he said.

"I never cook, *ya Baba*," she said. "You know this." She was fighting to be as patient as possible, but the summer heat was bearing down on them. It was hard to breathe, and her shirt was soaked with sweat. Also, Ben was double-parked on Arch Street, provoking conniption fits from the driving public.

Baba was insistent. "Maybe you will throw some big FBI party and need to make *fetta*."

Nora pulled the ladle and stock pot out of the back of the Rogue. She pressed them gently into her father's hands. "I couldn't make *fetta* if I wanted to. Keep your kitchen. I will come visit and you can make me *fetta*."

"What are you going to eat there?" he demanded.

"Same thing I ate at Quantico, Baba. Big juicy ham and bacon sandwiches."

Her father's face convulsed in disgust.

"That would be even worse than dating *him*," he said, nodding toward Ben.

"I know," Nora stage-whispered. "That's why I said it. See? It's not so bad. I still haven't gone over to eating pig."

"So there's hope," her brother Ahmad declared cheerfully, joining them and gingerly setting a pile of CDs on the floor of the front passenger seat.

Ben peered at the stack. "What's this?"

"Old CDs of my mom's," Ahmad answered. "Symbol of *her* rebellion against my grandfather—who wouldn't let her listen to music."

Nora looked at her brother, refusing to get weepy. "You would never let me touch those before," she said gruffly.

"Yeah, well, you'll need something to keep you from freakin' out in that little town."

"Don't hate on little towns," Nora said. "I've rented a bigger apartment than you've ever been in for half what we pay here."

"I don't understand why anyone would name a town Erie," said Ahmad. "It sounds like something out of Scooby Doo."

"Believe me, I have no idea," Nora answered.

Her father, still clutching his stock pot, said, "But why did you have to pick *that* town, Nora? Who would pick a town with a name like *that*?"

She shrugged. "I told you, Baba. It was Lincoln, Nebraska, Birmingham, Alabama, or Erie, Pennsylvania. It was the closest I could get to home."

"Well, I don't see how it's close at all. It's the furthest part of the state that you can go and still be in the state. Who can get there if you need them?" His eyes flicked over Ben, then he said sourly, "Not even him."

"He has a name, Baba. It's Ben. And Ben will come visit, and you and Ahmad will come visit, and it's no big deal. People move all the time."

"Not my people," Ragab grumped.

"Besides, I'm a big bad FBI agent now," she said with a grin. "I don't need anybody at all."

Her father wiped at the sheen of sweat on his forehead and gave her a baleful look.

"It's true, sir," Ben added, trying to be helpful. "She got first in her class in mixed martial arts."

Ragab's lip curled ever so slightly as he staunchly refused to look at Ben.

Nora rolled her eyes. "Give me a kiss. I'm going. Don't pout."

He dutifully gave her a kiss on each cheek, then patted her hair. "Call me every day."

"I will call you. Not every day."

"Call *me* every day," said Ahmad, pulling her into a hard hug.

"Maybe," conceded Nora.

She draped her long arms around both of them, breathing them in, then reluctantly released them. All three smiled at each other's wet eyes. Nora slid quickly into the SUV as Ben waved goodbye. He'd long ago given up hoping Ragab would shake his hand.

Ragab and Ahmad stood rooted to the sidewalk, still waving at the retreating Nissan. Nora stayed turned around in her seat, watching and waving until Ben turned right onto 22nd and started heading toward the Ben Franklin Parkway and the Schuylkill Expressway beyond.

He glanced over at her. "You okay?"

She nodded in silence.

He lay a hand on her knee. "Not convinced."

She shrugged. "I'm good, Ben. Those two are going to have a hard time, though."

"They aren't your job, Nora."

"We're all each other's jobs," she answered softly, her gaze falling on the parade of flags adorning the Parkway. They passed in front of the Art Museum and began traveling up Kelly Drive; he always took this way when he could, she'd noticed. The river snaked along beside them while craggy cliffsides stretched skyward. She'd run along the river thousands of times, but she still watched it as though seeing it for the first time. The pathways were dense with runners and dog walkers; several rowing shells were slicing through the still water. Nora squeezed Ben's hand, then started sorting through her mother's CDs. There was a lot of Amr Diab, some Warda and Isala, a few Kazim al-Sahir albums, and the ubiquitous Umm Kulthoum. She glanced at Ben, trying to assess what he'd be able to tolerate, and decided on some Amr Diab.

It wasn't the first time she and Ben had had a road trip together. He'd driven her to Quantico and picked her up at graduation, although Ahmad had been with him that time. As they logged more and more miles away from the city, Ben's tension seemed to increase.

Finally he switched off the music.

"Look," he said, clutching her hand. "I'm just saying that if you ask to transition into anti-terror you will end up with a job in a real city."

"Erie's a real city. They have a mayor and everything," Nora said.

"Nora, look—"

"Benjamin, I get it. But I have never wanted that."

"But you want to be with me, right?" he insisted.

"Of course I do. But we both know why anti-terror isn't for me."

"Because Eric Burton once thought you were sketchy?"

"Because on some level I've been coping with terrorists who happen to look like me since I was a kid. I don't want it to shape my whole life that way. I gotta figure out who I am outside of that box."

He looked over at her, frowning.

"How about 'the country needs you' argument?"

Nora burst out laughing. "You are so self-serving. You just tried to work the 'Ben Calder needs you' angle. When that fails, you go after my patriotism?"

"Well, maybe you need to think about it that way."

"You yourself said they recruit people like me every day. So maybe they're in good shape."

"I think you're being short-sighted."

"I think you're being pulled over." She pointed at the flashing lights of the State Trooper as Ben swore.

The first few weeks in Erie, Pennsylvania, were a swift and unrelenting blur of meeting new people and learning to live in a quiet apartment in a quiet city.

She found a routine, though. It was, she realized, one she hadn't necessarily anticipated.

One issue for which she was thoroughly unprepared was having a neighbor.

The floor overhead groaned as Nora frowned into the dimness.

"You *cannot* be serious," she said aloud, as the music began filtering down into the stillness of her ground-floor bedroom.

On some level, she preferred the music to the pacing, but both kept her from sleeping. She glanced at the clock, only to confirm that it was just past one in the morning, which was, in Nora's mind, the wrong time to be playing the violin.

She would not have played the violin at that time.

She would not have paced around on hundred-year-old hardwood floors at that time.

But she was, apparently, the only rational tenant of the two who occupied the old brown-brick house on French Street.

Her landlord had not shown her the apartment at one in the morning, however, so she'd had no idea that her upstairs neighbor could be so malevolent. Since taking up residence in June, Nora had prepared in her head three or four polite speeches and several carefully-constructed patient pleas for respectable hours. Somehow these would crumble on her tongue each time she saw the slight woman with the pale blonde hair. Her neighbor would nod at her and pull her thin lips into a thinner smile. Nora would always end up feeling regretful of her irritation toward this wispy woman whose name she did not know.

Now she lay in her bed, a box fan aimed strategically at her, feeling powerless against her tiny violinist neighbor. The crusty, peeling windows of the brown brick house seemed to usher in the July heat (something else the landlord hadn't mentioned), and so Nora had invested in a fan to help the one window air-conditioner in its labors.

She finally turned on her side and, taking her BlackBerry off of the bedside table, texted Ben.

He called her immediately.

"Hey," he said.

"Hey," she replied, grateful for his voice.

"How's Erie?"

Nora paused, wondering how much to bombard him with at this time of night. *I hate it*, she responded in her head. *I hate it so much. I run. I work. I work out. I sleep. I wake up. I do it all again.* It was late, though. She didn't want to waste their conversation complaining. At last she settled on the word: "Boring."

"How's the neighbor lady?" he asked intuitively.

She couldn't resist spouting out, "*Killing* me. I don't get the walking as she plays. There's no reason to walk, is there? Can't you just stand still and play the violin?"

"I have no idea, Nora. But you need to talk to her. Or complain to the landlord."

Nora sighed. "If I complain to the landlord, she'll know it's me. And the few times I've seen her it just hasn't felt right. I feel like I could squash her. So I'd feel like a jerk for having that be the first thing I ever say to her."

"So ask her out for coffee, get to know her, and then talk to her about it," Ben answered sensibly.

Nora smiled in the darkness. "You and your coffee."

"Did you get any ticks yet?" he asked.

She shook her head into the darkness. "Not yet. But that thing about deer ticks I sent you . . . that wasn't even the half of it—83 percent of the countryside is apparently insane because of Lyme disease."

"What's your source for that figure, Special Agent Khalil?"

"The server at the Eat-n-Park."

"Well, she would know," Ben confirmed. "How's the world of child pornography?"

She sighed. "Scary. Ugly. Sad."

"Your team?"

"Good. Fine. Whatever. Boring."

Nora was silent, thinking, then said, "I haven't figured Pete out yet; he comes off as some sort of hard-drinking frat boy, with this crazy Southern drawl. Which totally makes him sound ignorant, right? But he's very sharp, very intense, about computers. Every time I say I don't understand something he says, all nerdy, *Well did you try to understand?* Anna . . . I don't know. She makes me nervous."

Ben laughed. "What? Why?"

"She's so intense, so, like, relentlessly capable . . ."

"Kinda like you?"

Nora made a "psh" sound. "I am waaay more subtle. Anyway, they aren't as fun to hang out with as you."

"Did you go out drinking with them yet?"

Nora groaned. "Oh my God, this is the drinkingest town I ever saw."

"You haven't seen many towns," Ben reminded her. "But of course it is. What else are they going to do there? Anyway, this whole violinist thing is your fault. If you were out at the bar you wouldn't notice. You don't have to *drink*. Have a coke. It's called *group bonding*."

She considered this, then said again: "They're really boring, Ben."

"Is that your way of saying you miss me?"

She shook her head, listening for a moment as the melody upstairs crescendoed and then eased into softness. "You know I do," she answered.

"Good. Now go to sleep. You have to be at work in seven hours. I'll come see you on Labor Day?" he was asking.

"Yes. Ahmad will be here. But come."

Ben was silent. "When is he coming?"

Nora noted the change in his tone and said slowly, "It will be his first long weekend after classes start, and he knew I'd want to hear all about it. . . ."

"So the whole time I'd be there. When will we get time alone?"

Nora sat up in bed and clutched her knees. "Ben, I don't know. But it's hard on him not having me around, you know this. It was just us for so long. He's so excited about coming. . . ."

There was a long pause. "Okay, Nora. I guess I'll talk to you soon, then. Get some rest."

His voice was both cold and hurt.

Nora held the phone against her ear, trying hard to think of something to say. "I—okay, Ben. You, too. Call me soon."

She replaced the BlackBerry and lay back down feeling so much worse than before they'd spoken. The violinist overhead seemed to sense this and began a slow, soulful tune that eventually lulled Nora into a dreamless sleep.

Nora liked to get to work first, to take a little time to get her bearings in a still-quiet office before Pete and Anna arrived. Typically, Maggie was the only one there when she arrived, but although Nora felt sure that she heard and noticed everything that went on around her, Maggie rarely spoke unless directly spoken to. Nora hadn't actually received more than a few curt nods and a grunt from her, and Anna had warned her from day one that it was best to steer clear.

The woman is madly efficient and a good egg, Anna said, *but if you talk too much at her she'll unleash hell on you.*

Nora had never heard anyone called "a good egg" before, so the two of them dwelt on this point for rather longer than Anna seemed to think necessary. Her next statement was, *Seriously, though. We can't function without her. So don't piss her off.*

As all this had occurred in the context of an office tour, Anna then showed her the room where useful machines went to die. *Every now and then we have to use a VCR to see a random videotape of something. That machine is in here. Some stats machines. Old fingerprinters with actual ink pads. Peter calls it the Room of Requirement. That nasty vinyl loveseat in the corner is where he sneaks off to for naps. When you can't find Peter, he's here. Just so you know.*

Nora now glanced periodically at the television hung on the wall just outside her workspace. It was usually muted, but Nora found it bizarre to have a TV on and going all the time. She felt as though they were trolling for work by waiting to pounce on something the networks dug up for them. A gaggle of older women Nora couldn't name were hotly debating something, and Nora felt like it was far too early for that much animated discussion with anyone. She tried to reposition herself so that her back was to the screen.

As she did this, Pete entered their large, shared cubicle and plopped into his desk chair. He brought with him the smell of sweat mixed with far too much aftershave. He also clutched a towering cup of Starbucks coffee.

"Miss Nora, how are you?" he drawled.

"Peter. Good morning. Isn't it a little warm outside for all that hot coffee?"

"There is a lovely young barista who I cannot disappoint," he responded lightly.

Anna issued a small, derisive snort as she walked in with some of the office Folgers in a public radio mug. "Thank God Pete's around to keep corporate America up and running."

"And the staff turnover high, I'd imagine," Nora added. Anna laughed out loud as Pete waved his hand at them both.

"What you cannot imagine is how happy she is to see me every morning," he insisted.

Sheila Biggs entered frowning. "I'm not happy to see you at all, though. I'd rather have everything in place for busting this guy and have you out bringing him in. Instead I'm not sensing any progress on any front with this thing." Each of the three gave full attention to the Supervisory Senior Resident Agent. "The Crime Victims Center just emailed me that there is more evidence of abuse, and the director is convinced that the porn in question is coming from our alleged perp in McKean."

"Do you think the ones who are old enough will testify?" Nora asked.

Anna said darkly, "I don't think any of them are old enough."

Nora's stomach twisted.

Sheila Biggs's tone was unpleasant. "Pete, even with the limited warrant you have you should be able to identify the IP addresses for the sites he's using. Nora, you still need to be cross-checking missing persons with the faces on the material we have so far. I want proof—fast—people. You've had plenty of time."

Anna, Nora, and Pete exchanged glances as she stalked out.

"Aren't the images testimony enough?" Nora asked. "Can't we make the arrest without the sources?"

Anna shrugged. "Sometimes. Not always. But the issue is that Burgess has disseminated porn before. There's more to the story this time. We want to figure out where he's getting it and get to *those* guys. And find the little girls they're using."

"Ugh, but Sheila just has no idea what I'm up against here," Pete muttered.

Nora looked a question at him.

"Frank Burgess is fat and perverted. But he also knows how to use the Internet. He's gone Dark Web on this thing, I'm sure of it. I'm going to need his computer."

"You want me to send for another warrant?" Anna asked.

"Yeah, it's going to have to be key to this thing. We might as well bust in and say we're after the computer—this stuff is coming from a dynamic IP address that's jumped all over. It could be in Erie. Or it could be in Thailand. But Burgess is just the small fish."

"Less likely it's in Thailand," Nora pointed out. "The girls are almost all Caucasian."

"I know," Pete replied. "But the point stands. We don't know where until we can go deeper. I'm trying now with what I have, but we need to just go over there and get the computer."

Anna pulled her reading glasses out of her hair and perched them on her nose as she wrote. "Internet Service Provider records are insufficient to fully establish browsing history . . ." she was mumbling to herself as she filled in the lines of the document. She quickly stood and crossed the length of the office to ask Maggie to submit the paperwork via email to the Assistant United States Attorney's office.

Nora followed her with her eyes, trying again not to weigh-and-find-wanting this tiny outpost on the seventh floor of one of Erie's few high-rises. She was a world away from the FBI's massive Philadelphia Field Office. Nora was one of three Special Agents here. In Philly, a senior Special Agent like Anna would have her own office and secretary. In Philly they would have handed such technical tasks as tracking down the mind-numbing IP addresses to the IT team; here the IT team *was* Pete.

Anna was fighting her weight and a relentless, thin line of gray that poked up from under the coating of red she gave her hair. She was a master at harmonizing the efforts of state and local authorities. Arresting Frank Burgess, when the time came, would be a group effort. Unlike in Philly, where Nora had worked as part of a team she saw day in and day out, the work in Erie was fluid. Two weeks into her post, Nora was realizing that the team members rotated in and out, sometimes including the police department and state police, sometimes including the Border Patrol. The territory was vast. Their office was responsible for seven counties, most of which were rural.

Erie was the urban center. Erie was where families trekked over an hour to visit the mall and eat at the Olive Garden, and where small-town kids who'd never before seen black people came to go to college. As Nora gazed out the long window beyond her desk, she watched a group of six motorcyclists making its way along State Street. Their mufflers, or lack thereof, resounded through the steel and glass corridor made by the rows of office buildings.

Only after the sound had finally died away did Anna remark, "It would have been nice to get this porn perp into custody before the Roar."

Nora looked up slowly from the computer screen, where she had just begun attempting to match faces from Burgess's porn files to the dense pile of missing persons reports. She decided she hadn't heard correctly. "Excuse me?"

Anna swiveled her head to regard Nora. "You haven't heard about the Roar?".

Clearly she had not, so she didn't repeat herself.

"Roar on the Shore," supplied Pete. "Erie's annual celebration of biker culture."

This she did repeat, turning the words over in her mouth. "Biker culture?"

Anna harrumphed. "Bandannas and leather jackets and tattoos and everything related to the mighty Harley Davidson, from insurance to how to keep your scrawny-granny-biker-chick from flying off the back when you hit a bump. Bikers. Bikers flood the city. Eighty thousand of them."

Pete, ever so slightly more cheerful about the topic, added, "They're gearing up for it now. It starts tomorrow."

Nora nodded. "And what is required of us?"

Pete and Anna exchanged glances. Anna said, "Occasionally Erie PD calls us in for help with special issues as they get stretched thin with crowd control. But in reality I've never had to do anything except turn up my TV to drown out the noise. They're harmless and happy."

"Beyond that," said Pete, "don't lean on anyone's bike."

Anna shook her head, looking tired, then added, "And no matter how much you are tempted, buy no leather halter tops. It's just skanky."

Her father's voice was gruff. "What are you eating? Where do you get food?"

Nora decided to work a very patient tone. "They have a

Wegman's here. We talked about this. That store we went to in Jersey once. It's way cheaper than Whole Foods. Their deli section thing with all those rotisserie chickens and stuff is pretty amazing."

"That chicken isn't *halal*," her dad said.

"Yes, but when there's no *halal* meat available you're allowed to eat regular and then just say the name of God over it before you eat," she countered. "Because God actually hates it when you *starve*."

She heard her dad laughing and envisioned him shaking his head. "Nora, I will freeze something for you every day and then bring you a cooler full of food when I come."

"How about you just focus on Ahmad," she replied, though her tone was gentle. "How's he doing?"

"Grumpy. He doesn't like working in the restaurant in summers, you know. Then again, he does like the new waitress, Madison."

Nora smiled, imagining. "Madison?"

"She has an earring in her tongue, which of course I didn't notice when I hired her. But I keep seeing her sticking out her tongue to show him, and now I need to figure out a way to fire her."

"For having a tongue piercing?" Nora asked. Other servers had had worse.

Her father's voice was full of frustration. "No, for flirting with my boy."

Nora said, "Baba, Ahmad's a man now, you have to let him be."

"So he can end up with a *kafir* like you have?" her father hurled.

And with that, the conversation, like most of their conversations, crumbled.

There were only so many times that Nora could relate the same problem to Ben, she felt, and so she stopped talking about her father's irrational anger and tried to speak mostly about work, and the city, and things they would do when Ben came to see her.

Ben had made fun of Erie when he helped her move in. *No skyscrapers. Not enough people. You won't last a week.*

She had been terse in response. *You still have no idea how tough I am, Ben Calder.*

She'd claimed toughness to Ben. In fact, she'd been terrified. She'd never really been alone before. Her little apartment in Chinatown had been just moments from home, moments from Ben, and in a neighborhood dense with people, alive with city clamor, and afloat in some of the best, most comforting smells in the world. Just thinking about it made her ache for dim sum. Quantico had meant almost no privacy; she constantly shared space with fiercely eager agents, chattering, vying with each other for the attention of their teachers, undercutting each other, occasionally bullying. . . .

Now, the only break in the quiet was the mad violinist one floor up.

Of course she hated it; of course she missed the city, even if she disliked proving Ben right.

She missed the paths along the Schuylkill River, haunted as they were by the gray clouds from Philadelphia's constant, creeping traffic. She missed the crowded anonymity of the sidewalks. Erie wasn't tense and teeming, wasn't a kaleidoscopic jumble. And so she felt as though she stuck out in a way she never could have in Philly, even when things were really bad.

Only Nora's morning runs kept her sane. She loved the bay, splayed out as it was under a wide sky that, like the water, fluctuated between bright blue and murky gray. The lake was somehow always different. Some mornings it was flat and serene, other mornings its surface rippled constantly, at a slow, steady boil. Often it foamed with whitecaps that made her wonder why boaters would leave the shelter of the bay for the even rougher waters beyond. She had never been on a boat, and the thought made her woozy.

State Street tumbled down the hill and into the bay, but not before providing an anchor for the Bicentennial Tower, a webby gauntlet of stairs that provided sweeping views from its top tier. No one ever seemed to run the tower stairs but her. In fact there just weren't that many runners period—in Philly, she'd had to fight for space. The runners were fierce and focused, with expensive shoes that would cause Nora to slow her pace as she passed, ogling. More than this, though, the trails she ran had been riddled with infants pushed in overpriced strollers and octogenarian speed-walkers in spandex that did them no favors.

Here she could really run. She would rip along the Bayfront and then into Frontier Park, along its footbridges and across its wide pathways lined with a universe of tall, softly swaying grasses. There were occasional walkers, a few joggers, but no one who was really serious about running. She wasn't yet lonely for competition. She liked putting on blistering spurts of speed and feeling the burning in her chest that eventually gave way to a hard, fast breathing that blotted out all other sounds and made her feel strong and self-sustaining.

But when she came home the loneliness really seeped in, and she wandered through the three large rooms of her apartment as though lost. She missed Ahmad's messes and his constant eating. She missed her father and all his blustery overprotectiveness. On nights when she awoke to raid the fridge, she half expected to encounter Baba sitting in his undershirt and shiny Adidas sweatpants on her couch, shouting advice at cooking show contestants.

Missing Ben was constant, a continuous twisting in her belly, and so she often walked around her apartment with her hand pressing against her navel as though to calm the churning within. There was some wisdom, she'd decided, in not falling in love. Just marrying some guy who was suitable and being done with it. She didn't have time for the distraction of thinking about Ben when she should be working, should be focusing on taking this new job by storm.

She didn't need to switch to anti-terror, but at the very least she was going to have to prove herself so she could get a better post. An East Coast post. A post near Ben.

PRELIMINARY
EVENING

She had to marvel at her neighbor's will. The passage she was playing seemed demonically hard. Nora had learned it by heart, because the violinist had played this particular passage no less than fifty times in the last hour. It was indeed becoming smoother. The times when the violinist stopped midway through and began again at the beginning had become fewer. Nora knew now what it sounded like when she got it right.

But Nora was starting to lose her mind. She had just rolled over and cast a resigned glance at her clock, which absurdly read one-thirty in the morning, when she heard the unmistakable sound of breaking glass. It sounded to Nora like it had been the broad, heavy pane that filled her oaken front door.

She was out of bed in an instant. She plunged her feet into her sneakers and, head tilted, listening intently, she crossed to where her gun holster dangled from one of the four posters of the bed-frame. Her neighbor had heard the sound as well, it seemed, because the music stopped midstream.

Nora didn't even have a chance to assess if there was an intruder in her own apartment. She suddenly heard heavy footsteps pounding across the floor above and a scream that stopped Nora cold. She dashed back to the bedside table and pounded the numbers 9-1-1 into her BlackBerry, even as she raced, phone in one hand and gun in the other, to her front door and out to the porch she shared with the violinist.

The intruder had smashed the glass front door which was the twin of hers, then unlocked it from the inside. It stood ominously open now, the heavy glass littering the porch in large shards. Just as she was about to enter, Nora's BlackBerry finally responded, "9-1-1, what is your emergency?"

From within, Nora heard another gut-wrenching scream. "Intruder, possibly armed, attacking a woman—100 French Street, second floor, *hurry*!"

Then she was in. As she mounted the stairs, she was met by the sound of a heavy lamp crashing against a wall and a bulb shattering, and a voice roaring out the word *bitch* over and over. Now she galloped up the stairs two-by-two, leaping into the room, gun drawn. The living room was empty; she continued to what had to be the bedroom.

The door had the same crystal doorknobs as her own bedroom one floor below; it was not fully closed. Through the gap, she could see figures, and the sound of her neighbor whimpering in pain. With a quick kick, Nora burst in.

The man was bigger than she'd expected, with wide, rippling arms spilling out of a gray muscle shirt. Tattoos rampaged across biceps, forearms, and neck. Sandy hair framed a wide face with chiseled features. His expression was already one of fury, but when he spied Nora's gun pointing at him, it turned to white-hot rage. Squirming beneath him, pinned to the floor, was the violinist. The blood dripping down her cheek and from her already-swollen bottom lip made a jarring contrast against her pale skin. Nora was surprised his position alone hadn't crushed her.

"Get off of her and put your hands on the floor, slowly," Nora said, mustering her angriest, most commanding voice. She begged God for a squad car with extra loud sirens, but nothing came.

"Fuck you," answered the man, his chest heaving, his tone scathing.

He didn't move. Nora scanned his clothing for a weapon and saw a bulge in his pocket that looked more pocketknife than gun. Still, she did not want to gamble.

"I'm Special Agent Nora Khalil of the FBI. If you refuse my direct order to stop this attack and surrender yourself, I will shoot you. Is this clear?"

She watched the man assessing her, weighing his options. She watched him assess incorrectly. He lunged at her, and she shot him twice, point-blank in the chest, as she deftly side-stepped his barreling mass.

The weight of his dying body splintered the door against which he fell. As the echoes of Nora's shots faded, the violinist's soft sobs became audible. The jockeying of nearing sirens struck a dissonant chorus.

It wasn't how Nora had intended to meet her neighbor, but it was certainly effective.

Nora looked from the corpse to the woman, whose eyes were not on the massive dead man but instead riveted on her violin. It had evidently been tossed on the bed where it lay now, face-down, the bow pinned beneath it. Nora, reading her mind, walked over to the instrument, picked it up carefully, and showed it to her.

"Not a scratch," she said, before replacing it on its back on the bright quilt. Then Nora walked over and crouched next to her neighbor. "Are you okay?"

The woman nodded, sitting up, feeling her limbs gingerly for breaks.

"Just a little bruised, I think."

Nora tilted her head, observing her. "A lot bruised. Should I assume that guy's a neighbor who couldn't take the midnight practicing thing?"

The violinist raised her eyebrows and then burst out laughing. "My ex-husband," she answered finally. "And yes, it always made him crazy, too." She stuck out a slim hand. "I'm Rachel."

Nora took it, noting the graceful, tapered fingers. "Nora," she said.

"You saved my life, Nora," Rachel said. "He intended to kill me this time."

Nora digested the words, "this time," and regarded her curiously. "Yeah, I got that impression, too. I'm glad you're okay. . . ." She couldn't help adding, "But that doesn't mean we aren't going to talk about suitable practice hours."

Three police officers rushed in at that point, guns drawn, and Nora and Rachel spent the next ninety minutes answering questions. The ex-husband had come for Rachel from Buffalo where she had met, married, and divorced him. His continual physical abuse had earned him a restraining order that Rachel thought she could bolster by moving away. She had taken a job with the Erie Philharmonic in order to make a new start.

But the ex had not been ready to let go.

One of the officers was attempting to call an ambulance, but Rachel insisted that she would walk to the emergency room which was, after all, only two blocks away. Nora recognized this as a move typical of those who don't have health insurance. When she further realized that Rachel wasn't going to call any friends or family to accompany her, she refused to let her go alone.

They walked slowly down French Street to the hospital, striking up a refrain. Rachel kept stressing that Nora should go home and sleep, seeing as she had to be at work the next day. Nora kept responding that she was trying to get Rachel in her debt so completely that she wouldn't dare play the violin at midnight ever again.

"What was a concert violinist doing with some burly biker guy?" Anna was asking, a frown creasing her features.

"I asked her the exact same thing," Nora said, swiveling in

her desk chair. "She told me she had married him to piss off her parents."

"Ohhhh," said Anna. "Yeah, I get that."

"Get what?" asked Pete as he walked in, clutching his Starbucks cup and reeking of cologne.

Anna supplied, "Female self-destruction as rebellion against parents."

Pete narrowed his eyes, trying to get his bearings in the conversation, then decided they were joking. "You're talking about Miss Nora's crazed nightlife?"

Anna grinned. "Actually, that's just the right description. But I guess you didn't hear? She shot a brute last night."

Pete gaped. "I wanna shoot brutes," he said crankily. "Why do *you* get to shoot brutes?"

Nora related the story, returning finally to the point about how the delicate violinist ended up with the tattooed attacker. "Apparently he was very appealing when he was sixty pounds lighter and fighting fires for a living. Then he started hitting her. When she left him, he just drank and rode his motorcycle."

"And he got drunk and rode his motorcycle to Erie to reclaim her?" Pete asked.

"To reclaim his *manhood*," Anna theorized.

Nora tapped her pen against the desk as she completed the paperwork. It was the second time she had killed someone, and she was trying to decide how she felt about it. She concluded that tea would clarify things, and she stood up to head for the kitchenette down the hall. "You guys want coffee or anything?" she asked.

Both declined.

As she scooped dried mint leaves into her mug from her secret stash behind the Keurig, she heard the SSRA behind her. "Well, Agent Khalil?"

Usually Sheila said "hello Nora," and hearing the "Khalil" this morning confirmed to Nora that she had been consciously avoiding trying to pronouncing her last name. "Hi, Sheila."

Sheila held a tall stack of files. "Child porn purveyors not enough for you, huh? Gotta go shooting wife-beaters. What's next?"

Nora shrugged, not sure how to answer, and added hot water to the loose mint and the waiting tea bag.

Sheila regarded her, her features easing into a look of real concern. "You okay?"

Nora dangled the teabag in the mug, watching the water darken, then looked at her boss. "I think so. Little sleepy, maybe."

"How do you feel about how things went down with this intruder thing?"

Nora thought about it. "I've been trying to sort out if there was any other way, but I don't see how there were any options."

Sheila nodded. "I get that. And I'll read your report carefully before sending it on to the police. I still prefer that you don't walk solo into such situations."

"I called the police first," Nora said. "They took forever to come, by the way."

"It was actually only six minutes. I checked. Look, Nora, you acted correctly and with bravery. I'm proud of you," Sheila said. "I also want to keep you, so be careful. I imagine you weren't wearing a vest."

Nora shrugged again. "I was wearing pajamas."

Sheila shook her head and walked back to her office, flicking through the stack of files.

By now, Nora desperately needed her tea. The warmth of the mug radiated through her familiarly, restoring her a little. Not sleeping was a wrinkle she hadn't foreseen in her strategy to excel in her new position. Appearing at work exhausted at seven thirty in the morning was not going to lead to stellar performance.

Nora blew across the rim of the mug, then sipped tentatively. Slowly, she walked to the cubicle and glanced at the papers on her desk, not eager to go back to scanning through the endless rosters of lost girls. It was like looking for a perverse lottery ticket. Nearly each of Frank Burgess's waking hours was spent in trolling the Internet. Nora felt her skin crawl as she imagined him, utterly sedentary, locked in his trailer, feasting his pale eyes on the flesh of little children. She hated him. She hated him so much.

She had just settled into her task when a text from Ben flashed across the screen of her BlackBerry. *On my way to NYC. Do you need anything?*

She texted back, *Six or seven I HEART NY t-shirts.*

Then she frowned at the screen, adding, *Why are you going to NYC?*

There was enough of a delay that she had turned back to her computer screen when the words *Long story* came through.

She sighed, then pushed the BlackBerry away. She didn't like long stories. She tried to go through her files again, but found herself staring at the BlackBerry. She did not want to pick it up, but was finally unable to resist. *What's the long story?*

Sarah is getting out of rehab and needs someone to be there for a couple days.

Nora shoved back her chair and stood up, then sat down again. Then she stood up again, glaring at the screen and its message. Her breath came only choppily, and she found herself looking around the office as though expecting someone to materialize she could show the message to. She almost walked over to Maggie. But she imagined herself showing Maggie the screen and demanding she share her outrage, then imagined Maggie growling at her to get out of her cubicle. She almost texted Rachel, but knew both that it was too soon in their friendship to start being needy . . . and that Rachel was surely still sleeping after the late night at the hospital.

Dammit, she whispered to herself. *He doesn't have time to come here. How can he go up there? To her?*

At least he's telling you straight up. You would never have known, she pointed out, playing in turn the role of both of the girlfriends she didn't have at a time like this.

She was holding the phone in her hands feeling utterly mystified when Anna said, "Yes!"

Nora looked a question at her.

Anna said, "I just got word that the warrant was coming through this morning for Burgess's arrest and confiscation of his computer."

Nora set her phone facedown on her desk and then sat up quite straight in her chair, willing herself to focus fully. "That's incredibly fast for a warrant to come through," she said. In Philly it would have taken longer, unless strings had been pulled or favors called in. There was just so much more to do to pin down a judge.

Pete actually grinned at her. "Yeah it's fast. Which means it's not just another mind-numbing day at the office!"

Anna shook her head, then smiled at Nora. "We're going to McKean! Lucky you."

"Oh my God," Nora said, her heartrate zooming.

"Did you wear your fabled running shoes?" Anna was asking, sliding into her desk chair and pulling her laptop out of her slick leather briefcase.

"Will I need them?" she countered.

"Hell no," Pete said. "Did you see that fat slob? He couldn't run to the bathroom."

As it turned out, her running shoes were the last things she needed.

The morning was filled with almost interminable waiting. The twenty-minute ride to McKean in Anna's SUV was the swiftest part of it—Nora still marveled at the near total lack of traffic to contend with. Both Pete and Anna tended to take advantage of this by driving extremely fast even when it was completely unnecessary to do so.

It was the state troopers who came late, though.

They discovered this as they were pulling into the small town, nestled innocuously amid vast stretches of green as far as the eye could see.

"Really?" Nora asked Pete, who was engrossed in his BlackBerry looking at his Instagram account.

He looked up. "Really what?"

"That's it? That's all there is?"

"Girl, what did you expect? People turn to porn out here out of boredom, not malice."

"My God."

It was over an hour before the state police finally appeared. McKean, like most of the towns in the area around Erie, had no police force. Three state troopers—one of whom Nora watched spit tobacco mid-sentence—and their sergeant would provide support for the arrest. Anna, who did not flinch during the spitting incident, was speaking to them calmly.

Conversation. Speaking into handheld radios. More conversation. More speaking into handheld radios.

The three state police cars had gathered near Anna's SUV in the parking lot of the local Sheetz.

Nora was refusing to answer Ben's string of *Why aren't you responding?* texts. Instead, she watched the cluster of law enforcement officers that had formed about Anna, almost obscuring her. Occasionally Nora caught glimpses of Anna's unnaturally red hair, which shone like a squat beacon from between the uniformed figures.

"Those are some amazing hats, I have to say."

The wide-brimmed gray wool hats bore shiny black bands and sat tall on the troopers' heads. Just below each hat's peak were two deep, matching indentations that made the hats look like faces with sucked-in cheeks.

Pete looked up. "Yep." He looked back down at the screen.

"I think we need hats. I would like a hat like that," she said.

"Like that?" Pete said, contemplatively. "Well, it's a pretty awesome hat. But I think I'd look better in a fedora."

She turned to regard him, then nodded lazily, her boredom weighing heavily on her. She said slowly, "Maybe. Theirs may be slightly much, now that I think about it."

Finally, Anna beckoned to them. She and Pete descended from the SUV with relief; Nora had thought Pete was going to kick a hole in the back of her seat.

Anna, reading glasses on, was holding a file with a computer-generated map of the area and the relevant warrants. She introduced Pete and Nora to the sergeant, who informed them that he went by the name of Buck. The way that he said this seemed intended to convey a rural mixture of power and friendliness, but for Nora it only served to undermine whatever assurances she'd been drawing from the hat.

All were peering at the route they would take to the trailer park where Frank Burgess lived.

Anna said, "He has a vehicle registered in his name, but it's an '84 Ford Bronco. I cannot imagine that it would provide a fast getaway. Either way, you should block it in when we pull up."

The men were nodding.

"If you can make us a perimeter, we can enter and make the arrest."

Buck said, "There's no evidence of anyone else in the trailer?"

Anna shook her head. "No. Just Burgess."

They agreed to lead the way without sirens or lights, and the three agents returned to the SUV. After Anna slid the key into the ignition, she turned to Pete. "Pull those vests out of the back, kiddo."

"Don't call me kiddo. And why?"

"Because we're in God's country, boy. *Thar be guns.*"

Reluctantly, Pete passed out Kevlar and then put on his own.

"Your vests are different than what I'm used to. . . ." Nora observed, fighting with hers.

Anna nodded. "Israeli Kevlar," she said. "People here have more rifles than handguns. You need more advanced stuff. With the right shirt you can conceal it, though."

Nora placed a hand against the hard material, already sitting up straighter in her chair because she had no choice. She was trying to determine if any of her work shirts could be worn over the vest. She had one that was baggy enough, she thought. *Still, though. Wouldn't look too fly.*

Glancing at Pete in the rearview mirror, Anna said, "Don't feel so emasculated. Do it for the Starbucks wench."

With that, she shifted into gear and tore off behind the state police. Although technically newer, Nora was slightly older than Pete and had a fuller resume. She appreciated his frustration at being patronized by the seasoned older agent. It was a dynamic she'd had quite enough of back in Philadelphia.

Frank Burgess's trailer was sandwiched in among a dozen or so others. The park was a mere five minutes from the center of McKean. All the trailers seemed to Nora to be carbon copies, give or take some variations in trim or the occasional awning. She took note of the Ford Bronco, however, and her blood began to race. It had been almost a year since she had been part of a bust. In that year she had trained hard, in both martial arts and firearms, but it was still different from being out in the field.

Anna closed the driver's side door quietly and motioned for them to do the same. "Okay," she said, looking them hard in the eyes. "As we discussed."

What they had discussed was that Pete would go to the back of the trailer and peer in through one of its grubby windows as

Anna and Nora approached from the front with their identification and stated intention to arrest.

This they did. Anna checked to see that the troopers and Sergeant Buck were in place before she rapped on the rusted outer door.

"FBI," she called out. "Frank Burgess, we have a warrant for your arrest."

Exactly four seconds elapsed before Pete called, "He's going for the gun cabinet!" This was followed by a crash as he kicked in the window. Nora and Anna leaned in hard against the locked inner door, then Nora stepped back as Anna took aim and fired her Glock at the doorknob, shattering it. The flimsy door swung open revealing Pete's flying lunge against Frank Burgess. The obese man teetered, stumbled, then fell against the very gun cabinet he had been trying to pull open.

The state police poured in after Nora and Anna, guns at the ready, but Anna was already securing Burgess's fleshy wrists with her handcuffs as she read him his rights. He was groaning in a loud combination of anger and pain. The open gun cabinet revealed at least a dozen rifles; a few of the weapons had tumbled onto the floor and Peter was careful to roll the man away from them before helping him to his feet.

Each of the agents, panting, regarded the other, confirming with gazes that they were all okay. Anna's look expanded to take in their backup. "You all alright?" she asked briskly.

All three nodded.

"Alright then," she said with a smile. "Not a bad summer outing."

Sheila was pleased. She was a different person entirely when she was pleased. It was all new for Nora who realized she suddenly felt rather unmoored. Their boss was smiling, clapping them on

their backs, and making optimistic predictions about good con-
quering evil. This last was even slightly more than Sheila herself
could tolerate, and she seemed to snap out of it and return to the
task at hand.

"Speaking of which, Anna, are you prepping for the meeting
with the AUSA—"

Anna indicated the pile of papers on her desk. "I have the full
debriefing ready."

Her boss nodded. "I assumed you would. I'll see you at three,
then. Again, good work team, but the hard part starts now." She
exited with a swift step, leaving the three of them to their report-
writing.

Pete had become fully alert, and his wide gray eyes were sharp.
He looked at both women. "Has Burgess retained counsel yet?"

"No, he's going with a public defender."

"Mason?"

"Who else?"

Nora listened intently. She'd heard Mason's name before. The
word "bitch" usually followed quickly behind.

"God, she's such a bitch," Pete muttered.

"Why?" Nora pressed this time.

Anna answered for him. "She likes to win. And she's good at
her job."

"She's a bitch."

"She's *assertive*," Anna insisted. "And she wins a lot because
she's smart. So we hate her."

"Do we have anything to worry about?"

"Only if Pete fails to find all this Dark Web mumbo jumbo he
was claiming would be on Burgess's computer."

He paused, his fingertips hovering in midair. "Oh, now it's all
on me?" he demanded.

"Of course," Anna said.

"Then call Ms. Mason because I want to see if Burgess'll just give me some information instead of making me spend a thousand hours breaking the encryption."

Anna shrugged. "As you like. Strike while the iron is hot."

"Sitting a couple hours in lockup will be enough to remind him how bad it sucks," Pete pointed out. "But yeah, let's just get the show on the road. We can make a deal, right? Because we want to know his source."

Anna nodded. "Sheila made that clear to me."

"Then we have some bargaining power," Pete said. As Anna put in the call to the public defender, Pete returned to tapping on his keyboard.

Nora sighed as she turned back to her laptop. "That was a lot of firepower for a sedentary man." *Five Shotguns. Had he known the Bureau was targeting him and so harbored some fantasy about a standoff?* Hunters, she assumed, actually had to leave their domiciles in order to shoot the woodland creatures. Burgess had seemed practically agoraphobic. Nora began printing up all the prior reports on Burgess, killing time until Anna came in to let them know that Maura Mason was in the elevator on her way up.

"Pete, you're on point for this," Anna said.

Pete shook his head vehemently. "Ew, no, I don't want to be in the same room with him."

Anna gave him a look. "Peter."

"What if he molests me?"

"I'll shoot him," she said, in the tone with which Nora imagined some Midwestern grandmother might dangle the reward of a cookie for good behavior.

"You're not a very good shot," Pete pointed out.

"But he's very large. My odds are good."

Nora watched them bemusedly. She was just as happy not to have to interrogate anyone. It was her least favorite thing to do. She sipped at her tea, asking herself what her favorite thing to do might in fact be. She realized it was running down and tackling someone. *That is not something I'm ever going to get to do here.*

Fat Porn Freaks Don't Run.

Pete glared at her. "What are *you* smirking about?"

"I was thinking up bumper stickers."

Anna said, "Look, Pete, you know that he hates women. He's resorted to a public defender, but she turned out to be a woman. Play the testosterone card. Be his bro. Win him over . . . and then dick him over."

Pete rubbed at his beard, a glint in his eye. "Did you seriously, and with a straight face, just ask me to go in there and use my gender as a tool to manipulate a subject?"

Anna thought a moment. "Yes. Yes, I did."

"*Seriously.*"

"Welcome to the Bureau. No one said you couldn't teach third grade instead."

Pete looked at her, wide-eyed; then he looked at Nora, who shrugged.

He sighed. "Jesus. Alright. Let's do this."

He entered the room, most of which was swallowed by Burgess's bulk. They watched him greet Maura Mason and then, as though he had forgotten something, suddenly excuse himself and return to the hall.

His lips were pursed and his nose was flared. "Also," he whispered loudly to Anna, "he smells really bad."

Both women gave him a sympathetic look and then burst out laughing as soon as he walked away.

"Who knew he was such a whiner?" Anna asked.

The monitor, however, showed that he was a whiner who was utterly charming under pressure.

"Hi, Frank. It's been a long day already . . . I apologize. Are you doing alright?"

"Of course I'm not doing alright," the man grumbled, frown

lines creasing the soft flesh of his wide forehead. His accent, slow and thick, was immediately grating to Nora, who knew her own expression reflected the revulsion she felt. Anna had been wise not to send her in.

"Now, I'll be honest with you," Pete said, his voice gentle, thoughtful. "There's stuff I can do to help and stuff I can't—tell me what you need. I know you had wanted a lawyer, and we made sure you had the best in town," he said, with a wide smile at Maura Mason.

Maura Mason gave him a dispassionate stare.

"I could use a sandwich," Burgess said.

"Of course!" Pete said quickly. "Preferences? Ham? Roast beef?"

"Ham," the man answered.

It figures, thought Nora.

"Absolutely," Pete was saying. "Ms. Mason, something for you?"

She narrowed her eyes. "I'm fine," she practically spat.

"Sure? Are you sure?" Pete asked, showing his dimples before he began walking toward the door.

She nodded, and he exited and went straight back to Anna and Nora. "I'm not getting him a sandwich, obviously," he said, his tone several registers lower, his words more rapid. He sighed, tapping his feet and killing time as though perhaps he were putting in an order somewhere.

On the monitor, Nora heard Maura Mason hiss at Burgess, "That man is *not* getting you a sandwich, by the way."

"You're a tease," observed Anna. "That poor pervert in there . . ."

Pete bared his teeth at her, then headed back toward the interrogation room.

Nora and Anna looked at each other and laughed again.

"See why we hate her?" asked Anna.

Pete had entered, saying to Burgess, "My assistant Maggie was actually just ordering in for all of us so we added yours. Okay? So just fifteen minutes, man. Jimmy Johns is, like, *insanely* fast."

Burgess cast a glance over at his lawyer as if to say, *See?*

Pete picked up the reins again. "Listen, Frank, I'm very sorry about this morning, man. I really am. That must have been difficult, having us all charge in there like that."

Mason jumped in. "My client is going to be bringing charges against you for unnecessary use of force."

"Unnecessary?" Pete responded, very slowly, very calmly. "Now Ms. Mason, your client was going for his gun. Guns, I should say."

Maura Mason's face appeared impassive, but it looked to Nora that this information had been left out of the version of the story she'd encountered from Burgess.

"That's my Second Amendment right to self-defense," intoned Burgess.

Nora was sure she saw Pete roll his eyes at the camera at this characterization of the Second Amendment. His gaze returned to Frank Burgess quickly, though. Pete was even nodding sympathetically. "I get that, I do. And you have a lot worth defending. That's an incredible computer system you have out there."

Now it was Maura Mason who rolled her eyes. "Were you planning on asking my client a question or just kissing his ass all day, because I seriously don't have time, Pete."

Pete looked surprised and even slightly hurt at her words. Nora watched the expression on Frank Burgess's face. He was actually frowning at his lawyer. "Oh my God," whispered Nora. "He's won him over."

Anna was smiling knowingly. "Pete's a flirt, plain and simple."

They watched as he looked intently into Frank Burgess's bloodshot eyes. "Frank, I'm sorry. I don't want you to think I'm wasting your time, here. See, I think you're important to us—I was just telling my colleagues that what we really need to be doing is asking you for help."

"Help?" Burgess asked.

"Here we go," Mason deadpanned.

Pete sat on the edge of the table and began tugging at his tie as though utterly exhausted. "I know that you are a hardworking man, and that you do things in your leisure time that are your own business. I totally get that."

Burgess sat a little taller in his chair.

"The thing is, some of the sources you've been using are pretty intense, pretty serious stuff. I think you can help us by helping us find the bastards who messed everything up for you, who set off our alarms, helping us dig a little deeper than we're able to. You're a victim, man. I know that—"

Mason interrupted him. "McCormick, can you spare us? Are you offering my client something?"

"I am explaining to him how much we would like his cooperation, ma'am."

"Don't . . ."

"But then again, you know, there's no need if—"

Burgess held up a fleshy hand. "What do you want?"

"You really know your computer stuff, and I'm struggling to keep up, Frank. The faster I can get in there and access the information we need, the faster this nightmare will be over for you. The slower I have to take, decrypting your files and, you know, stumbling around in the dark, the longer you'll have to stay in lockup."

"Are you offering him a lighter sentence, Special Agent McCormick?" she asked.

"I am offering to advocate for him for a lighter sentence, certainly. If he makes my job easier, if he helps me access the bastards responsible for him being here, I will go to bat—"

"He's giving you nothing," Mason said, with a dismissive wave of her hand.

"It's an app called Telegram," Burgess blurted out.

Nora's jaw dropped.

"*Frank*," Mason objected. "You don't have to—"

"You can join groups. You can message people securely who are plugged in, but also see all the public conversations that are going down within the group itself. You can post things. They put a lot of exploding pictures up there, you know. Lotta stuff," he was saying, his eyes seeming to look well beyond Pete and the walls of the interrogation room.

Maura Mason looked green. "I encourage you to exercise your right to silence, Frank—"

"There was a guy there. Claimed to have some live snuff, you know. So, yeah, I wanted to see that, always have. He couldn't produce it but he had . . . other things."

He picked up his lawyer's pen and scrawled something on her legal pad. Then he looked at Pete. "Whatever it takes to just move this shit along. I got high blood pressure."

Pete nodded, managing to look sympathetic and moved at the same time. Then he turned to Maura Mason. "May I?"

"Oh, for God's sake," she snapped, shoving the legal pad at him.

Pete copied down what Burgess had written, then thanked them both. "Maggie will be in shortly with your sandwich, Frank," he said.

"There's no fucking sandwich, Frank," Mason said, standing to leave, as Pete slipped out of the room.

"Nicely done, sir," said Nora.

"All in a day's work, Miss Nora. That's how we southern gentlemen fight crime. Through flattery and doublespeak."

She grinned at him. "But will it help you unravel the mysteries of the Dark Web?"

"Well," he said, looking at his watch. "We have done twice as much work today as we normally do, and so I am willing to continue masquerading as a federal agent until 5 P.M. If the secrets are not yet revealed, then I am willing to show up again tomorrow morning with my coffee and start afresh."

But it seemed that the password he had taken was all he'd needed. In no time, she heard Pete congratulating himself behind her. He shoved back from his desk, spinning around in the swivel chair.

She paused to look at him. "Success?"

"Why, yes," he responded. "I believe that is the proper word. It's a start anyway," he said.

"What did you find?"

"The technology he was using was dark but pretty basic at the same time. There are ways of communicating with like-minded folks in order to have private conversations. These are encrypted so the good guys—you and me—can't listen in or follow. Unless I can masquerade as Frank Burgess, I can't see the stuff that comes to him, all of which is, like, tips to new kiddie porn sites or the infamous live snuff, exploding pics that disappear from the Web once they've been sent."

"So with the information you got today—"

"I can find several other nasty fat men like Frank. And from them . . ."

"Several more?"

"Yes. Yes and no. But if they don't know we're following them, and we monitor closely, we'll get several steps closer."

"Do we have enough to prosecute him with though?" asked Nora.

Pete smiled. "Does Miss Scarlett wear a corset?"

Nora frowned. "I'm—is that some kind of southern thing for 'yes'?"

Pete flared his nostrils. "Oh, you have much to learn, Miss Nora. Much to learn."

When five o'clock rolled around, she realized it had been the least boring workday she had yet spent in Erie, Pennsylvania.

Pete was stretching. "Come on, Nora. Me and Anna'll take you out. Your first official bust means we *officially* have to buy you a beer. Contractual obligation."

She shook her head automatically, searching for an out. "No, you know, I have to . . ."

He looked at her sharply, his tone changing. "What's your deal? Why don't you ever want to go out with us?"

Her eyes narrowed and she returned his gaze fiercely. "Seriously? Would you talk that way to—"

But Anna stepped in to defuse. "Pete, you just bore the hell out of her. Time to own that. You and your dimples just bore us all to death. And in fact Nora doesn't drink." Anna smiled at Nora in a way that evoked John Wansbrough's fatherly gazes. "But we will take her out this evening because she deserves it, and she's still new in town, and we should spend some after-hours time together so that she learns to love us."

Nora realized she had been biting her lip as she slowly exhaled.

Anna continued, "And you can eat and drink whatever you like. Okay? It's on Pete."

"Hey!" he protested.

"It's on both of us. Come on. Commodore Perry's?"

Pete sighed. "Of course. That's where all the boring people go."

They headed down State Street toward the landmark pub. Traffic was light, lazy even. The streets were swollen with people. There was a preponderance of black or faded T-shirts and jeans or black leather pants. Nora looked curiously at bushy beards adorned with beading or small braids. Some had scraps of ribbon woven into them. Merchants were hawking every imaginable motorcycle-related product, and bright yellow barriers had been erected to demarcate the areas where pedestrians should walk and browse and where cars could still pass. Neatly aligned motorcycles were reveling in the special dispensation to monopolize the city's street parking during the Roar.

Ten minutes after leaving the office, all three had settled into a tall, uncomfortable wooden booth, and Pete was dutifully explaining that the Commodore was not a dive bar. "It's an after-work bar for the professional class," he said. His shock upon discovering that Nora had never entered a bar before had now transformed into some sort of mandate to explain Erie's bar culture. "Because Roar on the Shore is starting, there are slightly more biker-types than office-types."

Nora, on cue, looked about her, taking in the excess of leather and ink, facial hair and bandannas.

"The altered atmosphere, however, does not affect the most important facet of the Commodore—the Giant Pretzel with the Outrageously Good Mustard Dipping Sauce." Anna's tone conveyed a childlike awe.

Feeling it was expected of her, Nora said, "Well, bring it on. And let's order me a Coke."

Anna ordered herself a mint julep. She then asked for a Coke for Nora, and, with what struck Nora as slightly more delight than the situation could possibly warrant, ordered the giant pretzel. Pete said to the server, "Eisernes Kreuz." The server nodded as though they had shared just such an exchange several times before. She walked away, weaving in and out of the tables in the increasingly crowded bar.

"Eisernes . . ." Nora started, then felt her tongue falter. "This is a beer?"

"Eisernes Kreuz!" exclaimed Pete. "Not just any beer. You should always hold out for the best local brews. Very old German family.

Perfected their approach in Holland before bringing their wisdom to these shores."

"Pete fancies himself a beer connoisseur," Anna explained.

"We all need talents," Nora said.

Anna laughed out loud.

"It's damn good beer," he said, not flummoxed in the least. He regarded her curiously. "Can you just help me understand something about this not-drinking thing though?"

Nora flared her nostrils slightly and looked at Anna. "The whole sensitivity training thing apparently didn't wash with this one?"

Anna shook her head. "He's his own beast, Nora. It's up to you, but I'd say educating him is actually to the collective benefit."

Pete had his hands up as though at gunpoint. "Look, I never met anyone that just didn't ever drink. There are people who used to drink too much and then had to stop. I get that. But to never even try it . . . it doesn't make sense."

Nora tilted her head to regard him. "Is there a question in all that?"

"Yeah, I want to know why you never tried it. You aren't even a little curious? You didn't have any friends who drank in high school? College? How could you have been a Philly police officer and not drink?"

Nora shifted in her seat. People didn't usually press her on this. Ben just went with it—she'd always assumed he was relieved she didn't drink because Sarah had been a drug addict. And though her cop friends had teased her, she'd been sure that most of them acknowledged it was for the better. It was too easy for cops to end up alcoholics at the end of a day full of brutality; she could name six of her cohort who'd had to leave already for that very reason.

Pete was looking at her earnestly. She was still on the fence about him. Frat boy? Jerk? Or someone who genuinely didn't understand and wanted to? She decided at last that his question wasn't an attack. She took a breath, then said, "Okay, let's think about it this way. In my house, alcohol might as well be crack cocaine."

She saw she had the attention of both her colleagues. They leaned in to hear her over the din. "Growing up, we never cooked with it, never splashed it into stew, never even bought cough syrup that had alcohol in it. My mom went out of her way to buy powdered vanilla so that there was no alcohol in it. Everyone had a story about someone who had just, like, imploded because of drinking. 'He drinks,' was, like, the same as saying, 'He's headed straight to hell.' Sitting in a bar—" she paused to gesture around her for effect, "—is only marginally less awful than sitting in a strip club."

Pete and Anna exchanged a look. Nora started to fidget, feeling uncomfortable.

"Shall I keep going?" Nora asked. "Or have you lost interest yet?"

"No, I'm with you," Pete affirmed.

"Okay. So, it's in popular culture, too, right? In Egyptian movies, the worst people in the world were the people who drank. The abusive husbands, the scary dictators, the drug dealers, the rapists. My dad's restaurant doesn't serve alcohol, and when someone brings their own bottle he won't touch it to open it. Just the servers do that. It's just something we feel is . . ." She stopped and searched for the words. "Scary. If you start, you can't stop, and it will make you a monster and wreck your life."

Pete seemed to be preparing a refutation, but Nora held up a hand. "I get that plenty of people are used to it. It's absolutely normal for them. I'm just answering the question of why I don't consider trying it. Because I guess I learned to be scared of it from early on."

But Peter clearly thought she was being ridiculous. "Nora, we got briefed on you. You shot some dude in the back of his head in the middle of downtown Philly. You got some kind of award at Quantico for Jiu-Jitsu. And you want to tell me you're scared of beer?"

Nora looked to Anna for help but got none as the mint julep had just arrived in a short tumbler. The drink therein was slightly murky looking. It immediately absorbed all of Anna's attention.

"I am scared of beer," Nora confirmed, accepting her Coke gratefully from the server. "And it was Mixed Martial Arts, not Jiu-Jitsu."

The server set down a dark brown bottle before Pete.

Pete happily received his drink, smirked as Nora took hers, then nodded at Anna's. "She is at heart a Confederate princess."

Nora didn't understand, but Anna's next words to Pete clarified.

"It is no dishonor to the Union to admit that you Southerners invented better cocktails." She tugged a bit of the liquid up through the tiny brown straw, then uttered an audible sigh of contentment. Crushed mint leaves were suspended in the liquid; a sprig of fresh mint was perched atop its surface.

Nora could not suppress her interest, given that mint tea was her go-to drink. She leaned in slightly to peer at the cocktail.

"What's in there?"

Pete, embellishing his accent for good measure, ticked off, "Bourbon and smashed mint leaves. Sugar. Water. This incarnation is all wrong, of course. The mint should only be spearmint. It should be with shaved ice or crushed ice. And in a pewter or silver cup. But, you know. It's Erie, not Savannah."

"I'd be happy to let you try it," Anna said, "but I was in fact paying attention to everything you just said."

Nora gave her a grateful smile, then turned to Pete. "So, I've told you why I don't drink. Now, you tell me why you're such a punk."

Pete blinked at her in mute surprise.

Anna was chuckling soundlessly, then she patted Nora on the shoulder appreciatively. "Nora, it's about time you came out of your shell. Welcome to happy hour!"

Pete shook his head. "I am *not* a punk."

"You act like some kind of obnoxious frat boy."

Anna raised an index finger, indicating she had the appropriate response. "Football player, not frat boy. Although you were probably that too. . . ."

"No, not a frat boy. But I was a quarterback."

"Much sought after by the ladies," Anna added.

Pete was nodding. "Once. Now I'm having a hard time getting past a Venti."

Anna and Nora exchanged knowing glances.

"But you disappoint me, Miss Nora. Or rather, I disappoint myself. Coming off as an obnoxious frat boy is not at all the vibe I was going for."

Nora took the bait. "And what vibe would that be, exactly?"

He shook his head. "Miss Nora. The South has three things going for it and three things only. Chivalry, barbecue, and the mint julep. Given your stances on pork and alcohol, all I can extend to you is chivalry. I shall, given the new blossoming of our friendship, endeavor always to impress upon you that I am not an obnoxious frat boy at all, but, indeed, a *southern gentleman par excellence.*"

As Nora digested this monologue, a loud crack tore through the air, followed by a thunderous crash. The walls of the Commodore Perry shook, its windows rattling in their frames.

"What the hell?" said Pete, rising and looking about him.

Screams erupted all around them.

"Across the street," Anna shouted.

The three tore toward the entrance, yanking open the heavy oaken door.

Nora saw smoke pouring out of the bank on the opposite corner and three figures clad entirely in black leaping onto three motorcycles. They were white, late 30s perhaps. One had a goatee. Each carried an over-stuffed backpack, and all three had rifles slung over their shoulders on wide black straps. The bikes started almost in unison, their engines adding to the uproar on the street.

Nora and Pete looked at each other, then dashed across the street in pursuit, guns drawn.

"Out of the way," Pete shouted.

Nora found herself crying out those same words, over and over, but the festival-goers had densely packed the area, and now all of them seemed paralyzed with shock, many screaming. The bikers were weaving in and out among the crowd, and both agents dodged left and right, in and out, desperate to catch up, intent on getting a clear shot and dislodging one of the men.

Their shouts did not go unnoticed, however. Each of the bikers had cast backward glances at the pursuing agents, and each one seemed to be increasing the speed and the determination with which they darted through the crowds.

Pete had collided with a pedestrian, knocking her down and unbalancing himself—but Nora agilely darted through the crowds. She heard the wail of police sirens behind her and knew that no police car could navigate the crush of pedestrians to reach the fleeing motorcyclists. The bikes now roared along State Street, and she knew that they were headed for the Bayfront Parkway. If she could just get beyond the pedestrian congestion, she could get a clear shot. . . . She ran as fast as she could, angry with herself for not having worn sneakers to work. The hard black loafers slapped against the pavement as she approached the third biker.

"Out of the way!" she screamed at an obese woman in a violently pink sundress who was standing, stunned, several yards in front of her, but blocking the most direct angle of pursuit of the bikers.

The woman scurried to the left as Nora's shoes slid slightly on the sidewalk. Nora steadied herself, then took aim at the third biker's back wheel. She fired. Immediately the bike skidded out of control, and the biker tumbled onto the street. The bike careened, spinning, toward Nora and as she dashed to get out of the way, the second biker doubled back in a wide, rapid arc. The unseated motorcyclist leapt onto the back of his partner's bike.

Once settled, the last biker swiveled in his seat and aimed his rifle at Nora.

She barely had time to throw herself behind yet another row of motorcycles, hoping the web of metallic frames would provide enough cover. Her eyes widened as she realized she could see the bullet streaking out of the rifle, its trajectory lit red. The round ripped into the gas tank of the first motorcycle in the row. The bike exploded, hurtling against the brick wall behind Nora in flames. Nora tucked herself into a ball as shards of scalding metal rained down on the pavement and the screaming crowd.

It was State Street's second explosion of the day—the second in its history.

The EMTs were fast in coming. Hamot Hospital was only a block away, after all. Nora sat on the sidewalk, with Pete next to her, as the paramedic treated the burns across her arms, neck, and back. The metal had burned right through her clothing, and Nora would rather have gone to the back of the ambulance than expose so much flesh to the paramedic, or, for that matter, to her partner and the passersby. But each ambulance she saw was already filled with festival-goers being treated for burns that were similar if not worse. The fat lady in the pink dress was not far down the curb from her, and her exposed left shoulder wore an angry burn.

Nora realized, too, that no one was concerned with the amount of skin she herself was showing as the paramedic wrapped her wounds. Shock and disbelief were visible on the faces of each person in the street. Even those uninjured seemed to need to sit on the sidewalk, dazed, until being shooed away by the law enforcement officers. The cops were moving the colorful sawhorses used for festival crowd control to block off the side streets, barring the media trucks from approaching. Overhead the NBC chopper occasionally dipped and then headed out again. Pete had just explained that the pursuing police cars had never even been able to catch sight of the bikers after they had reached the Bayfront Parkway. It was as though they had simply disappeared. The news station gave access to the police for aerial searches in a crisis. There would be two cops riding along with a reporter, following possible routes they thought the motorcycles would have taken.

Nora gazed at the helicopter with its overly-cheerful peacock emblazoned on the side.

"Any bank robber is going to have figured that part out, though, right?" she asked Pete. "They wouldn't just cruise down the interstate until they get to Mexico or wherever. They're going to go somewhere close, some temporary safe house. Switch vehicles. Then go on."

When the EMT had finished with the bandaging, he looked at Nora and told her she needed to go to the ER. "Sure," Nora said, thanking him and determining that that was the last thing she'd do.

"You got some kinda hospital phobia?" Pete was asking.

"Got a time phobia, Peter. I'm fine, and I don't want to waste time."

Pete looked at her. "You were pretty zippy, there, Agent Khalil."

Nora smiled at him. "Pretty poor results, though."

"We have a motorcycle we would not have otherwise had."

Nora nodded, gazing at the motorcycle that still lay on its side on the street. A few police officers were staking it off with yellow tape. "I don't know how much we'll get off it. He was wearing gloves. They all were."

Gloves, leather . . . a goatee . . . Nora was raking through her memories of the men, trying to recall hair color and skin tones.

"We'll be able to figure out a VIN number, probably."

Nora considered this, then got lost a moment, reflecting on what she'd just seen. "Pretty tough, that guy, huh?" she said finally.

Pete agreed. "I saw what happened. You made an excellent shot. He popped up like a daisy after falling off that bike. I don't think I could have done that. And then have the presence of mind to take that shot at you. Ballsy."

Nora cringed, remembering how he'd made eye contact with her. His eyes had been hard and angry. She could not recall their color. It bothered her.

"Who does that, though?" Pete asked.

"Huh? Which part?"

"Robbing a bank. It's the age of the Internet. I thought we were all just raiding each other's checking accounts now or charging shit up on strangers' Visa cards."

Nora smiled despite herself. She didn't know. She had never dealt with robbers. At least not since she was around six or seven, when she'd proved herself a virtually uncatchable robber in Coxe Park.

"That was a legit bank heist," Pete said. "Like in a movie."

Nora gazed at him bemusedly. "I swear sometimes you sound twelve to me."

Pete smiled. "Part of my charm."

Anna walked up to report that what was left of the bank guard's body was being retrieved from the scene. She plunked herself down on the curb next to Nora. "You okay there?"

Nora nodded. "Fine. Do we have tape yet?"

"Yes, it's being taken to the office now. As soon as you're ready, Pete, we should go. But Nora, we'll take you home first."

"I'm fine," she protested. "I want to come."

"You're covered in bandages and your shirt is in shreds."

Nora pursed her lips. "Pete was about to gallantly hand me his blazer."

Obediently, Pete shrugged out of his blazer and handed it to Nora. Anna shook her head. "Double-teaming me already? Good. I like the bonding."

"We got numbers yet?" Pete asked.

Anna nodded. "They let the branch manager walk out with the two tellers. She said the haul was probably slightly north of 900 K."

Pete whistled, extending his hand to Nora who allowed him to help her up from the curb.

The three started walking south on State toward the office. Sheila was standing on the sidewalk, speaking to the police officers who came and went. Their office had no bomb squad. As with so many other things, they relied on the local talent. There were five police officers—three from the Erie Police Department, one from the Sheriff's Department, and one from a suburb called Millcreek. Sheila watched as they trolled through the wreckage, one ear pressed against her BlackBerry, the other tilted toward whoever came up to report back to her.

Nora's eye fell on the cop standing with her. He had taken off the ballistic helmet and Kevlar jacket of the bomb disposal suit, but still wore the bulky, steel-plated pants and over-shoes. His sweat-soaked T-shirt redundantly proclaimed the words "Bomb Squad." Sweat streamed from a thick shock of gray-streaked blond hair. He wore his badge around his neck on a lanyard that flopped against his prominent gut. He nodded at the trio. "Hey, Anna. Pete." He nodded at Nora. His blue eyes were tired, his face grave.

"Nora Khalil," Anna said, by way of introduction. "New kid. Nora, Abe Berberovic."

"Nora. Hi."

"What do you think, Abe?" asked Pete.

"Not much to think. It's pretty straightforward. Easiest home bomb ever. Ammonium nitrate, fuel oil. Witnesses say they heard a gun fired. I assume they shot it with an incendiary bullet as they walked out."

"Tracer? He shot a tracer at me," Nora volunteered quickly.

"Yes," Abe nodded. "I'd figured that's what ignited the fuel tank on that motorcycle. You okay?"

Nora nodded.

"Well, the bank guard wasn't as lucky. They let the two tellers and the manager go, but they'd strapped the guard to the bomb."

The agents nodded somberly. Abe wriggled out of the rest of his suit, then went to place it in the armored bomb squad vehicle. Then, he fell into step with them, wiping his flushed, sweat-streaked cheeks fruitlessly against the wetter sleeves of his T-shirt. "I'll come back and look at the tapes with you. But I assume we'll see these guys walk in with a big bag of some sort. I'm guessing they knew that the armored car would be coming to collect today."

"Still, they had to know that no homemade bomb could break through a bank vault," Sheila was saying.

"Certainly," Abe agreed.

"Then why bomb it if they had already gotten the money at gunpoint?"

The cop shrugged. "That's going to be your driving question, I reckon."

Sheila sighed. Then she dropped back to walk next to Nora. "Pursuing rifle-toting bank robbers on foot and without Kevlar, Agent Khalil?"

The mispronunciation made Nora's skin crawl, but she nodded, waiting.

She didn't have to wait long. Sheila's tone was terse, irritated. "Not my favorite move."

Nora said nothing.

"Still, I appreciate what you were able to do. At least we have one vehicle. You didn't harm any civilians." Sheila paused in her walking. "Even so, you drew his fire and put many in harm's way."

Nora looked at her boss. She bit back several different responses. *Sometimes . . . you just go.* She'd learned it from five years on Philly streets. *Sometimes you just click into gear and there's no thinking, there's no calculating. You just go.*

Sheila didn't look like someone who had ever felt it. Sheila looked like she and her desk were inseparable. Nora knew she was flustered now because this bank robbery was the biggest thing that had ever happened in Erie and she was worried about how to manage it.

They had arrived at the building that housed their office. Before entering, Nora cast a glance over her shoulder at the blackened maw of the bank's front lobby. She recalled the biker's hard eyes. She decided that Sheila's worry was well-founded.

Abe Berberovic was in love with Anna. It took about thirty seconds after they all sat down to go over the tapes for Nora to observe this. First surprised, then bemused, she took to watching his eyes skate over Anna's face. No one else seemed to notice. They all sipped at the coffee Maggie brought them as Pete booted up the laptop and tried to sort out the operating system required to display the footage rendered by the bank security cameras.

Nora had known better than to ask Maggie for tea; she was clearly pissed that, on a day when she had elected to stay later than usual to finish up some work, she had gotten roped into staying extra late. The explosion and loss of life thing apparently left the woman wholly indifferent.

But when Nora realized Abe wasn't touching his coffee either, she said, "I'm going to make some tea. Abe?"

He looked up at her, his tired eyes kind. "Yes, actually. Sounds great."

Without looking up from the report she was filling out, Anna said, "Nora, you should put mint in Abe's, too." This was said so casually that Nora's suspicions were immediately confirmed.

The crinkles around Abe's eyes intensified now as he recognized Nora's look of comprehension.

Smiling, Nora took an extra moment to stop by her locker. Her old blue backpack still held the Penn T-shirt Ahmad had given her the day he got his acceptance letter. She dug for it and then headed for the restroom. Cautiously she slid out of Pete's blazer and her tattered Oxford shirt, twisting right and left to get a full sense of the bandaging job the EMT had done. There were half a dozen small burns, the largest being on her lower back. She felt grateful none of the hot metal had rained down on her face; she had curled herself into the tightest ball she could—that Quantico training kicking in. The most annoying of the burns was on the back of her neck, just below her chignon. She would have to wear her hair higher, as already the friction of the thick knot of hair against the bandage was uncomfortable. She tugged the elastic out and let loose the tumble of curls. Her hair smelled acrid. She gathered it into a quick ponytail for now, and headed back to the conference room.

By the time she came back with their teas, the footage of the robbery was ready to play.

It had all happened very, very fast. One of the men had smashed the lobby door with the butt of his rifle and then all three burst in. One was indeed carrying a huge duffle. While the first man subdued the startled guard and began duct-taping him to the duffle itself, the other two held the three female employees at gunpoint. It seemed clear that all of the men were shouting and gesturing. Once the guard was bound to the duffle, all three men leapt over the teller counters and a rapid exchange ensued with the bank manager and both tellers. Two men began stuffing their backpacks with the money sacks which had evidently just been taken out of the vault for armored car pickup, while the tallest man aimed his weapon at the women. Each woman stood with raised, trembling hands, her gaze riveted on the rifle that swung back and forth like a hypnotist's watch. Finally, their backpacks zipped, all three men shooed the women out through the broken glass doors and into the street. Upon exiting, the tallest man whirled, pointed his rifle at the duffle bag and fired.

The streaking bullet was visible even on the black and white tape.

And then blackness.

Sheila looked around the room at them, then said, "Pete, please play it again."

Pete moved the cursor back to the beginning. This time, when the men entered the lobby, Anna said, "Pause."

Pete paused the feed.

She was frowning, watching the video from over the rims of her reading glasses as she made notes on the legal pad in front of her. "Can you zoom in?"

The faces on the screen were grainy, but for the most part clear.

"God, here's the part where we need facial recognition technology."

"Someday reality will match the movies," Abe said with an old-man chuckle. "But you have to admit they're plucky, right? No bandannas, no panty hose, no Halloween masks. Just the faces God gave 'em."

"Plucky. Right," Sheila said. "At the very least let's zero in on the door frame, catch the height markers?"

Nora watched as Pete used the mouse to select parts of the screen to zoom in on. Security measures in banks and businesses dictated that subtle markers be notched into the doorframes for just these occasions. Now Anna, Abe, and Sheila were squinting at the screen.

"6 feet," said Pete, zooming out now from the first man. He allowed the video to advance a few milliseconds. "5'9-ish, right? . . . 5'11," he said at last. The group jotted this down.

Abe interjected, "The last one is weighted down, slumping, you know. With the duffle bag. He'll be slightly taller as he exits."

"Are your guys going to be able to get us pieces of that bag?" Sheila asked.

"The bag? Maybe a scrap of metal if we're lucky. If our crime scene isn't contaminated too badly."

"It's locked down," said Sheila assuredly. "Just keep your boys focused. But we are going to need speed. The Roar brings millions of dollars to the local economy. We have to sort this out immediately." Nora thought she saw Abe and Anna actually roll their eyes at each other, but it was so subtle and quick that she couldn't be sure. Sheila continued, "Can we figure out a source for the ammonium nitrate?"

Abe laughed out loud. "Sure, every farm supply store in the region."

Pete said, "That will be about a thousand."

They all ingested this as Abe said, "Unless it's clear that someone is amassing ammonium nitrate in vast quantities, the farm supply stores have no obligation to keep a record. If I want to stockpile, I can go from one store to the next and just buy one bag." He stood at this point, stretching. "Alright, I've got to get back to my team."

"We'll be back down to the bank in a bit," said Sheila. "Thanks for coming up, Abe. Thanks for pulling in whoever got us this tape so fast."

Abe gave a grin that fell largely on Anna. "I live to serve," he said.

"Well, they can't have just disappeared," Anna was saying into the phone.

Pete looked at Nora. He stage whispered, "That sort of statement usually means that's exactly what happened."

Nora nodded, waiting.

Anna sighed and pulled her BlackBerry away from her ear. "Nothing."

"The chopper?" Pete asked.

"The chopper, state police, sheriff, PD, no one's got even a lead."

Pete hopped up on his desk, his long legs dangling. "You know, they get a lot of credit. Those are some bold bank robbers . . . robbing our little hamlet in broad daylight like this."

"Bold? Desperate?"

Anna harrumphed. "Probably both."

"Men on a mission," Nora surmised.

Her partners turned to look at her.

She shrugged. "They want to show strength, not sneakiness. They want to look badass in a way that attracts others—which is why they robbed a downtown bank in the middle of a motorcycle festival . . . on motorcycles. That heist was advertising."

The two were silent. Then Pete said, "Hey, Philadelphia. You sound like some kinda college girl."

Nora shook her head, but suppressed a smile just the same.

Anna stood. "I have to go with Sheila to oversee the evidence-gathering at the bank. Nora, how are you holding up, all those burns?"

Nora shrugged. She hadn't been thinking about them and

suddenly felt vaguely uncomfortable. "Nothing, Anna. Really, I'm fine."

"Ok. Then head out with Pete. Sort out where those motorcycles went."

Pete was nodding. Gingerly he said, "It's getting dark outside, Anna."

She put on her angry face, and both Pete and Nora were slightly taken aback. "Use a fucking flashlight, Peter. And don't come back until you have an answer."

She stalked off to Sheila's office without another word.

"I was just sayin'," Pete defended himself.

Nora shrugged. "She's in crisis mode. She didn't mean anything by it."

"Crisis mode," he repeated, leading her to his car.

"Shouldn't we walk?" she was asking.

"You do understand that it's like a thousand degrees outside," Pete retorted.

"Peter, as your accent clearly indicates, you are from the south. Why are you giving me a hard time? This is your climate."

"*Was*. Was my climate. Now I like air conditioning. I like snow tires. Sweat is . . ."

"Cramps your style?"

"Cramps my style," he affirmed.

"Doesn't help get the honeys?"

"Cramps my style," he said again. "And you sound ridiculous when you use words like that."

"Okay, we can take the car at least to where they disappeared from our line of vision, but then we need to start entertaining the idea that they ditched the bikes and are hiding, or that they hid the bikes somewhere nearby. It's just not possible that they got far."

"Fine," he said grudgingly, cranking the AC for the eight-block ride. He plopped the flashing light down on the roof of the steel gray Ford Fusion, and Nora recalled Ben's old car with a pang. She wondered why the Bureau kept giving its agents small cars that could be easily crushed. In the movies everyone got tank-like SUVs that shone like black mirrors.

Pete guided the car out onto State Street from the garage. They did not get very far until they were forced over to French by the impassable swarm of emergency vehicles. Some onlookers lingered as well; despite the fact that the bomb squad had issued an order to clear the area, some of the festival-goers, beer-emboldened, could not be daunted.

"What did you think that walking was going to achieve?"

Nora glanced at him and then at her own place as they passed it going the wrong way. "Look, in Philly I walked or ran everywhere . . . I felt like I knew the city better than the guys who were always in their squad cars, or their . . . whatever, their Bureau-issued vehicles."

Pete considered this. "I like my car."

"I know you do. But you don't really know the city, right?"

"I'm trying not to." He shrugged. "Also, this isn't really a city."

"Dude, it has a mayor. Come on."

But Pete only snorted.

Nora looked at him. She realized suddenly that Pete was biding his time as much as she was. "What's your ideal post, Peter?"

He looked at her wistfully. "Aw, now . . ."

"You can tell me. I know you're wishing you were somewhere else." She thought for a moment, then admitted, "So do I."

Pete inhaled then said, "Well, I've always wanted to live in California."

"Really?" Nora asked.

Pete nodded. "Yeah. Just, you know, live the dream a little. My family . . . well, my family isn't very well off. So."

The way he spoke these words left Nora assured that they were a massive understatement. She regarded him thoughtfully as he drove. "So Cali is the answer?" she asked.

"Nah. But I thought it'd be cool to have one of those Hollywood girls. You know, just once."

"Some hard-core beer-drinking girl?" Nora teased.

"Hell yeah," he said, grinning.

"I'm pretty sure Hollywood girls like sweet drinks in pretty glasses," Nora said. "I saw it in the movies, brother."

Pete threw back his head and laughed. "Don't believe everything you see, Miss Nora. The girl who loves beer and former quarterbacks—"

"Crime-fighting former quarterbacks, mind you," Nora interjected.

"Yes, crime-fighting former quarterbacks . . . she's out there."

Nora smiled. "I do believe that she is. That said, what do you see here?"

They had looped around to the east side of the hospital and were now overlooking the bay. They lingered for a moment at the traffic light, their eyes scanning the view. The bay stretched out, dark blue-gray in the twilight. The road descended toward the Maritime Museum, the library and harbor, the convention center and its hotel, and the small bayside restaurants.

Nora tilted her head, her eyes scanning the water. "Could they have gotten on a boat?"

Pete glanced at her. "With their bikes or without?"

Nora shrugged. "I don't know."

He considered for a moment, then said, "They could have shoved their bikes into the bay and jumped on a boat. Sure. The scenario where they get motorcycles onto a boat would be . . . I don't know, unwieldy at worst and attention-getting at best." He pulled the car into the Erie Sand and Gravel Works. He slid the gear shift into park and they descended into the evening's heat.

"I mean, they could have headed to Canada, right?" Nora said. "It's only, what, twenty-five miles away?"

"Canadian bank robbers?"

"It'd be funny, right? Canadian bank robbers. Dressed up like prototypical American alpha males?"

Pete laughed out loud. "On behalf of the prototypical American alpha male, I'm offended that such an absurdity could even flit across your brain."

A squat-looking administrative building seemed ill at ease holding sway over what looked like acres of gravel piles stretching as far as the eye could see. A long, empty road meandered between the piles.

Pete looked from the road to Nora. "Dump trucks take the gravel all over the city," he said thoughtfully. "But also to the end of this road for loading onto barges."

"Well, who do you call for warrants to search the gravel company?"

It turns out that John M. Finch, owner of the Erie Sand and Gravel Company, was more than welcoming, and no warrant was necessary at all. But there were also no abandoned motorcycles and no employees who'd seen any boats approaching the docks.

Anna narrowed her eyes at them when they returned after 10 P.M. empty-handed.

"Not even a track?"

Pete shook his head. "Trucks run in and out of there until dark. Any bike tracks would have been obliterated."

"Lot of brush out there. You're sure?" Anna insisted. She had clearly liked the idea.

"There are no abandoned bikes. You want to look in the bay, that's another story." His tone was borderline disrespectful but Anna was too tired to push back.

"No, I don't want to order a sweep of the bay yet. But I'm not ruling it out, either."

Finally she said, "Well, the state troopers are continuing to search. We gave them the outside perimeter and they've stuck to it efficiently. But nothing. I'll see if I can't get the coast guard in on the fun. Pitch your Canadian idea to them."

"They're in the city," Pete opined. "Biding their time."

"Til what? Heading for Rio?" Anna demanded.

Pete shrugged. "White men in leather with money. Definitely Vegas."

Nora drummed her fingers on her desk. "They had the money. Why bomb the bank and kill the guard? It puts them in a whole other felony class. What was the point?"

"Makes a statement?" Pete offered.

"That they . . . don't like banks?" Nora rejoined.

"Banks are institutions," Anna said softly. "Institutions of the American government because they are federally insured."

"Anti-government types then?" Pete asked, rubbing the stubble along his jawline.

Anna shrugged. "Maybe. McVeigh used the same kind of bomb, you know."

"So, what I said. Makes a statement."

"They walked away with almost a million in cash. What are they going to do with it?"

She shook her head. "Better rifles?"

Nora thought of Abe's assessment of the homemade explosives used at the bank. "Better bombs."

"Jesus," Pete whispered.

Nora and Pete exchanged glances, waiting.

"Alright, you two. Let's give it a fresh start in the morning. Be here early, though. The whole city is in an uproar. They're this close to shutting down the festival."

"They should shut down the festival," Nora said.

"It's not a festival," Pete interjected. "It's Roar on the Shore. Festival makes it sound like there's maypoles and wine tasting."

"Whatever the hell it is," Anna said testily, "it may not be for long. If we can't make a quick arrest here, they're going to cancel the non-festival's festivities. Got it? So we're not lingering over Starbucks wenches and we're not taking our morning runs, we're showing up early and fixing this thing."

Nora and Pete nodded and headed out the door.

"What about Frank Burgess?" Nora asked, as they started descending the stairs.

Pete shrugged. "A few extra days getting brutalized in prison won't hurt that fat fuck."

Nora winced, but found that she agreed wholeheartedly.

Her neighbor Rachel had been keeping an eye out for her return. This was disconcerting for Nora. The feeling transformed swiftly when she found that her neighbor was handing her a large Tupperware container, still warm, with several pieces of buttery garlic bread resting precariously on top of it. "I made gnocchi today. Had plenty to share."

With a rush of gratitude, Nora realized she hadn't eaten anything for almost twelve hours and she was ravenous. "Rachel, you shouldn't have. I still feel like it's too soon for you to be up and around like this," she observed.

"You heard the doctor. A few bruises. I got off easy this time."

She had. Nora had been in the room when the nurse recorded the legacy of broken bones, a knife-slashing across her belly, and a pot full of boiling water dashed at her back as she tried to dart away.

"Anyway, you should come in," Nora said.

"No way, I heard the commotion, saw the news, and I know you must be wrecked. I wanted to insist you come up to my place, but I knew you'd be too tired, so I brought you this to-go deal here. Not pretty, but it works."

"You're . . . you're completely amazing. Thank you."

"Hey, now that I've got a new door, there's nothing stopping me," Rachel said cheerfully.

Nora took in the bland, cream-colored fiberglass door the landlord had apparently installed that day. It would have been better suited to some suburban subdivision than their character-heavy, early 20th-century brown brick abode. Nora wondered where the thick oak frame had gone, and suddenly realized how vulnerable her own door, more glass than wood, looked in comparison.

"Well, let's hope none of the other neighbors sleeps with open windows," Nora teased.

"Got a brick through the window just before you got here."

For a second, Nora had believed her, but then saw that Rachel was laughing. Nora hated to admit she'd actually fantasized about sneaking out and throwing a brick through the window with a "*practice in daylight hours*" message attached.

"If I weren't practicing for an audition in Pittsburgh, I'd ease up. So the food is a way to say I'm sorry, too. I can't stop just yet, but soon, I promise."

Nora reached out and embraced her tightly, careful not to knock the garlic bread to the ground. "You do what you need to do. I'm lucky to get to hear it, Rachel."

Rachel grinned. "Thanks, Nora. Be safe in all this. Let me know if you need anything."

She was just nestling into bed when she heard Ben's ringtone. She rolled over and grabbed the phone.

"You knew I'd be worried about you, but you wouldn't answer my texts or calls. What the hell, Nora? The story's all over the news."

"I've been busy," she said.

"You're being passive-aggressive or something."

"I'm being tired."

"Are you injured?"

She gazed down at the gauze circling her forearm. "Nah."

He was silent. "Are you seriously still angry at me over this thing?"

"I was trying not to think about it."

"She's not a threat to you, Nora. You know how I feel about you."

"I know. But you had a relationship with her that . . ." Nora stared at the swirls in the plaster ceiling, groping for words. Finally, she said, "I don't know how to be that person. Yet. And you've been . . . well, patient for a white guy."

"I'll continue to be patient until you run out of patience," Ben insisted. "I told you that from the beginning. I'll never pressure you, Nora. I know it's all still . . . new."

She inhaled deeply, trying to smother the fear in her. Ben could get any woman, should have any woman, shouldn't have to wait for her to get over a lifetime of lessons about waiting til marriage. They were lessons that were starting to feel like they'd come from a different world altogether.

He too was silent, then said, "Look, for the sake of an old friendship, I need to be there for her. I am not going back to her. I'm just being there."

Nora felt a surge of emotion. "Well, I could use a friend too, Benjamin. You might think about it that way."

"Well, every time I schedule time with you, I'm also scheduling time with your family," he snapped.

It came too quickly. Nora turned his response over in her head, then said softly, "I guess I get it now."

"Look, Nora, I—"

"Enjoy your stay," she said, cutting him off. She ended the call. Then, uncharacteristically, she turned off the ringer completely. She would trust that the Bureau did not need her for the few hours remaining until she reported for work. It only took half an hour of crying until she fell into a fitful sleep.

FIRST **DAY**

The Bureau had called seventeen times in the night. When she saw the phone screen she used every swear word she never had, then tore out of the house without brushing her teeth, running the length of the nearly-deserted early morning sidewalk between her home and the office.

She had remembered this time to wear her sneakers.

The office was in chaos.

"Nora, where the fuck have you been?" Pete demanded. "I was about to come see if you were dead or something."

"I'm so sorry, I never turn the phone off and I just . . ."

"Picked the night of our biggest case to do it?" His eyes were incredulous.

"Sheila's pissed?" Nora asked tentatively, her stomach twisting into knots.

"Sheila's too busy to be anything right now, but she will eventually remember she should be pissed at you."

Anna was on her phone and talking to Maggie simultaneously. Every phone in the office seemed to be ringing. Nora felt lightheaded with a combination of regret and anger at herself. She immediately balled that anger up and transformed it into fury at Ben. Somehow this was going to be his fault.

"What happened?" she demanded.

"We got a claim of responsibility. And then a murder right on its heels."

Nora laid a hand on the nearest desk. "No."

Pete nodded. "It's been insane."

"Claim of responsibility from whom?"

"White supremacist patriot group, sent out a very scary webcast." He typed on his keyboard and a face filled his screen. "Gabriel Baker. Who is apparently actually a truck driver. But he happens to be calling for Armageddon."

Nora stared at the face of a middle-aged white man, pale blond hair, tanned skin, neatly-trimmed facial hair. "Demands?"

Pete shook his head. "So far he's demanding we pay attention. Wants our illegitimate government to step down; wants to expel all foreigners and non-Christians from the country. He sent it to all the news stations and so half the night was spent trying to convince them not to air it and start a panic."

"Who was the victim?" she asked Pete, her eyes scanning the room, trying to deduce information from the level of chaos.

Peter's face was grim. "Judge Bernstein. Seventy-one years old. Federal judge. Drive-by shooting. He was returning to his house after a dinner out. Just got out of the car when he was nailed. Wife sustained no injuries."

"Don't tell me motorcycles."

"Okay. *Motorcycle.* Eyewitness saw one guy driving, one guy shooting."

"Semi-automatic assault rifle?"

Pete was nodding.

"Backpacks?"

"Good question but no. If it was the same crew, they've dropped them off somewhere."

"Where was it? Close by?"

"West Sixth Street," Pete said, pointing behind Nora's head in a rather useless gesture.

In the neighborhood. Nora shook her head. The murder rate in Erie was assessed quarterly instead of daily. People often didn't lock their cars or even their doors in some neighborhoods. Nora herself had taken to leaving a spare key behind a crumbling brick on her front porch so she could run unencumbered. No one had threatened her—not once. Not even any of the grizzled homeless men who occupied Perry Square at night. To gun down an elderly judge on Erie's nicest block . . . She shook her head.

"Leads?"

"No! No leads." Pete ran vexed fingers through his hair, a deep frown on his face. "They disappeared just like the others did. And I've spent the whole night trying to trace the IP address on the webcast and it was completely fucking impossible. All we can say for sure is that the Pennsylvania militia movement is alive and well and way more tech savvy than we previously assumed."

"How long you been here, buddy?" Nora asked, forcing herself to be and sound very calm.

"All night, Nora. I was just getting into bed when the call came through."

"Okay, then I'll call it a stroke of good luck that one of us got some rest. Show me the reports and then go curl up in the Room of Requirement. And do not drink any more coffee. You look like you just walked out of a crack house."

He looked at her askance.

"All wild-eyed. Got the crazy hair," she added. As though to answer his unspoken accusation, she pointed to herself and said, "Philly PD. I've seen things, brother."

He smiled despite himself, then showed her all the info on his laptop, printing up the most recent police and coroner's reports. Then he went into the storage room, saying the words, "Ten minutes," over his shoulder.

Pete had just vanished when Anna and Sheila both walked into the cubicle.

"Nice of you to join us, Nora," Sheila practically spat at her. Looking up from Pete's laptop screen, Nora could see the stress etched across her face, and it scared her slightly more than images of men on motorcycles.

She tried to convey how badly she felt without sounding melo-dramatic. "I'm so sorry—"

"Later, later," Anna said quickly. "We have a new issue to deal with. Where's Peter?"

"New issue?" Nora asked, rising.

"Yes, there's been an abduction."

Nora looked from one face to the other. "Really?"

Sheila looked furious. "Of course, really," she hurled, as though Nora's response were the stupidest possible thing anyone could have said. "April Lewis, the first black councilwoman Erie's had."

Nora blinked, thinking rapidly. "Details?"

"She didn't come home last night," Anna said. "The family got a call. They're very wealthy, so they were tempted to pay the ran-som right away without contacting us. But when they heard about the judge's murder this morning, they finally called it in."

"Who did they think they were going to pay?" Nora asked.

Anna checked her notes. "The call they got was very short. It said to leave 1.5 million dollars in unmarked bills in a couple of trash cans in Perry Square."

"These things usually go into bank accounts—it's a very old-school ransom request," Sheila observed.

Anna shrugged. "I guess we've seen how they feel about banks."

"Cell phone or landline?" Nora asked.

"Hmm?" Anna asked.

"The call came in to a cell phone or a landline?" she repeated.

"Oh, no, a landline. Where's Pete?"

"Sheila!" Maggie's voice somehow managed to clear the forest of other sounds in the office. "Sheila: TV."

All three women swiveled their necks to see Vance Evans fill-ing the screen, an air of gravitas infusing his carefully powdered features.

"Oh, no . . ." Anna murmured. "We begged him to hold off until we could determine if this group was legit. . . ."

"NBC News regrets to share with the general public the video, sent last night, detailing the agenda of a local militia—"

"I am going to fucking kill him. I am going to fucking kill that man!" Sheila's shouting drowned out Vance Evans. "He's going to set off a fucking city-wide panic—" Then, she interrupted herself to yell, "Maggie! Get me Washington on the line and call in the CIRG. . . ."

Sheila's eyes shone with rage. She turned to the agents. "Conference room!"

"Wake up, Peter," Nora said, crouching next to him.

He rolled over, squinting. "That cannot have been ten minutes," he whined.

"Well, it was close. We need you."

Cursing, he came to a sitting position on the vinyl loveseat. He rubbed desperately at his eyes, trying to make them focus, then followed her to the conference room where Anna had already called up the webcast.

Anna glanced at them and then back at the screen. As the conference room door was closing, Nora overheard Sheila shouting through the closed door of her office. Her voice was a full register higher than Nora had imagined it could go.

"You're so fucking bored with broadcasting about Ox Roasts that you're willing to terrify the public and publicize for terrorists?"

Pete looked a question at Nora.

"NBC went ahead and broadcast the webcast. 'Breaking news.'"

"Fuck. Fucking idiots," he said.

"That's apparently Sheila's take on it," Nora said.

Anna nodded to Nora. "You didn't hear this yet. I guess we'll be getting to know this video inside and out."

She pressed play on the remote in her hand.

They all remained standing around the conference table, waiting for Gabriel Baker's words.

"*The Jewish judiciary is strangling the vision of our president. If we wait any longer for real change, it will be too late. We thus declare open warfare against all enemies of traditional Aryan values. With the fourteen acts of violence that will come, we begin the task that we must accomplish. We must secure the existence of our people and a future for white children.*"

Pete leaned against the wall then ran his fingers through his hair.

Nora felt her whole body slacken. She, too, found herself leaning against the wall for support.

"You recognize it?" he asked softly.

She nodded.

"Fourteen, huh?"

"Fourteen."

"*We have been growing, my brothers and sisters. And now it is time to act. We welcome our fellow militia members to join us. We open our hearts and our doors to like-minded preservers of tradition. The time for radical action is now. The time to banish fear is now. . . .*"

Anna regarded Pete. "This bullshit is supposed to be regional. What'd you do, Pete, import it?"

"Oh, come on, Anna. There are more Confederate flags flying off of Girard pickup trucks than back in South Carolina," he snapped.

Nora noted that when he was angry his Southern accent intensified exponentially.

Sheila burst in, slamming the conference room door behind her. Her chest was rising and falling rapidly and she was clutching her BlackBerry, her tablet, a legal pad, and three different pens. Taking her place at the head of the table, Sheila asked,

"What's the story with the number fourteen? Is there something important about that?"

Reluctantly, all three of them sank into seats around the table. Pete and Nora let Anna explain. "Fourteen is a white supremacist symbol, very current in alt-right discourse. There are fourteen words in that slogan, maybe the most popular slogan for the movement—the one about securing the future for white children."

Sheila's lips pursed hard against this news, her frown lines deepening. "Fourteen acts of violence . . ."

"Four down," Anna said softly.

Pete frowned. "Four?"

Sheila said tersely, "There's also been an abduction. City councilwoman. Black woman."

"You think it's important that she's black?" asked Anna.

"Now I do," said Sheila.

"The bank guard was black?" Pete asked.

There was a general nod of confirmation. Nora was starting to feel desperate for tea.

"*Preliminary evening* means what's coming today can only be worse, right?" Pete asked.

Both Anna and Sheila looked at him. Sheila looked slightly queasy.

Pete seemed lost in thought, though. He was rapping his knuckles on the table, saying, "I didn't think there was a significant armed militia presence in Pennsylvania. I knew Michigan, Ohio—"

Anna chimed in, ticking off on her fingers, "West Virginia, Washington State, even Minnesota . . ."

Pete said, "After Obama took office there was an eight-hundred-percent increase in anti-government patriot groups. With all the energy generated by the last election, there are well over three thousand out there now. Some three hundred of them classify as militia. They got on high alert, thinking they'd have to take back the country after a 'rigged' election. Money was rolling in to fundraising sites—a lot of it was through the Dark Web but a lot was pretty brazen, out in the open. The alt-right was suddenly awash in money and firepower. Hard to redirect."

"What changed?" Nora said. "Why are they materializing now?

"Someone must have decided change wasn't coming fast enough."

"But Erie? Here?"

"Sure, why not? We had one of the biggest flips in history, right? Hold on to that anger, wait for something to get better. If nothing improves, well, Roar on the Shore, sister," said Pete. "Noise, bikes, white folks doin' their thing. At the very least, it's good cover."

Anna shook her head rapidly. "There's never been a problem with Roar on the Shore before," she said. "The worst that's happened is public urination or a few bar fights. People come to shop and swap and show off."

"And dance," said Pete. "White Snake came last year."

Sheila nodded, looking at Nora but not looking at her. "We need to identify the catalyst. Let's look at this thing a minute together."

"Can Maggie make a transcript for us so we can parse it bit by bit?" Anna asked.

Sheila hesitated. "I hate to lose time like that but let's ask her."

The *let's* in this case meant that Anna needed to go do it if she wanted it done. Anna rose and went to talk to Maggie.

The TV meanwhile had gone back to the local "breaking news" newscast. Vance Evans was busily gathering public reaction.

The cameras had headed out into vendors' alley along Perry Square. A heavily bearded man was standing outside one of the Harley-Davidson kiosks. The small amount of flesh visible on his face glowed pink with sunburn. A skull and crossbones bandanna crowned his head, pulled tightly across his forehead and knotted in the back.

"Nobody defiles Roar on the Shore, man," he was saying.

Vance Evans asked him, "What is the mood among the festival-goers?"

"You mean the bike rally, right? It's not a festival, man."

"I mean those attending Roar on the Shore," said Vance patiently, a look of patronizing interest cemented across his tanned features. Belatedly the screen ran the interviewee's name: *Jerry Walsh of Fredonia, New York.*

"People are pissed, man. People look forward to the Roar all year round, man. This is a peaceful gathering of people who love to ride. I can't see no bikers doing that. Blowin' up a bank. The Roar is beautiful, man. Keep that terrorist shit outta here."

The live broadcast couldn't bleep out the expletive.

Evans asked him, "What do you think of the broadcast from the Pennsylvania Patriots? Does the message of revolution resonate with you?"

"I think that's bullshit, man," Walsh said. He gestured at the shiny bikes in the kiosk. "The Harley Revolution is the only revolution I'm interested in."

Vance Evans walked to the next kiosk, where a woman with a shock of gray curls and, in Nora's opinion, alarmingly tight blue jeans stood, pale blue eyes swimming with tears. She was unpacking her goods—dream catchers, hand-painted leather jackets, hair clips with attached eagle feathers, and a variety of knick-knacks—in preparation for the 11 A.M. opening time.

"By this time last year I'd made a thousand dollars. Now nothing! That madness happened right at opening! And now look, look at the streets—it's like a wasteland."

Vance Evans turned back to the camera. "And that's the word from the street. Mr. Baker will have to work much harder to convince these frustrated bikers that the mission and message of the

Pennsylvania Patriots warrant disrupting this all-important week with violence and bloodshed."

Nora and Pete looked from the screen to each other.

"Play the video again while we're waiting for the transcript," Anna said, coming back in. "It'll take a while."

Gabriel Baker liked to clench his fist and hold it aloft. He also liked to use big words, although Nora, ever averse to big words, felt as though he occasionally stumbled over them.

"Most of the message is recycled, right?" Pete said, rubbing his hand over his beard. His laptop was open and he was tapping phrases into the Google taskbar to see if they had come from other sources.

"Yes and no," murmured Nora. "The Order. Anti-government stuff. But there's other stuff. Stuff I didn't see in class."

Sheila looked lost. Anna explained, "The Order is a white supremacist terrorist group. Guy named David Lane was its best articulator. Can you pause it, Pete?" she asked.

Baker had just said, *"Diversity is code for white genocide."*

Anna nodded. "Yes, this is also classic Order stance."

"Do we have a new David Lane on our hands?" Sheila was asking.

They each considered this.

"Lane was a thug," said Pete, eyes riveted on his laptop screen. "I don't have anything on Gabriel Baker; not yet, anyway. We can run an extensive search but I have nothing matching so far."

In the background, Baker was still speaking.

We must disavow our liberal bedazzlements and relearn the meaning of fear. Only the stupid know no fear. Not fearing our enemies is the ultimate form of stupidity. Refusing to rise up and reclaim the future for our own white children is self-annulment. If these mud-peoples will not take the necessary step of deliverance through self-annihilation, then let us unburden them. If all of us rise, then no one can imprison us. If our ruler can not

purge our material soil of foreigners, those who would unseat
their masters and presume to rule, those who lack art, who lack
history, whose gods are their own and who defile Nature as un-
pleasant freaks, wholly and forever disagreeably foreign, forever
creatures of a sick twilit moral code . . . then we must extend the
righteous hand of aid to this leader for whom we had had such
high hopes. For even under his eye, those who would destroy us
flourish.

Nora snapped her fingers, recognizing a catch phrase.

But Anna was already nodding.

"Mud-peoples—that's straight out of the Christian Identity
lexicon," she said.

Sheila tapped her pen on the table, waiting.

"Christian Identity is a spinoff of British Israelism," Anna supplied. "They incorporate very racist, very anti-Semitic interpre-
tations of the Bible. Anyone not created when God created whites
is lumped in with the beasts of the field, and so any non-white is
a 'mud person.'"

Nora suddenly perceived that each person in the room was
carefully refusing to glance at her caramel-colored skin. She
drummed her fingers on the tabletop, enjoying their discomfort.

"One of its early voices was Wesley Swift."

Baker's voice had grown louder, surer, as though settling into
his role. Nora tilted her head to listen to him. She wondered if
any television preachers would endorse such a message.

"What was that church Swift founded?" Nora asked. "Christian Christians or something?"

"Church of Jesus Christ-Christian," said Anna.

Sheila asked, "Is he alive? Dead?"

"Oh, way dead," Pete said. "Must have been the sixties."

"1970," Anna volunteered. "His disciple Richard Butler founded
the Aryan Nations."

"Who've been racists without a country for a while now—they

lost big in a lawsuit. No more compound, no real leadership," Pete said.

Emancipation from the yoke of Judaism was once the greatest of necessities . . . and now we add to this the yoke of the black, the Muslim, the Arab, the Asian, the African, and all the unwashed migrants swarming over our sovereign borders. What self-deception it is to pretend we do not hold a natural repugnance against all of these, instinctive as it is primal and born of self-preservation, preservation of a noble race.

"I don't think ransom is going to help April Lewis," Sheila murmured. "Not a federal government representative, true, but a government official. A black one."

"Do we have proof of life yet?" Pete asked.

"No," Sheila responded, shaking her head. "Chief Nichols and I are going to visit the family as soon as we're finished here and discuss how to proceed. And listen, people. *You* are all representatives of the federal government. Which means we don't set foot outside this office without Kevlar from now on."

Pete glanced at her skeptically.

"Even just to go for coffee, Peter," Sheila said, putting on the scary face. "Does each of you understand me?"

They all grunted assent. Anna was leaning forward, as was Pete. Nora, too, was riveted.

"He's kinda hot," Anna admitted. "Married, though. Nice ring . . ." Baker made yet another solidarity fist. As the camera zoomed in, the hammered silver band came into view. "Nice teeth. All in all they picked a good spokesman."

Nora looked at her, a little repelled by her callousness.

Anna seemed self-assured though. "Well, look, they needed someone to bring together all these alt-right groups, didn't they? Christian Identity and Patriots and whatnot . . . I mean did you ever *see* John Trochmann? It's only logical that someone easier on the eye should step up this time."

Baker had his fist up again, inciting his people.

An act of rebellion every day to take back our country once and for all; a purging of the country's impurities. A replicable plan for those who know that only through revolution will we regain what has been lost; the lie of democracy is not enough.

Fourteen acts of violence will collectively work the deed that redeems the world.

Pay attention. Pay careful attention and repeat this formula over and over, in your towns, in your cities, in the furthest reaches of the globe.

Fourteen.

All four of them looked at each other.

Finally, Sheila said, "Pete, do you think your Starbucks friend could be convinced to deliver? It's going to be a long week."

The Critical Incident Response Group had taken rather more of Nora's time at Quantico than she'd deemed necessary. She had not elected to tread a path that led to being part of CIRG, but it felt to her that, in response, the Bureau made her study the division and its organization even more, perhaps to cultivate the necessary level of awe. CIRG had emerged out of the post-Waco self-flagellations and remained as a sort of bloated beast, feeding off the Bureau's fear of failure. Those training for either its Aviation and Surveillance or Tactical Operations sections tended to walk with a particular swagger, while the Behavioral Analysis people cultivated a mystique that fluctuated between brainiac and seductive psychotherapist. Those in the Critical Incident Intelligence Unit, meanwhile, spoke to no one but each other.

Nora knew that the CIRG sweeping into Erie would be transformative. Both the scope of the CIRG and the egos of those directing it were massive. Sheila would be eaten alive, and whatever limited sense of power the three special agents on staff had attained would vanish.

She looked at Pete and Anna, feeling like she needed to brace herself.

Anna said, "Anyone feeling nostalgic for pedophiles?"

"Ooh, me," Pete said, immediately.

Pete was assigned the task of sorting out a source for the webcast link that had originally been emailed to them. Anna and Nora were to parse the text for any concrete indications of a plan, including any possible threats against local institutions. Sheila was busy calling in the cavalry and managing the councilwoman's abduction, an issue that both the family and the FBI were desperate to keep from the media.

Anna's reading glasses were perched on the tip of her nose as she made a grim list using her trademark incongruous purple felt tip pen. "Blacks, Jews, Muslims, Arabs, immigrants . . ."

"Mexicans . . . Latinos generally. Illegal immigrants generally. And then probably refugees, right?" said Nora. "The writer is complaining about the government letting people in, and you have a refugee population here. . . ."

Anna looked up as though remembering something. "We got a call, actually. Two or three days ago. Wait."

She popped out of her seat and began rummaging about on the shelf over her desk, her orange hair looking particularly unkempt. Nora just had time to peek at her BlackBerry, the screen of which was now blank. Ben had given up trying to talk to her. By now, the field office in Philly would know about Gabriel Baker. She wondered if Ben were back at work after "taking care" of his ex-girlfriend in New York City.

"There was some graffiti," Anna said, finally seizing a different legal pad than the one she'd been jotting notes on. "They called it in as a hate crime."

"Who's this?" Nora asked.

"You said refugees. I'm saying, the Office of Refugee Resettlement in DC has a local office here, and they called in some graffiti on their building on Monday." Anna looked slightly guilty as she said this.

"I take it we didn't get back to them?" Nora asked.

"Well, Monday and Tuesday we were knee-deep in Frank Burgess, right?" Anna replied, looking, it seemed to Nora, as though she were seeking absolution.

Nora gave her none. "What did the graffiti say?"

Anna checked her notes.

"*Go back where you come from.*"

"Unfriendly," Nora observed.

"Nothing more unfriendly than a dangling participle," Anna rejoined. "On the other side of the building they wrote *Rabid dogs.*"

"Better. I like to see good old campaign rhetoric take root."

Anna gave a small shrug and seemed to be scanning the notes for anything else that might provide insight.

"Why would you come to Erie as a refugee?" Nora wondered aloud.

"Why do you go anywhere as a refugee?" Anna responded absently.

Nora shrugged, hesitant to admit she was a little vague on the process.

"Anyway," she said, looking up from her notes, "since the natives are leaving the area in record numbers, the refugee population has boosted the city's numbers."

"Given Erie's overall lack of diversity, should I assume the natives are leaving because the refugees are coming in?"

Anna tsked softly, shaking her head. "Nah. The natives are leaving because there are no good factory jobs and fewer white-collar positions. Same old story. Still, the cost of living here is easier on a new resident than, say, Philly or Pittsburgh. Getting by in Erie is more doable."

Nora contemplated this. The rent on the French Street apartment was seven hundred dollars. In Philly, the same rent would have landed her in a roach-roiling death trap. She shivered. Her current home was more spacious than the apartment in which she grew up.

"Well, I guess that we have a pretty good idea where to start on our list, then."

Anna nodded. "Let's pay them a visit and see if we can't suggest they get some emergency plans in place. Or maybe just shut down for the next couple of days until we sort this out."

Nora had taken to wearing light cotton undershirts in case she needed to add the Kevlar vest to her outfit. The vest was hard to disguise under her Oxford shirt, but with the blazer it wasn't too noticeable. The summer heat made the blazer seem like the accessory of an insane person, however. She and Anna exchanged knowing glances as they headed out into the July morning.

Nora liked the way Anna drove. She was calm, assertive, and never swore. She drove as though she expected the traffic to part for her, and as far as Nora could tell, it actually did. They took State Street all the way up to 26th. It was not a pretty drive. The sedan passed several abandoned factories, their many-paned windows broken or blackened. Small, weedy lots were occupied by used car dealerships and shuttered businesses. Turning onto 26th, they traveled past shabby row houses with limp aluminum siding and listing window air conditioners.

The Office of Refugee Resettlement's International Institute inhabited a long, low building on East 26th. The two agents entered, their eyes adjusting with effort to the dim lighting after the fierce July sun. The mismatched chairs outside the office area held an array of people, and Nora regarded them curiously as Anna showed her badge to the intern.

The intern asked them to wait in the waiting area. Nora settled into a folding chair, listening carefully to the soft buzz of languages around her. The faces were drawn, tired, and used-to-waiting.

A tiny woman in a cream-colored headscarf spoke rapid Syrian Arabic to a gaunt teenaged boy with a thin layer of down on his upper lip. A little girl, no more than four, rotated between them, leaning against each set of knees, occasionally careening in her trajectory slightly beyond mother or brother and then skidding to a confused halt as she got too close to a stranger. With wide, blinking eyes, she would walk backwards and then begin again.

One object of the girl's fascination seemed to be the towering magenta wrap perched atop the head of an elderly African woman. The woman did not even glance at the little girl, though, and instead sat regarding Nora steadily. Her wide black eyes, the whites laced with a web of red veins, conveyed a total lack of interest. Nora felt that the gaze had been there, long and heavy, and Nora had accidentally sat down in it. Two tall men sat to the woman's left, talking softly in a language Nora couldn't divine.

The heat in the room was intense, and Nora began to fidget. "What's the name of the director?" She had just murmured these words to Anna when the intern tugged the sliding glass window aside and said, "Regina will see you now."

They stood and were given access to the office. Regina's office was small and crowded with towering stacks of paper. The bright light barreling through the window at Regina's back made her hair seem to glow. She was herself thin and gaunt, her face pale. Her half-hearted stab at makeup seemed to accentuate her paleness: two dark streaks of eyeliner weighed heavily on her eyelids, a jarring contrast to her blond eyelashes and eyebrows. She wore an orangey shade of lipstick. Nora, who wore no makeup at all, suddenly wanted to lean across the desk and do something she'd never done: offer girly advice. *That look is all wrong for you.* Maybe in just the way she'd heard women do occasionally—in the hushed tones of professional women who want to maintain professionalism. *You have lipstick on your teeth. There's mascara in your bangs. Your tag's sticking up in back.*

Regina looked irritated.

As though sensing this, Anna led off. "We apologize for the delay in getting back to you. We're grateful that you contacted us."

Regina nodded gravely. "We've had an uptick lately in incidents. You know. It's a different world now . . ."

"Incidents?" asked Nora.

"People come in. Kids. Bullied in school or walking home from the bus. Veiled women are getting yelled at more, headscarves being pulled off. But it's a general xenophobia. My kids from the Congo are having a hard time. All it takes is an accent and even the other black kids go after them."

Anna tilted her head. "You have many from the Congo?"

Regina nodded, her face pained. "Yeah. Often they're kids who've been child soldiers, you know? So they get bullied like that, it's like brushing off flies. Sometimes they'll ask me, though . . . how much are they allowed to react. . . ."

Anna nodded. "But nothing serious, no threats?"

Regina looked at them with a steely gaze. "I think the graffiti is serious. And a threat. Which is why I called you for help."

Nora appreciated the firm response. She realized this woman didn't give a damn what Nora thought about her makeup.

"Has anything like this happened before?" Anna asked.

"Never. People are generally pretty welcoming. With the exception of the incidents I mentioned, I'd call Erie folks very giving, very tolerant. Proud they are a host city."

Nora saw that Anna's phone was vibrating with an incoming call. Anna glanced down. Sheila's name filled the screen. Anna frowned, then stood up to walk to the hall. "Forgive me," she said to Regina.

Anna walking out did not help Regina's mood. She watched Anna leave, then let her eyes rest on Nora.

Nora shifted under her gaze, searching for something to say. "How many refugees are in Erie now?" she finally asked.

"Upwards of nine thousand. There are five thousand Bhutanese alone."

Nora wasn't going to confess she had no idea where Bhutan was.

Regina sighed impatiently. "Look, you clearly have no idea what goes on here. We are the ones who greet refugees at the airport. We set them up in apartments and make sure they understand how to use flushing toilets and gas stoves and—"

At Nora's frown, Regina interrupted herself. "Look, not all of them are urban Europeans like the Bosnians. We get people from the Congo and remote areas of Sudan who've lived the last ten years under a tarp in a refugee camp where they had to dig their own latrines."

Nora nodded, feeling ignorant, as Regina continued.

"We show them where the doctor is, get them plugged into English lessons, get them social security cards, get them jobs, help them fill out their tax forms, call their landlords to explain they have no hot water, teach them how to ride the city bus to get to work, enroll their kids in school. . . ."

"So the people in the waiting room there—"

"Have had their homes blown up, their daughters raped, their husbands shot, their brothers beaten. They've spent anywhere from two to twenty years in a filthy, over-crowded camp where you have to wait in line for clean water. They've spent years being lost. And we're just trying to help them find their way." Regina's eyes were tired. Nora weighed the woman's words in silence.

Anna pushed open the door, her face drawn and tense.

"Okay, so Regina, I do not want to rush through this, but I'm here to suggest that you get a solid emergency plan in place. More than this, I think it's essential that you shut down for the next few days."

"Shut down?" Regina asked. "You're kidding, right? These people rely on us for services, for—"

"No, I'm afraid I'm not kidding. We have good reason to believe that this refugee community is a possible target of domestic terrorism."

Regina blinked. "Domestic terrorism," she repeated incredulously.

"There are patriot groups and white militia organizations all over the country," Anna explained patiently. "We got a message from a local group that they have some issues with—"

"—Everyone," Nora supplied.

"Well, with everyone not white," Anna continued.

"And so we were hoping—"

But Regina was not listening. She had tilted her head slightly, narrowing her eyes as she listened to a near deafening roar coming from the street. The glass pane in the window trembled. Each woman rose to standing. Nora instinctively put her hand on the handle of her gun as she and Anna exchanged a look. *Motorcycles. A lot of them.*

And then the window exploded inward. The sound of rapid gunfire mingled with screaming filled the air. Regina tumbled forward over her desk as Anna yanked Nora to the ground; both women threw up their arms to avoid the shower of glass and bullets as they sheltered in front of Regina's desk. The screaming in the lobby intensified, and the sound of gunfire grew even louder.

Anna tugged the unconscious Regina all the way over her desk and onto the floor. "No pulse!" she said to Nora.

Nora released the safety on her gun.

Anna placed a hand on her arm, her eyes wide. "Those are semi-automatic weapons, Nora."

"And I'm a very good shot," she said, shaking her off.

She cracked open the door to Regina's office and felt Anna immediately at her back. The scene unfolding took her breath away. Two women in jeans and T-shirts stood firing into the waiting room and reception area. One had a long blonde braid, the other medium-length brown hair that swung with every discharge of her weapon.

"Hey!" Nora screamed, but she could not even hear her own voice over the thunderous sounds of the gunfire and the screaming. In horror she saw that the little Syrian girl was lying face down, her soft curls spilling onto the floor.

Nora took aim through the smoky air and fired two bullets into the back of the woman with the braid; she fell forward immediately. Her brown-haired companion whirled to face Nora, a look of fury on her face. Before she could open fire, Nora plowed three shots into her midsection.

The force of the bullets caused the woman to fly backwards and collapse onto the lap of one of the very tall Africans who was now slumped dead in his chair. The woman's weapon spewed a few more bullets into the drop-ceiling before clattering onto the floor.

Nora flattened herself against the wall of the corridor and met Anna's eyes as she emerged fully from Regina's office. She looked the way that Nora felt. Her face was white, her eyes wide. Her gun hand shook.

Nora felt herself shaking as well, and she fought for breath amidst the swirls of smoke. But she had to see if anyone else was coming in. She peered around the corner and out through the gaping holes where the glass doors of the building had been. Three more women stood on the lawn, their guns at the ready.

A police siren could be heard in the sudden silence; a neighbor must have called 9-1-1, for Nora and Anna had had no time to do so. At the sound, the three women slung their weapons over their shoulders and mounted their motorcycles, gunning the engines.

"No!" Nora shouted. She tore through the lobby and leapt out through the shattered glass of the entryway, skidding onto the lawn as the bikers peeled away.

She raced into the middle of the street, planting her feet.

This time she did not aim for wheels. She shot directly at the closest woman, who crumpled.

The motorcycle wobbled out of control and plowed into a parked car with a crash that reverberated throughout the street. The approaching sirens drowned out the sound of the engines as the remaining motorcycles turned down State Street and disappeared.

No. Not again . . .

Nora galloped toward the squad car. The driver slammed on the brakes at the sight of her, and she hurriedly holstered her gun and pulled out her badge, holding it aloft.

"Follow those motorcycles!" she shouted as she ran up to the window. She was gesturing wildly at the place where last she had seen the women. "Call for backup! Do *not* let them get away!"

"I need to see your fucking credentials!" the policeman shouted back.

"I'm showing you my fucking badge," Nora, outraged, screamed at him.

"You don't just shove something in a cop's face and expect him to chase off wherever you order him," the cop shouted back.

Anna was on the lawn now, shouting. "Do what she says, goddammit, Mike!"

At a word from his partner, the driver of the car punched the accelerator and the car tires squealed as the car flew down the street, skirting the wreckage of the third biker.

Nora sank to the pavement in the middle of the street, overwhelmed. Anna ran to her side. "Are you alright?"

"I'm fine. We need ambulances, Anna. Those people . . ."

"I called them."

"That little girl . . ."

"I called them," Anna said. She knelt on the ground next to Nora and clutched her shoulders. The late morning air was suddenly swollen with the sound of sirens.

Even as his PD colleagues were attempting to keep the television cameras at a reasonable distance from the crime scene, Mike Szymanowski was under attack from all sides and wasn't going quietly. "What was I supposed to do? All of a sudden a black woman with a gun is running through the street and then telling me what to do—"

"What bothered you more?" Nora snarled. "That I'm black or that I'm a woman?"

Mike snapped, "That you had a gun, okay? It's not an everyday occurrence in the streets of Erie."

"We have a problem with vanishing bikers, Mike," Sheila was saying. The forensic team borrowed from Erie PD had finished photographing the scene. Now, they were all standing in the middle of the street outside of the International Institute, as the ambulance and EMT workers began the work of carrying out the nineteen bodies from within. The third biker had been disentangled from her motorcycle and carried off to the intensive care.

"They can't just have vanished," he said petulantly.

Sheila looked at him fiercely. "They vanished. Again. Now, what are we going to do about it?"

"Well I imagine you are going to question the only perp that your agent didn't kill and get *her* to tell you what's going on." The accusation of incompetence was explicit in both his tone and his words.

Nora's anger burned dangerously hot. Anna saw the look in her eyes and jumped in. "I think we understand now the importance of cooperation. Now that you have met Special Agent

Khalil, you will be able to work together in the future for a better outcome."

"Yes, well, working together doesn't mean bossing me around, either," Szymanowski said.

"So it isn't that I'm a black woman, it's that I dared to give you an order?" Nora asked. "In the middle of a fucking firestorm?" She wasn't usually one to swear. She particularly disliked the word *fuck*, but she found it was spilling comfortably off her lips, providing exactly the emphasis she needed to deal with Officer Szymanowski.

"Nora isn't black, by the way, Mike," Anna supplied.

Nora held up a hand. "It's all the same to them," she said, walking away.

"*Them*? Who's *them*?" Mike shouted after her.

Various reporters overheard this and took up the cry, brandishing fat microphones. "Who's 'them'? Agent Dixon! Agent Dixon!" they called to Anna, who ignored them with a practiced air.

Nora strode into the International Institute, trying without much success to shake off her anger. The broken glass doors had been removed altogether to allow the teams to enter and exit more easily. She found she was hugging herself tightly as she walked through the lobby. She stopped to stare at the place where the little girl had lain.

An acrid smoky smell hung heavy in the air, but this was not what was making breathing difficult.

"Nora?" She turned to see Special Agent in Charge Joseph Schacht bending slightly to pass under the low doorframe.

She felt a rush of relief. *A familiar face.* Her SAC was famous for being florid of face, wearing ill-fitting shirts, and sporting the ugliest neckties in the Bureau.

He shook her hand hard, then grasped her elbow with his left hand, immobilizing her arm as he looked intently into her face.

"You're looking well," he said, after a searching gaze in which he seemed to reassure himself she was alright. After a moment he smirked. "New position agreeing with you?"

Nora gave him a half-smile. "Well, if you'd asked me two days ago, I'd have said it was pretty boring."

"You shot three violent criminals, Nora. You're to be commended."

"Shot them too late, sir. A massacre occurred while I was in the next room."

"Under a hail of gunfire."

Nora inhaled, swallowing. "You got here fast."

"Every once in a while the good guys get to use the company jet."

She nodded distractedly.

"We were just about to land when we heard the latest development." Schacht surveyed the room and then said, "Let's debrief a little in the car, shall we? Air conditioning."

She followed him to a blue minivan, clearly a rental from the airport as the Erie agents had been unavailable to retrieve this Philadelphia delegation. Anna saw her following Schacht and gestured that they would meet back at the office. There were two other agents in the van. Nora remembered seeing their faces back in Philly, but she couldn't recall their names. Schacht solved the mystery by introducing them as Special Agent Derek Ford and Special Agent Venkatram Chidambaram. They looked young and a little haughty. Ford had rugged good looks, but for an ugly scar that marred his right cheek and caused his right eye to slope a little. Chidambaram looked to be of South Asian origin, with skin darker than hers but soft, wavy black hair that framed his face. He was short and slim; his suit looked more expensive and a little tighter than necessary for a day at the office.

She figured the shock of having to travel to Erie, Pennsylvania, wasn't sitting well with them.

Schacht and Nora settled into the middle row of seats as Agent Chidambaram plugged the office's address into the GPS and began navigating through the crush of reporters and television cameras.

Nora said, "It's just . . . just turn on State Street and go north. It's not, you know, GPS-worthy."

Schacht smiled at her. "Busy week?"

"I feel like the world just turned upside down. We had nothing to do except stalk the perverts. And now all of a sudden . . . we can't keep up."

"It's very serious. They've been warning us about domestic terrorism for a long time now. We've been able to head a lot of things off at the pass. But rapid multi-pronged attacks, carefully planned, with several different teams . . . We are under-equipped to deal with it. We're going to try, though, Nora."

"Head things off like what, sir?"

Schacht shrugged. "Well, we had a bank robbery a few months back in Virginia. The express purpose was to rob the bank in order to get money to buy arms for a race war."

"Race war?" Nora asked skeptically.

"That was the plan, Nora. Sounds nuts to you and me, but it was very real and very imminent for those involved. They had been training and needed more funds for their arms suppliers. Who were, absurdly, Mexican."

"Pretending to be," Agent Ford interjected.

"Yes, pretending to be. They were our guys. Actually Honduran and—where, Derek?"

"Honduran and Chilean. But those idiots couldn't tell, of course."

"Of course," Nora said softly. "You think that's what this bank robbery is about?"

Schacht shrugged. "Don't know. Just saying there's precedent. War costs money."

She looked out of the window at the crumbling factories, then back at him. "What kind of arms?"

"Everything. Rocket launchers. Automatics, semi-automatics . . ."

"Bombs?"

"No bombs. Grenades, though."

"You think these guys here can get rocket launchers and stuff?" she asked Schacht.

"We both know anyone can buy a rocket launcher off the Internet. Do they know how to use one? That's different. They'll need someone ex-military. And the way we treat our vets, it's certainly not impossible to find disaffected ex-military."

Nora shook her head.

"But why here?" she demanded. "Why target this backward little city that doesn't even matter?"

Schacht looked at her as though she were a very poor student indeed. "Nora, it's urban hubris to suggest that the rural areas don't matter. Rural poverty is far more widespread than urban poverty. The latter just makes for better movies. There are more discontented country folk than there are city dwellers. Their opinions are deeply entrenched. The last election taught us that they'd felt unheard in all the previous ones. Their man promised them jobs, promised he'd get rid of the foreigners, promised they hadn't suffered for nothing. But the system could only allow for so much. So . . . maybe they can get their views across with arms. Collectively, the gun owners of America have more firepower than the armed forces of certain countries."

Nora took a deep breath but found she had no way of responding. It had taken her a very long time to overcome her distaste for her gun. She knew she needed it. She had saved lives with it. But still . . .

Schacht continued, "Many Americans are angry. Truly angry in a way that you can't fathom. They see their way of life under assault. Language issues, religious issues, the way we teach kids in school, the way we interact with each other. For some people, multiculturalism means the death of tradition, and tradition links them to their fathers and grandfathers and their *people*. . . ."

"Keeping you mired in racism . . ."

Schacht tsked. "Loving your roots and wanting to preserve them isn't wrong. This methodology is wrong, of course. But then again it's the whole freedom fighter versus terrorist argument. Their cause is noble. Get back to . . . well, someone's interpretation of what the world should look like. The guy they had hoped would lead them there showed them quickly enough that his own self-interest and gold potty were his real concerns. Even though he's in office, they're expected to pay taxes and tolerate foreigners diluting the gene pool."

"So the logical response is shooting up women and children at a refugee center?"

Schacht shook his head sadly. "Tragic. But what a message! How many women engage in mass shootings?"

"One prior to this," she said.

"And now five women. Five women on motorcycles. No helmets, no Kevlar. Just walking in and taking matters into their own hands. If the women aren't worried about shooting other women and even children, then what does that say about the mission?"

"Urgent?" Nora ventured.

"Urgent and clear. Unambiguous and just. And finally . . . necessary. So women are called in from whatever other things the group envisions women should be doing. They're called to fight. And they're normalizing the fight for other women who might be watching."

They fell silent.

Nora thought for a moment about her father and everything that he hated about her life and her choices. She wondered if she could boil it all down to a love of roots and tradition. She had always seen it simply as an effort to control her.

She dug deep into memory and found her mother's voice reading to her in classical Arabic, making Nora read poetry aloud, making sure Nora did not lazily elide any letters that did not exist in English.

"*These words are a living bridge to centuries of love and pain and joy and desire and loss,*" *she would say, tucking Nora's unruly hair behind her ear.* "*Don't ever forget how to walk across this bridge.*"

Nora looked at the men in the front seat. "Do you have more reinforcements or did you just bring these two guys?" she asked Schacht.

Ford twisted in his seat to cast a scathing gaze upon her.

She would not be cowed by either the good looks or the scary scar. "What?" she demanded. "I'm not saying you're not a genius, man. But we need bodies. Since yesterday we've had a heist, a bomb, a murder, an abduction, and a massacre. We don't even have a forensics guy. Not one." She realized part of this rant was a poorly-veiled complaint to Schacht for consenting to such an exile for her.

Schacht said, "Sheila wisely called in the CIRG, but it generally takes about four hours for them to get themselves together. These two are CIRG but based out of our office, so I brought them with me—my own private brain trust. We have press handlers coming from DC. Chid here is our behavioral analysis expert and Ford specializes in domestic terror groups and militia movements. Pittsburgh is sending a whole forensics team and their best hostage negotiator. It's handled. You just have to show up for work."

Nora scoffed, then leaned forward to direct Chid where to park. He glanced at her, then back at the road. "Khalil, is it? Arab?"

She pursed her lips at him. "Irish," she said caustically. "Turn here into the parking garage."

"Y'all validate parking?" he asked.

"Not for city slickers," she declared.

When they walked into the office, the plasma screen was full of Vance Evans's face.

"Public reaction to the shootings at the refugee center was strong and clear: this is not Erie."

He was standing about a block from the building that Nora had just left in ruins. Around him, onlookers milled, awaiting their moment of fame on the camera.

The first to speak was a black woman whose eyes were red from weeping. "My neighbors. These people comin' in here were my neighbors in my hometown. They weren't foreigners. They were new Americans. . . ."

A biker was next. "I heard these women were on bikes. I'm here to tell you, that ain't us. Bikers just wanna ride, you know? Disgustin' what these people done. It's disgustin'."

The camera fell on a thin boy weeping on the curb. Evans explained that his family had been inside the center when the shooters entered. They had survived war in the Congo only to be separated permanently here.

With a grave voice, Evans peered into the camera.

"Just say, '*Oh, the humanity!*' and get it over with," snarled Sheila, muting the TV and stomping into the conference room.

After multiple introductions, and Maggie grumpily appearing with a tray full of tea and coffee, they all gathered around the conference room table.

Nora wasn't keen to speak up first, but she had forgotten to ask Anna about the call she'd received while they were at the institute.

"It was Sheila," she said. "This Baker fellow had made another announcement. Released it to Vance Evans."

"What did he say?"

Pete called it up on the screen. Gabriel Baker looked fit; his blue eyes gleamed with energy.

He was handsome, Nora thought. He was handsome in a way that would attract people. It wouldn't be easy to write him off as just some wild-eyed redneck.

Fellow patriots, all those who want to take back our country from the filthy parasites besieging it: now is the time to rise up and join our cause. Do not fear your strength—wield it! As to the rest of you: Welcome to the First Day. It will be stormy.

"First day?" Nora asked. "First day? How many days are we looking at?"

"Shit," Special Agent Chidambaram said. He started to laugh. He shook his head, as though shaking it off, then burst out laughing again.

Silence descended on the room as the other agents stared at him.

Pete spoke for the group. *"Dude."*

Special Agent Chidambaram shrugged. "The last piece just fell into place."

There was some shifting in seats. Finally, Sheila, utterly exasperated, said, "You wanna be slightly less cryptic? We have no time here. None. The world is exploding all around us, Special Agent Chidambaram."

"I go by Chid, if you don't mind, ma'am. And actually there will probably be several more explosions," he said. "There will be body counts that are way more than the ones we've had so far."

Again, the agents around the table seemed on the verge of pummeling him.

Special Agent Chidambaram looked at the printout he had with him. "Look, the words 'preliminary evening' in and of themselves could have meant nothing. Coupling them with 'first day' might also have been nothing. But when you throw in the word, 'stormy' . . ." His voice trailed off.

They continued to stare at him.

"No?"

Even Schacht was losing patience at this point. "Chid, you'd better just out with it."

"Ring Cycle. Opera. Richard Wagner."

It sounded to Nora like he'd said "Vogner," but she saw Anna write "Wagner" on her yellow pad. They all exchanged glances. Sheila frowned rather menacingly.

Special Agent Chidambaram sighed dramatically. "So, Wagner wrote opera; well, he would have said he wrote dramas set to music. Major exponent of German culture generally and Aryan culture specifically. In addition to writing music he wrote essays. That first message of Baker's swiped liberally from Wagner's essay on Jews."

Anna drew in her breath sharply. "Can you tell us about the essay?"

"Sure," said Chid. "He was trying to say that Jews by their nature have no original thought—he was trying to win whatever competition there was to win between himself and a composer like Felix Mendelssohn. A Jew, if that's not obvious. But mostly it was all about pointing out the 'repugnance' of their nature. Their inability to assimilate. That they're physically repellant. He contended that the scars they had from years of persecution had colored—indeed damaged—their intellectual output. Meanwhile, the true guardians of the German intellectual heritage were most certainly white men like himself."

Anna continued dutifully taking notes, but Pete and Nora and the rest were just watching Chid carefully.

"I mean, look, he was trying hard to become a *thing*, right? He was jealous of his contemporaries, especially the ones filling the great opera houses and theaters of the time. And so his project became at one point to discredit at least one group of his competitors in order to take more of the market share. He determined in the end that those Jews who did not willingly self-annul, or in another translation, 'self-annihilate' . . . well, they were deluded at best. Clinging to a cultural heritage not their own."

Sheila leaned in, desperate. "What on earth is your point, Chid?"

He looked at her in surprise. "The Ring Cycle," he answered, as though it were obvious. "Wagner's masterpiece. The Ring." He raised his hand, ticked off on four fingers: "*Das Rheingold, Die Walküre, Siegfried, and Götterdämmerung.*" He lowered all four fingers, then ticked off again: "Preliminary Evening. First Day. Second Day. Third Day."

He watched as Anna wrote all this down in purple ink.

"It's both a celebration of German or Aryan—in this case, most specifically, Norse—culture and a promise of fire. Revolution. The deed that redeems the world. But the Nazis . . . well, the Nazis used Wagner for their own ends. There's a phrase, a magic spell in the operas that invokes *Nacht und Nebel*, 'Night and Fog'—Hitler devised the Night and Fog Decree in 1941. Anyone resisting Nazi rule could be disappeared into Night and Fog."

These words were met with absolute silence.

"How many days?" asked Anna, her voice barely a whisper.

"Four days," Chid confirmed.

Pete's voice piped up from nowhere, it seemed. "Stormy."

Chid looked a question at him.

"Why did he say 'stormy'?" Pete asked.

"*Stürmisch*," Chid answered quickly. "It's German for *stormy*, but more importantly it's a . . . well, it's like a stage direction for the conductor. The music should be stormy. It's, like, the first thing you see when you open the score for the Valkyries—Jesus!" He started laughing again, shaking his head.

"What?" Nora demanded fiercely.

"The attack this morning. Women. Women on motorcycles." He looked around, then finally started to accept that no one was on the same page with him at all. "The Valkyries were women who decided who lived and died in battle. But they rode horses— they were pretty badass. . . ." Chid's voice trailed off. "Anyway. If he's keeping to the Ring for a framework, you've got four days. In the end, everything's going to go up in flames. So. Yeah."

Only Schacht could come up with something to say after that. "Maybe you could help us better understand Baker and his message."

Chid sighed, looking at his notes. "Yeah, okay. Sure." Having said that, he lapsed into silence.

"Now would be good," said Sheila testily.

"Okay, of course, no . . . I was just, you know, gathering my thoughts." He took a rather languid sip of his tea. "It's a little problematic because Baker really . . . See, I was working on this on the plane, reading the transcript, you know, and, well, some parts of the profile fit and others don't. I guess this part needs sorting out still. But someone who's using this level of rhetoric is going to be a highly educated white male. Because even if it's overblown, his prose is *correct*. Grammatically on point. And the sources he's citing, well, some of them are very erudite. Who reads Wagner's essays, anyway? Like, three musicologists and maybe four or five history nerds. But Baker's a truck driver, is he not? Anyway, this rhetoric makes those Bundy guys sound like hillbillies in comparison, right?"

"Maybe," said Pete. "What do you think he represents exactly? Are we talking more patriot movement than white supremacist, or a mix?"

Ford leaned forward to respond. "Well, that's where it gets interesting. It's a little unclear. I think he's invoking various patriot and radical Christian groups in order to pander to their members, but it's a mish-mash, really." Chid was nodding even as he doodled on his legal pad, thinking as he wrote, not looking up at the agents around the table.

Anna asked, "Does he have to do this in order to issue this appeal he's laid out to all militia members throughout the country?"

"Yeah, I'd say so," Derek Ford answered. "Like a candidate for president. You have to appeal to everyone, bring the disparate groups together."

Only the scratching of pens on legal pads broke the silence.

Anna looked up. "Why do you think he timed this with Roar on the Shore?"

Chid smiled. "Your motorcycle festival thing?"

"It's not a festival," Pete insisted with a surreptitious wink at Nora. "*Celebration of biker culture.*"

Chid shrugged. "Whatever the case. If he's sending his army out on motorcycles for this phase of it, well, you can't just stop everyone on motorcycles when you have an extra 80 thousand of them in the area. Plus, that's about the whitest bit of white culture I can think of at the moment. So there's that box ticked off. . . ."

Nora piped up. "Recruiting?"

The three Philadelphia agents nodded.

Derek Ford said, "Bikers are usually non-violent, but disaffected. And predominantly white. He may think he has a potential pool for expansion."

Schacht said, "But we know that usually recruitment is going on online and at gun shows and . . ."

"Preparedness expos," all three Philadelphia agents said at once.

Pete laughed. "The end is coming!"

Finally exasperated, Nora slapped the tabletop. "The end just came, people! Five bitches on motorcycles just slaughtered an old woman and a little girl and everyone in between," she said furiously. "Now tell me how to fix it. Give me something doable."

Silence descended quickly. Pete, looking chastened, said,

"You're right, Miss Nora. Chid—can we work with this number fourteen at all?

"What about it?" asked Chid.

"If Baker's saying they'll engage in fourteen acts of violence, and you seem to think there's a framework of four days, can you help us with the breakdown?"

Anna added, "Are we going to be able to prevent any of them, or do we have to keep watching people get massacred?"

She and Nora held each other's gaze. Nora realized she too was fighting intense surges of emotion after all they had seen that morning.

Nora looked down at the screen of her BlackBerry and found that Ben had indeed called and texted six or seven times. Her anger at him had vanished; she wanted to talk to him so badly. She needed to tell him what she had seen. She needed to tell him how she had failed to protect even one person in that center. She needed to tell him about the tiny body of the Syrian girl, and the soft curl of her hair.

And if today counted as but the first day . . . She shuddered involuntarily.

Chid was looking at her sympathetically. "Fourteen. Yes." He scrawled something on his legal pad, then looked up triumphantly. "Yes. Super smart, actually."

"How so?" asked Schacht.

"Fourteen. So, let's think of *Das Rheingold,* which is really about a robbery, by the way, as having four acts. Technically it's four *scenes,* but I think it's fair to think of it as four acts for our purposes." Chid paused dramatically to have another sip of tea. "*Valkyrie,* which is, for all intents and purposes, about biker chicks, is three acts. *Siegfried,* about the hero who learns to fear, is, what . . ." He wrinkled his brow, figuring, then said, "Yes. Three acts. *Götterdämmerung,* about vanquishing the gods and setting the world, aka the corrupt system, on fire, is three acts—BUT! There's a *prologue*." His voice was positively sing-songy.

Sheila was looking at him with a deeply impatient nerd-loathing etched across her features. "So?"

"So what is that?" he prodded, looking around expectantly.

"Fourteen?" Pete answered slowly.

Chid grinned. "Fourteen!"

Nora stared at him, trying to decide whether he was growing on her. He was simply too frustrating to watch in action. Yet somehow he reminded her of her mother. Her mother had had an almost infinite tolerance for finding pleasure in things that Nora had found utterly useless. She watched Chid shift in his chair, realizing they were a pretty tough crowd of exhausted agents.

"So in the end," she said, making her voice as sarcasm-free as possible, "what are you telling us, Chid? Besides that this guy wants to set the world on fire."

"That your perp is quirky. A lover of classical music—and really good classical music, mind you. Not, fucking, Pachelbel's fucking canon. He's probably pretty well-off. Super smart. I imagine he's got a wine cellar and a fondness for risotto as well as a mind-blowing gun collection."

They were all silent, digesting this.

Suddenly Chid added, "Oh, and he's a *mother-fucking racist*."

Nora tried to reconcile these quirky aspects with the images of Gabriel Baker they'd watched over and over that morning. It didn't all seem to jibe.

Derek Ford had been sipping from his coffee mug as Chid spoke. As Chid fell silent, Derek placed his mug on the table with a slightly-too-loud thud. "Crucially," he added, "he has the ability to motivate people to do his bidding."

"Well, what's the point if you can't have minions?" asked Pete, then he looked over at Nora and seemed to bite his tongue.

"So how do we find him?" Anna asked.

Chid looked thoughtful. "It's safe to bet he's got a place in the country. Somewhere that people can train."

Special Agent Ford nodded, affirming this.

"So basically anywhere around here," said Sheila.

"Well, yes and no," Chid said. He's not going to be living in a trailer. So that's going to narrow it down. You're looking for a very nice house surrounded by at least twenty to fifty acres."

"Aryan Nations had only twenty in Idaho," Ford said.

"And you'll have to have a barn," added Chid. "At least one."

Ford said, unnecessarily, "To store the weapons."

Silence descended once more as the agents considered this. Then Nora said, "So our risotto-eating friend wants to launch a revolution. Why is he giving us hints? Doesn't that mean he wants to get caught?"

Chid and Ford both shook their heads, but Ford was first to speak. "Look, when you're a terrorist you've built an organization and you've spent a lot of time offering your people fame in exchange for their insignificant little lives. You have to do what you can to get attention for your cause, on the one hand, and to make your opponents look bad on the other."

Schacht chimed in. "He's convinced that he is very smart and that we representatives of the government, by virtue of being lemmings, being sheep, that we are deeply stupid. He's got vision, we've got none. These acts of violence are to teach us a lesson. He may say it's about revolution, but it's mostly about him."

"Which is in keeping with the Ring theme," Chid said, excitement surging across his features again. "What does it mean to possess the Ring of Power? What shall we do with it? He's saying, I can bend people to my will. And I can do it with an agenda that is totally opposite to yours. The agenda ultimately may not matter. The power does."

Sheila was shaking her head. "But how can he think this is

going to play out? Race war? Are people really going to rise up and join his cause?"

Schacht replied, "They were prepared for revolution, armed rebellion. Collectively they have the means. What's been lacking is the right voice to assess when the new leader has failed. How much of a chance does he get? You need someone who appeals to all the disparate voices of discontent. If Baker can organize them and unite them, they will be a force."

"Look, the media has, in the space of a few hours, made this man the stuff of legend," Chid said. "He's taken the darkest xenophobia, the deepest racist sentiments we harbor, and the filthiest remnants of campaign rhetoric and shown us what all that can look like made manifest. He's done exactly what many have fantasized about. All the groups he appeals to will point to this for a long time and imitate it if they dare. So he's already won. We may wipe out his army today or tomorrow, but the precedent is now in place for action."

Chid had scarcely spoken these words when the Erie agents' BlackBerries started buzzing on the tabletop. Each agent sprang up as though electrocuted.

Sheila threw open the door and dashed out of the conference room.

Anna addressed the visiting agents, her voice a whisper. "Abe from the bomb squad—they're trying to defuse a bomb at the synagogue."

Chid held her gaze, then said softly, "Fire."

Anna's usual veneer of calm while driving had evaporated completely. She blazed across the sun-baked pavement at top speed, shouting insults at anyone who dared impede the SUV's path.

"I don't get how they knew," Pete said.

"Rabbi Potok showed up to give the summer Bar Mitzvah class

and saw a U-Haul truck parked outside, still warm—she must have missed them by thirty seconds. She's no dummy, not on a day when we've just had a mass shooting at the refugee center. She called the police immediately." The wheels shrieked as Anna made a hard right turn.

"Were they waiting for the kids to arrive to detonate?" Pete asked.

Anna said, "What do *you* think? Why blow up an empty synagogue when you can blow up one that's full of prepubescents?"

Schacht had insisted they should not use their sirens in order not to alert the press; it would be a tricky stunt to pull off, however. Nora knew that so few newsworthy stories happened in Erie that any congregating of emergency vehicles, particularly after what had occurred that morning, would draw attention.

Temple Beth Torah occupied the corner of 21st and Peach Streets. It was an innocuous enough tan brick building. It was squat and simple, if wide. A large stained-glass window, a kaleidoscope of bright colors, soared atop the northwest corner.

A firefighter was holding up his hand and staunchly refused to let Anna get any closer despite her threats. The three agents thus descended, all staring at the building from a block away.

The U-Haul truck sat in the designated handicapped space near the synagogue's main entrance. The jet-black armored bomb squad van was there, and Nora spied Abe in his EOD suit along with the rest of his crew.

"Their initial report is that there's as much ammonium nitrate as Oklahoma City," Pete said softly.

"But there's a remote trigger mechanism this time hooked to the—what did they say, dynamite?" questioned Nora.

"Yes, that's what they're trying to figure out, apparently."

"Maybe they need you, Peter?" Nora said.

Anna had heard them. "I already volunteered him," she said, without looking at either of them.

"What did Abe say?" Pete asked.

She shrugged. "I doubt he can text back effectively at this moment. But someone will have relayed the message."

Schacht had kicked into high gear. He took Anna and Sheila and began doing the only possible thing in such a scenario. He began forging a Unified Command Center, drawing senior law enforcement and rescue people under one roof to coordinate decision-making. He was, Nora knew, a master coordinator, and Anna—unlike Sheila—had the connections and relationships with the various branches of law enforcement that they now desperately needed.

Agents Chidambaram and Ford joined Pete and Nora where they stood. Chid was looking at the scene like he might analyze a text. His black eyes were calm and clear, taking everything in at once. His face was grave. He had not spoken at all since they'd arrived.

It was only a few moments before Anna jogged over to the cluster now made by Ford, Chid, Nora, and Pete. "Sheila's calling in evacuation notices to every mosque and black church and ethnic community center," she said in a rush, panting. "This trigger mechanism is wired to the dynamite and apparently has a password—they think you have to log in from a device, iPad, iPhone, something like that . . . We pulled matching iPhones off the dead women this morning and the one you sent to the hospital in a coma, Nora, so the idea they have a network going might be valid."

Nora was nodding, remembering watching Anna collect them from the scene.

She continued breathlessly, "Abe thinks they set it up that way in case something might go wrong and they need to abort along the way—it's not just a small bomb they can shoot and run from; if it goes off we're losing a whole city block. Abe's trying to hack it now before the bomber connects with it and gives the okay."

She looked directly at Chid and Pete. "They need you guys. We've got seconds."

Abe was running toward them with a laptop, his helmet dangling from the back of the suit. Chid and Pete jumped into the back of Anna's SUV, Abe handing off the MacBook to Pete, even as Anna helped disentangle him from the top half of the EOD suit. Nora and Ford stood on either side, peering through the open windows.

Abe sank into the backseat next to Chid while Pete stared at the screen.

Pete scanned what to Nora looked like a cascade of numbers. "You want me to try to remote into the device?" he was saying.

Abe nodded, sweat streaking his cheeks. "Can you?"

Pete allowed himself a bemused look. "A network-connected Apple device? Timmy Cook said no."

"But you're not trying to get into the Apple device, you're hacking into the trigger mechanism, which is far simpler," insisted Abe.

"He's right . . ." Ford broke in, poking his face through the window. "If you can keep up a steady stream of interference, your attempt to connect with it will be enough to keep the bomber out."

"Are you sure?" Chid asked.

"No, he's right," Pete said, his voice tense, fingers flying over the keyboard. "Someone's trying to put in a code now."

They watched tensely as a *W* appeared in one of the six spaces.

Pete immediately began filling the other spaces with the letter *X*. Each *X* was quickly erased but Pete backspaced in order to fill it up again; it immediately became a heated race. The first *W* was followed with another *W* as Pete rushed to fill in the remaining spaces and prevent the bomber from replacing them. His eyes were riveted on the screen; the index finger of his left hand remained pressing the *X* key, while his right thumb slid continuously over the laptop's touchpad.

"Will it lock us out?" Anna asked worriedly.

"An Apple device would," said Ford. "But this is not; plus the combination is clearly not simply digits. This could go on forever."

The bomber had managed to insert a third letter, a *V*.

Chid frowned and leaned forward intently; Nora watched as calculations and considerations registered in his sharp eyes.

"But in the meantime, while the mechanism is distracted—" Abe began.

"You can cut the wire," Ford finished for him.

Abe was already halfway out the car door, and both Nora and Ford started zipping him back into his suit. They had barely secured his helmet when he began running full speed for the van.

Pete had not moved from his vigil over the *X*s. "Tell him to hurry," he said through gritted teeth. "They have four out of six."

Ford shouted at the top of his lungs, "Four out of six, Abe!"

Nora shifted desperately from foot to foot, wanting to run over to urge Abe on. She looked at the computer screen and saw that an 8 had taken the fourth space.

Sweat was dripping into Pete's unblinking eyes. Nora tugged her sleeve down, then said softly, "Pete, I'm going to wipe your forehead, man."

He did not acknowledge her but also did not flinch as she reached gently through the open window and dabbed at his forehead.

"Five out of six," he whispered as a 6 appeared on the screen.

Ford relayed the message. Nora strained to see what was going on in the U-Haul.

"Come on Abe," Pete said, and Nora realized she'd stopped breathing.

Chid said, "B."

They watched in horror as the final space on the screen filled with a *B* and the entire screen went black. All of them swiveled their heads to look at the U-Haul.

A long breathless moment gave way to another and then another.

Abe emerged from the U-Haul tugging at his helmet. He held aloft the wire cutters and then made a mock salute in the direction of the SUV.

Pete's shoulders sagged in relief and he flopped back against the seat.

Nora exhaled. She looked long and hard at Chid. "You knew the code," she said.

"I figured out the code," he answered. "That's different."

"What was—"

But she was interrupted by Schacht.

Schacht had appeared at the SUV window, his face flushed and grim. "Good work, Pete, people—don't sit still though. Whoever it was has to be close by, watching. We need to find them. *Now.* You're all wearing vests?"

Pete and Nora nodded. The other two were silent. Nora sensed that Chid would think a bulky vest would defile his carefully crafted look.

"There are extras in the car," Anna said curtly. "Report in to me every ten minutes via text."

Schacht said, "If we don't hear back every ten minutes, we will overreact. To say the least."

All four nodded. Nora saw that Anna had already spied the Chief of Police. Anna wove her way over to him and drew him over to the group Schacht was forming. All of them began conferring, their heads bent together, and Nora knew they'd be asking for police backup. It was essential to make a perimeter around the area so the would-be bomber couldn't slip through their fingers.

Nora realized that Schacht's assumption had to be true. *Of course they'd be watching. Something this massive, a strike this profound . . . You don't just run away after that. You watch the chaos unfold, you record it on video for later. . . .* Nora began scanning the surrounding area, her eyes resting on each house.

She had memorized the figures from the bank video, the shape and size of the man on the back of the third motorcycle and his friend; the shade of their hair, the tone of their skin. But surely she wouldn't just trip over them on the street. She studied the neighborhood. There was a sagging VFW outpost, and many rundown houses on the verge of collapse. Mixed in with these were a few stately old homes, many with cupolas and wide front porches.

She looked at Pete. "Can you access the office network and try to find out if any of the homes around the synagogue is uninhabited?"

He looked at her thoughtfully, his face more tired than she had ever seen it. "I think I can. But it's going to take a minute. And more than that, I'm going to need a little air conditioning."

Chid and Ford were wriggling into the vests they'd found in the back.

Nora looked at Chid as Pete availed himself of Abe's laptop. "You going to tell me?" she asked. "About the code?"

Chid nodded. "Wagner-Werk-Verzeichnis," he answered.

"Pardon?"

"Wagner-Werk-Verzeichnis," he repeated. "It's a way of cataloging Wagner's musical output. WWV for short, and then you add whatever the number of the work you're referring to."

"So 86B is . . ."

"The Ring Cycle is collectively the 86th work, and B here is for the second opera, *Die Walküre*."

Nora sighed, exasperated.

"Don't shoot the messenger," Chid snapped, looking irritated as he buckled the straps of his vest.

Nora stood over half a foot taller than he did, but he did not seem to find this disconcerting. He looked up at her, his keen eyes observing her with unabashed interest. "So you're Arab, then?" he asked.

It was hardly the time for the categorization game. "*Flemish*," Nora replied, and Derek Ford gave a little snort of laughter. Nora ignored him. "Chid, I want to know what's in Act Three today. How can we prevent more of this?"

He raised a hand in protest. "Look, it would be silly to suggest he's trying to mimic every act and scene of the Ring. On one level it's just silly Norse myth."

"What are the other levels?" Nora demanded.

"An analysis of power dynamics. George Bernard Shaw wrote a whole Marxist interpretation of it. Maybe it's about empowering the underclass and putting an end to capitalism. The actual Ring goes back to the Rhine maidens in the end. The gods-slash-our-capitalist-masters fail to keep their immortality."

Nora listened carefully, trying to understand.

"Edward Said saw Wagner as stuck in history. His characters can't break free of being damned to fulfill dire predictions. Hopeless. Adorno saw his use of violence as a criticism of the obsession with myth even while he was glorifying the main character as a man of the sword."

Peter made a gesture. "But how does it all apply here?"

Chid shrugged. "He's going to put on it the spin he wants. He thinks he's being clever. He's evoking images in a particular framework that's motivational for him. Wagner fancied himself a revolutionary, right? Had to flee after participating in the 1849 May Uprising. This guy . . . Baker . . . I doubt his people even know what he's doing or understand this elaborate framework . . . or even care. They're probably just feeling victimized and angry . . . disenfranchised . . . while on some level he has to provide for himself—and his legacy—a synthesis."

Nora said impatiently, "Okay, then. What's our next step? What can we expect from his particular brand of *synthesis*?"

Chid sighed. "My guess is he's going to kill the black council-woman. Probably pretty gruesomely." He paused to consider, then continued, "His people are absolutely going to blow up a mosque and maybe a black church. Probably they'll occupy a federal building at some point. Just for, you know, flourish." He sighed, effectively dismissing her. "Let's go, Derek," he said, and the two of them started their walking tour.

Nora was left standing next to the SUV, the window still open, but the air conditioning blasting. "This day is fucking unbeliev-able," Pete said, fingers flying across the keyboard. "If ever I needed a beer it would be in this actual moment right now."

Nora watched Derek and Chid walking along the sidewalk. They passed the cluster of law enforcement agents and contin-ued on, seemingly assessing and discussing each house as they passed.

Finally, Pete looked up at her. "2129 Peach Street," he said fi-nally.

"Let's go," Nora said. They walked, their direction opposite to the one Chid and Derek had taken. Despite the efforts at subtlety, onlookers had gathered to see what had drawn police and fire-trucks to the area near the synagogue. Nora knew it did not take a genius to add up the presence of the bomb squad at the syna-gogue. The news crews would soon descend.

They found themselves in front of the house, and Nora looked desperately at Pete. They locked eyes instantly and both knew, wordlessly: *back door*. She joined him behind a towering, bram-bly hedge.

"What's your plan?" he asked softly.

"Was I supposed to have a plan?"

He narrowed his eyes at her. "Fine, no plan. We're just check-ing it out."

"Just checking it out," she confirmed.

They began darting across the backyard, crouching low as they went.

Once they reached the back porch, they both drew their weapons. The wood was worm-eaten and creaked underfoot as they mounted the steps. The back door, paint peeling, held a wide pane of murky glass; a jagged section was missing from its lower half. Pete extended his free hand and tried the doorknob. It turned. He looked at Nora and she nodded.

He pushed the door open gently.

Nora, whose eyes had been scanning the street from which they'd come for anyone alert to their presence, inhaled, steeling herself, then followed Pete inside. It was darker than she expected, for the dirt-caked windows let in very little light. They found themselves in a dilapidated kitchen. Cabinet doors hung askew. A grease-covered stove crowned an oven with no door at all, and the fridge was blackened, its handle broken. The July heat had baked the mold and dust into a potent stench.

Nora squatted, looking at the floor under the light of her phone screen.

Pete watched her.

She looked up at him, nodding slightly, then said quietly, "Someone's been here. Can't say how recently." The dust was disturbed. The tracks led in one direction up to the set of stairs that emptied out into the kitchen and in the other direction they dead-ended at a closed door. A basement, perhaps.

"We should go," Pete whispered. "Let's check in with Anna and come back."

Nora looked at the stairs. She was so sure what they wanted was there.

"We have to look, Pete."

He rubbed his beard, thinking. "Nora." It was all he said, but she could see he was conflicted.

She took another step toward the stairs that led to the second floor, then said softly, "Haven't we all failed already today?"

"That's for damn sure," came a voice behind them. Both whirled.

Pete and Nora leveled their guns at a man with graying hair and a goatee; in the dimness his eyes did not even register a color. He held an assault rifle, and it was leveled at their chests.

Neither agent had a chance to fire, however, as the floor beneath their feet suddenly gave way.

The fall was painful. Nora fell on top of Pete who immediately started clutching his right side, especially his ankle. Nora sprang up, her gun pointed into pitch blackness save for the square of light left by the trapdoor that still swung overhead, creaking.

Nora saw Pete reaching for his BlackBerry when the first kick barreled out of the darkness behind her. It landed on her wrist, sending her Glock flying. She bent double, clutching her wrist, and Pete began scrambling to rise and come to her aid when he was tackled. Nora watched him collapse to the floor, unable to fend off the huge shadowy form that pinned him to the ground.

In pure panic, Nora whipped around to try to see where her own attacker was. That was when her legs were kicked out from underneath her. She landed hard on the cement floor, and she inhaled a thick layer of dirt, then coughed, gasping for breath. Someone heavy with rough, calloused hands tugged her wrists behind her as a crushing weight settled on her back. The wrist that had been kicked sent shockwaves of pain through her entire body. A scrape on her cheek dripped blood into her mouth.

The trapdoor was suddenly pulled shut, plunging the basement into inky blackness. Almost as soon, however, the door at the top of the basement steps opened, casting a dim pool of light.

Nora tried to move her head so she could meet Pete's eyes, but the man holding her down pressed her cheek hard against the floor. "Don't move, bitch. If you know what's good for you."

Pete managed to call out, "Nora—you—?" before a hand crashed against his mouth with a sickening thud.

"I'm fine," she choked out, but the man sitting on her yanked her hair hard and she was forced to end her attempt to reassure Pete with an unwilling yelp of pain.

They all heard footsteps descending into the basement. "They'll be here soon," came the man's voice.

Nora could hear Pete's BlackBerry vibrating angrily; no sooner did his stop than hers began to quiver in her pocket. The attacker felt it, and he patted her down and then extracted the phone and took it himself.

"What should we do with the phones?" came the voice of the man immobilizing Pete.

"Smash them," said the man with the goatee. "Can't risk anyone tracing them using a GPS. Just wait til we get to the tunnel. Otherwise they might find the pieces."

"So we done here?" asked Nora's attacker.

"Tracks all covered," Goatee reassured him.

"Next step?"

"Get our new acquisitions out."

"I think this one's gonna have a hard time walking," the man holding Pete said.

"He'll walk," Goatee spat. He pulled a flashlight out of his pocket and switched it on. He seemed to be searching for something on the floor, and then the light came to rest on Nora's Glock. The man bent to retrieve and pocket it. Then he turned the light toward the group. Nora squinted as the bright light moved from Pete to focus on her, moving over her face and down the length of her body. "It's a better haul than I'd hoped for."

She flinched inwardly at the tone. That tone scared her more than the overt violence of the moments before.

"Bring them. Let's go. Like I said, it won't be long before someone'll be coming."

Nora and Pete were forced to stand, their wrists still cinched behind them, and both captors and prisoners followed the man with the bandanna. He led them deeper into the basement, then pulled aside a filthy Steelers banner to reveal a low wooden door. He inserted a key and then twisted it quickly, shoving hard against the door which groaned loudly as it swung open. He ducked, pushing through it, and the others followed. Nora was sure that Pete had broken his ankle from the way he was hobbling and leaning on his attacker.

Nora had eagerly been stealing glances at the other men's faces as the flashlight darted across them. She was almost certain the one with the goatee had been one of the bank robbers. The other two were pale, both equally wide. The one with Pete had dark hair and the one holding her had sandy hair that somehow flourished on his face but not his head; he wore a thick, if trimmed, beard. Both were tall, over six feet, and she estimated the one holding her to be at least two hundred and thirty pounds. Like Nora herself, both had to bend down to pass through the small door.

Even as Nora's phone vibrated again, her captor threw it to the ground and then stamped on it with a heavy boot. Pete's captor handed over his phone for the same treatment. Nora's eyes lingered on the boots; not summertime wear, surely. She winced as she stared at her phone. She hadn't been without it for over a year.

The tunnel they entered was dank and musty. Nora found herself gagging slightly as they began to walk. She wanted to ask why such a tunnel existed beneath the city, but she knew it was no time for a guided tour. Still, she was fairly certain that Erie had never had a subway. The tracks they walked over were much smaller, not nearly as wide as would be necessary for a train of any kind. They reminded her of tracks erected for minecarts, but in all the movies she'd seen, no coal mine had been located in the center of a city.

She watched Pete's progress with increasing fury; occasionally, and despite his best attempts at playing the stoic, he would cry out in pain. He needed the emergency room. She tried desperately to figure out what she could drop as a clue; surely there weren't that many possibilities and their trail would be instantly obvious to anyone who half tried. She wondered where Ford and Chid were at that moment. Had they reached the same conclusion about the house? What sort of perimeter had the Unified Command established?

They walked endlessly. Rivulets of water snaked down the walls here and there; in other places, cars overhead shook silt down upon them. Her wrist ached so painfully she could barely tolerate it. She felt claustrophobic in a way that was making it hard to breathe. *Don't panic.*

The tunnel was getting wetter the farther they progressed, and so it began to dawn on her that they were going north and getting closer to the lake. Goatee's flashlight finally revealed a low door with a heavy lock. He worked patiently at the lock and then tugged on the door which opened reluctantly, cement grinding across cement. The lapping of water was loud, and Nora's stomach twisted. They had emerged at a deserted dock just beyond the ornate Erie Water Works, a vast old art deco building. The low door to the tunnel was camouflaged perfectly behind vines and brush.

Nora looked left and right in desperation. They were fully exposed, in broad daylight, but there was simply no one around. The yacht club and the marina were all several hundred yards away. She weighed the idea of beginning to scream. She eyed the waiting speedboat with abject fear. Her heart began to race even faster. She had never been on a boat, and did not want to begin today, here, with these men.

"Get in," Goatee said.

Pete was already being dragged bodily.

"His foot is broken," she said to Goatee.

"*Doctor* Federal Agent, is it?" he said.

"Look at his foot, man. He needs medical attention."

"Then maybe his employers will take our demands extra seriously."

"And what asshole demands do you have?"

He eyed her. "Mind your manners, girl."

Nora narrowed her eyes, but Pete gave her a warning glance.

Goatee looked away from her. He began tapping on the screen of his phone then realized she was still refusing to get into the boat. He waved the rifle at her.

"Oh, *now* you're going to shoot me?" she demanded.

She saw his eyes harden. "You're right." And he pulled back his fist and slammed it against her cheek.

Nora reeled backward, collapsing against her captor. Pete shouted in protest. Her vision exploded with light and darkness at the same time; shooting pain coursed through her entire face. She pulled wildly at her wrists, trying to strike back, but this only resulted in her getting shoved even harder into the boat.

"Put them both in the berth." And the men were suddenly shoving them into the cramped forward area of the boat.

Despite the confined atmosphere, Nora experienced a moment of relief. She could talk to Pete at last. Her relief faded immediately as the engine turned over, making a soft rumble as the boat began to move. She swallowed hard, trying to suppress her fear. "How's your foot?" she whispered urgently.

"It's okay, Nora, it's not broken, it just hurts like fuck."

"Who uses trapdoors?"

"Fuckin' Scooby Doo villains, that's who."

"Or someone who is lying in wait to catch some federal officers. I guess *we* are Act Three."

"Yeah, you know, if I didn't fucking hate the opera before this I sure fucking hate it now." She could tell he was straining at his wrist binders.

"What are we going to do, Peter? Where do you think they're taking us?"

He was silent for a moment. "Schacht and Anna are going to be looking for us."

"Looking where?"

"I guess we're going back to their base as hostages. Now I guess it's lakefront. But what kind of balls do they have taking us out of here when the city is going to be shut down?"

Nora nodded in the darkness. "Do you think the Unified Command or CIRG will have notified the coast guard?"

"I hope so," Pete said. "And border patrol."

"Pete. I've never been on a boat before."

She heard him exhale in disbelief. "Never been to a bar. Never been on a boat. It's one fucking adventure after another."

She smiled, despite herself. "I'm just warning you because I have a feeling I'm gonna puke if we go much faster than this."

Pete sighed audibly and seemed to be fighting to produce patient words. "On an open lake, they'll be going very fast, and it's going to be very choppy; the front part of the boat here is going to be rising and falling very rapidly."

Nora gave a soft groan.

"So, like, puke the other way."

"I'm sorry ahead of time."

His accent flared up. "Not as sorry as I am, woman."

They moved slowly at first, and Nora held out hope that they wouldn't really go any faster, nor would the boat do what Pete had predicted. But she was wrong. She tried to press herself hard against the turf-covered floor of the boat in order to keep from bouncing. She and Pete ended up bouncing into each other.

Pete was becoming angrier with every mile they put between

them and Erie. "I want a beer, and a huge sandwich. In fact, you should take me to Commodore Perry's right now, Miss Nora Khalil."

He had to practically shout to say this. She wondered, given the fact that he'd been up all night, how Pete was still functioning.

"You're insane," she called into the darkness.

"Yes, but I'm dying here. It's been like a hundred thousand years since anyone gave me food."

"I don't know how you can think of food when all I'm trying to do is not throw up."

"You will prevail!" Pete practically yelled. "You are going to receive a commendation, my friend! Now, what I really need is some ice for this ankle."

"I'm so sorry about your ankle, Pete. I wish I could help you!"

"Beer would be good," he responded. Having to talk so loudly made his request sound rather more desperate. "Three Eisernes Kreuz beers. Four. Four Eisernes Kreuz beers! And two giant cheeseburgers and a truckload of french fries and . . ."

"And an outrageously big pretzel, or whatever you call it."

"Yesssss!" called Pete. "Now you're catching on!"

They fell into silence, each listening to the drone of the boat's motor.

Then Pete cried out, "I'm so fucking pissed at these people, though."

Nora had been thinking that, too. "They're just . . . uneducated, right? That's what we're going to tell ourselves about how this could happen?"

Pete didn't seem to have an answer. Then he replied, "Or overWeb-educated. Instead of ever meeting an actual person, they just rely on the Web to tell them what's what."

The strain of trying to talk over the sound of the motor was intense.

She didn't feel like continuing to try to talk, but suddenly Nora had formulated what she thought was a pressing question. "So, I don't get it. I thought the government was replaced with government outsiders who would give them what they want. So now they're against the government?"

"The country has a lot of angry people in it. Everyday people who were struggling had gasoline poured on their frustration fires during the election. To govern you have to compromise, though. And that means betraying the cause."

They were both silent. Finally Pete got as close as he could to Nora's ear, rather beyond her limits for personal space but she preferred it to the shouting.

"I grew up with a rifle in my hand, Nora. There are plenty of families where you can do that peaceably. But my family wasn't one of them."

"Are you some kind of militia dropout, Peter?"

"Very much so. Well, not me. My dad. When the Brady Bill was signed and then assault rifles were banned in the '90s, people got angry. A lot of militias popped up. They thought normal guns were gonna be next. I was poor, I told you. I maybe didn't say I was poor white trash. But that was it."

Pete went awhile before saying anything else, and Nora thought maybe he was done speaking. But he continued. "When you're poor, and no one listens, and you're always on the margins . . . for people like that, the only real sense of power they have in their lives is in their gun cabinet. Any limitation on the 'Second Amendment Right to Bear Arms' is a death sentence."

As she processed this, he added, "Three of my daddy's friends went right off the grid. Took up arms and started hatching plots."

Nora had nothing to say, but digested this as the boat thumped over the rough lake waters.

She adjusted her face so she could aim right for his ear. "What happened to them?"

"They'd pop up to beat their wives and go back to training."

She wished she could see his eyes in the dark. She sensed that they had clouded over.

"What about your dad?"

He said nothing.

"Did he do that? Did he hit you, too?" she pressed.

"Maybe. He became one of the disappeared, anyway." He said nothing for a long while, and Nora cast about wildly for something worth saying. She could think of nothing at all.

Several minutes passed before he placed his mouth close to her ear again. "Like Schacht said, it's a storm that's been threatening to burst for years. Public discourse gets amped up, people stop being scared to say all the bullshit they're thinking, and then . . . other people end up getting hurt."

"I have a bad feeling we're some of the people that're gonna get hurt," said Nora, mustering a laugh.

"Not if we can help it, Miss Nora," he called into the darkness. "I saw your shoes today. You wore the super sneakers!"

Nora smiled ruefully into the darkness. The Mizuno Wave Riders had been Nora's last purchase from Philadelphia Runner, her favorite store on Walnut Street. "Just because grownup shoes go with your suit, doesn't make them the right choice."

"Sounds like a bumper sticker."

She considered this. "Might need tweaking first. . . ." She listened to the motor for awhile, then turned to her partner. "Pete, your dad missed out on a lot by leaving you."

"Hell yeah he did," Pete answered immediately.

"I'm sorry."

He was quiet, then said, "Me, too, Miss Nora. Me, too."

She didn't actually puke. But it was a very hard trip that took well over an hour.

They climbed out onto a temporary dock that stretched twenty feet into the lake. The dock shuddered and groaned and bounced under the onslaught of waves. A setting sun tinged everything around them deep magenta, such that the aluminum of the dock seemed aflame. Nora stumbled as they led her out of the boat; she fought hard to get her bearings, but her legs couldn't seem to function. She wobbled, and her captor supported her, grumbling as he did so. Pete still limped painfully.

There was another long walk ahead of them. They tottered over a stretch of rocky beach and then began making their way up long wooden staircases built into the tall, forested bank. She saw no harbors or other collapsible docks and no signs of anything but rocky, deserted beach for as far as her eye could see.

At the top of the stairs they were forced to walk again. A path had been trampled and well-worn in the dewy weeds. Nora's running shoes were instantly soaked through. A ramshackle old farmhouse had come into view as soon as they reached the top of the bank. The cylinder glass in the windows caught the sunset's fuchsia flush across its wavy panes.

Their captors gave no indication that the house was their destination, however. They walked well beyond it, heading away from the lake, and soon came upon the first of three large barns. This first one had a huge silo alongside it.

Pete was trailing far behind her, so she could not share a look with him. Nora was at a loss, and merely walked, exhausted, sweating, and famished through the barn's towering door. After Pete and his escort finally entered, Goatee slid the door shut with a bone-jarring thud. The barn was spacious, with two levels and innumerable stalls. It was rough-hewn in every aspect, as though it had been hastily constructed. Electric lightbulbs dangled nakedly from the ceiling. A few box fans noisily engaged in churning up the heat, but there was very little ventilation, so the air was heavy, close, and moist.

The rustic motif was disrupted only by the presence of plasma screen TVs placed equidistant from each other on each of the four walls. These conveyed a constant stream of images, a parade of people in camouflage carrying rifles and shotguns, Gabriel Baker appearing periodically to speak, fist clenched and raised. Both women and men flashed victory signs and proudly displayed their weaponry; Baker's voice could be heard in the background. Nora could not make out the words, nor could she focus her attention on the images, because Goatee had begun speaking to them as soon as Pete entered.

"Welcome," he said, without a hint of actual welcome. "You'll be having your pictures taken. The rules are simple. If you're good and quiet we will occasionally feed you. If you make problems we will beat you until you die. Understood?"

Pete and Nora exchanged glances, then nodded.

"Good." He shoved them against the wall of the barn. Then he pulled out his smartphone and began taking their pictures. He posed their captors next to them as well.

"Make them hold up their badges," he insisted.

Both agents had their pockets searched for their badges and then were forced to pose with them. "Smile," Goatee said.

"What, you're posting it on Facebook?" Nora fished.

He scoffed. "Facebook." He only shook his head, plucked the badges out of their hands and pocketed them, then turned his back, saying to the other two over his shoulder, "Put them in with the nigger."

As he walked away, however, he seemed to be studying the pictures he'd taken. He stopped. Then he turned to regard Nora carefully. "You black, too, girl?"

"Welsh," she snapped.

"You fucking wish," he said, and stalked away.

Pete was shaking his head, and Nora could see that he was laughing without sound. Poor Pete had been awake for something like forty hours now, and he looked like he was about to collapse.

They walked along the length of the barn. The stalls were either open entirely or had curtains strung up for doors. They saw a few people milling about, some wearing blue jeans and T-shirts, some wearing camouflage fatigues. Those who passed them seemed to smirk. Two different women clapped their captors on the back and told them they'd done well. Nora looked at them with open disgust, but they were supremely uninterested in her opinion.

They could finally hear the messages emanating from the TVs.

Building walls, my friends, is the only way. We must keep out the filth, the killers, the rapists. They're hungry for what's ours. And they're bad.

It was a different cadence than Baker's other speeches, and the words were far less tangled and clunky. It suited him better, Nora decided.

Our Constitution guarantees our right to defend ourselves, our way of life, our families, our freedom. To keep America pure, to keep America strong. We will build walls to protect our country. I will be the first to stand atop that wall with my gun and keep out the rabble and defend my true Christian, Caucasian, American family.

When they arrived at the last stall on the ground floor, they saw that it was the only one in the barn with a very solid looking door; it sported a heavy metal bolt. Outside of it, a burly man with raging biceps stood glowering. Upon seeing them he slid the bolt open, opened the door, and they were unceremoniously shoved inside.

They fell to the floor. Each breathed for a moment, trying to regain bearings.

"You okay, Peter?" Nora asked. She was grateful that a ribbon of light penetrated from the slim gap in the doorframe. She could just barely see Pete in the dimness, and she began to discern the contents of the room as her eyes adjusted. It looked like there were crudely fashioned bunkbeds with no sheets on the mattresses.

"I'm okay. How about you?"

"No, I'm fine, just fine."

A voice cut through the silence. "Well, I'm not fine *at all*."

Both turned to see a plump black woman sitting cross-legged on the floor.

"April Lewis?" Nora breathed.

She was eyeing them curiously. "If this is the rescue effort, I'm going to have to confess discontent."

April Lewis looked to be in her mid-forties. A crown of innumerable braids framed a face of wide, open features; laugh lines emanated from her mocha eyes, and her high cheekbones made her look truly regal. She wore a rose-colored tunic that strained slightly to contain her expansive chest. The blouse was stained with sweat and dirt visible even in the dimness.

Had Nora's wrists not been cinched behind her, she would almost certainly have hugged her. "I'm so relieved to see you," she said, trying to keep her voice down.

"Did you think I was dead already?"

Pete didn't hesitate to nod. "It never occurred to us that they would spare you, given the other things they've been doing."

"Yes, it seems they're still hoping for the ransom money," she said. "What other things?"

"Mass shooting at the refugee center. Bomb at the temple. We defused it, but only barely."

April Lewis shook her head. "In Erie."

"Yes, in Erie. Seems to be some blueprint for race war," Nora explained.

"Are you hurt?" Pete asked her.

"Nothing being brutally murdered won't cure," she remarked.

"We weren't sent to rescue you," Nora admitted.

April Lewis's eyes were tired but kind. "I'm so relieved. You're spectacularly bad at it."

Pete and Nora exchanged wry smiles.

"What are you kids, FBI?"

They nodded and introduced themselves.

"We were abducted," Nora said unnecessarily by way of explaining why they were bound.

April Lewis nodded, unsurprised. "I think having a council-woman isn't enough of a government representative. They're gunning for the feds. Then again, I think I *might* just count because I'm ever so slightly *black*."

April Lewis was a very unequivocal shade of black. Nora tilted her head, regarding the woman, carefully taking in her strong features, and finding herself smiling for the first time that day.

"And rich. Right?" Pete asked.

"Oh, hell yes. But not rich enough to have my own militia."

"Well. We all need a five-year plan," Pete said.

"Anyway, they don't seem to be discriminating between minority populations," Nora said.

"Well, they have a mission, right?" the councilwoman said.

"What have you figured out?" Nora asked.

"Nothing new," she replied. "Just that the woods are full of angry 'patriots' who somehow believe that their patriotism gives them license to overthrow the government and take as many non-whites with them as possible."

"No, it's *new,* I'm sorry. They are killing mercilessly, indiscriminately. Kids, women. It's mind-boggling. Unprecedented," Nora insisted.

"Sorry, how is that different from shooting up black churches?" Lewis demanded. "Because it happened on the same day?"

"Well, yes . . ." Pete began.

Nora added, "And it's all so brazen. They don't care if you see their faces."

"Yes," April Lewis replied quietly. "They don't care if you identify them and they aren't afraid to die. Once it gets quiet in here

at night you'll be able to hear some of their propaganda; it's coming out of the TVs they have around. It's very deliberate and very
scary. *I'm* starting to worry about the black threat and I've only
been here a day."

Pete looked around. "Do you have any idea about their numbers?"

She shook her head. "No. I think they really can't do too many
training drills; that kind of noise carries. I'm pretty sure they've
got us out in vineyard country—it's the only way they could keep
this many people around in broad daylight. No neighbors, right?
But still."

Nora and Pete considered this.

April Lewis went on, "This barn seems to be like a bunk house,
you know? A lot of people walking back and forth." As though
for emphasis, the ceiling overhead creaked loudly with footsteps.
"I didn't see anyone but the guards at the door. There was a rota-
tion of three of them."

"No clues about who's behind all this?" Pete asked.

She shook her head. "You think there's just one person?"

Pete shrugged. "There's a man named Gabriel Baker. He's been
sending out webcasts. I think it's his voice on the videos here. . . ."

Nora held up a hand, listening.

*Today we are fighting for our lives, for our rights, for the rights
of white children everywhere to grow up away from the onslaught
of cultural assault. Fight against white genocide, fight with all that
you possess! Together, we can make America great again.*

"Definitely Baker," she said.

"Our analysts think they have some clues about the person responsible. A certain profile, you know? But not typical racist
redneck."

"No, it couldn't be, could it?" April Lewis mused.

"Seems to be trying to appeal to all possible constituencies in
order to launch these massive efforts," Pete offered.

"As a politician, I get that," Lewis said. "Still, it doesn't really bode well for us, does it?"

Nora was looking around their stall. "Not even a little," she confirmed. "We have to figure out how to get out of here."

April Lewis emitted a sigh. "I've been trying to think that through. It's impossible."

"Why impossible?" Pete asked.

"Well, there's like fifty heavily armed, angry white folks outside. And we're in the middle of fucking nowhere," she retorted. "Just getting outside of this stall is impossible. It's bolted from the outside and the giant man outside is holding a rifle."

"What about going to the bathroom?" asked Nora, who was desperate to pee at this point.

The councilwoman gestured with her head toward the corner of the stall. "They leave a bucket. They don't want to take any risks."

Pete looked her over. "At least your arms aren't cinched behind you. You can unzip your pants."

She gave him a once-over. "I'll unzip your pants for you, baby." April Lewis grinned.

Nora smiled, grateful for the tension-reliever. "They know we're a threat, Pete. Trained law enforcement."

"Well. We are." Pete rose with a soft groan and limped into the corner of the stall to look at the bucket. It was a large metal bucket, suitable for hauling ashes from a fireplace. Then he returned and bent over, peering closely at the flooring. The boards were about four inches wide. "What's under here?"

April Lewis looked at him blankly. "What's under the *floor*?"

"Have you seen light coming up from here, or heard any noises? Is it a basement or a crawlspace?"

She shook her head. "I haven't heard any noise. Crickets maybe. Frog or two. No light."

He squinted hard at the floor and then returned to the bucket. "Please come help me, Ms. Lewis."

A disgusted frown contorted April Lewis's features. "I'm pretty sure I explained what that bucket was for," she said as a disclaimer.

"Yes, I heard you." Pete's face was impassive. "I want you to try to unhook this handle."

She looked at him, then began attempting to do so. When she struggled, he gave his back to the bucket and clutched the sides with his hands, attempting to hold it tightly despite the cable tie cinching his wrists.

April Lewis pushed and wrangled, finally squeezing the arc of the handle until she could jimmy one end out of the bucket's eye. Success on one side made the other side easier.

"Okay," Pete said. "If you can, try to shove it down between these two floorboards and then we can work together to wedge one of them up."

She looked at him skeptically.

He asked, "You got some other idea?"

She shrugged.

Pete crawled on his knees across the limited available space until he found the two boards separated by the widest gap. He indicated the gap with a nod of his head. "Here."

April Lewis came to kneel next to him. Then she started attempting to shove the bucket handle down between the floorboards. The gap wasn't big, but she could just slide the metal between the two boards.

"If we're lucky," Pete said, "the hooked end of the handle will catch on a nail and we can pull it up."

April Lewis frowned, working intently.

After a few minutes, Pete began to grow nervous. Nora knew that neither of them could do this task with their wrists cinched behind them. Quietly she asked, "When was the last time someone came in?"

"Before you were shoved in here?" The councilwoman was

grimacing as she concentrated. "I don't know, twenty minutes maybe."

"Did they feed you today?" she asked.

April Lewis nodded. "Yes, earlier."

"Do they bring utensils? A knife maybe?" Pete asked.

She shook her head. "No need. Finger food. Nothing hard, metal, or jagged necessary."

"Okay, then," Pete said with resolve. "Then this is actually our only shot. So take all the time you need."

She grew increasingly frustrated, and Nora, subjected to the drone of the television in the hall, became increasingly unnerved. After some fifteen minutes, in which even in the dimness Nora could see sweat streaming from April's face with the effort, the hooked end of the handle caught on a nail from the underside of the floorboard.

"Okay, hold it for me and put it in my hands," Pete said.

The councilwoman placed the wire in his hands and he closed them as tightly as he could and began to tug. The task was unwieldy. Pete refused, however, to accept defeat. He pulled, repositioning himself several times until the small gap began to widen.

It continued to widen, until April Lewis said, "Enough. Let me try."

She inserted her fingers and pulled. The wood groaned slightly as it moved.

"Cough," Pete instructed Nora, who obediently began to cough as April pulled harder on the board. After a few fits of pulling and coughing, the board popped free.

"Yesss," April Lewis said. "Now what, FBI guy?"

"Now we use those nails to puncture these cable ties," he said, indicating the underside of the board and the nails poking out of it.

"Who's we?" Lewis demanded.

"You just have to keep us from impaling ourselves."

Nora asked, "Then what, Pete?"

"You should go first, anyway. If we can pull up a couple more of those boards you can squeeze down there and crawl out."

Nora eyed the five inches of inky blackness they had exposed. "And do what?"

"Umm, get help, obviously."

"You did hear the councilwoman? Angry white folks. Weapons."

"It's dark. They won't expect anyone to bust out so fast. Get to the beach and run west until you get to a phone. Get help."

"Run west," Nora repeated. "Peter, we rode in a boat for over an hour."

"I didn't say it would be easy," Pete said. "But as previously noted, you are wearing your super shoes."

Nora shook her head at him.

"Couldn't she just steal the boat?" April Lewis asked.

Pete scoffed. "That boat will have to be under constant surveillance. Soon as it's rough enough they will have to fold up that dock or lose it. They'll have to send the boat back where it came, probably, no matter how rough it is. Their entrance off the main road will be too tightly guarded to get by, I guarantee it." He looked long and hard at Nora. "Run along the beach til you're well beyond all this. It's the only choice."

Nora sighed. "You scare me when you don't get enough sleep, man."

That was the assent he needed. He swiveled his head toward April. "Ms. Lewis. Can you help position that nail for Nora?"

She knelt behind Nora and looked doubtfully from the tip of the nail to the thin hard plastic of the cable tie. "I see tetanus in your future, honey," she murmured.

"It's okay," Nora said. "I'm actually still wearing Kevlar under my blouse, so even if you ram me with it, I'll be fine."

"So your back is covered, great, but your pretty little wrists here . . ."

Pete said, and his anxiety was starting to color his tone, "Nora's tough, don't you worry. Time is short though."

Ms. Lewis harrumphed. "Alright, but come over in this tiny bit of light. I don't have my reading glasses, you know. I need all the help I can get."

Nora complied, and the councilwoman had her lean backward over the board with its exposed nails. The work was slow going. Nora's injured wrist blazed with pain as the cable tie was pulled more tightly while Ms. Lewis worked. The nail kept sliding across the slick plastic. The board was wide and difficult to work with. Getting punctured with a nail was less problematic than the splinters Nora was getting as the board slipped and slid over her wrists and arms. Ms. Lewis kept apologizing softly and Nora kept murmuring absolution. Pete said, "Scrape it up a little with the nail and it'll be easier."

So the councilwoman scraped at the plastic and then returned to attempting to puncture the cable tie. Finally she said, "There's only a tiny bit to go. Can you twist your wrists and pull it apart?"

Nora did so and the cable tie broke at last. She rubbed at her wrists in relief, and then went ahead and hugged the woman. "Thank you," she whispered. "Thank you so much."

"Just put that freedom to good use, baby."

Nora nodded. "Let me get you, Pete," she said.

"No way," he answered. "There's not enough time. Work with Ms. Lewis to get two more boards up and then get the hell out of here."

The two complied. The sound was disconcertingly loud, but Nora realized that the propaganda spinning through the hallways was actually doing them tremendous favors. Her coughing didn't hurt either.

At last she was looking at a big enough hole to shimmy down into the crawlspace. She tentatively stretched her leg to see how far down it went, but she quickly found the ground and that the hole was only thigh high.

"West, huh?"

Pete looked at her, his eyes full of concern. "I swear I would do it, Nora. I'm so pissed about my foot right now."

"I believe you, Mr. Quarterback. Mr. Gallant Southern Quarterback guy."

"Umm, Mr. Gallant Southern Quarterback . . ." Ms. Lewis began.

"Yes?" he asked.

"What if there's no vent down there she can exit out of?"

Pete looked at Nora, and she could tell by the resolve in his gaze that he was refusing to accept that possibility. "Find the vent that lets in the outside air and you'll be fine. If you can't find it, come back. No harm, no foul."

"What if I'm too big to get out of it?"

"You will think of something, Nora. Too much is riding on this."

She nodded. The pressure felt enormous, stifling.

Pete continued, "You need to get Schacht to call in an airstrike on this place, do you hear me?" he said fiercely.

"Hey, *I* heard you and I didn't like what I heard," April Lewis interjected.

"You make sure Ms. Lewis is safe," Nora replied, acknowledging and ignoring her in one swoop. "I'm going to do everything I can to get them back here by morning. Maybe we can head off the *Second Day*."

"You better be a hell of a runner," the councilwoman said.

Nora and Pete exchanged slow, tired smiles. "I'm alright," Nora said.

Pete was nodding. "She's alright."

"Not so good with bugs, though," Nora said, positioning herself over the crawlspace.

"Aren't there scorpions and scarabs and shit in Egypt? This is nothing, girl," Pete said.

"I'm from Philadelphia. I don't do nature."

Pete smiled reassuringly. "You'll be fine. But Nora . . ." His expression became dead serious. "Every single person you encounter will be heavily armed. There'll be surveillance cameras everywhere. Don't use the beach stairs, they'll be monitored—go over the bank on foot, even if you have to take an hour to make it down to the water."

Nora listened intently, nodding as he spoke. She looked up at him, feeling desperately scared.

He held her eyes. "Go."

April Lewis leaned over and kissed Nora's cheek. "Be safe, baby," she said.

Nora took a long breath, nodded again, and sank down through the floor and onto her knees.

"Nora," Pete called softly as she started to move.

"Yes, Pete?"

"Tell the Starbucks wench I love her."

"No you don't, Peter. The crisis scenario is messing with your brain."

He seemed to be considering this.

Then he said, "Well tell her I want her really bad, then."

"Badly," April Lewis corrected.

"I'm going to introduce you to my violinist neighbor Rachel," Nora whispered.

"Is she hot?" Pete asked.

Nora sighed and looked at April Lewis.

"Get outta here," Ms. Lewis said with a wink. "I'll deal with this one."

There were indeed bugs. Even before Pete and Ms. Lewis began tapping the floorboards back into place, Nora realized that she could see absolutely nothing and had to feel around with her hands in the dark to find the outer limits of the crawlspace. Each time she felt about with her hand, it seemed to her that she touched something crawling. The entirety of her self-discipline had to be summoned to prevent herself from screaming.

They hadn't been too far from the north wall of the barn and so she headed that way and soon found the gritty cement wall.

Was there even a ventilation grill? She wished she'd brought one of the nails, anything sharp, anything reassuring. She hated feeling so powerless. Phoneless, gunless. Hungry as hell. And she had to pee so bad. *Badly,* she whispered to herself.

The floor overhead creaked as people walked over it. Nora felt like she could barely breathe in the hot, enclosed space and the pitch blackness. Her hands were patting along the side of the wall until she realized that a small pool of light was leaking in, just a few hundred feet down. The outside lighting at the barn's entrance was making it into the crawlspace through what had to be the ventilation grill.

She reached it quickly and began feeling around its edges. It was just about as broad as her shoulders. Pete wouldn't have made it through, even had his foot been in any shape to carry him. She crouched for perhaps far more moments than she had, peering out to see if anyone was passing by. She watched as the light from the big house's windows fell across a small cluster of women. But they walked past it, continuing out of Nora's line of vision.

She sighed and began trying to coax the grill out of the wall. The screws required more time than she felt she had, however, and she ended up with bleeding fingertips. When she had finally pulled the grill away, she attempted at first to scramble up and out. She immediately realized that the Kevlar was making her bulkier than normal.

She dropped back onto the ground and unbuttoned her blouse with trembling fingers, then shed the vest and dressed again. She looked at the vest for a moment.

I'm going to get shot at. I'm about to seriously get shot at.

She heard her father's voice in her head, swearing in Arabic. "Zift."

She sighed and shoved the vest through the opening and then followed it out. She lay on the ground for a moment, then slid the vest back on over her blouse. She watched as the vest rose and fell with her rapid breathing. *Calm down, sister. Just take it easy. We have a long, long way to go yet.* She thought about abandoning her navy blazer, but realized that her white shirtsleeves would be a liability if she were trying to fade into the darkness.

Just to the left, the barn door suddenly slid open, spilling a huge swath of light across the grass just beyond where she lay. Nora tensed and huddled into as small a ball as possible.

". . . Baker said we have to do things in order, that's all I'm say-ing."

"People are starting to get restless, though," came the re-sponse.

"Well, all I know is we don't do anything not on the list."

"Well, it should be on the list," the other voice insisted grumpily.

Nora's heart thumped in a way that struck her as perilously loud. Some sort of spider ambled over her hand and she had to resist shrieking. Just as quickly as the two men had emerged, though, the barn door slid back into place, the noise covering the remainder of their exchange.

Nora clenched her eyes tightly shut, and then opened them, trying to find some sort of courage. She began uncoiling herself, looking about for the best path across the morass of weeds to the bank beyond it and the beach below. She squatted, surveying the area, fighting to keep her breathing even and calm. More starlight than Nora had ever seen gleamed above and the air smelled impossibly sweet. A chorus of insects sang loudly, pulsing, one group responding to the other in a constant refrain.

The soft glow of a lit cigarette exposed a guard posted at the top of the beach stairs. This meant she couldn't take a direct line through the tall weeds, for she would pass too close to him.

Surveillance cameras. Where would you be if you were a surveillance camera? She peered hard into the darkness.

Corners. She looked up at the top of the barn. The light perched above the sliding door cast everything behind it into what felt like deeper darkness, but Nora decided to simply assume there was a camera there and give it a wide berth. Still, there would be cameras around the edges of that house. How well would they pick up a dark-clad, dark woman sprinting in the dark?

Motion sensors? The group of women hadn't triggered any by the farmhouse. She would have to run behind the farmhouse in order to stay as far from the beach stairs and the man stationed there as possible. Should she go for the shortest distance between two points or just dart in some crazy pattern?

She decided to trust her speed. She would aim for the furthest edge of overgrown land beyond the house, the point where the towering forest loomed darkly. Then she would follow the tree line north and finally duck into the trees at the top of the bank and make her way down. It was at least five hundred yards of exposed running. But maybe, maybe if the cameras thought she was an aberrant blur—at least at first—then she would get away with it.

She placed her left hand on the side of the barn to steady herself. Then she inhaled, exhaled, and shot away from the side of the barn. She immediately slipped on the dewy grass, but quickly regained her balance and gave it everything she had.

She expected to hear gunfire, but there was none. She pushed herself as hard as she could and cleared the house then barreled toward the lake, chest heaving. As fast as she was running she found that the night air felt cool and refreshing against her face. She felt sharp and in focus, aware of the way the weeds caught at her legs, and, on some level, frightened anew of ticks.

She swept past the farmhouse, now brightly lit in the dark. As she sprinted past she saw an imposing fireplace. The heads of some heavily antlered deer had been mounted on the wall above it. And then she had cleared the house and was almost to the trees. She veered toward the lake.

Easy. She had done it. She paused at the edge of the bank, looking back. The man with the cigarette was now some five hundred yards to her left. He had not moved. Chest heaving, she stared woozily at the edge of the bank. The descent seemed impossibly steep, and the trees swayed in front of her, black and ominous. Far below, the waves were thumping rhythmically against the shoreline. She tried to catch her breath, steeling herself for the next step and casting a quick glance backward at the barn where Pete and April Lewis remained captives. It looked still and benign.

Nora clutched a thin sapling and took a step over the edge of the bank.

That is when the floodlights set high in the trees sprang instantly to life, illuminating, it seemed to her, every contour of her body.

Nora froze.

The man at the top of the beach stairs swung about, the cigarette plummeting from his mouth. He stared at Nora in confusion for a moment, then aimed his rifle directly at her.

She plunged into the trees just as the spatter of gunfire punctured the stillness.

Immediately, she slid several feet. Branches scraped at her cheeks and hands, and she fought to find footing in the brambles along the ground. An eruption of shouting followed the gunfire and she heard what seemed to be a thousand voices, men and women, calling to each other, issuing directions. The voices seemed to be descending on her, and gunfire whizzed past her thudding into tree bark.

She charged headlong through the trees, scrabbling, sliding, tumbling down the side of the bank. It seemed that her pursuers were materializing out of nowhere; she realized that the beach itself must have had several people posted there who were now climbing up to cut her off. She darted toward the stairs, climbing upward again, and trying to take advantage of the dark shadows created by the floodlights. Then she scurried down again toward the lake, clinging to low-hanging branches to keep from toppling over. Several tore off in her hands, causing her to slide swiftly down the steep embankment. Others held and she continued running, zig-zagging. She could not duck when she heard the gunshots behind her. There was no way of telling if she were putting herself more directly in the path of the bullets or dodging them, and every instant was different as her feet could not find solid ground for more than a moment. Just ahead of her two men pounded up the wooden staircase, flashlights bobbing. She gasped, halting, wondering how to get over the stairs or around them. Then she realized that there was a big enough gap that she could pass between the stairs and the bank if she flattened herself. She listened, desperately trying to assess if anyone else were coming up or down the stairs. But the crashing behind her and the sound of the rifles spurred her on. A bullet barreled into the staircase just inches from her face, sending shards of wood flying, and she threw herself against the bank, feeling cool earth against her cheek. She shimmied under the staircase to reach the other side.

West, west, west, she repeated to herself. Fear now overwhelmed her, and all she could do was run and dart and untangle herself from groping branches. Shouts of men and women behind her seemed to electrify her feet while terrifying her brain so intensely that she could not process, could not plot a course, could only plunge ahead, fired by a mad hope of reaching the beach.

And then she was there, skidding down the last few feet to land on an unwieldy layer of flat rocks. She found herself just beyond the last yellow pool cast by the tree-suspended floodlights. She glanced back. The boat that brought her bobbed in the waves, the dock still groaning. She could see a shadowy figure not far from the boat, and as soon as she turned to run she felt the bullet slam into her back. She pitched forward from the force of it, the wind knocked out of her, more grateful for Kevlar than she had ever been. Her knee screamed in protest where she landed, heavily, on a sharp rock.

"She's down!" called the man by the boat. His voice drew nearer. "She's down, hurry!"

Nora did not stay down. She rolled back the few feet she had descended from the bank, and, grabbing the undergrowth, pulled herself into the cover of the trees again, fighting for breath. The pain in her back felt as though she had been sucker-punched. She heard footsteps clattering across the rock, and flashlight beams scanned the shoreline, even boring into the lake itself. Nora crawled some distance and then arose to continue running. Only when she had gotten beyond the range of the flashlights did she descend again and begin dashing along the beach.

The beach was so rocky. She tried to lighten her step, scared to put too much weight on one foot and ultimately twist an ankle. Her knee ached from the fall, though nothing like the roar of pain in her back. On the upside, she had fallen on her hurt wrist and seemed to have jammed it back into alignment, for its pain had subsided.

The shouting had just begun to abate and fall away when she heard the unmistakable sound of gunning engines.

She thought for a moment that they had brought motorcycles to the beach, but suddenly realized it was much worse. Four wheelers. Four wheelers with headlights were bearing down on her. *Trees or water?* she asked herself wildly. *Trees or water?*

No. She was not a strong enough swimmer, and the pulsing black waves terrified her. She knew there were massive rocks under the surface against which the waves could hurl her. More than this, she was certain that if they thought she had gone into the water, they would send the boat after her. She galloped back into the shelter of the trees, trying as hard as she could not to slow down. She had to keep running. She could not stop.

They were hunting. Cries of outrage had turned to whoops as the four-wheelers careened across the rocky beach. Each bore two riders, one with a rifle, the other driving. Nora climbed as fast as she could but kept heading west with every step. She did not look back, trying to play hide and seek the way she had as a child: surely if she did not look at her seeker he would not see her. She could not tell if the light that occasionally fell across her legs and back was enough to indicate her location, or if the four-wheelers were traveling too fast to really see her. Up, she whispered. Climb up. The lakefront portion of the compound had to end eventually. There had to be a limit as to where they could come down from and where they could ride.

Not that trespassing was going to be a law that impeded them. *Idiot,* she said to herself. *These people aren't going to stop out of deference to some border or boundary line.* They would keep coming. They would hunt her all night if they had to. She paused, her chest hollowed out by pain and cramping. She clung to a sapling, listening to the engines and the laughing below.

She was sport.

She began to run again, and then suddenly, unexpectedly, she ran out of trees. Bank erosion had made for a bald mudslide of land. In the moonlight, it seemed to stretch for at least five hundred yards. She skidded to a halt and then fled back to the trees, praying they hadn't spied her in the moment she had been exposed.

She was stuck. She couldn't swim for it, and if she ran along the beach now, they would catch her easily.

What am I going to do?

Her chest heaved up and down as she looked all about her. The roar of their engines seemed to taunt her. They had arrived at the eroded stretch, and they too had circled back.

Well.

Well, they would not add her head to the group above the mantel of the farmhouse.

She didn't have time for that.

She darted to the edges of the beach, skirting as best she could the bobbing of their lights, gathering the heaviest lakestones she found. Most were disc-shaped and she weighed them anxiously, wondering if she could propel them with sufficient force; her wrist felt better and yet not in peak form. *Perhaps two-handed . . . yes.* She made three piles behind three wide trees, engaging as she did so in a dance of feinting and falling back, dodging her hunters as they circled and swooped.

When she was ready, she picked two large rocks, each the length of her forearm and slightly heavier than she could carry comfortably. She cradled the first in the crook of her arm like a discus. Then she slipped down a few feet below the tree she'd chosen and crouched at the line where the beach met the bank. The first ATV was just making the edge of its circuit and heading back toward her, its headlight bobbing. She ducked behind some of the tallest brush, her chest heaving. As the four-wheeler approached, she saw that the driver was aiming his headlight on the woods behind and to the right of her.

She waited.

A hundred yards. Fifty. Ten. *Now.*

She popped up and slung the rock as hard as she could at the shadowy form in the driver's position; without waiting to see if it had hit its mark, she crouched down, grabbed the other, and heaved it too before diving into the woods, rolling slightly. A shout went up and an explosion of gunfire ripped through the night.

The headlight now glanced about as the four-wheeler careened out of control. She had flattened herself against the tangled underbrush. She realized that the other rider must have subdued the ATV, for the engine was idling then, and only one of the four-wheelers was still making its circuit, its headlight scanning the trees. She began dragging herself with her elbows toward her next stockpile of rocks.

She heard a woman yell, fighting to be heard over the roaring engines, "He's hurt. I need help."

"Find her, dammit!" countered another voice.

Both machines idled now and their headlights were trained on the bank. One woman and two men on foot, equally spaced some fifty yards from each other, started into the trees.

Apparently I did not think this through. . . .

She clutched the next two stones and waited, struggling to control her breathing. Left flank. A man was drawing near. The four-wheeler's headlight framed him in a hazy halo of light, and Nora could see that he carried a flashlight in his left hand, the rifle resting on his right hip. He was looking left and right, but his footsteps were steady.

She did not hesitate. She sprang up, slinging the heavy stone directly at his throat. There was a sickening thud and he fell backward. For once, the weapon did not discharge, exposing her, although the flashlight now lay in the underbrush. Nora pounced, grabbing and extinguishing the flashlight. Then she tugged the strap of the rifle down the man's arm to disengage it. The ATV headlight showed his chest heaving up and down as he gasped for air. Blood dribbled out of his mouth. The lakestone had crushed his windpipe.

She pocketed the flashlight, shouldered his rifle and dashed toward the beach.

Afraid that one of her first two stones might have damaged the first ATV, she leapt astride the second one.

Be easy. Be easy to figure out.

She had never ridden a four-wheeler, of course. She could hear Pete's voice in her head. *No bars. No boats. No ATVs. What the hell, Nora?*

Okay, Pete. Help me out.

It had brakes like a bicycle. *Oh my God,* she whispered, staring blankly at the machine. She clutched the handle bars.

Gear shift. It was idling, so it was on, so that was done. *Gear shift?* She punched at a backlit button with an up arrow, and saw a number light up on the dashboard. *Okay. First gear. Gas?* She looked at the handlebar grip and realized she had seen enough motorcycles in the movies to have an idea. She twisted the grip forward and the machine surged forward. *Zift.*

She clamped down on the brakes, then aimed her rifle at the other ATV and shot at its wheels.

Quickly, she turned the handlebars to maneuver out from behind the other ATV, aiming the headlight straight ahead as she did so. Shouts and gunfire poured down from the bank as she accelerated. The ATV started whining and she pushed the up arrow quickly. Nothing happened, so she released the gas and tried again, grateful that it sped forward even more quickly. It seemed to resist her and she struggled; all the muscles in her arms strained as she tried to control the handlebars. The rocks made it difficult, and there was a hail of gunfire coming from the beach behind her, but she continued accelerating, shifting the gears doggedly until she dared not go any faster. She kept closer to the edge of the water, fearing the piles of driftwood as much as the rocks.

She kept going for what seemed like miles, expecting all the time to be pursued via boat or four-wheeler or helicopter. She did not know the limitations of the group and its leader's wealth and resources. How easily would they give up? She had injured one of them and probably killed another. It was as close as she'd gotten to killing with her bare hands. She remembered the man's face as he choked on his own blood, unable to make a sound in the underbrush. The memory made her squeeze her eyes shut and the vehicle swerved, jolting her back to reality.

She drove on for over twenty minutes until she was forced to stop at a long low wall constructed of six-foot cement blocks jutting out into the water. There was no driving around it, and no way to get over it. Where this wall met the bank, she spied a wooden stairway threading its way upwards.

She needed a telephone. But she had no money, no ID.

Let it be just some mellow hipster couple living by a vineyard. Some Downton Abbey-*watching couple. Cardigans. Let there be cardigans.*

She soon found herself on a well-kept lawn; it was a modest two-story house, well-lit. No high ceilings. No dead deer. She ran to the deck and paused a moment. She stowed the rifle she'd swiped out of sight, then mounted the steps and knocked as calmly on the sliding glass door as she could muster.

A wide-eyed teenaged girl in a tank top and pajama bottoms came into sight in the living room. She stood gaping at Nora. Her bright blonde hair hung in two matching braids. She did not open the door.

Nora could only imagine how filthy she looked. She knew she

had an ugly bruise from where Goatee had punched her. She waved, ridiculously, then said, "I'm Special Agent Nora Khalil with the FBI. . . ."

But the girl vanished from sight.

Nora suppressed a scream of frustration, and was about to take off running again when the girl came back into sight with a rifle cradled in her arms. She approached the deck doors with a slow and steady step.

Okay, at least she's giving me a chance. I look scary. I get that. I'd want my gun, too.

Nora tried to introduce herself again. She engaged in a bit of pantomime as she did so, holding her thumb and pinky finger up to her ear like a receiver. "I desperately need a *phone*. If you have a cell phone you could just call the number for me and hold it up without letting me in. I can shout through the door or FaceTime them or something. Please?"

The girl stared at her, incredulous.

Nora tried again. "I understand how rough I must look right now. If your parents are around, please call them out here and have them supervise."

"You got some ID?"

Smart girl.

Nora shook her head. "I was abducted by some bastards down the beach from you. I swear. Please just call the number for me. You have nothing to lose, I promise." She held up her hands. "My hands are where you can see them. But lives are at stake. Please."

She saw the girl thinking about this. Then she reached into the wide pocket of her pajama bottoms and pulled out an iPhone.

Relief flooded over Nora. "Thank you! Thank you so much. Dial 814-555-6218."

The girl keyed in Anna's number rather clumsily, for she was still holding the rifle in what was clearly her phone hand. She hit the speaker button and waited, eyes riveted on Nora.

"Please pick up," Nora whispered against the glass. "Don't let it go to voicemail."

"Special Agent Anna Dixon speaking." Anna's voice could just barely be heard through the glass.

"Anna!" shouted Nora, her palm against the glass.

The girl was sufficiently convinced now. She cracked open the sliding door, just wide enough so that Nora could speak into the phone she still held. Her rifle stance relaxed somewhat.

"Oh my God, Nora. Where are you? We've moved heaven and earth looking for you—is Pete alright?"

"Yes, Anna, for the moment—they took us both—some kind of compound on the lake. We need . . . We need to move right now. They have April Lewis, they have Pete—his foot is hurt, he couldn't get away. They have . . . weapons. People . . . I'm scared they'll hurt them because I ran. . . ."

"Nora, you've got to calm down—Where are you?" came Anna's voice.

Nora looked hopelessly around her, as though some sign might appear. "I have no idea, Anna."

"Planer," said the girl, her eyes even wider.

"Planer," said Nora. "Can you trace this call? I ran to this house but these guys aren't that far off—there's, like, this compound, barns and stuff—They took our phones, our badges, guns. . . . Tell Schacht we need like . . . SWAT teams and . . . fighter jets."

"We're tracing you now, Nora. Don't hang up. Stay where you are. We'll send as many people as we can."

Nora held the girl's gaze. "Okay? Is that okay? Don't hang up, okay?"

The girl nodded, mesmerized.

"I'm gonna just sit down a minute." She slid down the door frame and sat on the wide slats of the deck.

The girl set the rifle on the floor and crouched down. She

spoke to Nora through the opening she'd made with the door. "You . . . you, um, want a glass of water or anything?"

Nora turned her head to look at the girl. "I would sell my soul for a bathroom," she said.

The girl's name was Brianna Ellis, and she was sixteen. Nora had never felt more gratitude toward another human being than she did at the moment that Brianna pulled open the sliding door and ushered her into her home. The girl even disappeared upstairs for a moment and returned with a Taylor Swift T-shirt.

"Really?" Nora asked.

Brianna shrugged. "I used to love her, but I fucking hate her now."

Nora nodded. "It happens."

But as she emerged from the bathroom, face washed, chest emblazoned with the word "Red," she realized she had probably endangered Brianna more than anyone ever had. *I should have pushed that ATV into the lake,* she thought.

Then again, a wall's a wall. Any fool would have figured out where she'd gone.

"Brianna," she said, accepting from her a glass of water. "There are some guys after me."

The girl nodded, her green eyes held a knowing look. "You can call me Bree. And you pretty much just led them here."

"Do you have a car?"

"Me personally? Not for another two months. It sucks so bad. . . ."

"No, I mean, is there a car here we can take? We need to leave."

"Oh. No. My mom's working nightshift. Dad's at bowling."

"Text them," Nora said.

"Oh, believe me, I already did. But they just never pay attention to their phones . . ." she griped. "Why even have a phone?"

"Call her actual work. Call the bowling alley."

"Call?" Bree looked disconcerted.

"Yes, the bowling alley. Tell them to tell your dad to come home right away and get you."

Bree looked at her askance. Then she shrugged, began Googling the number. "It's all the way in Erie though."

"Oh, for . . ." Nora spluttered. "Neighbors?"

"What about them?"

"How close? I didn't see any other houses or lights around."

Bree shook her head. "Well, it's not like walkable or anything. Well, I mean, it is for some people. But I'm not a big walker . . . and it's totally dark. . . ."

Nora felt trapped all over again, then remembered the rifle she'd left leaning on the railing outside. She slipped out to get it, listening intently as she did for the sound of ATVs. Everything was, for the moment, quiet except for the sound of breaking waves. She locked the sliding glass door behind her.

"Nice AR-15," Bree observed, twisting a braid around her index finger. "Yours or theirs?"

"I took it from . . ." Her voice trailed off, and she saw that Bree knew instantly she had had to kill for that rifle.

"You okay?" Bree asked softly.

Nora nodded.

"How many are you expecting?"

"Hmm?" Nora asked, trying to gauge how many rounds were left in the cartridge.

"How many bad guys are about to come over the bluff?"

Nora blinked. "I'm not sure, Bree."

"You need more ammo?" she asked. "You look like you need more ammo."

"You just happen to have ammo for a Bushmaster? Just . . . sitting around?"

"Not sitting around. In the den. Come on." Bree headed into a thickly carpeted den.

Nora, casting a worried glance at the bluff, followed.

A gun rack occupied one wall of the wood-paneled den. On it, from smallest to heftiest, were a dozen rifles.

"Thirty round capacity, I'm guessing," Bree said, assessing the weapon.

Nora watched, feeling appalled and appreciative simultaneously.

Bree yanked open a drawer to display tidily arranged boxes of ammunition for the various guns in the room. Nora noted that there was a rifle quite similar to the one she held; Bree pressed a hefty box into her hand, which Nora accepted. There was also a gap where Bree had pulled down the Luger she'd walked into the living room with when Nora first appeared.

Nora studied the guns and the ammunition displayed in front of her. She could not help but ask, "Do you have any handguns?"

Bree tugged at another drawer and showed her two different handguns lying prone in form-hugging Styrofoam insets. Nora seized the Glock with a sigh of relief, checking that its cartridge was full.

"Okay," she was saying. "This is great. Now, look, Bree, you need to . . ."

But the girl was pocketing several rounds, apparently for the Luger.

"What are you doing?"

"Helping," she answered, as she walked back into the living room to load up.

Nora flustered, followed her. "Look, we need to get these lights off, Bree, and then we should talk."

The girl complied. Then, before Nora could direct her to go into her room, she plopped herself down on the floor, rifle on her lap, and began tapping on the screen of her phone.

"Wait, you left the line open for Anna to track us, right?"

"Of course—I was just about to Instagram this though—do you care?" she said.

Nora wasn't sure she'd heard her. "Sorry?"

"Instagram us, you know, hanging out with our guns for the shootout. Selfie? I'll use the flash. Real quick."

Nora stared at her. "Bree. Some really bad guys may be coming up your beach stairs, *like right now.* I didn't invite you to a shootout. Just, if you could lock yourself in your room with your weapon, I'd feel better. I can handle things down here."

"I've gotten a hunting rifle every year for Christmas since I was twelve," Bree said. "I can help you."

Nora struggled to recalibrate what she knew about white people and Christmas celebrations. "Charming. Look, I believe you. Now go to your room."

"You're going to regret it. . . ."

"Why's that?" Nora, patience exhausted, demanded.

"Because they have more guns than you do," she said, nodding toward the lawn. "Here they come."

Nora looked at her wildly. "Give me that phone."

Bree passed it to her.

Nora picked up the Kevlar vest from the couch where she'd tossed it after changing into the Taylor Swift shirt. She walked over to Bree and, over her huffing protests, forcibly tucked her arms through the arm-holes, buckling it up for her. "Get to your room," Nora hissed, putting on the scariest expression she could muster. She was relieved that Bree gave her a fierce frown in return but whirled and began ascending the stairs.

"Anna," Nora whispered urgently. "Anna, six armed men just walked over the bluff."

"We're in the car, Nora," came Anna's response. "But we're still about fifteen, twenty minutes away. Do you have to engage with them?"

"God, I hope not. There's a teen in the house."

"Get her out of there, Nora. It'd be better to take a car and go."

"There's no car. No neighbors. Nothing but grapevines and . . . white power."

"Get her out of there, keep your vest on. CIRG has sent one of the SWAT teams. We'll be there as fast as we can. Keep the line open."

A plump, silvery moon illuminated the lawn in a way Nora hadn't expected; she couldn't decide if the added light would work in her favor or not. As soon as the figures hit the Ellises' lawn, they split up to encircle the house. Nora didn't know which one of them to track. She crouched by the couch, instructing herself to breathe in and out. Her fingers closed and opened around the handle of the Glock. She toted the Adaptive Combat Rifle over her shoulder, its magazine filled with thirty fresh rounds. Six people. Thirty rounds. She could miss four times on each.

Stop trying to do math, she whispered.

Anyway, her chances were better with the Glock. She had far more training with that.

She watched as one of the figures crouched low and mounted the three steps that led up to the deck. It was a woman. Her ponytail swung like a pendulum as she tugged at the sliding glass door, attempting to open it, then stood and took aim at the lock with her rifle.

Nora stared, still disbelieving what she was seeing. Even as she reluctantly aimed her Glock at the woman's chest, she heard a crash and knew that the front door had been kicked in. Nora prioritized quickly, firing three bullets through the glass at the woman on the deck and then leaping over the back of the couch.

There were three of them. Nora was suddenly hyper-aware of time and motion. In the darkened room she could not see their faces, was only vaguely aware of their stances, the way their bodies curved around the rifles they carried, and the way they shouted at each other. Their words ran together and Nora could not divine them. She was suddenly beyond words; there was no way to contain in language the fear she felt or the level of overwhelming panic.

Sometimes you just go . . .

She was kneeling. She depressed the trigger on the Glock over and over, moving the gun's barrel from one dark form to the other. Exposing her position drew their fire immediately and so she crouched, hoping she hit something, anything, and began firing up from the floor.

The angle proved effective for at least one, for she heard a shouted command interrupted by her last bullet.

Get out of there. Lead them away from Bree. . . .

She hurtled across the living room floor, praying her earlier shots had met their mark. She shouted incoherently as she ran, hoping to draw their attention, hoping to pull the remaining two out of the house and into the woods. She shouldered the shattered sliding door, pushing the rest of the glass out of it, then jumped over the body of the first militiawoman.

She hadn't anticipated that one of them was crouching in wait for her in the shadow of the deck. As she ran down the steps from the deck, he tackled her with an animal grunt. Both of them went sprawling on the slick grass of the front lawn. Nora fought to find a way out from under him, but encountered only a thicket of arms and legs.

"Not so fast, bitch," he hissed. He yanked the rifle from her hands and tossed it aside as he stood.

He grabbed her by her chignon and dragged her upwards until she was on her knees. His breaths were coming hard and fast, and Nora felt his knuckles grazing her neck. The skin was rough and hard. He pressed the tip of his rifle against her right temple.

Nora, panting already, took a deep, gasping breath, a breath that encompassed sky and lake and trees and stars.

She squeezed her eyes closed.

But the crack that came seemed to emanate from well behind her. Somehow it was the gunman who crumpled onto the lawn, and not Nora herself.

Nora whirled to see Bree holding up her rifle from the second-story window of her bedroom. "Told you you needed help!" she shouted.

Nora shook her head in disbelief as she let out a sigh of relief. She wanted to shout something up to Bree but found no words. Instead, she patted her own face and head, making sure she was still alive, still whole. She wanted to crush the girl to her in a hug or break into some sort of dance.

But she realized quickly there was one man left. She twisted left and right, scanning the moonlit lawn for movement. The sound of the waves was audible again, beating steadily against the rocky beach below, matching the sound of her own breathing. She sprang up to search for the rifle that had been tossed aside.

A smashing sound shattered the stillness.

Nora knew instantly that exactly what she had feared had happened. Bree's scream confirmed this, although the girl seemed to have fired off a shot; an identical crack to the one that had felled Nora's attacker shook the night. This was followed by more screaming.

Nora raced back into the living room, leaping over the prone forms in her path, and she bolted up the stairs, taking them three at a time. The landing at the top of the stairs revealed a hallway, but finding Bree's room was no mystery. A figure in camouflage pants and a black T-shirt had pinned Bree's arm behind her and had pushed her against the wall.

Nora hesitated, cursing herself for not having yanked a rifle off one of those lying dead in the living room. But she did not hesitate for long. She pounced, wrapping her right arm around the man's neck and grasping her own wrist hard with her left hand. She pulled backwards with all her might, squeezing with everything she had; her left wrist, not unscathed from the fall in the basement, launched daggers of pain that emanated throughout her entire body.

His hands went from pinning Bree to groping at Nora's arm which was vise-like but weakening fast. Bree, now released, reeled and fell onto her twin bed as she tried to get her bearings. Nora saw she was looking for her rifle which was nowhere in sight.

"Just run!" Nora gasped at her, but the girl could not get by them as the man staggered from side to side, Nora clinging to him.

She felt her arm beginning to give way and tried to redouble her efforts, but found to her horror that he was overcoming her.

She knew if she let him pull her off that he would throw her immediately. So she quickly yanked her arms away and slid down his back into a low crouch. As he whirled to face her she punched as hard as could at his groin, then whipped her right hand back, fingers arched to expose the palm. As he doubled over, she shoved the base of her palm upward with all of her might, catching the bottom of his nose and propelling it up into his skull.

The bones shattered, and blood began spurting out of his nose. Bree darted away, but could not escape a spattering of blood. The man fell facefirst onto her bed, gushing blood onto a comforter emblazoned with neon peace signs.

Nora and Bree both sank to the floor, looking at each other, chests heaving.

"Is he dead?" Bree asked.

"Maybe," Nora answered. She looked around for his gun.

Bree saw her. "I shot it out of his hand. Didn't mean to, actually—meant to kill the fuck. But I was just . . . surprised to have someone kicking in my door. It was new. And he was very close. It happened very fast."

Surprised, Nora looked at the part of the wall where the impact from the man's rifle had smashed a hole in the drywall. The weapon lay warped on her fuzzy pink carpeting; it had singed some of the pile around it. Nora tilted her head, getting a better glimpse of the man's right arm, and found that it had a huge burn mark on it. "You did great, Bree. You did so great. Any other kid would have freaked out."

"You saved me," the girl said.

"You saved *me*," Nora said.

Bree grinned at her. "We're fucking amazing."

Nora laughed. "Yes we are."

Bree looked from Nora to the man sprawled on her bed. "So *now* can I Instagram it?"

The man groaned and Nora sprang up from the floor. "I need . . . well, do you have cable ties?" She so wanted to tie his hands as hers had been for hours.

Bree considered this. "Nah. What about my bathrobe belt?"

Nora sighed. "Is it pink?"

"What do I look like?" She went to the closet and extracted a turquoise, leopard-print robe with a matching belt. "Pink," she scoffed.

As Nora tied the man's hands tightly behind him, they heard several car doors slamming. "And there's my team." Nora patted along the length of the man's body, making sure she hadn't missed any weapons. She winked at Bree. "These guys are only, what? How late are they?"

"Like, a million hours late."

"Yes," Nora agreed. "A million hours late. Let's go." She draped her arm around Bree's shoulders and gave her a quick squeeze, before releasing her to pass through her door. "We trashed your room, Bree."

The girl twisted a braid around her index finger and said, "It was a little trashed before. I'm not gonna lie to you."

Anna was the first one through the doorway, skirting the door that hung now from only one hinge, her gun at the ready.

Bree flicked the light switch as she began descending the stairs, bathing the foyer in light, and Anna turned quickly, then just as quickly lowered her gun when she saw them, exhaling with relief. "I didn't know what to expect," she said.

"I hope you expected dead bodies," Nora answered. "Because I have no clue what to do with all these."

Anna followed her gesture to take in the living room. She let out a small gasp despite herself. Agents Ford and Chidambaram had stepped in and were looking about.

Schacht followed. "Any risk that there are more coming?" he asked immediately.

Nora nodded. "Yes, there's definitely a risk of that. These came up from the bluff there." She pointed beyond the living room to the lawn and beach beyond.

Schacht turned and directed the rest of the group outside to form a perimeter around the house, concentrated by the stairs leading down the bank.

Anna froze, holding up a hand to Nora and Bree where they were on the stairs. "I'm glad you're both okay. I'm going to ask that you sit right there on the stairs until we can take some notes and digitize this scene, okay?"

The male agents held their positions in the foyer, surveying the damage and murmuring to each other.

Bree frowned as she watched Anna leave. "Where's she going?"

"Anna, in addition to being a super tough agent, is our photographer person. I'm thinking she went out to get her camera."

"She doesn't look super tough. She looks a little like a Strawberry Shortcake doll."

Nora pursed her lips. "And you look a little like a Barbie doll. I'm trying not to hold it against you."

Bree laughed. "NRA Barbie!"

Nora burst out laughing. "Home Invasion Barbie! Little miss crack-shot from the second floor."

Schacht, Ford, and Chid looked up at them where they sat together laughing on the sixth stair.

"What's so funny?" Schacht asked.

"Brianna Ellis, aged 16, meet Special Agent in Charge Schacht, Special Agent Ford, and Special Agent Chidambaram. Bree here used a Luger rifle to shoot a very bad guy in the head . . . from the window of her bedroom," Nora said. "She saved my life."

All three had the good sense to look suitably impressed.

Nora continued, "She needs some kind of Instagrammable commendation, SAC Schacht. Stat."

"I promise," he said very seriously, "that I will see to something that recognizes her action just as soon as we are not in the middle of a crisis."

Bree smiled brilliantly.

"But you're going to have to bear with us for a minute. Do you mind if we spend an hour or so sorting ourselves out here?"

She nodded enthusiastically.

"I'm going to need you to park your cell phone with us for a while, though. Okay, Brianna?"

She nodded much less enthusiastically at this, but managed to say, "Okay."

Nora looked at Schacht gratefully, then gave a nod toward the group outside. "Glad to see we got some backup now."

He nodded. "Yes. Our media liaison is still downtown, and I left several of the Pittsburgh agents onsite at the synagogue. The local bomb squad is a little irritated with us right now, got a little defensive over territory since I inflicted the DC crew on them."

Nora said, "Abe seems pretty level-headed. He'll recover."

Schacht continued, "There's another Philadelphia agent currently on his way, Nora. Just to . . . let you know."

Nora flushed, understanding the import of Schacht's words.

"Seemed to think that our ongoing war on drugs back home warranted his attention less than this madness."

Nora shrugged. "They come for the madness, they stay for the . . ." Her voice trailed off, unable to fill in the blank.

Anna, who was by this time trolling through the room with her camera, supplied, "Sunsets. We have amazing sunsets here."

"There ya go," Nora said.

She saw that Ford was on the phone, presumably calling in the coroner. She leaned over the railing and mentioned there was another guy in bad shape upstairs who might require an ambulance. She refused to say it in a way that might suggest to Ford that he should rush that request.

Sheila finally appeared, haggard, her blazer exceedingly wrinkled and sweat-stained. She looked up at Nora and a small smile played across her lips. "Well, Special Agent Khalil. Looks like you made a lot of people sorry they chose to abduct *you.*"

"**What the *fuck*** is this?" Mr. Ellis, slightly balding, slightly paunchy, very flushed, stood clutching a bowling bag and staring at the mayhem in his living room.

Nora tried to look at the scene with his eyes. Front door scarred and unhinged. Four different windows adorned with spider-webbing from the passage of bullets. The sliding glass doors shattered. A long, near-contiguous red blood stain on the living room floor where three bodies had lain. The pseudo-suede sleeper sofa riddled with bullet holes. Six federal agents standing around the living room; eight out keeping watch on the lawn. His daughter Brianna, light of his eyes, in blood-spattered pajamas, cheerfully holding a coffee pot.

Bree was the first to respond. "Those assholes down the beach, Daddy. You were right about them. Total douches."

Mr. Ellis fought for composure and words. He plunked his bowling bag on the floor and crossed to embrace his daughter. She held the coffee pot out wide so it wouldn't spill.

"Are you hurt?" he asked gruffly. "Is that your blood?"

"No, Nora kicked a guy's ass who was trying to kill me though. It was kind of awesome. So, yeah, his blood, not mine. I was gonna change but I figured I needed to take a picture of it first. Oh, and Daddy, I totally killed this guy who was about to shoot Nora in the head. I used the Luger! And then all these FBI guys were like, we have to launch an assault on the crazies down the beach, so I'm like, oh, I'll make you coffee!"

Tears of relief were leaking out of Mr. Ellis's eyes as he patted his daughter's hair, hugging her, releasing her, then pulling her close again.

Nora knew what was coming though. She counted down to herself.

Mr. Ellis kissed his daughter's head, then whirled on them.

"Are you people out of your goddam minds?"

Schacht crossed to him, offering his badge, and asked gently if they could sit in the den and discuss the matter. Nora thought she heard him mention compensation for any and all damage to his home and property as the two walked away.

She and Bree exchanged a look. "You want some coffee?" the girl asked with a grin.

Nora laughed. "Do you have tea?"

"Ooh, tea!" Chid perked up, then came to stand next to them, extending his hand to Bree, whom he'd been ignoring until then. "I'm Chid. Tea would make my day."

Bree gave Nora a *who's the weirdo* look, then went to track down a kettle.

"Nora, we need more details from you," Sheila was saying.

Her face looked positively gray. She had aged in the past two days.

"We've narrowed it down to two possibilities. There's a fifty-acre tract of land about ten miles east of here that belongs to a Joseph Geyer. It's zoned for a house and a barn, not three barns, like you said."

Anna looked up from her laptop, and Nora could read the response tempting her tongue. Something about violating zoning ordinances through stockpiling weapons. Sheila saw her look, but directed her to work up a quick bio on Geyer.

"The other possibility is slightly further on, five miles beyond Geyer's land, a property in the name of Emmett Mertens."

"It's always the Emmetts," Ford said knowingly.

"Really?" Nora asked, interested.

"What about barns?" Anna asked.

"Horse farm, apparently. Two barns on this one," Sheila replied, but Ford had his laptop open. "Google Earth?"

Nora shook her head as she peered at the horse farm. "This one's all wrong. Not enough trees." She waited while the camera moved west. She leaned forward. "That's it. Barn with a silo, two more barns, house fronting the lake."

"Surprised they didn't cover it with camo."

"Nothing surprises me about how brazen this whole thing is," Nora said. "Are there beach stairs?" She leaned over Ford's shoulder, realigning the Google Earth camera. "Yes. Okay," she said, straightening. "That's it. Let's go? Can we go? Can we go now?" She said all this as she accepted a mug of tea from Bree.

Schacht had just emerged from the den with a significantly calmer Mr. Ellis. "There's no we," Schacht said. "This is where CIRG comes in."

"Then what are you waiting for? Can't you give them the go-ahead?"

"Of course, but you have to understand that this means they

will be going in with their Hostage Rescue Team first and foremost. It could take a very long time. Force will be the very last thing on the list of strategies."

Nora turned her back on him and walked away.

"This is serious, Nora, I'm sorry. This is much bigger than you realize," Ford said. "We don't want another Waco."

"These people are armed to the teeth, Ford. I saw it with my own eyes. I've got the bruise from the round that hit me in the back," she patted her lower back.

"And a pretty good shiner on your left eye," Chid noted.

Nora pointed to her eye, having forgotten all about it. "Plus, April Lewis is being held hostage. A federal agent is being held hostage. What else do you need?"

"Negotiation. More intel. Are there kids on the compound? If so, where are they being held? We need a better sense of what we're facing," Ford said. "They won't just launch an attack on American soil without the attorney general's permission, and the attorney general will not give permission until every peaceful avenue has been exhausted."

"You saw the videos, man!" Nora said, trying again to keep from shouting. "They declared *war* on the federal government!"

"We hear you, Nora. We all know this. We've seen what's been going on. But we have got to find a peaceful resolution or it's going to be a slaughter, and that slaughter is going to breed generations of haters who felt like we did the wrong thing."

Nora wilted. "Come on, man. I think they're going to kill Pete. April Lewis has money. Pete is just . . . Pete. Representative of the federal government. They killed a judge for as much, and he was a little old man."

Ford leaned forward, as dispassionate as Nora was agitated. "It's out of our hands."

Nora looked to Anna for support. She was listening, frowning, her reading glasses perched on the end of her nose.

"CIRG does nothing but this, all day, every day," Sheila said. "Trust them."

Nora walked immediately over to Schacht. "We can't just leave him there," she implored.

"Nora, we can't just bust in there when we don't know what they have stockpiled," Schacht answered. "With the amount of cash taken from the bank they could have bought several rocket launchers, innumerable M-16s, grenades . . . The U-Haul at the synagogue contained almost as much ammonium nitrate and nitromethane as Oklahoma. God only knows what could go off if the wrong rounds hit the wrong storage facility."

She struggled to suppress a white-hot fury. "I *promised* him I'd be back for him," she said, working hard not to shout.

Schacht's calm had no calming effect on her as he replied, "And so you will, but there's no point in getting you and all of us killed in the process—that would be to their benefit, I'm sure you agree."

Nora leaned her head against the wall, trying hard not to curse at the Special Agent in Charge.

"More than this," Schacht continued, "you have to be aware that they could be baiting us."

Nora glared at Schacht. "What do you mean?" she demanded.

"Look," he said. "Nothing did more for the white militia cause than what happened at Waco. To provoke a confrontation, to make us invade that property and fire on Americans, that is gold for this organization from an advertising standpoint. The corpses of the Waco children radicalized more people than anything else the government has ever done."

"Hey, I studied Waco, alright? I'm not asking you to go in on the suspicions of some UPS man. These people hunted me like a dog. And we've seen the results of their weapons-stockpiling for the past two days. Assault rifles and bombs . . . the case for taking them down is airtight."

Ford snapped, "Which is another reason to let CIRG do what it does best."

"Easy, kids," Schacht said. "As we were saying, Nora, it's clear to us that they were lying in wait for you and Pete. It was inescapable that we would find that house and find that tunnel. There are only so many places on this shoreline that we can look, only so many places that are big enough and remote enough to support this sort of activity."

"Why that house?" Nora asked suddenly. "Is there some connection?"

"None so far. It's listed as being owned by the Benedictine nuns. It was a soup kitchen for a while and has stood empty for much longer," Anna said. She had clearly already looked it up when they were initially deciding whether or not they needed a warrant to enter so they could search for Pete and Nora.

"Why is there a tunnel leading out of its basement?"

"Maybe it was part of the Underground Railroad," said Anna. "Erie was a stopover on the way to Canada for a lot of runaway slaves."

Chid blinked skeptically at this, then lapsed into contemplative silence.

"Whatever its original reason for having a tunnel," said Schacht, "the point is, whoever picked the house, Nora, picked it for the tunnel, and probably even picked the synagogue as a target so they could use the tunnel. They wanted to abduct one or two agents, and we think they did so to bait us. Which is why we're going to be extra cautious. End of story."

Nora sank back onto the Ellises' couch, feeling overwhelmed. "So you're telling me that either way, whether I'd gotten out to tell you or not, they'd have been expecting you to find them and launch an attack?"

Schacht and Ford looked at each other, and Schacht nodded. "It's reasonable, Nora."

"Probably they were hoping for the Third Day, though," Chid said. "In fact, I would bet everything on it."

Nora regarded him, frowning. "Because everything goes up in flames in the fourth opera?"

"Valhalla burns," said Chid simply.

Schacht asked, "Did they photograph you? Badge shot?"

Nora nodded, remembering.

"See, we didn't get that yet," Sheila confirmed. "They were holding on to it. I think this theory is sound."

Nora looked at her colleagues and then at her hands.

Sheila walked over to her and squatted down. "We're all worried about Pete, Nora. I swear. But for this moment there is nothing anyone can do. You've had a hell of a day and night. I'm giving you a direct order: You need to go home. You need to rest. We have to defer to CIRG on this one. They will let us know what we can do and when we can do it. Those of us who *weren't* abducted and hunted down by a crazed militia will stay close to the compound. In the meantime you are to sleep, wake up, head to the office, and try to find solutions from there."

Nora looked from her to Schacht.

"Listen to your SSRA," said Schacht.

Nora sighed, feeling defeated.

Bree called out from the kitchen, "That's bullshit, Nora. Take your little Glock and go rescue your friend!"

"Go to your room, Bree," said her still ashen-faced father.

She gave him a devious grin. "Can't, Daddy. There's white supremacist blood, like, all *over* the place."

It was approaching midnight when they left the Ellis home; it was truly much the worse for wear for her having been there. They left several of the Pittsburgh crew on the Ellises' lawn. Anna, Schacht, and Sheila piled into Anna's SUV and headed to rendezvous with the CIRG command team. Nora was glad to hear the sound of the SWAT helicopter splitting the still night sky as they stepped outside.

The air smelled sweet and moonlight spilled onto the lawn and the grapevines beyond. Bree stood on her front stoop and called to Nora as she started to get into Chid's rental minivan.

"Nora!"

Nora turned back to meet Bree halfway. She had come out in her bare feet, clutching her newly reclaimed phone in one hand and Nora's Kevlar vest in the other.

"Hey, if you need, like, a sorcerer's apprentice or something, you could call me in," she said.

Nora took the vest from her and gave her a quick hug. "You did great tonight. No talking about it on the Internet, though, okay? Lives are at stake."

Bree nodded. "I get it. My dad sorted me out."

"Okay," Nora said, proffering a fist.

Bree bumped it. "Imma look you up at your office in town, okay? We can get some mani-pedis or something."

Nora laughed. "That is exactly what Home Invasion Barbie does in her downtime!"

After hugging the girl once more, Nora got back into the van and gave Chid and Ford her address. Ford was still working on his laptop from the front seat of the car as they drove her back into town. Despite herself, she fell asleep in the backseat. She awoke with a start when they pulled up in front of her place.

"You gonna be alright, Nora?" Chid was asking.

She nodded sleepily. "Yeah, I'm good."

"Alright, we're gonna go back to the office and let Maggie know she can go home. You'll come there when you get a little rest?"

"Yes, assuming all hell doesn't break loose."

"You remember orders: even if it does. Sleep."

"Yes," she answered. She was suddenly conflicted. She had

never offered her place over to any man other than Ben. "Do you—do you need a place to sleep awhile?" she asked, hoping desperately they would say no.

"We've been told about the Room of Requirement," answered Chid. "That's all we need, right, Derek? Half an hour here or there and we're good to go."

"Philly boys. Tough as nails," said Ford, in a monotone.

Nora nodded. "Alright, Philly boys. See you soon."

She slid the heavy door of the minivan back into place, then walked up the front walk to her place.

Nora pulled the spare key from behind the crumbly brick and opened the door. She gave the van a completely unnoticed wave and shut the door once again behind her.

She knew instantly that something was wrong. The foyer's inner door was slightly ajar.

She froze. Her hand flew to where a holster should be. She remembered instantly that she had no gun, no phone. She sighed, furious with herself, and cast futile glances out the door to where the van had been before it drove away. Finally she readied her fists as she pushed into the dim living room.

The floorboards of the hundred-year-old home did not welcome attempts at stealth. She walked as lightly as she could into the room, but the floor creaked with every footfall. Nora's adrenaline had shot up again, coursing through her limbs, sharpening her brain.

How did they find me?

She scanned the living room and listened carefully. There was a sound coming from the back, near the bedroom. Footsteps like her own falling across a protesting floor.

They were coming toward her now, swift and steady.

She darted right, flattening herself against the living room wall, tensing. Then she arranged herself in guard stance, weight on her rear leg.

A figure emerged from the dining room, and Nora unleashed a roundhouse kick.

And suddenly Ben was lying on her floor.

"Ben!" she gasped, falling to her knees beside him.

"Jesus!" he coughed, doubling up, clutching his chest.

"Oh my God, Ben, I'm so sorry—"

He took a few moments to cough, then opened very green eyes to look up at her.

She bit her lip, patting him gently. "Sorry?" she said again.

He grumbled, "This isn't the reunion I was hoping for."

Nora curled her legs under her and helped pull him to a sitting position. "Messing around in my apartment, huh?"

"Um, you did give me a key."

She smiled. "Of course I did. Took you long enough to use it."

He shook his head, observing her. "You look like complete hell." He winced as he ran his fingertips along the large bruise on her cheek where Goatee had struck her.

She patted her hair. "Yes, well, next time call and let me know you're coming. I'll pretty up."

He adjusted his position and pulled a shiny new BlackBerry out of his blazer pocket, handing it to her. "You didn't actually have a phone. Which is why the secretary lady gave me this to deliver."

She leaned forward and gave him a kiss on the cheek. "Thanks. Any chance she sent you my gun and badge with that?"

He gestured with a backwards nod of his head to the dining room table.

She peered up and saw a Glock in a new shoulder holster. Next to this were the requisite papers to sign checking it to her name. There was also a new set of credentials. "Okay. Three presents from Maggie. Where's my present from you?"

"Brought you a pony," he said earnestly. "It's in the backyard."

She smiled, despite herself.

"Maggie told me you'd also been burned in the downtown scene two days ago." Frowning, he ran his hand along her arm to where the gauze was still wrapped. "I'm sorry. I'm sorry I wasn't there for you."

She shook her head at him, trying to convey without words how deeply his trip to visit his ex had upset her. In the apartment above them, Rachel had launched into a meditative piece that drifted down through the floor like a warming mist.

He leaned back, listening, and then brushed his fingertips along her cheek, looking into her eyes. "You still mad at me?"

She nodded. "But I had a bad day. Sheila and Schacht sent me home and wouldn't let me go help Pete."

"Pete's gonna be okay, Nora." He reached over and squeezed her hand.

"You don't know that," she said, shaking her head.

"CIRG is good, Nora. Let them do their thing. You're no good to anyone if you've collapsed. . . . Rest."

She returned his long look, feeling something unfurl within herself. Her breath suddenly came easier.

"I didn't mean to hurt you, Nora. I was trying to do the right thing."

Nora studied his features. The sandy hair and strong jaw, the soft lips. "I have zero interest in talking about this now, Ben," she said quietly and without anger. "I'm just really, really tired. And I probably have a tick from having to hide facedown in the forest. Ten ticks. I probably have ten ticks."

He carefully came to a standing position, groaning slightly and rubbing his chest, then extended a hand to her so she could join him. She took his hand and rose slowly. She tried not to moan with the effort; her whole body hurt in a way it simply never had. He gently tugged the elastic out of her hair and began running his fingers through it, touching her scalp each time.

"I don't feel any ticks," he said. "But you should probably wash this hair. This is not city-girl hair, for sure. There's like, twigs and stuff stuck in it. Maybe a possum or something . . ."

She nodded reluctantly; showering sounded as if it'd be an inconceivably difficult task.

"I'm gonna tuck you in. And then I'm gonna go hang out with my buddies Ford and Chidambaram and let you get some sleep."

"Make them get my partner back, Ben. He's a . . . good egg."

"I will," he said. Then he wrapped his arms around her, kissing her lips very gently. "I heard you were a superhero out there," he murmured.

She leaned her head on his shoulder. "I think my best moment was just now when I kicked your ass."

SECOND DAY

Nora slept deeply and without dreaming. If Rachel played anything, she did not hear it.

She jolted awake, covered in sweat.

It took her a long time to sort out that she was not in the small apartment over her father's Arch Street restaurant in Philadelphia. She rubbed her eyes and ran her fingers through her hair, finding it at odd angles. She was grateful Ben had made her take a shower before getting into bed, although she should have remembered to braid her wet hair before sleeping.

She sighed. Her stomach ached with hunger again, and she mentally began running through the contents of her pantry. There was a box of Cinnamon Toast Crunch, she knew. *But was there milk . . . ?*

Suddenly she became fully awake. *Pete.*

I have to check in. The glowing hands of her wristwatch told her it was almost four in the morning. She went to find the new phone Ben had brought her.

It was lying on the dining room table where she'd left it next to the Glock and her credentials. The screen was just fading into darkness after having recently received a new text. She peered at it. It was from Ben.

No change. Hostage Rescue Team is still negotiating. A few of us are at your office. Come when you can.

Nora gathered her mass of bent and twisted curls into a tight knot at her neck, still slightly higher than usual to avoid the burnt skin. Then she slipped on a clean Oxford shirt and holstered her new gun. She hesitated, looking at the Israeli Kevlar, then remembered Sheila's direct orders. They were targets now. She strapped on the vest, reluctant to submit again to its grim weight.

She grabbed a PowerBar and a slightly bruised banana out of her kitchen, slipped her feet into the purple Wave Riders, then headed out into the darkness.

Perry Square was well-lit for the pre-dawn hours. A bent man, his reddish beard as thick as it was unruly, was sitting on the low wall that rimmed the park. He watched her as she approached. "Strange times, lady."

She nodded and continued her brisk pace without answering.

He raised his voice slightly, but his words were slow and clear. "Just because I'm a white man, don't mean I support all this shit goin' down."

Nora paused to regard him. Then she handed him her banana and PowerBar. "Let's hear it for assuming the best about each other," she said.

He grinned, accepting the food, revealing a few precariously dangling teeth.

By the time she got to the office, she was ravenous. Ben greeted her in the foyer after she swiped in. She could tell he wanted to lean in to kiss her, but held himself back with an *it's the office* sort of look. "You okay?" he asked as she unstrapped her bulletproof vest.

She nodded grimly but gave him a small smile. "A little sleep goes a long way. But I need, like, food. Anything at all. Anything not still walking around."

"We ordered pizza from some sketchy all-night place," he said. "Might be a little cold now though. . . ."

"Oh, Nick's? Nick's isn't sketchy, it's, like, perfect. Please tell me you got something without pepperoni. I'm beggin' you."

"I did. These guys were all, no, get all meat, and I was sure you'd pop up at some point so I insisted on a non-pork option."

"My hero," she said.

He grinned at her. "Say it again."

"My hero," she said, and for good measure she pecked him on the cheek. "Let's eat!"

He led the way toward the conference room, but Nora stopped dead in her tracks.

"What happened to this place?"

"CIRG descended. Those who aren't Enhanced SWAT needed somewhere to leave their stuff—there was no time to check into a hotel. Everyone had gone straight to survey the refugee center and then the would-be bombing site, and just as they were packing it in for the night, Schacht gave them the call that they needed to begin negotiating out at the compound. Those who could, dropped their things here and spooned some Folgers crystals into their mouths before heading out again."

The office was strewn with carry-on luggage and abandoned suit jackets. In front of Maggie's empty desk was a pile of plastic bags. She saw a pair of black high heels, and wondered if the woman they'd brought in to deal with the press had finally realized she wasn't going to get to sit down anytime soon, said, *Screw it,* and found some sneakers.

"Alright then. Welcome," Nora said to the room. Then she added softly, "I hope they know what they're doing." Her fear for Pete felt like hands tightening around her throat.

Ben saw the anxiety in her eyes.

"He'll be alright, Nora. Those idiots have everything to gain by letting him go unharmed."

Nora shook her head. "Ben, they don't care if they live or die. Why would they care what happens to him?"

Ben gazed at her, and she saw him make a conscious decision not to give her false promises. "Well, maybe here in the quiet we can figure something out that will help him."

Nora took a second to savor the sound of his voice. "I'm glad you're here, Ben."

"I'm glad I'm here, too. Philly's so . . . *boring*," he said, and they both laughed, recalling their phone conversation of three days ago where Nora had used that very word to excess.

Ben pushed open the conference room door. The long table was littered with more paper than she had ever seen. An extra-large pizza box sat in the center of the table, two-thirds of its contents having been consumed. Each of the agents was holding a slice of pizza and looking sleepy.

Ford waved to her; under the brightness of the halogen bulb, she found herself studying him, wondering again how he got the scar on his cheek.

Chid mustered a kind smile. "Nora! How are you?"

She was silent a moment, wondering how to frame the response. Desperately worried about Pete, shell-shocked from all she had seen in the last two days, and her body ached from a long list of burns and bruises. . . . Finally, she said, "I'm clean. That's about all I got at this point."

Even Ford cracked a smile. "Welcome to the war room."

"How did you get out of standing vigil outside the compound?" she asked.

"The Hostage Rescue Team is very territorial," he said. "It is unlike anything I've ever seen before."

"Washington boys," Chid said with a shrug. "Lot of dick waving going on."

Nora gave a knowing nod, although she was foggy, and felt it best to remain so, on the dynamics of dick waving.

"Anyway, we came to be Schacht's brain trust," said Chid. "So we are doing what we do best."

"Eating pizza at 4 A.M.?" asked Nora.

"And rockin' the laptops," said Chid with a grin.

Nora walked to the middle of the table and seized a slice of pizza from the grease-splotched box. Ben had gotten her mushrooms and green peppers, her favorite, but it had apparently had few other takers.

"Oh," she said. "That is so, so pretty." She took a bite and chewed rapidly, then said, having not quite swallowed, "What are we working on?"

"Gabriel Baker," answered Ben.

"He's pretty, too," Nora said. "Maybe a little too pretty."

"Chid was saying the same thing."

Nora looked at him and asked, "What were you saying, Chid, and why?"

"I was saying that he is spouting all kinds of rhetoric that doesn't seem to mesh. I mean, look. He's clearly a smart enough guy for a . . . what is he again?"

"He was a truck driver," Ford supplied. "I don't have any records for a while now. No employment, no health insurance, no taxes."

"He's never been out of the country. Joined the NRA at the age of sixteen, member of the local rifle club. Volunteer for the fire department when he was living in Lake City. He was on the roster of a church. . . ."

"What kind of church?" asked Nora.

Ford shuffled papers, looking. "Lake City Baptist Temple."

"Extremist?" she pushed.

"It's not on anyone's list, if that's what you mean," Ford answered.

"Is it one of those scary mega-churches?"

Both men shook their heads.

Chid said, "This area really doesn't have the population to sustain a mega-church."

"Doesn't rule out being extremist country though," Ford said. "Most rural churches are preaching that immigration and the concomitant religious pluralism are the primary reasons for the country's downfall."

"Preachers and politicians," Ben muttered.

"Well, yeah. Exactly. Like we said, the typical militiaman isn't a big reader," Ford said. "He opens his ears to the rhetoric of a good speaker, then asks himself the all-important question."

"What's the all-important question?" asked Nora.

"Are you a man of action?"

Nora nodded. "Except now women are asking it, too," she pointed out, remembering the scene at the refugee center, and deciding against the second piece of pizza.

"Yes, now women as well," Chid said quietly.

"Is Baker one of those 'traditional values mean my woman's traditionally in the kitchen' kinda guys?" Ben asked.

"Hard to say," Chid answered. "Calling on women to take up arms isn't any indication that you're convinced of their equality. It's done when they're needed. Manpower. The U.S. allowed women into the war efforts in World Wars I and II because of need, not desire. And most were sent back where they started when it was all over. The Israeli Defense Forces draft women because they need warm bodies." Chid gave Nora a pointed look. "Even Yasir Arafat did it in Palestine . . . his so-called 'Army of Roses,' right? Not a feminist."

"I'm not Palestinian," she whispered loudly.

"I know," he whispered back just as loudly. "I looked you up."

Nora scoffed. "In the middle of, like, the apocalypse here, you were so irritated that you couldn't figure out my heritage . . . that you *researched* it?"

Chid waved her off. "Solving puzzles is what I do. Do fish apologize for swimming?"

"And now that you know?" Nora pressed. "Have you figured me out?"

Ben perked up in his chair. "If so, can you tell me?"

Chid laughed cagily. "We were talking about Gabriel Baker."

"What radicalized him?"

"Well, we can make some guesses," Ford chimed in. "He's not from here, for one thing."

"More urban or more rural?" asked Ben.

"More rural—the town of Ulysses in north central Pennsylvania."

"Ohhhh," said Nora.

"You remember?" Ford asked, eyeing her with interest. "You must have been a pretty spectacular student."

Nora could feel Chid observing her with that look he got. She shrugged. "I'm a nerd," she said.

"That's a lie!" Ben protested. "You're the *jock* in our relationship." He gestured at her as he looked to the others for help. "She's the jock, I swear."

Nora gave him a small smile. "Yes. Well. I guess I found myself at Quantico."

"And! Empirically speaking, domestic terrorism is fascinating," added Chid. "She couldn't help herself."

Nora said nothing.

"Come on, it's a *little* fascinating," he pushed.

Ben intervened. "Come on. What's significant about Ulysses? You know, for those of us who are apparently not nerdy enough to retain information?"

Nora sighed. "There was an Aryan Nations World Congress there. 2002."

"Oh, shit," Ben said, swiveling in his chair, a frown etching into his features. "But no one takes that shit seriously . . . right?"

Ford looked up. "Baker didn't leave Ulysses for the region up here until 2003."

"Three hours away," said Chid, goading. "Three hours away from all that delicious ideology. Edible, digestible, delicioussssssss . . ."

"You think he met Kreis?" Nora asked Ford, ignoring Chid.

"August Kreis? I can't think why not," Ford answered. "What could be going on in Ulysses PA that was more interesting than August Kreis training the Aryan Nations?"

Nora considered this. "I can't think of anything, frankly," she said.

"Exactly," said Chid and Ford together.

"Oh, *that* August Kreis," Ben said. "The one who declared his support for—"

"Yes, well," Nora said curtly. "We can't all be enlightened voters. Some of us need guidance from neo-Nazis. I still don't get it though. How anything those guys could say would stick with anyone. Anyone!"

Chid took a deep breath, thinking. "For many different reasons, not all of them the same for each person who thinks this way. One is the sense that their language is losing ground, one might be that they can't put the nativity scene out at schools and courthouses. Another problem comes up when schools can't start their kids' day with prayer—and all of a sudden they feel challenged. Everything they assume about the world is thrown into jeopardy. You start asking questions about God and that's it!" He snapped his fingers. "Everything unravels."

Nora frowned, listening carefully.

"Anyone who attacks God is fair game. It's always been that way."

"What do you mean, attacking God?" asked Nora.

"I mean suggesting that *God*," he paused to make air-quotes around the spoken word, "has a chosen people beyond the borders of your tribe, or suggesting that he communicates in a language other than yours, or that he has more than one way of being worshiped—or, worst of all, that he has rules about living life that are less strict than the ones you follow. This diminishes his power, right? If he isn't almighty and all-powerful—if his power isn't absolute, then what power does he *really* have?"

Nora pondered this, feeling how the breath entered and left her body as she listened to Chid's voice.

"Anyway," he continued. "Looks like Baker doesn't have to cope with how Pennsylvania schools handle *God*—if they're schooled at all they're homeschooled. No registry anywhere."

"Tried and true coping strategy," murmured Derek.

"Taxpayer?" Ben inquired.

Ford tapped the keyboard of his laptop and looked nonplussed. "He's been off the grid for some time now."

"Where? The compound?"

"Maybe. Quite possibly his family has been holed up there with him. Part of the problem with storming in is all the possible kids. We can't forget Waco, right?" Derek said this, his tone affirming the fact that he was the one at the table who brought it up the most and was forgetting it the least.

Nora looked at him, then dropped her eyes to her laptop unseeingly. "What does he have planned next?" she asked finally.

Chid sighed. "I think if I were running this revolution I'd do what militia in other states have done but only inelegantly," he said finally.

Nora, Ben, and Ford looked at him.

Chid spread his hands wide as though it were obvious. "Occupy something!"

"Inelegantly?" pressed Nora.

"Well, large groups of men usually get snacky midway through a good occupation. It gets ugly," Chid said. He and Ford started chuckling.

"What?" asked Nora.

Ford shook his head and looked back down at the screen.

"*What?*" she asked again.

Chid said conspiratorially, "When they appealed for food and supplies, we joined the movement sending sex toys to the Oregon militia, care of the Malheur Wildlife Refuge."

Nora and Ben glanced at each other, processing this, then burst out laughing in unison. Ford actually blushed. In that instant, Nora adopted the theory that he and Chid were together. That would be twice in one week she'd uncovered a romance around the conference room table. She started sneaking glances at the two men as they chewed their pizza.

Ford, eyeing the last slice, said, "This would be so much better with beer."

Nora saw that as an obvious attempt to change the subject.

Ben grinned, winking at her. "Nothing like beer at dawn . . ."

The beer references brought the specter of Pete to the table. Nora frowned, leaning forward. "So what do we really know about Gabriel Baker?"

"Pretty normal guy," said Chid.

"For a racist psychopath," said Ben.

Chid shrugged. "Those are usually the scariest. The ones you don't expect because they seem so normal. But the thing is, he has to be a very . . . well, a very . . ."

"What?" Ben demanded.

"Some of his discourse is just . . ."

Ben gave Nora a look. She shook her head. "Chid does this. We are learning to cope."

"Okay, look, listen to what I mean. Where's that webcast of his . . ."

Chid pushed the remote. The plasma screen TV sprang to life. Chid started jumping from minute to minute through the webcasts Baker had sent the press. He frowned hard at the screen, as though chastising it for not rendering up that which he sought.

Finally, he leaned forward. "Oooh, yes, here . . ."

Gabriel Baker stood, his back to a copse of trees. He wore an olive green T-shirt. He was tanned, with a neatly trimmed beard and searing blue eyes.

Nora listened carefully.

"*And now it's time to reach out. Not just to the patriots as we have done, but to the larger populace. It's time to make America great again. It's time to reclaim this country for its Christian heritage, its Christian values, its foundational vision.*"

"He's reading from a teleprompter," Ben said.

"Yes, it looks like it," Nora agreed.

"Shhh," Chid said.

They looked at the screen and back at Chid.

"What?" asked Nora.

"The thing he just said, just now!"

Annoyed, he waved the remote, sliding the cursor backwards. "*We cannot shy away from antinomianism if the laws are themselves perfidious and base.*"

"See?" Chid asked.

"What? What's that, antinomianism?" asked Nora.

"Exactly," said Chid, crossing his arms and looking satisfied.

"*What?*" she said again, irritated.

"Well, it means freeing oneself from the necessity of obeying the law because the law is perceived as unnecessary, but the point is he *mispronounced* it."

Nora blinked. "So?"

"So, if you're writing a speech to present your views to planet earth, you would probably pick *words you know.*" He was making little karate chops into the palm of his hand for emphasis as he spoke.

Nora looked at Chid warily. "Okay . . ."

Chid leaned forward, tapping the remote against the table, black eyes flashing. He gestured with the hand that still held a crust of pizza. "*Unless* you are presenting someone *else's* words."

"Someone else? Someone like who?" asked Nora.

"Well, that's the trick, isn't it?" asked Chid.

Nora raised her eyebrows. "Apparently?"

"Yes, apparently, yes, definitely. So, the question is, from whence all these references to nineteenth-century German cultural elitism and from whence the reference to Wagner's essays and from whence—"

"Yes, we get the picture. What's your theory?" asked Ben.

"He's got a handler," Chid said, polishing off the last of his pizza crust. "He's . . . a lackey. A pretty face. Maybe even a fall guy."

They sat around the table digesting this.

"Do you think there's a connection with the owner of the property out on the lake?"

"Well, yes, but we can't find a real-life existence for him, can we?" Chid sighed. "The phantom Joseph Geyer. I mean, there are Joseph Geyers aplenty, but there is no logical connection to anything going on here. He doesn't seem to own any other property in the area. A man without history."

Nora thought about this at length, then asked slowly, "You guys have, what, four motorcycles now. Do they match?"

Ford nodded vigorously. "Only in that they're pretty cheap. Not something you'd ride to a biker festival."

"It's a rally, not a festival," Nora said.

"Yeah, Derek," added Chid. "No maypoles here, man."

Ford laughed. "I stand corrected."

Silence fell. Nora realized she too needed her laptop, and so went to get it from her desk. She took a moment to pace among the maze of desks, muttering the name, "Geyer," over and over and sounding slightly unhinged even to herself.

When she hadn't returned in five minutes, Ben emerged from the conference room, looking for her. They fell into step together, skirting the clutter, then ended up by the bank of windows overlooking State Street.

She turned to him, saying, "I think we should go. I can't stand this waiting. I want to be there."

"Schacht asked us to hold off, asked us to work behind the scenes. CIRG is all about this stuff. We need to do exactly what we're doing," Ben said.

"Technically CIRG is all about *this* stuff, too," she pointed out. She set her laptop down on a now-cluttered desk.

"Well, it's all hands on deck then. But the fast-roping out of helicopters thing is not in my skill set."

Nora sighed at him. "I knew you were too good to be true."

They stood for a while in silence, looking down at the just-stirring city. A city bus rumbled by, mostly deserted. A few people made their way along the sidewalks in the half-light. Nora wondered how to get it back, how to trust the person across the street not to shoot you.

Ben seemed to sense this. "This isn't real, Nora."

"How can you say that?" she demanded. "Of course it's real."

"No," he said, shaking his head, and sitting down on the window ledge. He looked thoughtfully out over the street. "This isn't the normal. They want you to think that this is some majority way of thinking about the world. But it isn't. Normal people don't want this. Normal people don't want pain and conflict and won't choose it. Life's hard enough."

Nora listened, wanting to believe him. "I had a pretty strong belief that people are basically good, you know? And then I watched a woman shoot a little girl. Just, shot her. For no reason except that . . ." She had not yet cried, and hot tears were suddenly spilling from her eyes.

Ben watched her, and she could see his concern. She had never cried in front of him before, and she saw him trying to decide if he should pull her into his arms. He finally extended his hand and she clutched it hard.

"She was shot because she looks like me, Ben," Nora whispered.

"Nora, it happens every day. Every single day," he answered. "We know this. And so the sane people have to call the crazies back from the brink."

"I hate how I feel about these people," she said in the same wet whisper. "It makes me doubt everything I know. About God, about the balance of good and evil, about everything."

Now he pulled her toward him, cupping her chignon in his hand, then sliding his fingertips along the length of her jaw, then brushing away her tears with his thumbs.

"They can't really have understood what they're doing, Nora. Don't you get it? The messages they've gotten have dehumanized all their victims. This onslaught of racist webcasts and gun-show rhetoric and campaign slogans and AM radio fear-mongering . . . So they don't even think of them as real people, just foils for whatever is wrong in their lives. . . ."

Nora was nodding. "And it's just a game. Some kind of Xbox deal." Nora wiped the palms of her hands over her wet cheeks.

"Yes," he said. "It's a game. And the more they play, the more they have to play."

She sagged against him and let him carry her for a moment.

"We should go back in," she murmured.

"We should," he agreed. "Just . . . give us another minute to stand like this. Just one."

They stood, still, silent. She had missed his breath in her hair and the expanse of his chest. She leaned against him, feeling the warmth emanating from him, and she decided she could pick what was real.

She planted a soft kiss on his cheek as they pulled apart, then she grabbed her laptop and they walked hand-in-hand back to the conference room. They disentwined their fingers as Ben pulled the door open.

She steeled herself.

Chid and Ford were talking together intently.

Her hopes rose. "Any word?" she asked.

Chid said, impatiently, "You know they'll call us if there's any change, Nora."

But Special Agent Ford held Nora's eyes, then turned to Chid. "Easy, man." He looked back at Nora, "Ask as many times as you want. It's fine."

Noting a change in the way he was talking to her, she looked a question at him.

Ford said, "I lost my partner two years ago. Trying to round up some neo-Nazis in Montana. They left me this," he pointed at his cheek. "Stephen wasn't so lucky."

Nora's eyes darted from Derek to Chid and she found that Chid's expression was complex; he managed to look chastened and grave simultaneously. It seemed clear, too, from the way Derek had said "Stephen" that Stephen had predated Chid as both partner and *partner*.

"So anyone with a partner on the line gets special consideration. It's an actual rule," Ford said firmly.

Nora looked gratefully at him.

"Thanks, Derek," she said.

"No problem, Nora," he answered, and she knew that he knew she'd put the pieces together.

"We interrupted you when we came in," Ben said. "What did we miss?"

Chid let out a long sigh. "We were complaining about not being able to track their communications. Even just a typical email account would help, but we really have nothing. The webcasts, as we've said, are coming from these dynamic IP addresses and we need time—so much more time than we have here."

Nora nodded. It was no time for Pete to be absent.

Ford said, "Look, it's the essential problem of dealing with any terrorist organization at this point. It's just too easy to encrypt anything, and we'll never have the manpower we need to break every encrypted site in order to monitor what they're saying to each other. So, say we're talking about Al-Qaeda or ISIS—first, get me enough Arabic speakers, and there are never enough, then get me my code-breakers, and there are never enough of those either. By the time we break into one site, they've abandoned it and started up another with a whole new encryption."

Ben said, "Okay, but we're talking about a bunch of rednecks in the backwoods of northwest Pennsylvania."

Ford replied, "Well, yes and no. Our militia organizations are not quite as tech savvy as the overseas terror groups. But their deep-seated conviction that the tyrannical U.S. Government is watching their every move has made them willing to do what it takes to set up very opaque communications webs. Ironically, they end up using most of the same technologies as the foreign groups they make so much noise about."

Ben grinned at Nora and began ticking off on his fingers. "Beards, check. Head-coverings, check. Love of wearing camouflage, check. Love of the semiautomatic rifle, check . . ."

She joined in, leaning forward in her chair, "Absolute conviction, check. Absolute lack of education, check."

Ford added, "Willingness to master the tech to get new recruits and keep the group up to date on goings-on, check."

Nora gave Ford points for trying.

"So what are we left with?" asked Chid.

Ben answered, "An impenetrable web of angry people."

Ford was nodding. "Short of torturing a password out of one of them, you can't gain access to the site unless you sort through the layers of encryption."

They sat in silence, each one thinking. Nora weighed the word *torture* and found it had chilled her. She felt slightly nauseous, loathing the militia, Goatee . . . what would she do to him to get information to save Pete? Or any other person on his list of Fourteen Acts?

She didn't want to think it through. Chid was staring into space, tapping his pen against the table, swiveling left and right, left and right in his chair. Ben and Ford both had their laptops open, and each one had gone back to tapping on the respective keyboards.

Nora started to boot up her own laptop, then looked down at her gleaming new BlackBerry. She picked it up, running her in-dex fingertip along its smooth edges. Suddenly she said, "Hey, what are they toting?"

"Hmm?" asked Ford. "What kind of weaponry?"

She shook her head. "What kind of *smartphone*?"

He narrowed his eyes in thought. Nora saw Ben and Chid were paying full attention.

She said, "I shot two women at the refugee center yesterday. Another one ran off the road and they took her to the hospital. She had no ID, nothing on her, so they listed her as Jane Doe. I assume we still have all their stuff."

Ford was nodding. "We logged three bottom of the line mo-torcycles, three AR-15 semi-automatics, and three iPhones into evidence. You want to look at their phones?"

"We can break into a smartphone, Nora, but it takes a very long time," Chid reminded her. "That's what Ford was saying—"

"Chid," she rejoined sharply. "I was listening. Unlike the BlackBerry, iPhones have fingerprint pads. Jane Doe is just in a coma—"

Ben's eyes widened. With a broad grin he finished for her, "—and so is still in possession of a warm thumb!"

"If the phone didn't get turned off or run out of battery . . ." Nora was saying, knowing she had to add that caveat, knowing they both knew it anyway. Still, she felt lighter, suddenly hope-filled. "Where, Derek? Where would it be?"

Ford had already pushed back his chair. "The portable stuff got hauled back here, and then just left because—" Ford strode out of the conference room, saying over his shoulder: "I think there was a box, you know—one of those cardboard boxes with the lids. . . ."

All three followed him. He scanned the room, then started pawing through the clutter. Nora watched, then asked, "Was Maggie here when you brought it in? She didn't receive it from you?"

Ford was nodding, "No, that's right—she was here, and I set it in her cubicle. . . ." He hastened his step and then uttered a, "Ha!"

He bent over a medium-sized box of sturdy cardboard. He squatted, tugging at the lid, and then pointed at three iPhones in plastic baggies.

Chid peered over his shoulder. "I like the camo case."

Nora looked, too. "Better than the one with the Confederate flag?"

"Glittery pink for me," said Ben.

Ford stood, his eyes bright. "They're all still charged, though it's pretty low. We'll take them and try each one. Hospital?"

"Six blocks down," Nora said, and with that they gathered their phones and badges, tucking their laptops into carrying cases. After bundling themselves back into their Kevlar, they all headed out the door at a jog. Nora was deeply grateful for something to do. She hoped against hope that her idea wasn't foolish.

Anyway, it's all we've got right now.

Pete, hang in there, man. . . .

"We'll take my car," she said.

"No way," Ben said. "Nora's gonna drive?"

She gave him look. "Only in a crisis." She headed for the dusty Chevy Malibu which the Bureau had provided her.

"They always seem to evaluate your personality and then give you a vehicle that is the complete opposite," Ben observed.

"You picked up on that, too?" asked Nora. "I thought I was the only one."

"Federal conspiracy number nine-thousand-and-twelve," Chid quipped. "They actually gave *me* a pickup truck."

Ford said, "I thought you said it was only six blocks. We could just walk."

Nora nodded, pleased to hear someone else suggest walking for once. "I did. But in case we need to head out somewhere straight from there." She pulled the driver's door open and climbed in. She, like Ben, slid her laptop under the seat; then she started the car.

They showed their badges to be allowed admittance with their firearms into the hospital. Chid and Ford's laptops were allowed to pass through without being scanned once they'd established their credentials. The woman at the information desk of the ER looked harried. Her gray curls framed features that seemed to have solidified into a frown. It had been a very busy two days at Hamot Hospital indeed. She gave the be-suited foursome a gaze that said, *Now what?*

They all pulled out their badges again. Ford said, "You have a Jane Doe in intensive care, brought in yesterday. . . ."

She narrowed her eyes.

Nora volunteered, "Motorcycle crash, came in in a coma. She'll have had some broken bones. . . . Late thirties maybe, early forties?"

The woman flared her nostrils at them, then looked down at the keyboard. She tapped slowly, deliberately, unmoved by the agents' apparent urgency. She then took each badge in turn and entered information into the computer.

Nora fought for calm.

"Room 216-B," said the woman, handing them "Visitor" stickers.

They all took off walking, Ben and Derek Ford in the lead. Nora sighed as she peeled the sticker and pressed it against her chest, falling into step next to Chid.

"It would be so much better if they left room for creativity," Chid sniped. "*Visitor*. It doesn't leave room for the multitude of possibilities."

"I think the category of *people coming to borrow a mostly-dead woman's thumb* isn't going to come up."

"It will when I rule the world," Chid said. "Just you wait, Nora Khalil."

"I can wait," she said.

"Yes." His eyes twinkled. Then he said, "You Egyptians have that . . ." he brought together the tips of all the fingers of his right hand, then shook it up and down in the traditional gesture, "that patience. 'Patience is beautiful.'"

She shook her head. "You don't quit," she said.

"So. Be honest. How is it being an Arab in the Bureau at a time like this? It has to be pretty satisfying, right, watching all these white terrorists running amok for a change?"

Nora stopped dead. "How dare you?" she demanded loudly, pulling herself to her full height and advancing on him.

She realized that Ben and Derek had stopped and turned to see what was going on.

Chid looked particularly small as he took a couple of steps backwards. "Hey, I didn't mean—"

"How dare you?" she said again, more softly this time, but no less contemptuously. The words crowding her mouth were so many and each was so dangerously anger-swollen that she couldn't speak at all. She walked away, brushing by Ben and Derek and taking as quick a pace as she could without breaking into a run.

Room 216-B mercifully appeared, a glass-walled intensive care room, filled to the brim with pulsing machinery. She stopped and stared at the prone woman. Her light brown hair was fanned out on the pillow. A rainbow of bruises decorated the right side of her face. She looked to be around forty. Rays of fine lines emanated out from her eyes. Nora took several deep breaths, determined to focus.

Seconds later, Ben and Derek entered, with Chid not far behind. Derek was still carrying the plastic baggies containing the three iPhones.

"You think she's a righty or a lefty?" he asked.

"Whichever hand's got slightly thicker fingers, thicker wrist, right?" said Ben.

Nora palpated each of the woman's hands. She expected to feel revulsion, touching her so intimately. But the comatose woman's flesh felt benign, warm. Grasping her hands in turn, Nora stared distractedly at the ribbons of veins.

"I feel like she's a lefty, but I'm not sure . . ." Nora said.

"Is she old enough to have one of those pencil calluses?" Ford asked.

Nora found it on the middle finger of the left hand. She held up the hand and waved it at them. "Let's do this."

Ford fanned out the phones. "Camo, Old Stars and Bars, or Girly Glitter?"

They all peered at their choices and then at Jane Doe's face.

"Girly Glitter," Chid declared.

Ford pulled out the phone and clicked it to life. "The charge is low, but there."

"If it's the right one we'll find a charger," Ben assured him.

"Nora? You wanna do the honors?" Ford handed her the phone.

Nora looked at the screen. The lock screen photo was of a toddler in a bubble-filled bathtub—no possible indication as to the identity of the phone's owner.

Nora picked up the woman's hand and pressed the thumb on the small circular pad of the home button.

Nothing happened. *Try again,* mocked the phone. She looked up, meeting each of her colleagues' eyes in turn.

"Try it one more time, for good measure?" suggested Ben.

"Okay, but it's going to lock me out," Nora said.

"Just try."

She wasn't breathing, she realized, and she took a deep breath. Pressing Jane Doe's thumb once more against the thumb pad immediately called up the keypad. She shook her head. "No luck," she murmured, handing the phone back to Ford.

Ford tucked the phone back into the baggie and handed it to Chid.

"Next candidate?" Derek asked.

"Camo," Nora said firmly.

This time there was no mistaking it. The lock screen image was of the woman herself, happy, laughing, a tall man outlining her body with his own, draping a heavy arm around her shoulders. Each wore camouflage pants and white T-shirt. Matching rifles were propped next to them.

Nora shook her head as she gazed at them, then seized the woman's thumb and pressed it on the home button. The lock screen photo faded instantly away.

Nora's sharp intake of breath was all the confirmation they needed. All three men took a step forward to peer at what had been revealed.

The Telegram app had been left open.

"She'd been taking pictures of the massacre at the refugee center," whispered Nora, feeling as though something within her had withered. "And posting them for the group to see it as it was going down."

"Okay, be very careful," Ford was saying. "We don't want anything to shut that app."

"Can you hit *Never Lock* in Settings?" asked Ben.

Ford nodded. "Yes. Good."

Nora handed the phone carefully to him, and he and Chid bent over it, talking quickly. It wasn't possible for all four of them to take in the requisite information from the small screen, so Ben and Nora sat back to let them work.

It was at this point that one of the Intensive Care nurses entered the room, her ponytail swinging, the V-neck top of her lavender scrubs stretched tightly across her ample chest. "Two visitors at a time, maximum," she said. Then she looked at them curiously, particularly at Nora who was still sitting on the edge of Jane Doe's bed. "What's going on in here?" she asked, attempting to sound authoritative. Her nametag read, "Lauren."

Ben stood, showing his badge. "Lauren, hi, we're with the FBI and we are helping this patient cooperate with a terror investigation." He pulled a card-holder from his pocket and handed her one of Schacht's. "If you have any issues with how we are running this investigation you may feel free to phone my supervisor at this number." He gave her a charming smile, then tapped Schacht's business card.

Lauren took the card and gave them each a stern frown. "I need to take her vitals."

"If you could come back in half an hour, that would be ideal," said Ben, kindly but leaving no doubt as to how serious he was.

"I'm going to speak to the resident about this," she threatened, turning to leave.

"Do that, Lauren. And please bring us back an iPhone 6 charger immediately."

Nora smiled at Ben. "We do need to preserve Jane Doe's life at this point, right? So there's no harm in the nurse doing her nursey stuff."

He shrugged, gesturing to Ford and Chid. "These two need to focus."

Chid was bent intently over the screen, eyebrows knit together in concentration, raking his fingers through his hair every few seconds. He flipped open his laptop and began tapping furiously, then went back to peering at Jane Doe's screen. Ford swiped carefully through the app, pausing when Chid said to pause, tapping on links that appeared.

"There's about a hundred and fifty in the app's private group," Ford supplied.

"That's not many," Nora said, looking around. Chid still did not look up. "That's not many, right?"

Ford shook his head vigorously. "But the public site it's linking to, the site where Gabriel Baker has been posting his webcasts, now has fifty thousand members and counting."

"Can you trace the IP address?"

"I can try, but it's dynamic, too. I want to see if I email the link to myself from this phone if it will show up differently. I need my laptop and for one of you to hold this."

He had been cradling the phone in his palm like some delicate preemie. Ben came and sat close to him. Chid kept pouncing furiously on his laptop, fingers flying, becoming visibly more agitated but refusing to speak to them.

"Check on the charger, will you Nora?" asked Ford, a note of concern in his voice.

"Right," she said. She entered the hall and spied the nurse's station.

"We desperately need an iPhone 6 charger, does anyone have one?" she asked, holding up her badge.

It was a nurse's station full of carbon copies of Lauren; each looked at Nora as though she had requested a kidney.

"iPhone charger?" Nora said again, miming plugging a cord into the heel of her hand. She finally reached into her pocket, pulling out a crisp bill. "Ten bucks? I will *pay* to borrow your cord."

The nurses exchanged quizzical looks.

Nora said, "Look, we're just here in room 216-B. Federal agents. Working for the public good."

One of the young women finally reached over and pulled her charger out of the wall and handed it to Nora.

"Thank you," said Nora, proffering the ten bucks.

"Keep it," she said, peering back at Nora from out of heavily lined cat-eyes and clumpy black lashes. "You have enough to deal with."

"Thank you. I think." Nora walked away, unsure whether she had meant she had enough to deal with because she was a federal agent or because she was not Lauren-esque in features and skin tone.

She returned to room 216-B and stuck the charger in the wall, then proffered its head to Ben who plunged it into Jane Doe's phone without a word of thanks.

Nora looked at Ben, then at the two men. She sank into the chair next to Ben.

"These guys gonna deliver?" she asked him in a stage whisper.

"They're good, Nora. Philly's finest," he said in the same fashion. He held her eyes and she could tell he wanted to ask her what had happened with Chid, but now was not the time.

She checked her watch and found it was after seven thirty. Fear for Pete was threatening to choke her. "Guys, we need to know their next move. What are you seeing?"

"One second," said Chid, without looking up. "I think I've almost sorted it out."

Nora rubbed her hands over her eyes.

Suddenly both Ford and Chid uttered the words, "Oh, no."

"What?" demanded Ben and Nora as one, both rising.

"We have to go right now," whispered Chid, his eyes wide, showing them the screen. "Right. Now."

Nora fought for breath, unable to tear her eyes from the screen, paralyzed as the Patriots' intended goal sunk in. Her memory paused in the hallway of the barn, where the drone of the television sounded, surreal, repetitive.

Together we can make America great again. . . .

And then all four agents were running through the hallway of the Intensive Care Unit. Ben was shouting into his phone as he ran, requesting every possible squad car, state trooper, border patrol, and emergency services vehicle, and shouting over and over the address he'd spied on the small screen.

Chid was calling Schacht, and Derek Ford was speaking rapid-fire with the director of the CIRG.

Nora cursed her car. "You have to drive," she called to Ben.

"Come on, Nora—seriously?"

She shook her head fiercely. "You come on, man. Assume I'm still injured or something!"

She pressed the key into his hand and beelined for the passenger seat, yanking out the siren and plunking it down onto the roof as she swung herself into the car.

"We're going to have a long talk about your driving skills," he said, swearing under his breath as he started the engine.

As they turned onto the Bayfront Parkway, Ford said, still holding Jane Doe's phone in his hand, "We're on an intercept path? In a Chevy Malibu?"

Nora ignored him and glanced over at Ben. "We'll be able to intercept them, maybe even beat them there," she insisted. "There are only three roads that travel west to east."

All four agents tilted their heads, listening for the sound of police sirens. Chid said, "There?"

Nora listened. "Yes—yes. They're heading out." She allowed herself to exhale a little, then called Maggie to get open lines for the officers answering the call.

Ben's eyes darted from rearview mirror to road to side mirrors as he pushed harder on the accelerator.

"Turn left at the light then right on Twelfth," Nora said.

It was rush hour; the east-west streets were dense with morning commuters heading into Erie from its sleepy suburbs.

Ford settled deeper into his seat, his index finger sliding along the phone's screen. Ford held the phone carefully. The nurse's charger dangled like an umbilical cord running to the car's USB port. "Here's the thing. I think he's set it up like a game. Like a . . . like a scavenger hunt or something."

Nora whipped around in her seat, eyeing him.

He met her eyes, looking grim. "You can't unlock the next activity until the one before it is finished. There's like a countdown clock. It says, *Eleven minutes until Act One.*"

"Well, it's good entertainment, right? It'll keep the members glued to the screen," Chid said.

"It'll take us a solid fifteen minutes to get to Fairview from here."

Ben shook his head. "Nah, the Malibu will deliver." For emphasis, he pressed his foot against the pedal and Nora watched the needle creep higher on the speedometer's dial.

A call came in from a number Nora didn't recognize. "Hello?"

"Mike Szymanowski," a voice said. "Your office said we could find out from you why we are speeding across the county on an intercept mission to Porter Farms in Fairview."

Nora said, "We have reason to believe that this Patriot group intends to harm a group of migrant laborers there. They posted that they're going to round them up and burn down the barn. It's going to be a statement against giving work to illegal aliens."

Mike Szymanowski was silent on the other end of the line.

"Mike?" she asked.

"What the *fuck*?" he said, finally.

"I know. The post said there will be five Patriots. So, unless they've changed tactics overnight, we're looking for motorcycles—bikers carrying semiautomatic rifles and/or big saddle bags. Big enough for rifles and probably portable gasoline tanks—maybe another fertilizer bomb."

Derek Ford leaned forward. "Maybe a sidecar kinda deal."

Nora repeated this into the phone.

She heard Mike Szymanowski say, "We can shoot them on sight?"

She could tell he wasn't joking, and, after yesterday, shooting them on sight was her most ardent desire. She took a jagged breath. "Let's just make sure they don't get to Porter Farms, and then hopefully they'll resist arrest."

Nora ended the call, hearing the distant sirens echoing the one on her car.

"Maybe the sirens will scare them off," Ben said.

Nora shook her head. "I think they have to finish their mission, whatever the cost."

"That's really stupid."

"It's a production," Chid said, not looking up. "Show must go on. They have viewers. Getting martyred or arrested will just stoke the flames."

Ford said, "The whole app here is designed so that we can't figure out what comes next until the last minute. Well, it looks like, from the previous ones, that it was somewhere between thirty and forty minutes prior. . . ."

Chid gave a bitter laugh. "It's intermission. Thirty minutes. Maximum forty, so you can stretch your legs and then get some champagne."

"Oh, for God's sake," Nora said, feeling queasy.

"But someone has to know, right?" Ben said. "Some elite group, some inner circle will have the whole plan."

Ford was nodding. "If we assume that Jane Doe was one of the insiders, let's see her last few calls."

Ford carefully placed the phone on the seat, and Nora watched as each man brought one of his knees closer in order to hold the phone in place between them. Ford began tapping on his laptop's keyboard, plugging in the numbers for the recent calls into the database. None of the numbers had been labeled with names.

Ford looked at Chid. "Call them or just look them up?"

"Ummm, no, you want to find who's being billed. Follow the money," Chid said.

At the risk of distracting them, Nora found herself asking, "Chid, you found something when you were at the hospital. You were concentrating hard as you looked through the app." They all braced themselves as Ben swerved to avoid an oncoming car that had not been deterred by Nora's siren.

"Yes," he said. "We were right. Baker is the face of this operation. In the inner circle there are multiple posts by this Geyer guy."

"Geyer, the phantom landowner. The one who doesn't exist otherwise?"

"Exactly," said Chid. "For example . . ." He leaned over the phone and carefully swiped into the app again, then read aloud:

The federal oppressors think they can stop us, further sullying their hands with our pure blood. They do not know that the movement has taken on a life of its own. The spirit of rebellion has spread. The call to action has been heeded. There is no stopping, there is no end in sight. Continue, brothers and sisters, with the agreed upon plan of action.

Fourteen Acts: the beginning of a global revolution.

Chid continued, "Baker also posts, clearly deferring to Geyer and his plans to prevent white genocide."

"*Diversity is white genocide*," murmured Nora, recalling the slogan.

"There's a real inconsistency in tone, in vocabulary . . ." Chid was saying.

"Is this Geyer the missing piece then?" Ford was saying, looking up from his screen.

Chid nodded. "I think so. It just hasn't made sense, you know?"

Nora was nodding, even as she cringed from another near miss Ben made. "I never felt like Gabriel Baker was quite right. Maybe for the brawn, but not the brain."

"Well, finding a phantom villain doesn't help us any more than having an unqualified villain," Ben pointed out, skirting a cluster of three motorcyclists. All four agents peered at them, Ben almost running into the curb as he did so. Two men and a wiry woman all sat at ease on large black Harleys. They were thin, deeply tanned, and all pushing seventy. It seemed strange that they were up riding about so early, and so Nora continued to peer at them, craning her neck even after they'd passed.

"Too old?" Nora asked.

Ford noted, "And no weaponry. No saddlebags for rifles."

"Right." Nora ceased peering out of the windows. "So. Geyer?"

"Well, unless I'm mistaken, it's just one more indication that we have a Wagner fan on our hands," said Chid.

"He's a character from one of the operas?"

Chid shook his head. "It was the name of Wagner's stepfather. Richard himself went by the surname of Geyer until his teens."

"*Christ*. Who's got time for this much esoterica?" Ben demanded.

"Clearly whoever's running this revolution, man," Chid responded rather testily.

"So how do we *find* him?" Nora asked.

Chid was silent, shaking his head. "He may well be out at the compound, surrounded by helicopters and hostage negotiators."

Nora considered the boat that had taken her to the compound. "Or on his way to Canada?"

"Maybe," Chid admitted.

"Or . . . back up the tunnel and now just walking around the city. Do you think that tunnel was really for the Underground Railroad?"

Chid frowned and began tapping the keyboard. "Nope."

"Why else would you need a tunnel under the city if you don't have a subway?" asked Nora.

Chid looked up. "Tell me the cross streets again, where that house was with the tunnel?"

"Peach and Twenty-first," Nora answered.

Thoughtfully, Chid tilted his head, scrolling down the screen. "You said there were tracks?"

"Small tracks, not big enough for a train or anything," Nora supplied.

He nodded. "Prohibition," he said at last.

Even Ford broke his pursuit of Jane Doe's phone directory to look over at him questioningly. "Prohibition?" he asked.

"There's an old brewery at State and Twenty-first," he said. "Used to produce Eisernes Kreuz Beer. *Iron Cross*. Popular—I will give the populace the benefit of the doubt and assume they did not know the significance of the Iron Cross for fascist Germany."

Nora nodded knowingly. "That's Pete's thing. Artisan beer. He's all about unique local flavor. Fascism—not so much."

"Well, they no longer produce it here at all. That label was acquired by Anheuser Busch."

"But you said *Prohibition*," prodded Ford.

"Back in the day, the Eisernes Kreuz folks didn't agree with the government's decision to help Americans curb their alcohol habit. So they continued to produce the beer clandestinely, and ship it out through the bay to like-minded consumers," Chid said.

Ford winked at Nora. "Sometimes the government just makes bad decisions. . . ."

Nora tried in vain to formulate a defense of such relativism that wouldn't render her existence as a law enforcement agent moot. Unable to do so, she stared at the landscape. They had left the city well behind. The car's GPS showed they were a quarter mile from the farm, and the distance was being swallowed fast.

They all saw the cloud of dust hovering over the farm's gravel driveway.

They had not intercepted the Patriots.

Nora was immediately calling Mike Szymanowski—"Bikers at the farm, Mike—we need *immediate* backup!"

The bikers had already descended and Nora watched in horror as they started walking and taking aim with the rifles in their hands. A handful of workers began to scatter at the sight, several of them running toward a large green barn set well back from Route 5.

Ben, fingers clenched on the wheel, accelerated into the turn, the car skidding over the gravel.

"Megaphone them—tell them to desist!" called Ford, pocketing the iPhone and then tucking his laptop into the seat pocket in front of him; Chid followed suit. Each pulled out his gun.

"There's no megaphone, man—" Nora shouted.

Ford had already rolled down his window. "Federal agents!"

Nora whirled despite herself, impressed with the volume he mustered.

Two of the bikers leapt back onto their motorcycles, gunning the engines.

"You three, out, now, after the shooters—I'll follow the bikes!" shouted Ben.

Nora, Ford, and Chid leapt from the car in a clatter of slamming doors and began racing across the wide gravel driveway. They followed the two men and one woman who, as they walked, peered through the sights of their rifles. Nora watched the woman advance, her long braid trailing down her back and swinging slowly as she walked. The men both wore black leather vests over T-shirts. Each of the three seemed to be utterly oblivious to the agents pursuing them.

Nora's breath was coming hard and fast. She saw the man in point position of the trio taking aim at a slight woman in frayed blue jeans and a worn Pittsburgh Steelers T-shirt. The woman, her face flushed with fear, was running, and the barrel of the rifle seemed to follow her movements.

"Put the rifle down!" Nora cried, just as Derek Ford yelled again for all three to stop: "Federal Agents! Put your hands in the air!"

But these words just seemed to enhance the man's focus. He did not look backwards, only paused in his striding. Nora saw him take careful aim.

"I've got the leader," Chid said, his voice tense. All three agents were jogging in a brisk parallel formation and closing in carefully on the Patriots.

Chid depressed the trigger of his Glock, aiming for the man's right shoulder. He fired twice in rapid succession and watched in satisfaction as the rifle fell to the ground, followed by the man himself.

Sirens announced two squad cars, but there was no time even to turn to look. The other two in the group had not stopped advancing on the barn and the scattering workers. Derek glanced over at Nora. "The more we shoot, the fewer we have to interrogate," he said.

Nora nodded. Without further conversation, Derek and Nora launched themselves at the bikers. In a running slide, Nora careened into the woman's legs, knocking them out from under her. The crack of the rifle she was holding resounded above the commotion as both women began flailing on the ground.

The woman's face contorted in fury. She launched a punch at Nora, who averted her already bruised cheek and slammed the woman's wrist to the ground. Nora maneuvered both her knees on top of the woman's thighs and then slammed the other wrist to the ground; she was pinned, sprawled beneath her, but arching her back as she writhed, struggling.

"Rather indelicate position there," Chid said, appearing with handcuffs and grinning at her. "But effective."

"No one said it had to be pretty," Nora said.

She looked over to where Derek, now aided by one of the cops who'd arrived on the scene, had flipped the large man he'd subdued onto his belly in the dirt. They exchanged a look and an exhalation. Derek surrendered his charge to the cop, then rose, dusting himself off.

"Ben?" she asked Chid.

"In pursuit," he answered, and, as Derek joined them, they all looked together over the wide expanse of fields beyond the barn. Even the woman Nora pinned swiveled her neck to look.

Nora saw that her Chevy was bumping over the field, pursuing the other biker, a tall, thin man who was bent over his handlebars. Nora gave him credit for being able to control the bike on such uneven terrain; the furrows in the earth were deep and the bike seemed to be aloft rather more than its wheels were connecting with the ground. Their trajectory was bringing them back toward the barn. Perhaps the motorcyclist hoped to regain the pavement and flee on Route 5.

Seeing this, Derek Ford took off running toward them.

Nora, still immobilizing her squirming, cursing catch, watched carefully as Derek ran at an impressive speed toward Ben and the biker. As he ran, he raised his gun.

It was only a moment before she heard the crack of his Glock. He waited a long moment and then sent off two more bullets in rapid succession. The third bullet met its mark and suddenly the bike began to spin uncontrollably.

Its rider tumbled onto the ground and the bike, still spinning, at last came to rest, pinioning him beneath it.

Nora allowed the officers on the scene to take the now-handcuffed woman. She and Chid jogged over to Derek. "Hey, Speedy," she said. "Nice shot."

Derek shrugged, accepting an understated pat on the back from Chid and then leaning slightly against him as he caught his breath.

Nora grinned at them. "I'm going to go catch up with Ben."

She picked her way across the field toward her car. Ben had emerged from the driver's seat and gone to stand over the biker, his gun pointed at him.

The biker was alive. Nora, gun drawn, gave Ben a nod and then got as close as she could, so close that she could feel the heat still rising from the prone motorcycle.

She peered more closely. She was relatively certain that the weight of the motorcycle had already broken one or two of his ribs. But she made no move to alleviate the pressure. She stood over him, pointing the gun, staring at him.

The man looked up at Nora and Ben. His hard eyes were focused and clear. Nora looked at him curiously. "Did you really intend to kill all these people?"

The man only smirked at them. "I don't gotta tell you nothin'," he spewed, his contempt for them swimming in his eyes.

Ben said, "No, you certainly don't."

Nora spied a tattoo on the man's neck below his left ear. It was a circle with a squat cross dissecting it. She remembered it as a white power symbol.

Ben and Nora holstered their weapons and then heaved the bike off of the man.

As soon as the bike hit the ground, both of them leapt on him, flipping him over, and cinching his thick wrists together. Ben cuffed him, patted him down, extracting his iPhone, and they rolled him onto his back again.

"Wallet? I.D.?" asked Nora.

Ben shook his head. "Neither."

Nora bent over the man, eyes flashing. "What's next? What are you planning next?"

"I have the right to remain silent," he answered with narrowed eyes.

She could tell he was hurting but did not want to admit it. She walked the opposite direction, trying to calm herself. She laced her fingers behind her head. Nearer the barn, Szymanowski's car had a gathering of officers about it. He and his partner had apparently stopped the other biker.

She watched, transfixed for a moment, then leaned against the passenger door of her car.

Ben crossed over to her. "You okay?"

She shrugged. "If okay means I'm glad we headed off a massacre, then yes."

"You hurt?"

Nora considered. "Grateful for long sleeves or all that gravel would have messed me up. But I'm fine."

Ben regarded her carefully, seeming to need visible proof she was indeed fine. "It's been awhile since we made an arrest together, huh?"

Nora's memory stretched back to a Philadelphia crack house and sprinting after Rita Ross and . . . she couldn't remember the other name. "It's prettier here," she said.

Ben looked around at the wide expanses of strawberry plants and the blue lake beyond them. "That it is," he confirmed. Several more squad cars were barreling along Route 5, scrambling belatedly into the parking lot.

Nora watched them come. She clutched at Ben's forearm, slick with sweat, the sandy hair matted against the skin. She looked over at the man sprawled on the lawn. He wasn't even attempting to come to a sitting position. "Ben, I'm starting to worry about how this is making me feel. I am so angry at that man there. I was really sorry Derek didn't kill him. I've never wanted to *kill* someone out of anger. Since this whole thing started, it's awakened something really ugly in me."

She looked at him imploringly, as though hoping he had a quick cure to offer. He only shook his head. "Nora, this is probably not the worst thing you're ever going to see with this job, amazingly enough. That you are worried about its effects on you is a million points in your favor. If you weren't worried about it . . . then you should worry," he said. He stretched his arm out and draped it across her shoulders. She allowed herself to rest against him for a few moments.

From where they stood it seemed that a representative from Porter Farms was deep in conversation with Chid and Ford. There was a lot of gesturing going on. Another wave of relief washed over Nora as she imagined how this morning could have ended. She felt so much gratitude to Jane Doe for having lent them her thumb.

Then her gaze fell on Mike Szymanowski's squad car.

"I should check in with Mike," she said.

"Yes. Thank him. I could never have chased them both down. They immediately diverged so I just picked this guy." He nodded toward the biker who panted amidst mangled strawberry plants. "Tell him I said thanks."

Nora kissed him quickly on the cheek. "I will. I'm glad you're safe," she said.

"I'm glad *you're* safe," he answered, with a crooked smile that made her wish they could take a few moments longer.

She walked toward Szymanowski's squad car. "Mike!" she called.

Mike Szymanowski raised his head. She saw him steel himself for another confrontation with her.

"Hey. Good work," she said.

"I hit her with the car," he said. "*Not. Actually. Good. Work.*"

Mike's partner walked over. His face was flushed from the pursuit; his chest heaved slightly. He looked at Nora rather defensively, as though perhaps expecting her to chastise them for running over a suspect. The embroidery on his chest spelled out *Hegel*.

"Thanks for your help on this," she said to both of them. "We couldn't have done it without you," she added.

Mike Szymanowski gave her a rather leery stare, and then nodded. "Yeah, you too," he said. "We're not gonna be able to book them until we get them some medical care, though. I called EMS."

She nodded to them. "We're waiting, we understand," Nora said.

Two police officers were walking alongside the woman with the braid; each held one of her arms. Her face was no less fierce or determined, it seemed to Nora, who took a long moment to stare at her. A long gash had opened on the woman's forehead and was dripping blood down the left side of her face. Nora realized she herself had probably caused it while subduing the woman on the gravel driveway.

Chid motioned to her and she joined the small group by the barn. Derek Ford was deep in conversation with a worker, and Nora was surprised to hear him speaking fluent Spanish as he jotted things into his notebook. She tilted her head, watching him, impressed, and almost forgot that Chid was trying to introduce her.

"Frank Porter," Chid was saying, gesturing to the tall man next to him. He had a shock of thick gray hair and sun-scorched features. Deep wrinkles traveled along his cheeks and creased about his eyes. He wore faded jeans and heavy boots. Chid finished the introduction: "Special Agent Khalil."

Frank Porter extended his hand. Nora found the hand was lifetime-of-farming rough but also warm and strong. She felt steadied.

Porter said, "Seems like y'all prevented a crisis today. We're grateful. My people here are grateful."

By *people* she assumed he meant the group of migrant workers milling around the barn. Her eyes found the woman in the Steelers T-shirt. Their gazes locked for a long moment. Nora cursed herself for having been so dismissive of Spanish class in high school. She wanted to ask the woman about conditions on the farm and about her journey to Erie—of all places. What had made her leave her home. . . . And were her children waiting for her to return. . . .

She found she didn't really know what to say to Frank Porter. She could only muster a tired smile. "We're happy to have been able to help." She looked at Chid and again at Derek. "I'm worried about Act Two," she said under her breath to Chid.

He nodded. "I'll extract Derek."

Nora felt desperate for a place to sit down and found herself leaning on the nearest squad car. Chid and Ford soon joined her, the latter holding Jane Doe's phone aloft.

Nora looked at the phone in concern. "It's still open, working, after all the commotion?"

He nodded. "It's going to need to charge soon. But it's working."

"What's going on then?" She wished desperately that EMS would arrive and they could process the bikers. Until then they were mired there on the farm. Her thoughts went to Pete at the compound.

Ford looked at the screen and then back at them, his face grave. "I think we just poked a bear."

"By not letting Act One go down as planned?" Nora asked.

Chid was nodding. "Of course. Of course this will make him crazy."

"*Crazier*," Derek said.

"What? What's happening?" Nora demanded.

"You're not going to like it," Ford said grimly.

"Of course I'm not," Nora retorted. "Go."

"There will be a live webcast showing an execution."

Nora snatched the phone out of his hand, making Derek Ford

flinch. There was a PowerPoint slide that read, *Second Day, Act Two, Execution of the Enemy.*

"I guess that's what they thought would get us there in force," Chid was saying.

"What's that mean?" she asked them.

Chid shook his head. "Is it one enemy or a *collective* use of the term enemy, so meaning both of them? Or all of us?"

Nora felt faint, and she returned the phone to Ford's hand.

He added, "There's an invitation to watch on live feed for all members of the group all across the country."

"Enemy. Enemy . . . which enemy?" Nora asked. "Pete? April?"

Derek shook his head again. "Impossible to tell. It might be someone new."

"Is it a reaction to what just happened or something new? Some new person taken hostage?"

Derek shook his head again. "Impossible to tell," he repeated maddeningly.

"How much time? *And don't say impossible to tell.*"

"No, that part's clear." Ford nodded at the small screen. "Twenty minutes."

Nora gaped and actually turned around in a circle. Then she said, "Can you send the link to Anna?"

Ford nodded, tapping on the screen. "I'm doing it now; I also sent it to Sanchez—Hostage Rescue Team. But I still don't think they can get access."

Nora ran over to where Ben was still standing over Tattoo-Neck. "We have to streamline this. We have to go. We have to get to Pete and April," she said, panting.

He looked a question at her and she filled him in.

"Call your boss," he said simply.

"But—"

"Call her."

Nora looked at him, her chest rising and falling, then she cast an angry glance at the handcuffed biker. Reluctantly, she punched in Sheila's number.

"Sheila, you heard from Ford? Anna told you what's going on?"

"Nora, finish processing the people you've just picked up. CIRG is on deck here, they're doing everything they can."

"Sheila, it really looks like the hostages are in mortal danger—"

"Nora, did you wrap things up out there? You know how the AUSA is about details."

"But I think that—"

"I'll expect a full report," Sheila said. The line disconnected.

Nora looked at Ben despondently.

He shrugged. "Okay, then. You did your best. She isn't hearing you."

"But Pete—"

"Even if you drove like a bat out of hell, which is inconceivable for you, we would not get there before twenty minutes—or now, fifteen—is up. It's not possible. We are spectators for this one, Nora, I'm sorry. Now, open your car door and start filling out the arrest forms for the lady with the braid. Explain why you kicked her legs out from under her so that your alternate viewpoint is there when she alleges police brutality."

She groaned, feeling like a recalcitrant teenager, and yanked open the door to her car. She tugged her laptop out from under the seat and switched it on. "I hate this job so much," she said.

"You do not," Ben corrected. "You hate rules and paperwork. Which makes you one of the good guys."

Nora considered this, darkly and grudgingly, as she called up the necessary forms. Occasionally she shot a glance over toward Chid and Derek who seemed to be pulling themselves away from the crowd at the barn little by little.

As she filled out the forms, she realized that Derek's ability to

take the stories of the migrant workers was an immeasurable service. None of them could really talk to a news crew without risk-
ing exposure. Maybe Derek's small interviews would be their one
chance to talk to someone in authority about the day the white
folks came to kill them.

Nora tapped reluctantly on the keyboard.

"I need my computer," Ford said, as both he and Chid entered
the car. Soon enough they were bent over their keyboards, tapping furiously.

Nora soon had her report filled out and filed, then, anxiously,
she got out of the car and paced next to Chid's open door, watching the EMS techs confer with the police. There were now six
squad cars in front of the barn and she saw that a press van was
attempting to enter the driveway, only to be deterred by a police
officer.

She listened to the tapping on the keyboard and tried to regulate her breathing. Each man would have a burst of activity and
then thump the *Enter* key. Nora started using this as her cue to
inhale deeply.

My brain is so foggy. . . .

"Make them wrap it up faster," she said to Ben.

"I'll see if I can hurry it along." He walked over to speak to the
officers. She saw him motioning to the man they had cuffed, asking them to take him into temporary custody until federal agents
could do so. They could not afford to divert their one vehicle for
that purpose at this point. Next, Ben engaged in conversation
with the EMS techs. Again he gestured toward the man in the
field.

The morning heat became intense. Nora felt sweat dripping all
along her back and pooling under her arms. She wanted to wrig-
gle out of the blazer and, more so, out of the Kevlar that was
pressed against her skin. She sighed.

She paused in her pacing to look hard at Chid. "Okay. So."

He turned his head to return her gaze.

"Yes, Nora?" He looked harried and rather like he didn't want to talk to her at all.

"How many Acts today?" she asked.

His face was grave. "*Siegfried*. Three Acts."

"Who's Siegfried?" she asked.

"Eponymous hero of the third opera in the cycle," Chid answered. "The boy too stupid to have fear. He learns fear when he learns to love." Chid looked at Nora trying to assess her reception of this. "I can say more. . . ."

"Yeah, that's plenty," she said, irritated.

Chid demurred.

"Would executing Pete and April Lewis be one act or two?"

"I don't know," Chid answered, his eyes bleak.

"Well what is it in the opera?" demanded Nora.

"Look," Chid said, barely masking impatience once again. "Wagner himself only *barely* paid homage to the Norse tales that shaped the Ring. For expediency's sake, this guy is going to shape this story however he likes. He already has."

She frowned at him, then looked away, frustrated. Finally she asked, "How does it end, Chid? I mean, you said this guy Wotan burned down the house of the gods. He was a god, right?"

Chid nodded. "Comic book fans might recognize him as Odin."

"So he died, then? When Valhalla burned?"

Chid drew in a long breath and withdrew his fingers from the laptop. "It was all predicted, as any good tragedy is. So Wotan was originally content to die thinking that Siegfried would take over. Metaphorically . . ." He gestured loosely to the handcuffed Patriot and the barn beyond. "Perhaps we can look at all these legions as Siegfried. Though it would be more convenient to find Wotan a grandson. Baker, maybe? Siegfried was the product of an incestuous union."

"White militias and incest. Shouldn't be hard," Ford chimed in. He had reconnected the iPhone to the nameless nurse's charger.

"Again, though, you're taking it too literally," Chid insisted. "It's a ridiculous story. Geyer's not going to take it blow-by-blow. He's using it as a vessel."

"Ugh, then why bother?" Nora said, frustrated.

"That's what I'm trying to figure out here," retorted Chid, losing his cool and raising his voice. "It would really help if we could find the actual person who's calling himself Geyer. I don't think we can fully sort out his intent til then."

"Just give us a second, Nora," Derek Ford said softly. "There are a lot of posts coming in about the barn and not all of them are positive. There might be a break in the ranks going on. . . . I'm trying to monitor. . . ."

Chastened, Nora began texting Anna. *Any word?*

—*CIRG asst dir has Enhanced SWAT at the ready. HRT continuing to try to talk to Baker.*

Nora sighed and darkened the screen.

The waiting was almost more than she could bear.

Ben walked over. "I need counter-signatures, here, here, and here," he said.

Nora shook her head, disgusted. "There's just no time for this. . . ."

Ben was starting to lose patience. "Look, I get how worked up you are. I would be, too. But you can't forget that if we don't process these guys right, there's a chance that they could walk away. We have to do it by the book, Nora. You know this. It's all we've got to ensure that a little justice comes out of this."

Nora listened and then signed without looking at him. Finally she turned her eyes on him. "I'm sorry, I'm being a brat, I know."

"No, you're just being a loyal friend. But at some point you have to realize that there's productive and non-productive behavior. There are twenty people out at that compound, Nora. Trust them to handle it."

Ford said, "Whether they are or not, the live feed just came on."

They all clustered around the screen, Nora and Ben peering in from either open door of the car, squinting to discern the action.

Gabriel Baker appeared, and Nora instantly recognized the inside of the barn where she had been held. It was hard to divine from the camera angle how many people were in the room. The camera's main focus was on Baker himself. Others who appeared had their backs toward the camera, faces turned toward their leader. Nora saw rifles on their shoulders and open-carry holsters at their sides. Some milled about, blurs of camouflage and cold gray metal.

Baker wore a pistol in a holster and a navy polo shirt, unbuttoned to expose the curl of his pale blond chest hair. Nora stared at the wedding ring on his finger and found herself wondering who the woman could be, and how they spoke to each other, and what it was like to interact with . . . defer to? . . . a man like Gabriel Baker. Did she live in fear of him? Did *he* live in fear, like Pete said, and the guns were the only sense of power he could retain?

Baker cleared his throat, then raised his hands for silence.

Friends, we are at a crossroads. I have issued a call, inviting my brothers and sisters in the militia movement to share with us in this moment, to share in our revolution, to go forward hand in hand.

Today our soldiers went to fight the cause of illegal immigration at the front, the cause that, more than any other, is dragging our country down into perdition. Our soldiers went to begin to reclaim our country for its citizens but they were thwarted by the forces of the federal government. Typical. Typical that the feds will protect illegals over our own people.

I say, there is no place for fear unless we are fearing the enemies at the gates, the enemies of our traditions and cultures.

No more.

We are forging ahead, setting up a model for action, definitive, sure, irreversible action in which citizens are no longer passive victims. No, this is a model for strong, independent citizens, lemmings no more, violated no longer by a system that caters only to the elite, to the New York liberals, to the Washington insiders, the compromisers, those who placate, those who surrender, and those who would take our guns in order to take our tomorrows.

Thunderous applause went up from the spectators.

The camera zoomed in on Baker who was smiling widely, exhibiting strong, even teeth.

I say—and please pay attention now—we have promised you Fourteen Acts that will shake this corrupt system to its foundations. We do this so that it can fall and then rise anew out of the ashes of sin, cleansed by fire. We have promised you Fourteen Acts that will shame this nation into realizing how far astray it has gone.

Now. We took this negro into custody.

The crowd shifted, murmuring, as April Lewis was led into the room. The same pink tunic Nora remembered was now far dirtier, and Nora was aghast to see blood stains on it. April's face was battered. One eye was nearly swollen shut.

We have been helping her to find humility. She came to us pompous and cocky. She was presuming to rule over whites, forgetting her rightful place, forgetting the mud out of which she rose.

He turned his attention on her. *You want to lead, girl? You want to wear this mass of dreadlocks into the halls of power? When you should be cooking my meals, working my fields?* The man who propelled her from behind now was attempting to force her onto her knees. But April Lewis was not going quietly.

With shaking hands, Nora called Anna. "They're in the barn, Anna—the furthest west of the three. Anna, they've got April Lewis, they're going to kill her—tell Schacht, tell Sheila—you've got to send the SWAT in, you've got to!"

Despite the fact that April Lewis was not bowing before him, Baker attempted to continue his speech. His smile was slightly less assured, though, as he tried to keep the microphone from picking up on her furious comments.

Others fear you, Baker was saying. *I do not. Others will defer to you. I will not. I know where I come from, and I know my role. And my role is to make sure that there are no more like you, rising from the mud to pretend to be other than what they are—*

It was at that point that April Lewis spat directly into his face.

Without another word, Gabriel Baker wrenched the pistol from its holster, held it to her forehead, and fired.

Nora screamed, and Ben, Chid, and Ford shouted in protest. From among the strawberry plants, the tattoo-necked biker laughed derisively.

"He killed her, he killed her!" Nora screamed again, feeling a hair's length from devolving into hysterics.

Ben came around behind the car and clutched her by the shoulders. "Easy, easy, you have to stop screaming! Breathe! Breathe!"

Nora looked desperately at him and then sank into him, sobbing. "We saw it. We didn't stop it. We just watched. Ben, we just watched...."

"There's nothing we could have done, Nora. Nothing. There's nothing we could have done, I swear." Ben held her hard, the palm of his hand open fully around her head, pressing her head to his chest.

But Nora pulled her head away from him, unable to keep from looking at the screen despite the tears crowding her eyes.

She saw that the cameraman had chosen to zoom in on Baker. Nora wondered at the move, trying from a distant corner of her own fear to analyze it. Would the sight of April Lewis's corpse gushing life onto the floor of the barn disgust and thus repel the viewers? Or would it incite Baker's followers to engage in activities other than those he had so carefully planned out for them?

Chid seemed clearly to be thinking the same thing. He looked at Nora, his gaze heavy. "I think Pete, like it or not, will now be the day's Act Three. It will need to be much more dramatic than originally intended. Baker inadvertently showed weakness. They will have to engineer his execution from a point of indisputable strength."

"Do you think they're cleaning up?" asked Ford.

Chid nodded. "Wouldn't you? A little? Before staging the next one? Maybe there'll be a change of venue even."

Nora felt bile rise in her throat. Ben held her gaze, centering her.

Ford said, "For now, though, there doesn't seem to be anything happening. They're running a feed of PowerPoint slides of people training and, you know, these white power slogans." He lowered the phone and they all moved back, taking some space.

She sank her fingers into the flesh of Ben's arm. "Ben, we've got to wrap this up and get out of here."

He nodded, his green eyes wide, and took the paperwork he had brought from EMS and started jogging it back to the ambulances.

Derek Ford watched her carefully. "Are you alright, Nora?"

Nora looked at him and at the cell phone in his hand. She thought of April Lewis, flirting with Pete and teasing them for being "spectacularly bad" at rescue efforts. She shook her head.

"No. We have to go. Now." She opened the door of her car and sank into the passenger seat, then gestured at Tattoo-Neck. "Derek, please, you and Chid get this. . . ." Words failed her. "Please just get him into the back of a squad car and let's go."

Both men exchanged glances and then stood up and complied with her request, Derek unplugging the iPhone and tucking it carefully into his pocket. She spied the glow of the screen through the navy material as he got out of the car.

Nora found herself texting Rachel. *What do you know about Wagner?*

As she waited for a response—and she truly had no idea what she thought Rachel could do for her—she stared at the endless emerald fields and the impossibly blue lake beyond them. It was, she thought grudgingly, one of the most beautiful places she had ever seen. Her memory drifted back to the desert-lined road that stretched between Cairo and Alexandria on the Mediterranean Sea. She recalled the long hoses that snaked along the parched earth, dripping precious water onto frail little fruit trees. Why is one person's field lush and fertile and another's barren and lifeless?

Rachel's text came through: *MMMMM. Bad boy. Gorgeous music. What's up?*

—*What if I told you the white supremacist bad guys are using the Ring Cycle as a framework for all these acts of terror?*

Huh?

—*Sequencing acts of terror with acts of the opera. We're on the second day now. Bracing for the third.*

Shit. Lot of fire in the third . . .

—*So I've been told. Was Wagner really this wicked?*

The wait this time made Nora fidget as she watched the tiny ellipsis float across the screen to indicate that Rachel was typing.

He was a lover not a fighter. Really audacious love affairs. But he wouldn't have shot a bunch of refugee women. Might have yelled at them for defiling German soil. But it would have been an intellectual protest: he thought he was a big martyr for his art, keen on preserving his culture, but he would have been too selfish to die for that stuff. Lot of silk shirts in his wardrobe. I imagine after verbally abusing some refugees he would probably have romanticized their plight and made one of them the heroine of his next opera.

—*If you wanted to thwart a crazy bad guy who's obsessed with opera, how would you do it?*

The response was immediate. *Play Bruno Mars at him.*

The three other agents had returned. With a clatter, Ben opened the car door and dropped into the driver's seat as Chid and Ford piled into the back.

"All set?" Nora asked.

"Yes. They're squared away. We've documented what went down here and covered our asses," said Chid.

"How much time do we have until they kill Pete?" Nora asked, trying to steel herself.

Ford answered, "Nothing's shown up yet, Nora. I think they didn't intend to move as early as they did on the last one, nor was it so supposed to end so soon, I assume. So they're recalibrating, tweaking the schedule."

"So maybe we have enough time to get there this time?" she asked.

Chid answered, "Maybe so."

She looked at Ben, mustering a half-smile. "You're going to really drive this time?"

He shook his head, tsking softly. "I find your lack of faith disturbing." He shifted into Drive.

"Does your Egyptian girlfriend get your Star Wars references?" Chid asked from the backseat, already flipping open his laptop.

"Never. It's actually quite painful," Ben answered, as he tore across the field toward the gravel drive and to Route 5 beyond.

Nora knew better than to engage on that topic. Any mention of space movies being ridiculous seemed to open some sort of mortal wound in Ben's heart.

"I had to study for that one," Chid said to Nora. "You can get up to speed. In order to talk to white kids like these—" he indicated Ben and Derek with a sweep of his hand, "you have to study up. Don't bother with the prequels. But you won't get the keys to the kingdom until you can quote a droid. It's not enough to speak English. You have to learn your man's language!"

Nora pursed her lips at him. "Is that why you know all this stuff about operas. To really learn 'the Man's' language?"

Chid smiled. "Touché. I learned pop culture for my man and high culture for the Man. But I lost nothing for it, you know?"

She considered this. "Benjamin and I learned really fast that the only show we had ever watched in common was Scooby Doo. I have never had time for space movies."

Ben looked at her aghast. "Space movies?"

Chid held up a hand. "I daresay, Nora, it's obvious that studying up on Star Wars will be central to the health of your relationship."

Derek looked up from the laptop screen to add, "Don't forget these are movies about revolution and throwing off oppression. . . . Fighting evil with your life. Resistance."

"God, you white folks talk a lot about revolution," she snapped. "None of you would know oppression if it walked up and bitch-slapped you."

Chid was chuckling in the back. "Hear-hear!"

Ben gave her a long look and then focused on the road without speaking. He was trying to make it to the interstate, but was caught behind a John Deere combine harvester.

"But I'll study up," she added, making her tone gentler, and allowing herself to pat him on the knee. "Because learning your language is important to me. Just as I'm sure you'll watch some classic Egyptian movies with me. Some Suad Hosny. A little Adil Imam?"

"Hey, I'm already a devoted Umm Kulthoum fan," Ben rejoined, his crooked smile returning to his face. "Bring it on."

Derek, holding the iPhone, coughed slightly.

Nora whirled. "What is it?"

"They've figured out that we are in their system. There was no warning this time. Act Three has begun."

"What?" Panic infused her voice. "Pete . . ."

But he was shaking his head. "It isn't Pete this time."

"Then . . . what?"

He twisted the phone so she could look at the screen.

"*Occupation*."

Nearly every flavor and brand of law enforcement had been either lurking outside the compound in Planer or out at the Potter farm in Fairview.

Thus when a panicked administrative assistant from the federal courthouse in downtown Erie had called 9-1-1 to say that the guards had been subdued and a stream of people in camouflage and leather were walking into the building, most carrying some sort of firearm, there was a massive delay in the response.

Chid was frowning at his screen. "They're broadcasting an appeal for other militias to join them."

"Of course they are," Ben said acerbically.

The media outlets had picked up on Baker's call to fellow militia organizations throughout the country. His right fist raised and clenched, he called for action.

They cannot kill us all. They cannot silence all of our voices. Revolution! Revolution! Revolution! A citizenry should not fear its government! The government should fear its citizenry!

Nora was immediately on the phone with Sheila who had found out only seconds before from the 9-1-1 call. "We're on our way to you . . ." Nora dared to say.

But Sheila was practically screaming at her through the phone: "You will report to the federal courthouse immediately. Immediately! And wait for the team we're sending from here!"

Nora hung up the phone and turned to Ben.

"We have to go downtown," she said.

He shook his head grimly. "I heard."

Nora's lips were pursed, her expression angry. "How can she send the team from there? They have to stay in Planer!"

Chid said, "Look, Nora, there's a method to this madness. If Pete wasn't part of Act Two then he's not going to be killed today. He just isn't. This is Act Three. Occupation."

"This is insane," she said bitterly.

"Every part of it, yes," Chid confirmed.

Ben had guided the Malibu out onto 12th Street and they were heading back toward town.

"What if they're just trying to call off the SWAT teams by distracting them with the courthouse. And then they kill him?"

"To what end, though?" Chid asked. "Look, Nora. Remember what we talked about the first time this came up? If there's a big finale then it's planned for tomorrow. Valhalla doesn't burn until the fourth opera, the 'Third Day'—in the Twilight of the Gods, *Götterdämmerung*."

"That's a ridiculous word," Nora said petulantly.

Chid said, "It is an *awesome* word, and German is *awesome,* and you should add German to your arsenal of languages, Special Agent Khalil. Some of the best Orientalist scholars were Germans. Wrote the best Arabic dictionaries by far."

"Thanks, I'll keep that in mind," she snapped. "So besides Valhalla burning what do you think is left?"

"Well . . . They've struck a blow at the judiciary. They've struck a blow at municipal government and minorities therein. They've struck a blow at refugee policies and the federally insured banking system. They tried to get across their anger at the Jews and illegal aliens, but we messed with the plan. So. Yeah, I think they *will* try to kill Pete tomorrow because he symbolizes federal law enforcement. I think Baker'll rely on our rage over that death to provoke the attack on the compound."

"So maybe if we can keep them from killing Pete then there won't be a need to have a giant firefight over the compound. And it's all moot."

Ben was nodding. "So we send in the SWAT teams tonight."

Ford shook his head. "No good. Number one, we've seen what happens when the plan doesn't work out. They get mad and keep moving. Two, they've got hostages now in the federal courthouse, man. Do we send SWAT teams for one guy or for fifty?"

"My *God*, why can't we do both?"

"Because there are American lives involved," Ford insisted. "And that's the last thing the Commander-in-Chief is going to want to authorize. Americans firing on Americans."

"These people are not Americans," Nora said angrily.

"Funny how they'd say the same thing about *you*, Special Agent Khalil," Ford pointed out.

They had arrived at the courthouse.

Nora stared at the scene. A few squad cars sat in the middle of the street, their lights flashing uselessly.

Nora's car had been allowed in close because of the flashing light on her roof. They descended from the car, leaving it parked on State Street and made their way to the front door of the courthouse. She realized that Abe Berberovic seemed to be in charge, and this made it all the more clear that the police forces were stretched thinner than ever.

"What's the story?" she asked, after introducing him to her colleagues.

"How's Anna?" he asked, his eyes concerned.

Nora reassured him. "She's hanging in there. Little sleep-deprived at this point, I imagine. But Anna's tough."

"Yes, yes she is. Sorry, okay, the story: a group entered from the front and back doors simultaneously and overcame the security guards—no fatalities reported though. They barricaded themselves in, and then started putting out this call for reinforcements from the public and from other militias. They hadn't even taken a hostage yet, only a few people had seen what happened with the security guards, so all of a sudden when this stream of people started entering the building, no one knew what was going on. Some fifty people got inside before the employees realized it was an occupation."

"Have they said anything about the hostages?" asked Ford. "What are their intentions toward them?"

Abe shook his head. "No, nothing."

"Did they let anyone go?" he pressed.

"No."

"Who are these people who got inside?" Ben asked, incredulous.

"By all accounts most of them were biker types."

"Biker types?" Chid asked. "I thought the Patriots were putting on this whole biker conceit to blend in with the bikers and make it more difficult to be spotted. But most bikers aren't . . ."

"Revolutionaries?" Nora asked.

"Blood-thirsty?" supplied Ben.

Chid considered both of these. "Exactly," he said finally.

"Well, that's what happened, and here we are." Abe was clearly uninterested in abstractions.

"How long since they locked themselves in?"

"Just about fifteen minutes really," said Abe, checking his wristwatch.

"Have they issued demands?"

Abe waved a printout at them. "Repeal of the Brady Bill, repeal of the assault weapons ban, ban on further immigration into the United States, deportation of all illegal immigrants, and a white homeland."

All four agents started to laugh. Abe just stared at them. "I'm kinda missing what's funny."

Chid began, "The absurdity . . ."

"*No*," Abe interjected, cutting him off, his eyes bright. "In my country, we all thought the Serbs were just being absurd when they made absurd demands. Then they began the ethnic cleansing. The absurd is no longer absurd when you have weapons and followers."

The agents immediately sobered.

"What do we do now, Abe?" Nora asked gently.

"What precedent do we have here?" he responded, the edge having left his voice.

Chid shook his head. "Oregon?"

"Oregon was ridiculous. We aren't going to ignore this," Nora said.

"Well, we also aren't going to storm the courthouse," Ford said tersely.

It was at that time that the SWAT Bearcats came rumbling up State Street from the Bayfront Connector. Nora felt her stomach twisting anxiously.

"I guess that answers that," Ben said. "CIRG to the rescue."

Abe nodded. "They're efficient anyway. Calm under pressure. My guys have been a little strained these past few days."

"Can't imagine why," Nora said.

The SWAT vehicles rumbled to a stop. Two men descended from the cab of the first Bearcat. Derek Ford spoke to Nora and

Ben as they watched them greet Abe. "That's Evan Sanchez, director of the Hostage Rescue Team, and there's Gray Rogers, SWAT leader. They're good guys, a little intense. But their teams are excellent, actually, the best there are."

"Then why haven't they rescued my partner?" hissed Nora.

Derek gave her a sympathetic look, but she knew he had no response. Sanchez and Rogers spoke at length with Abe, getting the full story again. Then Sanchez asked that a call be put in to the main line of the federal courthouse, hoping to find someone in charge who would be able to negotiate with him.

"Can't you just call Baker back? Haven't you been negotiating with him all day at the compound?" Ben asked.

"No. Only underlings. They won't give up his cell phone number. And there's no record of him having a cell phone even though we've even seen it on him in the webcasts."

"I think I have it," Ford said. "It's the most frequently called and received number from this phone." He wrote it down for Sanchez and then allowed him to look at the phone in his hands.

"This is gold," Sanchez said, his eyes wide. "How did you get this?"

"Long story," Ford responded, giving Nora a quick grin.

Sanchez extended his hand to Nora and then Ben.

"You're Special Agent Khalil, right?"

Nora nodded, eyeing him. He had a rather grizzled look to him. White hair frosted his temples and the stubble of his day-old beard, though most of his hair was coal black. His honey-colored eyes were underscored by deep circles.

"Anna had shared with us all the intel you gave them on the compound, the setup of the barns, the physical structure within; we figured out that the far western barn is not the arsenal and that probably it's the middle of the three. The third might be more bunkhouses, possibly a mess hall. So. Thanks."

Nora looked at him, waiting.

"Your escape is remarkable, you know. That doesn't happen every day."

She worked her jaw back and forth and gave Ben a *What does this guy want* look. Then she could not stop herself from saying, "The hostage you just let die is responsible for my escape."

Sanchez nodded. "I understand your anger, Nora. If it were my decision alone . . ."

"Everyone keeps giving me that line!" she said, furious.

He continued in a level voice, ". . . things might have gone very differently. Anyway, I just wanted to let you know I get where you're coming from. We want to explore every option. And the wild card is still, *what's in their arsenal*? We have to manage this in a way that makes it very clear that we value human lives, theirs as well as those of our agents."

Nora leaned forward. "How about you value the human lives lost so far by taking these people down?"

He nodded. "We're doing our best, I promise you." And then the conversation was over as he keyed in the number Ford had given him.

And so the negotiations began. And so began the wait.

Chid and Ford headed back toward Nora's car. Ford had his laptop open again and actually climbed up on the hood.

Feeling panicky, Nora headed over to them. "Any change?"

Sweat was trickling down the sides of Ford's face. He checked Jane Doe's phone. "There's nothing about Pete, Nora. Nothing at all. It's all about this siege here."

Chid looked at Nora and gestured to the hood of her car. "Come sit?" he asked, flipping his laptop open. Ford sat closest to the front of the hood.

Nora's shoulders sagged. "Fine." She clambered up on top of the hood next to Chid, closest to the windshield. The metal was hot, but it was better than sitting on the curb.

She sat very still, clutching her folded arms. "I thought we don't negotiate with terrorists," she said finally.

"Of course we do. And then we *mess them up*," Chid said.

"Huh?"

"Come on, Nora. Everyone negotiates. Life is negotiation. Even not negotiating is a form of negotiation."

She frowned at him.

"In the end we will storm in and win the day. But we have to look like we're worried about the coming bloodbath. Plausible deniability."

Nora stared at him. "*What?*"

"Look: Saying we learned lessons from Waco doesn't make the agenda of the Branch Davidians any more palatable. They were still traitors who would have engaged in active warfare with the U.S. government at the drop of a hat. Not to mention being psychotic religious fanatics."

"So . . . saying we feel badly doesn't mean we didn't want to exterminate them?"

"Or that they didn't need exterminating," said Chid. "Plain and simple."

"So callous. I can't . . ."

"If they could have, the Branch Davidians would have done everything that the Pennsylvania Patriots have done if not more. Was nipping their movement in the bud wrong?"

She shook her head. "I have no idea, anymore. Maybe. Surely, right? Because so many other movements have sprung up because of that?"

"Racist insurrectionists. Who would just as soon exterminate you and me because of the color of our skin."

"And me," chimed in Ford.

"And you," added Chid. "Because you're a devilishly handsome queer."

Ford blushed, but managed to say, "Not to mention a counter-revolutionary sympathizer."

They all laughed and then sat in silence for a moment as Chid and Ford tapped on their keyboards.

Then Chid said softly, without looking at Nora, "I'm sorry about the hospital. It was out of line."

She patted his back. "*I'm* sorry. I overreacted. I think you were trying to joke with me on some level."

"Yes, on some level," Chid affirmed. "On some levels I was dead serious. But that doesn't mean I should say everything I'm thinking. Sometimes I need to remind myself to invoke the filter."

Nora smiled. "It's a problem I have myself," she admitted. "Do you think we're all getting out of this alive?"

"Not a chance," he answered swiftly.

"*Filter?*" Nora prodded.

"Oh yeah . . . Nah, not a chance." Chid smiled. "*Filtering* doesn't mean *lying*—especially not to an Egyptian. Y'all got the curse of Ra and the eye of Horus and whatnot. . . ."

Ben walked over to where they were sitting. "Ford, that phone number thing might have saved the day," he said. "Sanchez seems to be making progress. Baker believes we're closing in on him because we've figured out his phone number. He's a little paranoid about it."

Nora nodded in heavy silence.

He turned his green eyes on her, the concern there intense. "Are you okay, Nora? That scene with Sanchez wasn't like you."

She looked down at the marks still on her wrists from the cable ties. Where the skin wasn't raw it was bruised. She held her wrists out to Ben.

"Without April Lewis, I would probably still be in the barn."

Ben gave her the *I want to hug you but we're at work* look again.

Chid said, "Strictures against workplace affection tend to slacken during an apocalypse. Hug your woman, Benjamin."

Ben obediently wrapped an arm around Nora's shoulder. "I'm glad April Lewis was there to help you," he said seriously. "I'm sorry."

Nora allowed herself to rest her head for a moment against Ben's chest.

"Thing about this situation," Chid said, "there really isn't any time to process. We're dealing in three days with more than some agents deal with in a lifetime."

"Three days, four days," said Nora thoughtfully. "If we mess with the schedule, will he adjust it or just stop?"

Chid regarded her. "Do you mean, if there were thirteen acts instead of fourteen, would the paradigm fail and all be rendered meaningless?"

She glared at him. "How do you even have time to put those words together? Jesus, that's . . . *yes,* I'm pretty sure that's what I just asked."

"I don't know," he answered simply. "The synagogue bomb was defused and so was one act less, but then they kidnapped two federal agents. Technically, one might have sufficed to constitute an act. So I presume it balanced out." He shrugged and looked apologetic, then said, "If Pete is part of the program and we save him, what will the contingency plan be? No idea."

Three hours into the occupation, the sidewalks were crowded with people. Some stood with anti-hate placards raised high. Others held up pro-gun slogans and white power symbols adorning old campaign posters.

Ben watched them too. "It's a new age," he said. "Protest is the new brunch."

Nora checked her watch, feeling useless, feeling trapped. The helicopters hanging overhead were fraying her nerves. At one point, a media helicopter got too close to the sleek gray CIRG chopper and a cry went up from the onlookers as the latter had to soar high into the sky to avoid an accident.

Police officers and Bureau agents alike kept trying to convince the onlookers to move back, to put enough distance between themselves and the courthouse that they would avoid injury in case of an explosion. Nora herself had been as assertive as she knew how to be without actually throat-punching citizens.

But to no avail. The scene was fascinating for people, and they would not be persuaded that their lives were in danger. Perhaps the memories of the last anti-government occupation were too deeply embedded as a laughable, sex-toy-steeped event.

To make matters worse, television cameras were stopping anyone and everyone and allowing them minutes of fame that aspiring actors the world over would never attain.

A man in a "Make America Great Again" T-shirt was railing into a microphone. "No one's had the courage til now to truly take a stand. I think that Gabe Baker is the bravest man in America. American jobs should be for Americans. We need a white homeland just like he's sayin'. There shouldn't be all this race-mixin'. Ending up with a bunch of mutts. Ending up with no culture. No future. I salute him and his movement."

Nora watched as the interviewer, a rail-thin blonde woman with orangey pancake makeup, pulled the microphone away. She looked ill.

Chid, Ford, and Ben had all given up and sought shelter in the air-conditioned car. They had in fact intended to go back to the office and camp out in the conference room, but Nora had insisted that being close to the scene would allow for more effective action should any be necessary. Each man had grudgingly agreed, although Ben insisted on getting sandwiches and sodas and forcing Nora to eat and hydrate. They all sat staring at their laptops; the two men in the back tapped away on their keyboards with rather more ferocity than Nora and Ben. The task of unraveling the iPhone's mysteries was still key.

Nora sat in the front seat with her legs folded under her. She responded to some frantic text messages from her father and Ahmed and even from Rachel, all of whom wanted to make sure she was okay in the midst of all the nationally televised upheaval. She texted Anna and Sheila, hoping they would both relent and let them stand vigil out there, but both refused to back down. She sent a few text messages to Ben, who, sitting next to her in the front seat, would shake his head and smile each time one came through to his phone.

At last she sighed, frustrated, and dropped the phone in her lap. "Why is there no *Stuck in a Chevy Malibu with Three Sweaty Guys* emoji?"

Chid retorted, "Because a mere emoji, my dear girl, cannot express Nirvana."

Occasionally she would lower the window in order to listen in on what was going on in the street.

Nora was sure that one of the women speaking to a CNN camera was the thin, gangly granny they'd seen that morning on their way to intercept the barn burners. She was only a few yards from Nora, but Nora could hear her clearly.

"My heart has never ached so much for my country as this week. This week! I look forward to this week all year long, every year! I came all the way from St. Louis to meet up with my friends. To ride by this beautiful lake. To drink a few beers . . . We've been robbed. We've all been robbed, haven't we? Such ugly people. Stealing away our beautiful days."

Nora watched her curiously for a long moment. *This is what it takes to get your heart to ache for the country.*

Not too far off, the woman they'd imported from Washington to speak in the name of the Bureau was holding court. Nora, noting that the woman's high-heeled shoes were back on, asked Chid, "What's her name, this spokesperson?"

"Lena Clark," he said, glancing over at her and then back at his screen. "She's smart. She has a master's from Johns Hopkins."

Representatives of the press were peppering her with questions.

"How many hostages are inside the courthouse?" a thick-haired man asked. Nora wondered if the position of his reading glasses was what gave him a particularly nasal tone of voice, or if his voice was simply *that way*.

"There are currently sixty-two hostages inside the building," Lena Clark said. "Our expert hostage negotiators are in constant dialogue with those responsible."

Nora looked over at Ben. "That's stretching it, isn't it? Is talking to Gabe Baker the same as talking to the actual captors?"

He shrugged.

"What's the main demand of the occupiers?" someone called out.

Clark read them the list that Abe had provided earlier.

"Which of these demands is the U.S. Government willing to comply with?" demanded a red-faced man in the front as he dabbed at the sweat on the back of his neck.

"The attorney general has been very clear: none of these demands is acceptable. The United States worked very hard to pass the Brady Act, or the Brady Bill as some call it, to address the violence in our country, which seems only to be increasing, as you can see. There is no retrenchment. As we all know, as we can all acknowledge, the victims of gun violence are most commonly those least able to defend themselves. We at the Bureau are committed to defending American citizens. We at the Bureau are committed to defending the law."

"Who's going to defend *us* from the Bureau?" shouted a red-haired woman in the back, her skin riven with early wrinkles and her voice hoarse from years of smoking.

She was quickly shouted down, however. This portion of the crowd seemed crisis-weary and was giving no quarter to such views—no matter how great a story they made for the evening's broadcasts.

"The situation is under control," Lena Clark was insisting. "The Bureau is able to meet the challenge of domestic terrorism head-on. We will resolve this crisis expeditiously, rest assured."

"How?" called a man in a baseball cap with the CBS logo emblazoned across it.

"Pardon?" she asked, and Nora could tell she was fishing for time.

"What steps are you going to take to get the so-called 'Patriots' out of the courthouse and into jail without killing the hostages?"

Lena Clark blinked, shifting her weight from one precariously high heel to the other, then said, "Now, if I shared that information with you, Mitch, I'd be sharing it with the terrorists themselves, wouldn't I?"

Ford observed, "She's got nothin'."

Ben said, "Well, that's no surprise, is it? Your PD friend is right. There's no precedent. It's one thing to bomb a federal building. Or a school. But to try to talk a bunch of willing martyrs out of their just cause . . ."

"Is like talkin' bears outta shittin' in the woods," said Chid.

Ford frowned at him. "Is that your best Tamil redneck?"

"Best so far. The day is young."

But the day was in fact receding, and the shadows that the federal courthouse cast across State Street were lengthening.

"Nothing from the live feed? They're not broadcasting the occupation?" asked Nora.

Ford shook his head. "Nothing since they entered. They took a few pictures standing in a judge's chambers and some of the hostages locked in a courtroom—no windows, right, so no problem. And that's it. Since then it's been that same PowerPoint feed selling the militia and calling for support from all the other militias in the country."

There was a bit of commotion and the agents swiveled their heads.

"Oh, hooray—it's the mayor," deadpanned Nora.

Indeed Mayor Vaughn, thick-necked and red-faced and sporting a "Don't Give Up the Ship" polo shirt, had appeared at the podium vacated by Lena Clark.

"What's the story with that slogan on his shirt? I keep seeing it everywhere," asked Ben.

"Something about Commodore Perry," said Nora. "Battle of Lake Erie. Lot of . . . white people shooting cannons at each other from boats. There's a museum about it over there." She gestured down State Street to the bay. "Mostly Commodore Perry is famous for his bar now. They have outrageously good pretzels, although I haven't tried one yet."

Chid perked up. "Perry? Ah yes—the epic struggle for the borders of the newly independent United States. The most ridiculous war in American history, the War of 1812. Imagine invading Canada and getting your ass kicked."

They all tried to imagine just that as the mayor began speaking. He looked utterly exhausted.

"The City of Erie has had a difficult week. We have had attacks on our people from all sides. No flood or fire or act of war has caused more loss of life for our city. I grieve for the families of those lost at the refugee center and the families of the PNC bank guard; I grieve for the family of Judge Bernstein, and most recently for councilwoman April Lewis. It is all egregious, all shocking. In addition to these acts, our courageous law enforcement officials have thwarted others and we are all indebted to them eternally."

"That's us!" said Nora, tugging on Ben's shirt.

The mayor continued, "This is not who we are. We will re-build. We will recover. We will continue to open our city to those who seek refuge here—we certainly now understand violence in a way that should inspire empathy for those coming from war zones. We will continue to celebrate diversity while affirming the tradi-tions of every culture. There is no way forward except through understanding."

His voice trailed off, and the reporters began shouting ques-tions at him.

"Mr. Mayor, Mr. Mayor! Can you elaborate on the failed at-tempts you referred to?"

He shook his head. "Not at this time, no, I cannot."

"Mr. Mayor! Couldn't it be said that the Patriot group is de-manding that they too be understood?"

Mayor Vaughn said, "There are ways of sending messages. Violence will never be one that is acceptable here. Not ever," he said. "But these people need to know that our people are not stupid; our people can understand the difference between mind-less, hate-filled propaganda and truth. Erie will survive. Erie is resilient. Erie will flourish again!"

"That's a line for the ages," observed Ben, rolling up Nora's window whether she liked it or not.

"Since when have *people* been able to tell the difference be-tween propaganda and truth?" Chid asked emptily.

"Yes!" Ford practically shouted, making them all jump.

"What?" all three asked him.

"I've been entering all the numbers that Jane Doe had called. All of them ultimately link back to one account holder—must have been some perk or punishment, but I guess he put his min-ions on a calling plan."

"Baker?" asked Ben.

"Nooooo."

"Who? A name!" demanded Chid.

"William S. Martin. I've got his name, date of birth, social security number. . . ."

"Any images?" Chid asked.

"Plenty. He'd been involved in litigation. Over beer. There's a bunch of newspaper articles about him. Erie boy, apparently."

"What does that mean, litigation over beer?" pressed Chid, leaning over Ford's screen.

Ford was skimming rapidly and speaking as he read. "This beer . . . so the factory, sorry, the brewery closed down in 2008. But because Eisernes Kreuz Beer itself is still distributed, it looked like they'd just downsized or shifted brewery locations."

Chid was now apparently skimming the same article. "There was some kind of court settlement involved. The company continued for a while after that but then apparently folded."

"Lawsuit?" asked Ben.

"Mmm-hmm." Chid nodded, picking up the narrative. "Anheuser-Busch claimed the original patent on the Eisernes Kreuz recipe. The settlement was so punishing that the board voted to remove Martin and gave his ninety-year-old mother controlling interest in the company."

"Jesus," said Derek.

Chid inhaled sharply.

Nora wanted to shake them both. "WHAT?" she almost shouted.

"Case was heard here in U.S. District Court. Judge *Bernstein*."

Nora felt dizzy. "You can't be serious."

Chid whipped his laptop screen around to show her the article he was reading from.

She shook her head. "Then it isn't just some . . . anti-government show where any old judge would have served the purpose. He had a plan!"

"You bet your ass he had a plan," Chid said.

"Eisernes Kreuz had better marketing and labeling, so

Anheuser-Busch retained the name even though they'd proved the original recipe. So it looks small-town and artisanal—limited distribution means they can charge big bucks," Ford said.

Chid narrowed his eyes as he scanned the information. "Martin's company had to declare bankruptcy. The settlement coupled with the financial downturn in 2008 was too much for them."

"It looks like the one thing William walked away with was the brewery building," Ford said. "His mother, Carole Martin, had disbursed the rest of the assets, leaving him emphatically out. She left most to the nuns—like the Peach Street house with its Prohibition tunnel . . . that connected to the brewery. . . ."

Nora nodded, thinking. "It wasn't clear when we first found the tunnel that it still hooked up to the brewery, but there's no other rational explanation. There must be some branch that Pete and I didn't notice, didn't know to look for, that links to the brewery. And it makes sense that that's where the motorcycles have been disappearing."

The others were nodding.

"But what's he been doing since then?" asked Ben, looking thoughtful. "Old brewery like that. Probably had farmlands where they grew the hops and barley. . . ."

Nora met his eyes. "Yes. When did the imaginary Geyer buy it?"

Chid tapped on his keyboard. The silence stretched, and Nora felt like she was hyper-aware of the breathing of all three men. Finally Chid spoke: "Martin had sold off some assets before the court case. Before he lost to Anheuser-Busch and his mother gained controlling interest in the company and then disbursed most of the assets without him."

"So perhaps he invented Geyer. He knew bankruptcy was coming," Ben said.

"Perhaps . . ." Chid answered, deep in thought.

"Wait, there's a breaking news thing . . ." Ford said, leaning in to his laptop screen. He began swiveling his head from laptop to Jane Doe's iPhone. "Wait . . ." He frowned.

Nora looked. Various news crews started huddling around their monitors, all staring down intently. "What's happening?" Nora demanded.

Ford plopped his laptop down, and all of them peered at it.

"What the hell?" asked Ben.

"Who's that?!" demanded Chid.

They all turned to stare at the courthouse, emerging as they did so from Nora's car, their eyes riveted on the building. Three windows had been flung open, and two bearded men appeared in faded T-shirts.

The SWAT team instantly aimed their rifles toward the windows, and the crowd made a collective gasp.

Then each bearded man began giving a dainty, regal wave to the crowd, until one tossed the other the end of a banner. As it unfurled, a cheer rose up from the majority of the onlookers.

Nora read the banner, then looked at Ben, then read it again to make sure she was seeing it correctly.

The gangly granny just down the curb from the car let out a whoop. "YES, dammit!" she began shouting. "Yes, goddammit! Preach it!"

The letters were crude, but the message was clear: *Long Live Roar on the Shore.*

What the fuck just happened?" demanded Chid.

The breaking news had come from Vance Evans who'd gotten a call transferred to his cell phone. He'd answered it at his post at the other end of the block.

The telephone interview he was still conducting was with one Jerry Walsh of Fredonia, New York.

"It was simple, Mr. Evans. Nobody was angrier than us bikers over this whole thing. One, they've been making bikers look bad by sending these nuts out on bikes. Two, they've shut down our favorite event of the year. Three . . . lot of us bikers look a bit like these assholes and so everyone is lookin' at us funny now. I reckon they call that racial profilin' and it just ain't fair. So when this Baker guy broadcast that he wanted more people to come take over the courthouse with him, we said, hell, let's blend in and sneak in and see what happens. Maybe we can get this shit over with and get on with the Roar. Do you know they had to cancel Dokken for this shit?"

"That's the word, yes," Evans said gravely, making sure the cell phone speaker was positioned close enough to the microphone.

"So we walked in," the disembodied voice of Jerry Walsh continued. "We hung out. We helped out. They weren't killin' hostages or nothin', they just said they wanted to keep the eyes of the world on the movement. We said, '*Hell yeah. We're with you.*' They said, 'Down with the government, any government not doin' the will of the people should be overthrown,' and whatnot. We said, '*Hell yeah, sure, whatever.*' They said, 'We're gonna occupy this building for as long as it takes to get them to change the laws and stop banning the guns the Founding Fathers said everyone should have—you know, cuz the Founding Fathers used to have assault rifles. Oh yeah, and to keep all the foreigners out. We're gonna send a message to all the foreigners not to even come here. They won't even fuckin' wanna come here once they see how serious we are.' We said, '*Go for it, man, we're with you.*'"

Vance Evans said, "What was the catalyst for revealing you didn't share their goals?"

"Well, we'd agreed we'd give them a couple-three hours to get comfortable with us and trust us and then we'd just jump 'em. But my buddy Sam—say hi, Sam!"

A disembodied voice was heard in the background, "Hey there, America!"

"So Sam winked at me and he started a fight. He said, 'Hey, man, you wanna occupy this shit but it doesn't look like you brought any beer. How we gonna get beer, man?' And so this Patriot fucker said, 'This isn't about the beer. We're here to change history.' And so my buddy Sam said, 'Any dumb fuck who wants to change *American* history without a beer in his hand should get his ass handed to him.' And then he hauled off and hit that guy so hard one of his teeth shot out of his mouth and skittered across the floor."

"It skittered, really?"

Nora for once thought she was getting a kick out of Vance Evans.

"Hell yeah. Skittered. And then we just started beating the shit out of those assholes and taught them not to fuck with real bikers. And that was it. Some of our wives'd sent this banner along with us—they'd made it, you know, to protest. So Foxy and Jim there just hung it out. Good work men!"

"Good work indeed," affirmed Evans.

"And here we are." As she listened to his voice, Nora envisioned the man giving a humble shrug. "You're welcome, America!"

America watched Vance Evans laugh so hard that he creased his pancake makeup.

"The only question is, what should we do with 'em now?"

The screen was filled with Evans mopping his eyes. At last he said, "I'm pretty sure you could start by opening the doors. . . ."

All told, there had only been ten of the Pennsylvania Patriots occupying the building. The group that had entered to help out had been almost entirely Fifth Columnists. CIRG and its SWAT team had a relatively easy task to take the militia members into custody, and then the processing was left to the agents on the ground once again.

Nora, Ben, Chid, and Ford worked side by side with a few of the up-from-Pittsburgh agents as day turned into evening in the chaotic, but mercifully air-conditioned, office on State Street. As they worked, they took turns envisioning the look on Gabe Baker's face when he got word of how his occupation had failed.

They holed up in the conference room. Every once in a while, Nora would try to sort out if Evan Sanchez was talking to Baker yet about Pete—now that he had the right number to call.

A few times, indulging her, Ford would disappear for a while and then return, shaking his head.

"Well, are they heading back out there yet?"

"The action on the Patriots' part won't be until tomorrow, Nora," Chid reassured her.

"But isn't it like we said? If we keep them from killing Pete they won't be able to provoke a confrontation? If we go and just snatch him . . ."

"They're working on it, Nora," was all anyone would tell her, before returning the room to the non-silence of tapping keyboards. Each one was merging the new information about William Martin into the story of Gabriel Baker and the still-unfolding drama.

It was pitch-black outside when Ford leaned forward again, studying the screen. "After the bankruptcy, Martin brought in a company to turn the brewery into some kind of shopping center," he said. "They had some investors but needed the city to buy into it—they were attempting to win the grant that the city sets aside for revitalization projects. Martin himself didn't have enough and his business's credit by this time was bad; the bank wouldn't loan him the money. The proposal was defeated by the city council."

Chid tapped his own laptop screen, smirking a little. "Any guesses as to its most vocal opponent?"

The other three responded, "April Lewis."

Nora asked, her heart beating in her ears, "I don't suppose the bank that refused him was PNC, was it?"

Ford gave her a look expressing that that would be too much, but started hunting anyway. "Right again," he finally confirmed.

They gave a collective sigh.

"So much for the crazed ideologue," said Chid. "These were very calculated crimes seeking very specific results."

Nora looked at him. "So what the hell, then?"

"So. High drama. He's played every one of his followers, like a *maestro*," Chid added, enjoying the metaphor. "He gets them to rob a bank, ostensibly to buy weapons. But I bet he also needed money. Even if he did buy more weapons for the stockpile, he probably kept plenty of cash for himself."

"Well, hell, his bombs didn't improve," chimed in Ford. "It was still ammonium nitrate at the synagogue, give or take a new trigger mechanism. Even though he made off with all that cash."

Chid nodded. "Then, he gets revenge on the judge who ruined his life, who happens to be Jewish. He gets revenge on the black city councilwoman who trashed his last attempt at a business project. He not only kidnaps her but tries to get some money out of *her* family. At the same time, he allows his followers to make mayhem, taking all the possible attention of law enforcement agencies off of *him*."

They all exchanged glances.

Ben eventually asked Chid, "Look, we've sorted out who Martin is, his motivations, but it seems like he could have done all this with significantly less hassle."

"Well, clearly," said Chid. "But all this . . . it's elaborate and erudite and he's made a splash."

"How do you think he hooked up with Baker?"

"That's the question that's making me crazy," Chid said frankly.

"What do truck drivers and beer magnates have in common?" Ben asked.

Derek Ford walked out of the conference room and returned with a large sheaf of paper.

"What?" Chid asked.

"I'd printed up all the tax information, remember? And all the penalty information from the IRS? I just want to look at the employment history, see if there's anything that could link him to Martin. Anything they had in common." He riffled through the papers.

"When did we say he'd moved to Erie?" he asked absently.

"In 2003," said Chid.

"He started working as a driver for the Erie Brewers in 2003," said Ford, tugging a paper out of the pile.

"Is that . . . ?" Ben asked.

But Chid was already nodding. "Martin's Brewery. As we said, shut down in 2008."

"And then all of a sudden Baker's out of work. And stays out of work. No options."

"I don't see any other evidence of employment after that."

"But somehow ex-boss and ex-worker hook up. Who radicalized whom?" Nora asked.

Chid ventured, "I would assume we have a symbiosis. Baker needed a visionary, someone to articulate and put a spin on his alt-right mayhem. Martin needed minions to enact his revenge."

"But he was poor, right? He had lost everything," Nora said.

"But he had kept enough land to train a militia," Chid replied.

Ford added, "And starting in the 2010s, the alt-right is piling up funds, kicking into full swing starting in 2014. If Martin offered land and vision, Baker could have used the networks he had tapped into back in Ulysses, August Kreis and all those fellows, to arm and support them. In election season, positing Martin as the intellectual mastermind of a truly comprehensive movement might push the Pennsylvania Patriots into the top spot for recipients of the windfall."

They rested a moment, each nodding slowly. It was a good theory, though still just a theory.

Nora, restless, tapped the screen of her laptop. "It looks like the Benedictine Sisters of Erie have another soup kitchen a block from here. By the baseball field."

All three men looked at her. "So?"

"So soup kitchens don't close for Armageddon. I'm going to walk over and see if anyone can help me understand the Martin family better."

Chid and Ford cast a skeptical glance.

She frowned at each one in turn. "You got a better way to kill time until they kill Pete?" she demanded.

Ben shrugged. "I certainly don't. Let's go."

They slipped out of the room and down the stairs, then out onto the street. The downtown was still crowded with people attempting to keep the "victory of the people" spirit alive and well since the failed occupation.

"What do you think we'll find?"

Nora shook her head. "I have no idea, Ben."

When they pushed open the door to the Ladles of Love Soup Kitchen, they were greeted by a plump elderly woman in a ratty yellow cardigan.

"Welcome!" she said.

Nora smiled at her.

The room they'd entered was painfully spare, though every wall was filled with pictures clearly drawn by small children and signed in uneven, wavery script. An open kitchen was visible beyond the dozen tables set up with folding chairs on all sides of them. The room smelled of slightly charred toast and chicken-noodle soup. About a dozen men and a few women and children sat scattered throughout the room.

"Are you hungry, children?"

It took a moment for Nora to comprehend that the "children" in question were herself and Ben. Nora was, in fact, starving. It always seemed to hit her when she least expected it. But she shook her head. "We're with the Federal Bureau of Investigation," she said in her least confrontational voice, as she and Ben discreetly showed their badges. "We would like to ask a few questions if we could."

The sister was unfazed. "Of course, child. I'm Sister Mary Catherine, director here. What is it concerning?"

Nora didn't know how to start.

Ben jumped in. "About ten years ago, Carole Martin left a house to your order. Designated as a soup kitchen? On Peach Street?"

But the sister was nodding. "Of course, yes. What about it?"

"We're trying to get a few insights into Mrs. Martin's decision. Is there anyone here who knew her?" Ben said.

"I knew her," said Mary Catherine, frowning slightly. "What is the issue?"

"Is there somewhere we could talk?" Ben asked.

Mary Catherine nodded. "Of course." She led them to the far table.

From out of the kitchen, a slightly younger woman crossed the room. Her mouse-brown hair was closely cropped. She wore an intent but curious smile. "Is everything okay, Mary Catherine?"

"Yes, Ann-Marie. These federal agents want to ask some questions. Could you find them some coffee?"

Ann-Marie nodded and went back to the kitchen.

"Sister Mary Catherine, why did William Martin's mother leave more assets to your order than to her son?"

"Ah," said the sister, her blue eyes clouding over. "Will," she murmured. "They called him Will. She had wanted to name him Wilhem, you know, after her brother. But she worried about anti-German sentiment even then."

Nora said, "She shared her thoughts with you?"

"She did. With very few in fact. But I happened to have been lucky enough to know Carole. She was . . . a gentle soul. Very kind."

"What happened with her son to upset her?"

Mary Catherine shook her head sadly. "Oh, poor Carole. You know, she loved that boy madly, but he was always in trouble."

"How so? We found no arrest records for him," said Ben.

"No, no, nor will you. I meant in trouble with other children. Bullying him—he was a small child, a frightened little boy, you know? Very sickly as a boy. And then he was always weak as a youth. The children in school tortured him, you know?"

"What was wrong?"

"Well, honestly, the doctors could never agree. But he just had a weak constitution—poor immune system, I suppose they'd say now. And I suppose because Carole was scared he would be hurt, she kept him inside most of the time. She kept him by her side."

"She didn't work?"

"Carole? Of course not! Carole was an heiress! Carole was a musician, unparalleled really. But her father had forbidden her to sing on the stage. So she was trapped in her home with her music. She could play the piano beautifully, children. Truly beautifully. But her dream had been to sing."

"Jazz?" Nora asked, by way of prodding, even though she and Ben both realized quickly what was coming.

"No, dear. Opera. She was . . . partial to Wagner, I'd say. I remember when I was visiting with her . . . she just stood up and sang the Liebestod aria from *Tristan and Isolde*—effortlessly, flawlessly. Rattled my teeth! I heard nothing to rival it until Jessye Norman sang it with Karajan in . . . oh, late in the '80s, I suppose it was."

Nora made a note to look up *Jessie Norman* and . . . *Kariyan*. She drew a few question marks onto the page.

"Then again, the sight of a black opera singer next to a former Nazi conductor was . . . well, that was something to behold. . . ."

At this point Sister Ann-Marie appeared with three Styrofoam cups of coffee. She deposited a small pile of plastic creamer pods and a few packets of sugar.

"What about her husband?"

"Her husband? Her husband worked at the brewery, though he stole from it, weakening it—crippling it. Drank himself to death, he did." Sister Mary Catherine stirred creamer into her coffee. "It's late for coffee," she said. Her blue eyes twinkled as she added by way of confession, "But it helps me get through evening prayers."

"Why did Carole Martin disown her son?" asked Nora. "Was it really because he had stolen the recipe for their most famous beer?"

Sister Mary Catherine shook her head vehemently. "Oh, no. This was certainly part of it, of course. She recognized his willingness to do anything for money, even if it meant dishonoring the family. But this last act, the thievery and the court case and the humiliation . . . this was the final straw in a lifetime of difficulties."

The agents waited as patiently as they could, fighting the weariness they felt in expectation of some window into Will Martin's life.

Sister Mary Catherine sighed deeply, then said, "Carole Martin's son did what I've seen other children do. The bullied boy became a bully. But he did it with a level of cruelty I was surprised at. This is the problem with rich boys sometimes. They can afford to be particularly cruel."

"Can you give us an example?"

Sister Mary Catherine sighed. "I think what disturbed his mother the most was that he was such a plotter. He would sit and brood and plan and devise and then an incident that all had considered forgotten would suddenly be avenged."

She sipped at her coffee, contemplatively. "He was angry at an employee of the brewery. A grown man with a family, mind you! But this man had teased young Will, made some laughing comment about him resembling a girl because he was so delicate."

Nora and Ben exchanged looks, waiting.

"Three months later there was an accident. He was a brewmeister, see? An expert. But somehow he fell into the vat itself. Drowned."

Ben said, "Not an accident?"

She shook her head. "There were ugly, persistent rumors that the boy—only twelve at the time—had paid one of the employees to push him in."

"Age twelve?"

"He knew the power of money over the poor," said Sister Mary Catherine. "Sometimes a soul is just weak, easily gives itself over to darkness. Even in the music, he found darkness. Wagner wrote some of the most beautiful music in the world. But Will latched on to the . . . well, to these threads of cultural superiority. . . ."

"But wasn't that Wagner's point?" asked Nora, recalling Chid's insights. "My colleague told me the Nazis used his music. Named efforts to round up and kill people after lines of his work. Doesn't that bother you?"

"Oh, of course, to some extent. But his characters also sing of the power of love to restore and rejuvenate." Sister Mary Catherine took a deep breath and looked about her, her limpid blue eyes taking in the forms bent over their meals and the artwork on the walls. At last she let her gaze fall on Nora again. The nun's eyes shone. "Music . . . music is from the divine realm, child," she said. "It is both prophecy and a testament to God's grace, isn't it? It can uplift like nothing else. It is a terrible disservice to art to suggest it should be limited by the borders of the artist's flesh . . . or even his intent."

Ben and Nora listened, waiting to see where she was going. Reluctantly, Nora sipped at the coffee. Then she dumped in as much sugar and creamer as she could, swiping Ben's share as well.

"That boy broke his mother's heart. And not because he was really . . . well, a rather poor, rather stiff musician."

She took a long sip of her coffee, her brow furrowed, recalling. "Carole had thought that, well, if her own career could not be, because she was a woman, because she had to submit to the will of her father and then to her husband, she was sure that if she taught the boy all she knew, that he would flourish where she could not. Instead of taking the musical education she gave him as the gift that it was, he found it to be one more area where he had failed. He was terribly afraid to perform and fail, to sit on the concert stage and forget the notes or stumble. I attended what was to be his great debut recital, a beautiful program from Scarlatti to Chopin. His hands shook so badly he could not play. He finally left the stage in shame. His father mocked him mercilessly, the attendees could not help but laugh and shake their heads. . . . It became another cross to bear for him. Sickly, anxious, and then simply not good enough. He never recovered and never played again in public."

Sister Mary Catherine's face was riven with sadness now.

"He broke her heart," she repeated. "Not because he could not perform. But because his relationship with music became so . . .

toxic. It became a cultural icon that he would hold up as an impossible, unattainable standard. She herself, beautiful accomplished musician that she was, became . . . repugnant to him. He was horrible to her."

Nora struggled to relate. For a moment she could feel again the weight of towering words teetering on her tongue. Her mother had been anxious to have Nora spout classical Arabic poetry even when she was little, even when the words were nonsense to her. Transplanted onto this soil, where poetry seemed scant and words weightless, Nora's mother had insisted. She had needed Nora to hear how the words were woven into the weft of timeless meters born of an ancient pulse.

Still, Nora thought. *I never got shaky over the idea of forgetting a line from Imru al-Qays. And even though he's a thousand times more advanced than Shakespeare a thousand years earlier, I never lorded it over anyone. . . . And,* her heart twisted at the memory, *I was always gentle with my mother.*

She glanced at Ben to find him watching her. She quickly focused on Sister Mary Catherine's gentle voice.

"Carole Martin tried hard to redirect her son who seemed to be foundering on all fronts. She even made him come to me, to come volunteer, feeding the hungry. But he could only see as far as their skin color, and here in Erie—well, at that time, there were few hungry whites. These days hunger does not discriminate. Either way, I was unable to cultivate in him compassion because he could only view poverty and powerlessness as failure."

"So Carole Martin gave up? Disowned him?"

"He disowned her, really. Walked out on her quite famously. Left Erie when she was most ill. When she made her bequests, she thought that increasing him in wealth might be dangerous."

"Why did Mrs. Martin pick your order for her gift?" Ben asked.

"Well . . . Carole always regretted not being more assertive, not standing up for herself, not doing more . . . and we Benedictine sisters have a reputation for being feisty. I've been arrested four times, you know!" She said this as though it were a badge of honor.

"What was the reason, Sister?" Ben asked.

"Protesting the war in Iraq. Protesting street violence. Protesting gun violence. And most recently protesting a candidate for national office who had the audacity to try to spread fear in our city. We sisters don't sit still too often."

Ben and Nora smiled, both looking around. "How many people do you feed a day?"

"Now? With so many of the old factories closed? Over fifteen hundred. All colors and races and creeds. We are united in our need to eat, you know. Our dependence on God's bounty. No matter who you are, or where you're from, eventually you're going to get hungry. We can't feed them all, but we do our best every day. It's all we can do."

They thanked her and walked out into the darkness. It was, by this time, past 10 P.M.

"She's amazing," said Nora.

Ben nodded.

"You gonna come camp out at the compound with me?"

"I wouldn't miss it," he said, kissing her temple and then wrapping his arm around her shoulders as they walked.

"You're kinda . . ." She wiggled, trying to find a position which wouldn't push her gun holster into her flesh.

"Yeah, it's not so easy. Switch sides."

They adjusted and shifted about until they found a comfortable way to walk.

"Well, of all the things I just picked up, there's one that stands out," Nora said.

Ben brushed a loose strand of hair from her eyes. "What's that?"

"I may have to give this Wagner guy a listen after all."

They shared what they'd found with Chid and Ford.

"Well," said Chid, "There's nothing like a disgraced and dis-empowered rich guy to be brooding for a decade and then un-leash hell."

For their part, the two had been sharing their discoveries with Schacht. Something like a plan was being hatched. The Telegram app had exploded with the rage of the group at having been sub-verted during their occupation. Promises of the Third Day being grim abounded.

But the Third Day would be the Third Day. Sanchez had at least secured from Baker the promise that no actions would be taken until the next day.

"Is that a promise Baker will keep?"

"He's been very deliberate so far," Ford said. "Geyer-slash-Martin's orders, perhaps, but they are obeyed to the T, not one bit more."

As such, Schacht had issued orders to all the agents to sleep five hours and then come to the compound at dawn.

Ben and Nora walked back to her apartment.

"We could just run in there," she said, pulling the key out from behind the brick.

"In where?" said Ben, yawning.

"Into that barn they're holding him in. Just bust our way in and grab him and go."

"Yes, Nora. We could," he answered, tired. "Let's do it first thing in the morning."

"Well, Benjamin Calder. I never thought I'd see you run out of gas."

"We're all half dead, woman." After they pulled off their hol-sters, they shed their clothes in a pile and fell into bed in their underwear and T-shirts. Nora shoved away her shyness about being so unclothed in front of him, finding some deep, distant place to store it. It was immaterial now, she knew. What was elemental was to lie curled next to Ben. She began thinking of what he'd said about losing patience with their agreement not to move to the next level.

But the still, dark room and the safety of his arm around her, her head on his shoulder and his almost immediate, even breathing, pulled her into a deep sleep that she realized she had never needed so much.

Even so, her sleep was brief. After only two hours, her eyes jerked open, and she found herself staring at the ceiling in the dimness. Soft strains of violin music seeped down from above. It sounded to Nora like a lament for the dead.

She carefully disentwined herself from Ben's arms. He stirred, frowning, and peered at her. "What is it?" he whispered.

"It's nothing. But I need to talk to my neighbor Rachel upstairs. I'll be back. Sleep. I mean it."

He squinted at her in the dimness. "I'll come with you."

"No. Sleep. I'll be right back."

She kissed him softly and then slid into her yoga pants. She was about to walk out barefoot, but then remembered her lesson about sneakers. *Always. I will always wear my sneakers. Sneakers save lives.*

She went outside into a warm, still night. Enough stars were visible overhead to convince her that growing up in Philadelphia had permanently destroyed her ability to understand what a night sky should look like. She pressed Rachel's doorbell, then took the extra measure of texting her that it was she, Nora, who was attempting to intrude.

The footfalls on the wooden staircase were loud and rapid.

Rachel pushed open her brand-new front door and threw her arms around Nora. "I've been so worried about you!" she declared.

Nora hugged her back. "Thanks, I'm okay. I'm sorry to bug you."

"I woke you?" Rachel said, guilt clouding her eyes.

"No. Well, I'm not sure. Maybe. But I need to talk to you if you have a minute."

Rachel nodded. "Of course. Come up?"

Nora followed her up the creaky staircase.

"Tea?" Rachel asked.

"No, nothing," Nora said. "Just . . . can you talk to me a little about Wagner?"

Rachel raised her eyebrows and asked, "Wagner again?"

Nora nodded.

"What do you want to know?" Rachel asked, settling onto her soft red couch.

Nora folded a leg beneath herself and sat down at the opposite end. "I don't know. What do you know about the Ring?"

"Alberich's Ring? Like in the Ring Cycle?"

"Yep," confirmed Nora.

Rachel thought a moment and then said, "I guess the key point is you have to forswear love to attain it. After that . . . well . . ." She ticked off on her fingers: "Don't turn yourself into a toad if you want to keep it. Don't bargain with giants for it. Don't trick Amazons into giving it to you. It's best left with the mermaids, frankly."

Nora ran her fingers through her loose curls. "Why a ring?"

Rachel considered this. Just as Nora thought she had no answer to offer, she spoke, her voice very quiet, very slow. "I rather think it's about taking a thing of beauty and using it in the wrong way for all the wrong reasons and ultimately destroying yourself. And a ring by definition has the convenient bonus of showing us the circularity of our habits in doing this."

Nora turned Rachel's words over, weighing them. "I really hate Wagner right now. I'm trying to sort out why I even have to know his name. A little old nun lady told me his music was divine. I want to understand from you, a musician, what the deal is."

"Ah," said Rachel, inhaling deeply. She flicked through the files on her phone and tapped one. The wireless speaker system glowed and sprang to life.

"The operas?"

"Dramas," she corrected. "This is *Das Rheingold*." They both listened a moment. Rachel studied Nora's reaction. At length, she said, "Look, the music is . . . well, you'd have to be nuts to think it was bad. It's exciting and stirring and unearthly and yet very real, very tightly constructed, very . . . sound. It's hard to back up a claim that it's outright bad, though some critics did at first."

Nora, who was still deciding, tried to listen around these words.

Rachel pressed on. "I think your real problem is, *Where does music start and the composer end*?"

Nora said nothing.

"It's the same with artists, too. I can name fifty horrendous people who produced some of the world's most transcendent paintings."

Nora tilted her head, considering. "Well, see, my grandfather would have said that is reason enough to discard their productions and listen to God's birds instead of music or look at his sunsets instead of pictures."

"Well, your grandfather would have missed out," Rachel said simply.

They sat listening in silence.

Finally, Rachel said carefully, "Look, as a musician, I can tell you that some bastard trying to link these works with acts of terror is devastating to me . . . and a terrible affront. It is as devastating, surely, as it must be for some pious person who reads scripture in order to connect with God . . . only to realize that some other bastard is using the words of scripture to call for violence."

Despite herself, Nora found tears pooling in her eyes as Rachel spoke.

"Whatever he was, or however the Nazis used him, or however this guy is using him, Wagner wasn't about bloodshed. Unlike God . . . well, or maybe *like* God, he was just sort of a dick."

Nora flinched.

"But still. He was all bluster and his music . . . well, someone like me would say its ability to endure might even absolve him, although some of my Jewish colleagues might argue that point. But ask Daniel Barenboim who dared have the Israeli Philharmonic play a bit from *Tristan and Isolde,* a passionate, tragic romantic opera. The audience itself debated it on the spot, invoking the Holocaust and concentration camps. They called Barenboim a fascist. But in the end . . . they gave him a standing ovation."

Nora murmured, "Brave."

Rachel shrugged. "If the musicians can't come together there's honestly no hope. It's the only language we have that's universal. Well, except math. But everyone hates math. It just can't compare."

Nora laughed.

"But, listen, Nora. I think he used racial arguments and cultural patriotism to argue for his own preeminence because they were convenient and because he was vain—he wanted to do whatever he could to convince people they should listen to him instead of the competition, which often happened to be Jewish. He was self-serving, you know? It was a means to an end."

Nora fell still, listening to the ebb and flow of the orchestra and unearthly voices of women interwoven with the instruments. At last she said, "So. That such arguments still matter in our day . . . ?"

"Means it's not Wagner who's the fuck-up. It's us."

THIRD **DAY**

Sunlight was just edging over the horizon when Ben, Nora, Chid, and Ford approached the compound the next morning. Barriers had been erected to prevent access from the east and the west alike. Ben showed his credentials to the earnest state trooper and was given access to the stretch of road leading up to the compound. There was no real driveway, although it occurred to Nora that perhaps once there had been gravel along this trail. Now, it was only a path that had been worn through the brush and weeds from cars or trucks repeatedly driving over it. The lot was otherwise overgrown with trees and brush, undistinguishable from any other thickly wooded lot along Route 5. The swarm of law enforcement vehicles seemed to have been pushing in incrementally, flattening weeds, pushing back against the edges of the compound. The array of cars and SUVs now littered the property's edges, striking a sharp contrast with the thick, wild stretch of green.

Ben pulled Nora's car alongside another unmarked car. He flashed his credentials at yet another state trooper. He was determined to get the Malibu up a little further into the thick of things and away from the gathering crowd of onlookers. Nora wondered if they were drawn by the sound of hovering helicopters. The SWAT helicopter was on the lakeside, a few miles in, but the sound cut through the still morning air and hung over the scene like a pall. Media helicopters were making a wide perimeter over the general area. Nora looked up and thought of vultures.

She shuddered.

Descending from the car, they immediately saw a cluster of people talking, Schacht at the center.

Schacht glanced up at the four of them. He looked as though he had several different things to say simultaneously, but he ultimately chose not to acknowledge them verbally at all and continued conferring with Sanchez and Rogers.

Nora noted that the Bearcat SWAT trucks were parked one next to the other, their idling engines spilling foul smells into the otherwise pristine air.

"Smells like Philly," Ben said.

Nora laughed despite herself. "That's where I recognized it. . . ."

Sheila and Anna pulled Nora aside.

"How are you?" Sheila demanded. "Do you have any details for me?"

"Nothing new," Nora said. "Just all the stuff Chid's been reporting about who Geyer really is. They're a good team, those guys, Chid and Ford."

Sheila nodded, her gaze falling upon the agents from Philadelphia.

Nora decided to use on Sheila the words she wanted to use on Schacht. "What are you guys doing for Pete? How are you going to get him out of this?"

"I swear, Nora, if it were up to me, we'd be swinging through windows, grabbing our boy, then firing missiles on their whole compound right now."

"The barn doesn't have windows," Nora pointed out. "So who's it up to?" she asked, knowing anyway.

"The attorney general, actually," responded Sheila. "They don't want—"

"Another Waco," Nora chimed in. "Yes, we get that. They ignored the Oregon militia because they didn't want another Waco. They're holding back now on the most repulsive criminals the country has ever known because they don't want another Waco."

Sheila heard her. "The Oregon militia was a joke—"

"We all know," Nora said hotly, "that it would *not* have been funny if they had been *any* color other than white."

Sheila had no response. "Give Schacht and these guys a chance, Nora. They're trying to avoid a bloodbath."

"The PR of it is ignoring the facts on the ground. These people are monsters."

"Yes, they are. And I know you know the story of the hydra." Sheila gave her a look that made it crystal-clear that she had, at most, slept four hours of the last thirty-six.

Nora was not sure at all that she knew any stories about a hydra and made yet another mental note to ask Chid.

"Give Schacht a chance," she repeated.

"His strategy got April Lewis killed."

"His strategy revealed to the world how small and cold-blooded Gabe Baker is," answered Sheila. "For better or for worse. That wasn't the intention, but it was the result. It's all we've got right now," she added.

Mike Szymanowski and his partner drove up in his squad car. Nora looked over at it and realized that three of the four Patriots they'd arrested the day before were all sitting in the back. They were bandaged and cleaned up a little, but definitely not in prison where she'd expected them to be.

Nora looked over at Ben in surprise. "What's this?"

Ford shrugged. "I told you they'd put together a plan."

"What sort of plan?"

"Schacht is finishing out the details with Sanchez and Rogers."

"What sort of plan?" Nora repeated, nervous.

"One that might get your boy freed," answered Derek Ford. "Breathe."

Chid nudged him, and he looked at the smartphone in his hand.

"Ten minutes til Prologue," he called out.

Nora looked at Chid. "Prologue?"

"Prologue and three acts today."

"So, four acts," Nora said impatiently.

He nodded. "Four acts."

"But they're no longer telling us what anything is because we've hacked their network."

He nodded again.

Schacht's steely voice reached them. "Okay, here's what we're not going to do," he was saying. "We're not going to let Pete die, but we're also not going to give these people the satisfaction of getting blown to pieces so that a thousand more militias can take up the banner. Now the way we are going to do that is a little unorthodox."

Nora looked from face to face, trying to figure out what they were up to.

Mike Szymanowski suddenly stepped forward. "We have the requested suspects, sir." He motioned to the squad car where his partner stood, his eyes riveted on the three would-be killers in his custody.

Schacht said, "Okay, people. For argument's sake, let's ask how can we best use three terrorists to get our man back?"

"Short of offering to webcast their executions?" Gray Rogers asked with an edge to his voice that Nora didn't dislike.

Chid eyed the circle. "Maybe the real question is, can we ignore the law for a moment in order to ultimately enforce it?"

Anna said, "Baker doesn't care if those people live or die. He doesn't send them out with vests. He doesn't expect them to come back. They exist to serve a purpose, that's all. Not even white lives matter to this guy."

"Maybe one of them matters," said Ford.

They all stared at Ford.

"The woman. I think she's his wife."

"What?" Sheila asked. "Did she say this as you arrested her? Did she have some ID?"

"None of them carries ID," Ford reminded her. "But her wedding ring matches his. I've seen Baker's so many times, you know, when he makes that fist salute thing. Chid noticed her ring when he cuffed her. It didn't take too much hunting to find out her name was Carly Baker."

He and Chid shared a small exultant grin.

Sanchez and Schacht conferred a moment, then said, "We've been going back and forth on this idea since it was proposed last night. We're going to tell Baker we have three of his people to trade for Pete, and that one of them is his wife."

From the looks of things, Sanchez was already calling in this new offer. Long moments of silence descended. The circle dispersed into smaller clusters.

Nora walked over to Mike Szymanowski. "Thanks for helping out again," she said.

He nodded. "I reckon we're all helping each other," he said. "We all live here, right?"

"Yes we do indeed," said Nora, holding his gaze.

Anna said, "They're getting ready to send them in. What's their countdown clock say, Ford?"

He checked. "Four minutes, Anna."

"Sanchez and Schacht and Sheila are going to walk the Patriots halfway up the drive. The others are supposed to bring Pete half of the way," she said.

"Why those three? Anyone could do that. The SWAT guys could do that."

"Baker requested the directors as a gesture of good faith," Anna responded.

"Couldn't they open fire on our guys?" Ben asked.

Anna nodded. "Sure. But they're likely to hit their own people.

Which is why they'll all be in Kevlar, and why we're keeping Baker's wife back. Once Pete has walked past the wife, the wife will be allowed to run toward the barn. And why also Gray Rogers will be standing ready. Helicopter snipers are ready. Helicopter fast-rope team is ready."

All of them swiveled their heads to look up at the hovering helicopter. In the distance, no less than six media helicopters waited to pounce on the scene.

"They're showing remarkable restraint, aren't they?" Chid asked.

"Rogers told the media point blank he would shoot down any helicopter interfering with this operation," Anna explained.

"I like Rogers," Nora said.

Schacht was strapping on anti-rifle Kevlar. He caught Nora's eye and gave a small nod. A wave of nausea hit her. Mike Szymanowski and his partner had pulled the three Patriots out of the squad car and were walking them over to where Schacht and Sanchez stood. Sheila's face seemed particularly white as she took the cuffed Carly Baker's arm with her left hand. The palm of Sheila's right hand rested just inside her blazer on the butt of her pistol.

Nora looked about. In addition to that of Mike Szymanowski, eight police cars sat with their engines running and blue and red lights flashing, sixteen cops standing alongside them, weapons drawn. Each SWAT team stood at the ready, rifles pointed in the direction of the barn. She watched them, admiring their black-clad patience under the morning sun's blaze. She saw Rogers speaking into his cell phone, and wondered if he was conferring with the helicopter suspended above the edge of the bank.

"Zero minutes," Ford said, shading the screen of Jane Doe's iPhone so he could peer at it.

Schacht and Sanchez began walking with the two men.

Nora watched, mesmerized, as Tattoo-Neck started making

his way up the drive under Schacht's guidance. She recalled the smell of him—sweat mingled with fire. Her stomach turned.

In the distance, the agents could see a burly man just emerging from the lake side of the western barn. He dwarfed a still-limping Pete who sagged as he walked, head dangling, hands still tied behind him. She recalled April Lewis's bruises. They must have beaten Pete badly. Nora wondered if they had freed his wrists since he'd arrived. She looked down at the red welts on her own wrists and felt a pang.

"He looks hurt," said Anna.

"He looks half-dead," said Nora, wishing they'd hurry.

Schacht and Sanchez had only gotten about two hundred yards away when Sheila took off walking briskly, dragging Carly Baker alongside her.

Nora watched Pete's progress, trying to remember to breathe in and out. He and his escort had almost reached the group of four men walking up the winding trail through the weeds and shrubs toward the barn.

"His beard grew," Nora said. "His beard—" She held up her phone and looked through the camera app's zoom.

She looked at Ben in horror. "It's not him! Ben, it's not him!"

Ben bolted around the side of the car shouting at Rogers: "It's not Pete, abort, abort!"

His voice carried, and Schacht and Sanchez whipped around to look, then seemed to realize in the same instant what had happened.

The land exploded in gunfire. They watched Schacht and Sanchez dart behind their charges as the two approaching men pulled out handguns. Schacht and Sanchez began firing, easily felling the burly man and the slim, bearded man they'd substituted for Peter. Tattoo-Neck pushed back, attempting to wrestle Schacht to the ground, while Sanchez's prisoner head-butted him. Sanchez stumbled, vanished into the weeds, then seemed to have rolled back to where his prisoner was. He rose with the man grabbing him firmly by his cinched wrists and shoving the handgun against the base of his skull.

It was at that moment that Carly Baker launched herself at Sheila.

With a shout of surprise, Sheila was suddenly sprawled on the ground, but Carly Baker had flopped on top of her, her hands, though tethered together, seeking Sheila's gun. The two were immediately locked in a tangle of tussling arms and legs that none of the agents could fully make out through the brush.

Rogers began shouting at his men in the Bearcat. Some of them took aim at the scene, looking for a shot that wouldn't injure the agents. Others slid the heavy locks of the armored vehicle into place as it began to move forward.

Sanchez and Schacht both turned, still holding their prisoners in vise-like grips, trying to make sense of the jumble of limbs that was Sheila and Carly Baker. Nora saw the two men raising and lowering their guns, attempting to get a clear shot at Mrs. Baker, who kept thrashing about and pulling Sheila with her.

Suddenly, a volley of shots poured out of Sanchez and Schacht's weapons and Carly Baker's body, that had just began to rise to a standing position, flopped down, disappearing, like Sheila's had, into the tall grasses.

Gray Rogers was screaming instructions, even as the compound's grassy lawn was suddenly thick with people in fatigues. Sanchez and Schacht half-dragged their prisoners toward the trees lining the trail as Patriots began showering the approaching SWAT team with gunfire.

Sanchez made it just to the forest's edge. From where they stood, Anna, Nora, Ben, Chid, and Ford watched him fall. They quickly realized that Schacht, still hurtling through the trees with Tattoo-Neck, hadn't seen him go down.

The man Sanchez had been guiding instantly attempted to divest him of his weapon, but as he grappled with Sanchez's limp form, Gray Rogers himself took aim and shot him. The force of the round sent him reeling backwards. He collapsed on the tall grass.

Nora and her colleagues crouched by the car, using it as a shield from the random rounds that found their way all the way down the long, twisting path.

Chid and Ford began calling for more backup and ambulances as the scene unfolded.

Paralyzed, they all watched a man run out of the barn with an RPG-7 rocket launcher on his shoulder. He took direct aim at the SWAT truck. A fiery cloud of exhaust framed his figure from behind as a rocket streaked out of the tube and straight through the bulletproof windows of the truck. The truck veered left and continued a slow path toward the copse of trees to the left. Flames poured out of it from the front and the SWAT team streamed out of its back end; each man clutched a semi-automatic rifle and had donned riot gear, but each was also coughing and several were doubled over from the smoke that had invaded the vehicle.

Nora watched, stunned, as a helicopter sniper sent several rounds into the man with the RPG-7. He collapsed, holding his neck. His weapon, however, was taken up by a woman. She had burst onto the lawn from behind the barn and in a swift and practiced motion, she picked up the grenade the man had been holding and shoved it into the mouth of the rocket launcher. Then she mounted the weapon on her shoulder and shot it directly into the open door of the hovering helicopter.

With an explosion that Nora felt in her belly, the helicopter burst into flame and then plummeted onto the lawn only a few yards from the farmhouse. The crash rattled the windows of every vehicle around them. Triumphant cries filled the air from the Patriots, even though the woman who had fired the grenade had just been shot in the head by one of the snipers stationed in the trees lining the path.

The second SWAT Bearcat started making its way up the path. Rogers was shouting indecipherable commands into his phone.

Schacht was still dragging his prisoner as he burst out of the woods nearest Anna's SUV. Each man was panting, his chest heaving; Schacht's face was haggard.

Officers Szymanowski and Hegel ran over to reclaim the remaining Patriot and hustle him into the back of the car.

"You're hurt, sir," cried Anna.

Blood had soaked through the lightweight gray wool of Schacht's trousers, from the thigh all the way down to his wing-tipped shoe. "I could use a place to sit down," he said simply.

Four agents rushed to his side and began coaxing him into the car. Nora had the presence of mind to turn on the engine so that Schacht could sit in the air conditioning. As she did so a grenade whistled past her and plowed into the earth not fifteen yards away.

Ben asked, "Was that meant for us?"

"Of course it was," snapped Chid.

Nora snapped back at him, "I think the CIRG approach isn't working," she said.

"It is for our opponents," said Derek Ford.

An EMS worker swooped down upon Schacht from the waiting ambulance. He looked woozy as the tech cut away the blood-stained suit and exposed the gaping hole in his upper thigh.

"Derek, what's their app telling them is going on in all this?" Nora called out over the gunfire.

"It's footage of the helicopter—someone's spinning it as a big win! Prologue: murdering high-ranking federal agents. Act One: taking down a whole chopper."

She got up close to Ben and clutched his sleeve. "We have to get Pete out now. Ben?"

Ben scanned the area, thinking. He shook his head. "The chances of getting in and out are—"

"Probably better than hanging around here to be firebombed!" she exclaimed.

Nora grabbed Ben's arm and dragged him over to Gray Rogers.

"Let us go in, Gray. We can cut up through the woods and then slip into the barn while their fighters are engaged with your SWAT teams. Please."

Rogers shook his head. "That's a death sentence."

"They're firing on the non-combatants back here—what's to say they won't fire on the whole civilian area beyond their acreage?"

"You Kevlar'd up?"

"Of course," said Nora.

"Then go. But you're going to have to move fast. The order from the attorney general to continue to hold off was last night. The newest orders are . . . different."

He said these words with effort, and Nora suddenly realized that Pete's life meant significantly less now that everything was going up in flames. Sheila and Sanchez were dead, after all. It was a different game. Gray Rogers had scores of agents under assault and a military threat that had to be dealt with.

Nora swallowed. "All we have are handguns," she said.

Rogers pointed at the abandoned Bearcat, the one that, burning, had veered into the trees and come to a stop. Smoke was still pouring out of the front cab.

"It's on your way. I was about to go secure it. Take anything you find in the back."

Nora and Ben nodded. "We can't be responsible for your safety," he added.

Nora looked at Ben, who nodded. He said, "We know."

"You have fifteen minutes," Rogers said, his face grim. "I can't give you any more than that. If you don't find Pete, or if it's impossible, you have to get out." He looked at Ben. "Drag her out by her hair if you have to."

"You call off the tree snipers, though," said Ben.

Gray Rogers nodded, casting a glance into the trees beyond them. "But take some extra magazines for Spence's assault rifle. It's on your way."

All three looked at their watches.

"I have 8:10," Rogers said.

The other two nodded assent.

"Fifteen minutes," Nora repeated.

They sprinted across the small clearing and into the back of the truck, coughing as the smoke within rolled out to meet them. Ben yanked two assault rifles off the rack, tossing her one.

"Four tear gas grenades," Nora insisted.

He found them easily and, after making sure their safeties were on, tucked one into each of their blazer pockets.

He held her gaze. "We'd better go."

She nodded.

"I'll follow you," he said.

She sprinted for the trees, wishing for the first time in her life that she had some camouflage gear. She darted from tree to tree but did not feel like the mayhem on the lawn would allow anyone to follow their movements. She cast an eye up to where the one called Spencer was perched high in the smooth branches of a maple tree. He had his eye locked against the scope of his rifle.

"Spencer!" she called.

He looked down distractedly.

Ben waved the magazine at him.

Spencer held out a hand and Ben narrowed his eyes, calculating, then tossed the magazine high into the tree. Spencer snatched it out of the air.

"We may need cover, Spencer, in a few minutes. Keep an eye out for us."

"You're goin' in there?" Spencer asked incredulously, gesturing to the barn.

But they had already taken off running. Nora crouched low, continuously looking to the right, trying to gauge how many of them were going in and out of the arsenal barn.

The SWAT truck was approaching and garnering most of the Patriots' attention. No one had yet picked up the RPG-7 from alongside the woman's corpse, and Nora wondered if this was because there were no more left who had trained on its use or if they were out of ammunition for it.

They gained the southwest corner of the barn. Chests heaving, they exchanged a look, then crouched low and stayed close to its wall, running as fast as they could toward the entrance. Nora would have done anything for a window to peer through, but she knew there was only the main entrance. She knew, too, that it was probably so designed for exactly this set of circumstances.

When they approached the lakeside, Nora stopped. She gazed at the lake peeking through the trees along the bank and fought for breath. Then she looked around the corner to the barn's main entrance.

She saw several people just beyond the barn, and she could clearly see the arsenal barn's entrance. People were running in and out, shouting words of encouragement or direction to whomever they met. She watched as two wounded men were dragged across the grass into the barn they were trying to enter. She looked back at Ben, eyes worried, then saw the same men who'd dragged in the wounded run out again to rejoin the fray.

"On your signal," he said, his eyes clear, filled with resolution.

She nodded, then took three quick breaths.

"Now!" she said, and she did not look back at him, only dashed along the barn and in through the massive opening.

She hadn't taken three steps into the barn when she saw the blood-stained floor where April Lewis had died. The sight made her stop in her tracks.

It was just enough of a hesitation to allow her to be tackled by a woman who seemed to have been standing there for just that purpose. The two crashed to the floor. Nora looked up, astonished, to see an animal look on the woman's face as she snarled, her breath hot on Nora's face. She was pulling at Nora's hair and scratching at her until Nora rammed her knee up into the woman's belly.

And then Ben was grabbing the woman's hair and wrenching her head backwards, dragging her off of Nora. Nora was immediately on her feet, scanning the barn for other attackers, but it was eerily still. The wounded men she'd seen brought in were lying in the hall. Perhaps her attacker was meant to nurse them.

Nora thought she did not look as though her bedside manner would be comforting.

"Keep holding her hair, Ben—drag her away from the door."

Ben encircled her neck with his arm and pulled her backwards, almost to the place where Nora and Pete had had their pictures taken. They were out of sight of the main entrance. Nora was scanning the barn as they walked, afraid that a group of Patriots would appear out of nowhere.

Nora leaned in. "Where's the federal agent? Where's he being held?"

The woman rolled her eyes. "*Seriously*. You think I'd tell you?"

Nora looked at Ben who yanked the woman's hair.

"*Where?*"

The woman gave a yelp and struggled, then kept silent.

"Kill her," commanded Nora, coolly. "We'll ask someone else."

Ben placed the muzzle of his pistol against her temple and pushed it into the skin.

"Okay, okay," she cried. "After the other one ran off they moved them to the farmhouse."

Nora's heart sank.

She looked desperately at Ben. Then she looked at the girl. "Well, we learned that they won't ease up to save a hostage, there's no point in bringing her."

He nodded, then cuffed her. Nora looked around, then grabbed the edge of one of the white privacy curtains hung over the stalls. She ripped it with as much force as she could muster, then shoved the piece of cloth in the woman's mouth.

Ben, almost with a flourish, put her under the cot, and put the bed leg through the chain of the cuffs.

As he did so, she said, "Time?"

"We have nine minutes, Nora."

"Dammit," she breathed.

The farmhouse, a hundred yards from the barn, had two visible defenders. There were two men pressed against the peeling paint of its west wall, firing their rifles south toward the SWAT team.

"Do you think they've seen us?"

Ben shook his head. "No way. But they're out of range for the pistols. Use the rifle."

Nora holstered her pistol and pulled the rifle into her arms. She despised its deadly weight.

They stuck close to the doorway, taking careful aim.

"I'll take the one who's lakeside," Ben said, raising his voice over the volleys of gunshot just beyond them. "You take the other," he said.

"Any point in aiming for legs or arms?" she asked.

"They're firing on federal agents, Nora. Take them down."

Nora nodded queasily.

"On three," he breathed. "One, two . . . *three.*"

They each squeezed their triggers, firing off the high-powered rounds, then ducking back into the barn.

They exchanged glances, then poked their heads out of the barn's entrance. Both men had crumpled to the ground. But there was more: the lawn was suddenly dense with smoke. The SWAT team had lobbed several grenades of tear gas onto the cluster of Patriots.

"Oh, no!" cried Nora.

"No, no—that helps!" rejoined Ben. "But we're gonna have to run like hell. Ready?"

"Front door?" asked Nora.

"Never did like being sneaky," he answered.

They took off, sprinting for the lodge, trying to avoid the billowing gas as it spread across the wide lawn.

The farmhouse sat unperturbed by the commotion behind it or by the ruins of the helicopter sprawled out, still smoking, in front of it. The morning sun bathed it in bright, unassuming light.

Nora reached the front door first, knowing that anyone inside would have seen her approach. As soon as Ben reached her, she stretched her hand to the doorknob.

"I go in first this time," he said.

"Go," she said with a quick smile. "Carefully," she added.

She flung open the door and Ben leapt inside, Nora covering him with the Glock.

The living room was deathly still compared to the cacophony of sound outside. The inside of the house was elegant, striking a jarring contrast to the dilapidated outer shell. Persian-style rugs crowded the floors. The sofas were swathed in damask silk. A grand piano sat under the east window. Only the deer heads seemed out of place.

"What if we find Martin?" Ben asked in a whisper.

"It will be my happiest moment," Nora whispered back,

walking with quiet footsteps over floors that groaned with aged discontent.

"I thought I'm your happiest moment," Ben whispered, moving across the ornate rug toward the dining room and kitchen area.

"Kissing you, killing psychos . . . I'll try to sort out which I want most."

"You do that," he said.

"Bedrooms?" Nora guessed.

"They'll have wanted them to suffer. Gotta be some sorta basement dungeon," he said.

"How many minutes?"

"Six," he said.

They both walked toward the kitchen seeking a basement door. It was immediately evident behind the bulky frame of a bearded Patriot. The man wore a NASCAR hat and held a shotgun that was leveled straight at them.

Without uttering a word of warning, he fired.

The shot rang through the stillness and Ben had just enough time to grab Nora's blazer and yank her to the ground. The round plowed into the kitchen wall, cracking the beige marble backsplash. Before the man could advance, though, Ben had fired his Glock twice.

NASCAR looked surprised. He turned wide hazel eyes on Ben and Nora where they lay on the cool tiled floor. Then he looked down at the red stain creeping across his paunch. He laid a hand across his gut, wrinkled his face in pain, and then collapsed on the floor.

Ben was up in a heartbeat, dragging the man away from the door. He and Nora tore down the steps two and three at a time. "Peter!" Nora shouted into the darkness. The smell of mildew assaulted her.

"Nora! I'm here!"

He was sitting on the cement floor, chained to an exposed-stone wall. His face had been battered; his right eye was swollen completely shut.

Nora looked him over, her heart contracting. "Oh, Pete!"

"There's no time," said Ben, tugging hard on the chain where it attached to a massive ring in the wall. "Get out of the way, Pete, I'm going to shoot the chain off the wall."

"Pete, meet my boyfriend Ben," Nora said.

"Nice," said Pete.

"Nice to see you, Peter," she said.

Pete turned his head to meet her gaze. "Took-you-the-fuck-long-enough, Miss Nora."

The shot Ben squeezed off resounded through the basement. He immediately began pulling the chain away from Pete's bound wrists.

"You responsible for the war zone outside?" asked Pete, rubbing his wrists and coming up to a standing position with great effort.

"We're out of time," Ben said.

"Pete, I know you're hurt. I need you to run, man. We're gonna get out and make for the woods on the west side, then run south back to our guys."

Pete looked exhausted but determined.

"After you, Miss Nora."

She galloped up the stairs, Ben and Pete on her heels. She burst into the kitchen, vaulted over the guard and then they were crossing the living room, and making for the front door. She realized that Pete had stumbled and Ben was supporting him as they ran.

The tear gas was enveloping the lawn by now.

Nora tugged her shirt over her mouth and nose. Ben and Pete followed suit. They looked around. There was still shouting peppered with gunfire from the south side of the barn.

She handed her two tear gas grenades to Ben. "Let's up our chances," she said. "I'll run with Pete, you throw these at the fighters."

Ben nodded. "Yes." He took the grenades as Nora looped her left arm under Pete's shoulders. She clutched her Glock and the two of them took off for the expanse of trees on the west side of the clearing.

She refused to look back, but she heard Ben's grunts as he lobbed each grenade, then heard him panting behind them, catching up easily as Pete's pace was painfully slow.

Ben was looking back and he answered a quick spate of gunfire with a few shots from his pistol. And then, miraculously, they had gained the woods.

Nora couldn't believe it.

"Yes!" she sighed, as Ben came up to support Pete's other side and they began running south.

But three armed men were suddenly behind them. One fired off a shot that thudded into a sapling next to Nora's right ear, splintering the wood.

"Spencer!" she screamed as the threesome hurtled through the trees.

Spencer did not need to be told twice.

A hail of gunfire spilled out of the top of the sturdy ash tree and onto their pursuers. Nora did not look back, trying desperately to get Pete as far away as possible before Rogers unleashed whatever was coming next.

But Ben glanced back. "Yes!" he called out.

They all looked back, then, and Nora saw that Spencer had dropped all three of the men—dead, dying, or just wounded? She would not know. No one was following them and Spencer himself was shimmying down the tree, his rifle now slung over his back.

"Go, go! We've gotta get out of here!"

All of a sudden he was running with them and then outpacing them.

"What's happening?" shouted Ben.

"Just go! Get out fast!"

Nora and Ben looked left and saw that the SWAT team was piling into the back of the Bearcat. A shout had gone up from the remaining Patriots, celebrating what seemed to be a retreat.

Nora and Ben mustered a burst of speed, panting and heaving with the weight of Pete as they maneuvered between the trees and underbrush.

They tumbled out of the forest to find Schacht, Anna, Chid, and Ford awaiting them. Nora and Ben shoved Pete through the ambulance's open doors and then flopped onto the ground, breathing in gasps. All three of them were completely soaked in sweat.

Nora lay back in the grass, completely unconcerned with the possibility of ticks.

The EMS techs began bending over Pete, tending to what Nora knew from experience had to be a broken rib—if not a few of them.

"What's going on?" Ben asked.

Ford said, "Rogers's team dumped enough tear gas on the Patriots to send them running into the barns. Now they're set to unleash the flash-bangs."

Anna added, "They'll probably start rounding them up after that."

Indeed, the Bearcat was drawing closer to the compound's main structures, crushing weeds and shrubbery along the way. The SWAT team, now wearing gas masks and ear protection, poured out of the Bearcat, unleashing the thunder of stun grenades.

———

The victory shouts turned to shouts of confusion and protest.

Nora stared at Ben, eyes wide, mouth open as she still fought to regulate her breathing.

"Shootin' fish in a barrel," Pete said from behind them.

They all looked back at Pete who was shaking his head, watching the scene the distant lawn. The black-clad SWAT teams, all wearing gas masks, were darting into the buildings and returning with one or even two Patriots at a time. These latter would be tossed on the ground with little fanfare and then the arresting officer would hurtle back into the barn or farmhouse and return with another.

From out of a multi-hued face, Pete gave Nora a glance. "Somehow I feel like Nora Khalil had a hand in making all this mayhem," he said.

"Your face is mayhem," Nora retorted. "I just showed up for work today. Not my fault it was a messy day."

Pete chuckled then immediately clutched his sides in pain. "Don't make me laugh, Miss Nora."

She came to a sitting position.

Pete sat too, his face contorting painfully. "I guess my bruises aren't gonna get much attention with this crowd."

They all looked at him sympathetically. "What the hell, man?" asked Derek Ford.

Pete shrugged. "They weren't very happy when they figured out that Nora had run off."

She shook her head. "I'm so sorry, Pete."

"*You're* sorry! I'm gonna pee a bit when I cough for the next couple *years*. But last I knew, they came and took April Lewis away. What happened? How did we get to *this*?"

His question was met with silence.

"They killed her, didn't they?"

Nora took a long time to find her voice. "We thought they were going to kill you, too. So someone thought up a hostage exchange. But they were pretty set on not giving you back," Nora explained.

"People love me," he said, rubbing his wrists. "What can I tell you?"

"And also they used it as a way of taking out two of ours. We lost Sanchez and . . . Sheila's dead, Pete."

His face grew dark. Anna looked away, tears streaking her cheeks.

Chid supplied, "They were bent on engaging. They had to provoke the confrontation, no matter what we did."

Pete shook his head. "And to think I once called this post boring."

Ben and Nora exchanged knowing looks.

Schacht's pant leg had been cut up past the thigh. He leaned heavily on Chid. If it weren't Schacht, Nora would have found his appearance absurd. But somehow the SAC brought a gravitas to the look that could not be dismissed.

"Sir, I'm telling you, that wound needs a hospital," Chid said.

"And I'm telling you it's fine," he snapped.

The EMS team was trying to wrap Pete's rib cage.

Rogers and his men had been charged with finding Gabe Baker and Will Martin among the barrel's fish.

"It's going to be ugly," Ford observed.

Three ambulances and a fire truck suddenly entered the compound in a howling tag-team. Rogers flagged down the first ambulance. He conferred with the driver and motioned to the growing group on the lawn.

Nora realized that he had probably called them, indeed that their window for getting Pete out had been predetermined by how long it would take for the extra emergency services crews to come.

"They know that if they find either of those two they must keep them alive at all costs?" Chid asked.

Schacht was nodding. "I discussed it with Rogers multiple times. He gets it."

"You think that Martin is on site?" Ben asked. "We were in the farmhouse. . . ."

"Description?" interrupted Chid, interested.

"Swanky," said Ben.

Nora nodded.

"Fancy?" Chid pressed. "It's my bet that the interior doesn't match the shabby exterior, that's all. That Martin had been fixing it up on the down-low with alt-right funds."

"That would explain the marble countertops," Nora conceded. "I'm more concerned with the fact that there's a big chubby guy bleeding on the pretty tiled floor."

"Did it look like a place where a truck driver would hole up? Or a mad beer magnate?"

Ford looked over. "Can you be called a magnate if your company went bust?"

Ben said, "The guy I shot didn't look like the old photos of Will Martin you found."

Rogers came jogging toward them.

"We have Gabriel Baker in custody," he said, a cascade of sweat pouring off his cheeks and dripping off the tip of his nose. "He's hurt though. It will be best to talk to him where he is."

"And where is he?" asked Anna.

"Next to the arsenal barn. The south wind was dispersing the tear gas so we have about fifteen there at this point."

"Casualties?" Schacht asked.

"I have at this count eleven dead, twenty-one in custody. Of the twenty-one, a third are injured. Baker is one."

"Kids?"

"Holed up in the third barn. About seventeen of them, all without a scratch. We're making sure there are no others stashed elsewhere."

The agents exchanged heavy glances. Nora nodded, conceding the point about the kids, relieved.

Rogers suggested that they would need to put Gabe Baker in an ambulance and thus it made sense that Pete and Schacht ride up in the vehicle.

"Yeah, turns out the third barn is also the garage. And gas station," Rogers offered as the group started walking north toward the lake. "Oh, and mess hall apparently."

They all walked slowly, unwilling to prolong the intense pace that the week had dictated. "Quite an operation," Ben observed.

Rogers shrugged. "I've seen bigger. Plenty of groups that if given half a chance would have done as much or more. Others were just too ideologically dispersed, or, when it came time, not resolved enough to take violent action."

"How did this group get their resolve?" Ben asked.

Nora volunteered. "Careful control of information," she said. "The TV system in the bunkhouse is . . . it's on a loop. Just cycling through a very selective smattering of images and ideas."

"Yeah, but they had to be convinced to come here." All of them looked out at the lake, the water reflecting a vivid blue sky. Now that the gunfire had subsided, the occasional chirping of a bird began to echo through the air. Nora could tell that the others had had similar thoughts: the nearly surreal beauty of the place had been violated.

Ford said slowly, "Easy enough to recruit from survivalist fairs and through Internet campaigns and gun rallies. The pictures on their site are showing otherwise marginalized people taking power with their own hands. Before the election, the rural poor were feeling weak and exhausted, disenfranchised. On the right day, in the right circumstances, all this white power stuff is going to look good. Blaming someone else for your woes is going to feel good. Easy enough to recruit your sister or your out-of-work neighbor." He paused as he looked down at the spot where Sheila died. "Or your wife."

They all paused again, the stillness amplifying the crash of the waves down below. The acrid scent of the tear gas hung over the rather wilted group of Patriots now sitting bound on the lawn.

"Pretty scrappy of Mrs. Baker, really. Picking a fight with the feds when she had fifty guns pointed at her," Ben said.

"She knew exactly what she was doing and she went for it," Chid said. "There'll be ballads written about her, don't you doubt it for a minute."

They walked on in silence.

"I should have known, really. I should have seen it coming. Brünnhilde rides her horse up onto her husband's funeral pyre after all."

"Really?" Derek asked. "Committed—what's that Hindu thing?"

"Sati. Not just for pious Indian brides," Chid said. "Still, that woman would have been rather a repellent Brünnhilde, I have to say, Amazon warrior though she fancied herself. Brünnhilde is a good sort in the operas. Motivated by love more than not."

"I'm not seeing it in Carly Baker," averred Nora. "She didn't even love her kids enough to keep them out of this mess."

"Yes, well, and their dad, our poor would-be Siegfried," he added, surveying the scene before them, "is apparently only *mostly* dead."

The ambulance had stopped just south of the barn. Schacht was already crouched over Gabriel Baker. Pete sat dangling his legs over the back edge of the ambulance; the EMS tech had given him his first food in two days and he was devouring a granola bar as he watched the interrogation.

"First, where is Martin?" they heard Schacht ask.

Gabe Baker only shook his head. His eyes, bloodshot and still streaming from the tear gas, scanned the cloudless sky.

"I bet," Chid added, "that our Mr. Martin is buying season tickets for the Canadian Opera Company right about now."

Anna shook her head, "Well if he is, he's doing it online because no boats left this compound. The coast guard was in place since you called it in."

Schacht turned to Baker. "Where is he, goddammit," shouted Schacht. Nora looked at him. She hadn't seen Schacht lose his cool before, not ever. Then again, she had also never seen him wounded, nor had she seen him watch a supervisory special agent and a CIRG director die.

Baker shook his head and coughed up blood, making the agents squirm out of the way. "I will never give him up. Never."

Anna sighed and then looked at Chid and Nora. "Who's gonna tell this asshole?"

Chid raised his hand. "I'm the brownest. It should be me." Without waiting for general acquiescence, he plowed right in. "Your fearless leader was using you, brother. You know that judge you killed for him? Hand-picked for having wrecked his business. You know the nice city councilwoman you kidnapped and shot? Wicked woman wouldn't fund his mini-mall. You know all that money you stole? Went into his pocket for his big getaway. He used you. He took advantage of your racism and your hatred and he put you to work . . . *for him*."

Baker closed his eyes.

He had to know it was true. He had to have had suspicions, Nora thought, watching the man carefully.

Schacht signaled to the EMS techs. They began the work of maneuvering Baker onto the stretcher.

Then Schacht continued addressing him. "You don't get to die, see?" Schacht said. "You get to stand up and talk to your followers and tell them that you were all victims of an epic manipulation. And then you get to call them off. And you get to apologize and you get to go to jail and stay there."

Baker was shaking his head ever so slightly.

"Why did he make *you* the voice of the movement, Gabe?" Chid pressed. "Real leaders take on the Man, take on the government, don't they? Don't you think it was so he could keep hiding? Even after you were dead and gone?"

Nora nodded, meeting Chid's eyes. "Baker was fearless. So Martin dressed him up as the hero, conferred the power on him."

"Knowing all along that Valhalla would burn," Chid said. "Yes."

"Where did he go?" Schacht asked, softly this time but no less menacingly.

Baker was silent, his eyes still shut. Nora began to worry he had died, but she watched his chest rise and fall. Finally he opened his eyes and looked at Chid. "He headed out the night the little black agent ran off."

Nora realized once again that this meant her. She leaned in. "Who're you calling *little,* asshole?"

Baker began to cough, arching his back, his face wracked with effort. Finally he managed to say, "He knew he had to get somewhere safe so he could still run things. Until it was all finished. He took the occupiers with him."

"Where?" Schacht demanded a third time.

"Where else?" Baker retorted. "The brewery."

"Why?" Anna said. "He must have known we'd have it under surveillance."

"Really?" Baker asked, his voice a low gurgling sound, yet still filled with contempt. "Even if you finally figured it out, you were still going to be putting out a thousand fires. You got time for watching an abandoned building?"

"He must have had something there," Chid concluded. "Something he needed before getting away. Was it the money?"

Gabriel Baker was silent; his eyes had shut again.

Schacht, frustrated, sprang up and cornered the EMS tech. He gave her a fierce look. "You will do everything in your power to keep this man alive, you got it?"

The technician raised her eyebrows and then, wordlessly, she and her partner lifted the stretcher into the ambulance.

Schacht turned back to them. "I know we're all tired, but Anna and Ford, I want you here to help me deal with the fallout from all this now that we've lost Sheila and Sanchez. Nora, Chid, Ben, you head to the brewery. Intercept Martin. See how it is that he's still conducting operations and see if our victory here means he's headed for Canada by now."

"He's got too much of a head start," protested Nora.

"Well, lucky for you Anna has Vance Evans on speed dial," Schacht retorted. He pointed a finger at the sky. "Hitch a ride."

The NBC chopper had maneuvered down onto the stretch of land just beyond where the SWAT helicopter had crashed. Still, to reach it, Nora, Ben, and Chid had to skirt the charred wreckage of the downed CIRG helicopter. She tried not to look, determined now to keep her composure.

She gazed at the ongoing activity of the compound. Photographers were wading through the weeds, recording every inch. The coroner was there with his ominous black truck. Emergency medical services were aiding in pulling bodies out of the barns. The helicopters hung above, throwing an impossibly blue morning sky into a confusion of glinting metal and sound. Their rotors sliced through the hot summer air, now drowning the rhythm of the waves below.

Ben hated Vance Evans instantly and viscerally. Nora watched it happen as they settled into the chopper and then solidify as they flew into Erie.

Vance was shouting at them over the roar of the helicopter's blades. "So that was a mess, huh?"

Each of the agents looked at him without replying.

"Messy week, I'd say. But it's made for some fascinating journalism."

Each looked at him in disgust.

"Never had so many opportunities to bring the story to the people," he said. "I feel like a man who's sitting on the cusp of history here."

Nora waited for Chid to hit him with a one-liner in the way that only Chid seemed able to do, but even Chid only looked at the man in silence.

Anna had told Vance to have his pilot land them atop the building that housed their office. They couldn't risk him putting them down at the brewery itself and obliterating the element of surprise, or, worse, letting the viewing public know what they were up to. As soon as they'd made their way into the building they bolted down the stairs to the parking garage and into Chid's rental van.

He peeled out of the parking garage and barreled up State Street. It was not a difficult trip as the streets now had become largely deserted.

The brewery sat on the corner of 21st and State Streets. Its smokestack soared into the air, making it the tallest structure for many blocks. Windows were boarded up in places and broken in others. Bold, intricate swaths of graffiti told tales of teen artists attempting to outdo each other in scope and creativity. Nora was most impressed with the *Viva Che* inscription that included a striking six-foot likeness of the fallen leader's face. In several places, small piles of red bricks lay at the base of the massive structure where they had fallen from the wall. A giant advertising mural had been painted onto the brick and now was flaking off. Enough of it remained that the message was legible, however.

"What does that even mean, 'Known for the collar it keeps'?" Nora asked. "What do beers have to do with collars?"

"The collar is the foamy part of the beer on the top," Ben replied. "Clearly your friend Pete needs to educate you better."

"Yes, well, he's having a rough week," Nora said.

"Aren't we all," Chid interjected, pulling swiftly into the parking lot.

"Anna was going to call for backup as we were leaving," Nora answered.

"Well no one's made it."

"Everyone is still at the compound. They'll get here," Ben said, evidencing an optimism Nora was sure he didn't really possess.

They forced open the wide front doors with a crowbar from the back of the minivan.

"Vests?" Nora asked.

They both nodded.

They all drew their handguns and stepped slowly into the cavernous building. They were assaulted by the smell of decay. It was hot, hotter than Nora expected, and she immediately felt as though she had to struggle for breath. She felt a creeping panic as her eyes fought the dimness to make out shapes and forms. How could they search fifteen thousand square feet? What if they were wrong and Martin was long gone?

They all exchanged looks and then began to fan out across the vast brewery floor.

Rats darted as they walked. But this part of the brewery had not sat idle. The floor was scuffed, and long black marks were visible in the dimness.

"People have parked motorcycles here," Ben said. "Right here on the floor."

"Not only that," said Chid. "Look."

There were massive piles of what looked like sandbags interspersed with 55-gallon drums lining the retaining walls. Chid walked over, gave a long, soft whistle, and then looked back to Nora and Ben. "Ammonium nitrate and what seems to be nitromethane . . . and drums of gasoline. It looks like there's a ton of it, give or take."

Their eyes scanned the room and they saw that he was right.

"Where are we in the program today?" asked Nora.

"Hmm?" asked Chid.

"Well, we just had Sheila and Sanchez for the Prologue and the chopper for Act One and then, well, I guess we saw Valhalla burn, right? Except we used restraint and didn't burn it for them even though they double crossed us. So what's left?"

Chid looked thoughtful in the dimness as his eyes took in the vastness of the old brewery. She could see he was imagining it filled with workers and the smell of brewing beer.

Nora laid a hand on Chid's arm. "Is he planning on dying in the end? It's all I want to know."

Chid's voice was mild. "No, probably not. He stole a ton of money. His model for the global race war is in place, which, again, I don't think he thinks has any hope of success, particularly since we were able to thwart at least parts of it. But he's given something to his minions—he's handed them martyrs like Carly Baker, if nothing else, and that will sustain the mayhem for the foreseeable future. And now . . . now it makes sense to me that he'd try to get out."

"Get out?"

"Yes, but, Nora . . . you're right about something." Chid did not look at her as he spoke. Rather his eyes scanned the piles of chemicals set against the soaring brick walls. "The compound didn't burn, and I bet he could have seen that coming. Was Act Two stabbing Siegfried in the back, the final betrayal of Baker? Because it looks like *this* is his Valhalla, his final act."

Ben listened, considering. "This is the one thing that Martin got out of the estate, isn't it? The brewery?"

"Yes," Chid answered. "If it burns . . . if we can't establish that Martin and Geyer are one, he'll get the insurance money."

Nora nodded. "I see. I see."

They turned their eyes upward. All three of them saw it at the same time. A faint light was coming from under the doorframe high above the brewery floor. They scanned the vast room for the stairway and then found a wobbly metal staircase at the north end.

"Can we get there without him hearing us?"

"He has to know we're here already, Nora. This place is surely wired. Look." Indeed, he motioned to two different corners and the contours of two different video cameras sharpened for Nora's eyes as they adjusted to the dimness.

She turned to Ben. "We have to catch him. To take him alive," she said.

"Let's try, then," he said. "He's an old guy. We're young and spry."

"Should we split up?" Chid asked.

"If we had backup I'd say yes," said Ben. "Better to stay together. There's just too much real estate here."

They began maneuvering their way up the staircase. It was precarious but not impossible, and they all soon arrived, winded, at the slim landing that overlooked the brewery floor.

Ben readied his gun, then extended his hand and rested his fingertips on the door handle.

"On my count," he said. "Three, two, one—"

And with that he shoved the door open and burst into the room, Nora and Chid hard on his heels.

The small room was empty. Elegant but empty.

It was about twelve feet by twenty, and lined with framed prints of masterpieces. It had a slick, gleaming hardwood floor and an antique desk atop which was a sleek computer system. Its two monitors were black and still. Soft strains of music filled the room. A porcelain espresso cup sat on a coaster.

Chid reached out and touched it. "Still warm," he whispered.

Nora looked desperately around. "Where did he go?"

It would have been impossible for him to have descended the rickety staircase since their entrance. They started exploring the room seeking another way out.

"Do you think he's gonna try to blow this place up with us in it?" Nora asked.

"I didn't until you brought it up," said Chid. "But now I'm pretty sure he is." He peered behind one of the prints. Then he looked back at them with a grin.

"What?" asked Ben.

"If I were hiding a secret exit, I'd definitely put it behind my Klimt." He slid the painting aside to expose a door handle. A few moments later the painting slid back on its own to hide the handle again.

"Jesus," Ben said.

"Shall we?" Chid asked, pushing open the door.

"Getting away from the ammonium nitrate sounds pretty good," Ben said.

The spiral staircase was of old and worn stone. It was dark and led down into pitch darkness. Nora sighed. They all whipped out their phones and turned on the light app.

"If he's trying to get away, it's going to be through that tunnel," Ben said.

Chid was nodding. "I'm betting this is leading straight there."

They followed him down for what seemed to Nora like miles in the close, musty stairway. Finally they made it to a door. The door opened onto a long corridor, the dark corners of which were dense with spiderwebs. The graffiti artists had broken in at some point. It couldn't have been hard, she thought, given the porous nature of the building, with its broken windows and webs of fire escapes. To Nora, it seemed as though the scurrying of rats was a constant, dark undertone. She tried to squelch the desire to bolt, and cast an eye back at Ben for courage.

He winked at her.

"Who winks at anybody anymore?" she whispered.

"I'm old school. Should I have flipped you off?"

"*Rude*." She looked around. "Is this the part where you start saying, 'Okay gang, let's build a trap?'"

"I can't," he whispered. "Forgot my ascot."

Chid paused at a low-hanging EXIT sign, long since burnt out, its plastic broken in one corner. He pushed open the door and they saw that it led to a long ramp that zig-zagged downward into pitch blackness.

Nora swallowed and felt her free hand reach for Ben. He squeezed her hand quickly, then stepped aside so she could follow the other three.

The basement was filthier than the brewery floor above, and harder to breathe in. The three walked cautiously through the darkness, picking their way across the floor as quickly as they could. Chid finally stopped in front of large wooden doors.

"Some of those fancy night-vision goggles would have come in handy right about now," Chid murmured.

"Or any backup. Any backup at all," added Nora.

"Or X-wings from Red Squadron," said Ben.

The right side of the door was on a runner, and Nora saw, as the flashlight beams moved over it, that it was designed to slide open. Chid yanked on the door handle and it began to move. When he had slid it all the way open, he peered in and then back at them.

"What do you think? He may still be upstairs, waiting for the right moment to ignite all those bags."

"Or he may have realized that hanging around to enact his vision will mean not getting away with the money," Ben said. "If I were him, I'd take the robbery money and cut my losses for this place. No matter how dramatic my dramatic flair might be."

Chid considered this, then nodded. "I agree. Let's go." He

poked his head through the door, then shone his flashlight app into the darkness. "Looks like there's a minecart of some sort. . . ."

Nora straightened her back and moved to follow when the sound of a gunshot exploded through the quiet.

"Chid!" she cried.

And suddenly Ben was pulling him back into the basement. Nora and Ben tugged on him, and Nora then leaned hard against the door, closing it again, as two more shots sent shards of wood flying through the air.

Chid was gasping in pain. Blood gushed down his arm from the shoulder wound; his pale pink Oxford shirt was immediately saturated.

"Chid! Chid . . ." Her hands soaked, Nora looked about desperately for anything to stanch the flow.

"Fucking rifles," croaked Chid. "That's gonna leave a mark."

Ben was wiggling out of his Kevlar vest and then ripped off his own shirt and used it as a tourniquet around Chid's shoulder. Chid was grunting in pain, his face gray under the beam from Nora's light.

"I'll call whoever is left to call—and get some EMS help. Where does this tunnel come out?" Ben demanded of Nora.

"Waterworks."

"I'll try to get someone to that side, too. But you have to get started—Nora, he *can't* get away." Nora was nodding, watching as Ben cradled Chid's head, trying to keep him from fainting.

"Peek through the bullet holes in the door, Nora. Shine your light—Check to see if the minecart Chid saw is still there."

She did so and then turned to him grimly. "No."

Ben looked at Nora and spoke very rapidly, his right hand grasping her shoulder hard. "He has a head start and firepower."

"Go on, I'll be fine," Chid rasped.

"Just give me a second," Ben said, ignoring Chid. "Get a head start, but look: you need me this time, don't go it alone."

Nora was nodding, attempting to rise, but Ben sank his fingers deeper into her shoulder. "We have to take him alive, Nora. Otherwise his cause will martyr him. We have to expose him as a fraud. If you do shoot, you shoot from a safe distance and you aim for a leg."

She nodded again, and jumped up, sliding open the door carefully. She and Ben exchanged looks.

"I'll be there as soon as I can," he said. He had already keyed 9-1-1 into his phone and they both heard the answering voice.

Nora shone her light down the tunnel and plunged ahead. She refused to say a parting word to Ben or to even look at him so as not to weaken her resolve. Soon she was rocketing through the dark tunnel, ears tracking the sound of the minecart far ahead.

The ground was uneven and made for rough going, with its challenging pattern of metal tracks and wooden planks. But she had worn the right shoes. And it was a radically different trip down this tunnel than the last time. She recalled the slow gait of the man guiding her along, her wrists tied behind her back, Pete limping painfully in front of her. She found a burst of speed at the memory, outraged anew over their abduction.

Sweat poured down her back and into her eyes. The humidity in the tunnel was almost intolerable and she quickly found herself gasping, wishing she had stopped to drink something at some point along the way.

There's a lake at the end of this thing.

Plenty of water . . .

He would have a boat, she knew. There would be a boat waiting. Would there be someone in it, she wondered? Or had they all been left to fight the battle at the compound?

She urged herself on. *I have to get there before he gets to the boat. God, I hate boats. . . .*

And then she saw a glint of metal ahead, and the minecart came into view. Empty.

Her steps slowed. She shone her light on the contours of the closed door in front of her.

She cast a glance behind her, but Ben was not yet close. She pressed her ear against the door and heard the unmistakable rumble of a speedboat engine.

She pulled gently at the door and found it did not move, so she tugged harder. It moved ever so slightly. The crack she'd made allowed for light to pierce the tunnel's darkness, illuminating the way for Ben, she hoped. She peered out through the crack and saw Martin heaving a backpack into the forward berth of the same speedboat that had carried her and Pete to the compound. He was smaller than she'd imagined. His hair was white and rather wispy. He was struggling with the heavy pack, and his shirt was sweat-stained.

There was no one else on the boat.

Nora spied another backpack on the cement, waiting to be hauled onto the boat.

Clear shot, safe distance. She aimed her gun through the crack in the door, preparing to fire. She inhaled, steadying herself.

At that moment the door to the tunnel was kicked open, and Nora was sent sprawling backwards, her gun skittering away. She expected gunshots and rolled behind the minecart. Immediately the minecart was shoved backwards and scooted several feet, exposing her. No shots were fired. It was Goatee, advancing on her, hands outstretched.

Why isn't he shooting at me? she asked herself.

All she could think of was that they didn't want to draw attention in broad daylight to the boat that was trying to escape. She tried to glimpse her gun, but it was lost in shadow. She pulled herself rapidly into a defensive position.

Where's Ben?

Goatee lunged, and Nora darted left, just out of reach of his huge arm. As she did so, she launched an uppercut into his throat. He clutched at his throat, enraged, and whirled on her. He threw a vicious punch into her midriff that knocked her against the door, slamming it shut again and throwing the tunnel back into darkness. She felt him hurtling toward her and she ducked, allowing him to crash against the door face-first.

As she came around behind him, she planted her left foot and unleashed several front kicks to his back, hoping to find his spinal column. She could see nothing but felt her right foot connect with a satisfying thud.

Goatee let out a loud groan just as Ben dashed around the corner. The light from his phone showed them that Goatee had collapsed on the floor of the tunnel.

Ben skidded to a halt. "What did I say?" he demanded, looking from her to the huge man.

"Help me pull him aside," Nora panted. "Martin's getting away!"

They yanked at Goatee and shoved him aside, Ben giving him a solid kick for good measure.

Indeed, Martin had pulled the last backpack into the boat. The moorings were untied and he was pulling away from the concealed dock.

"No!" Nora howled.

But Ben surprised her by running out of the tunnel and flinging himself from the dock toward the boat. It was just beyond his reach—he connected, but then slid down its fiberglass side. He had fallen almost totally into the water when his fingers caught on the small aluminum ladder attached to the back of the boat. As Martin slammed the throttle into high gear, attempting to shake him, Ben got both hands onto the ladder and began hauling himself into the boat.

Nora watched in horror as Martin pulled his rifle from over

the dashboard. "No!" she shouted again, overcome by her powerlessness.

Ben had pulled himself into the boat, soaking, and just as Martin was taking aim, Ben tackled him, pinning him and slamming his head onto the boat's hydroturf flooring. Gathering the older man's wrists together, he shoved the rifle out of reach. From his position on the floor, he groped around the driver's console; he felt for and found the throttle of the boat. Still holding Martin's wrists with his left hand, with his right hand he yanked the throttle to the idle position.

The boat came to rest in the calm blue water. Ben, sitting now atop Martin to keep him immobilized, looked back at Nora, chest heaving, as a cascade of sirens sluiced across the afternoon air.

Will Martin was slim and wiry. His eyes were as keen and penetrating as Chid's, Nora thought. Sharp. She watched him with trepidation as Ben tugged him off the now-docked boat. Squad car doors slammed from not far off.

Martin stood on the dock, his chest rising and falling. She saw that he was attempting composure. But he was also scared. Cornered. His gaze fell fully upon her, and she felt herself cringe.

"Ah, the plucky young escape artist, isn't it?" he said. When he spoke, Nora heard every consonant. His words came out slowly, thoughtfully. Nothing about Will Martin seemed hurried or without calculation.

She said nothing, only observed him, knowing that her curiosity about him was evident on her features.

"Do you think by capturing me that you can end this?" he asked her. His eyes were blue and very, very clear.

Ben interrupted. "I did mention already that you have the right to remain silent. . . ."

Martin smiled the smile of a benevolent grandfather. "But

that would prevent me from encouraging you to solve the next riddle."

Nora felt her whole body tense. "What do you mean next?"

Six police officers, led by Mike Szymanowski, were barreling down the steep incline from the Waterworks parking lot. Ben, lacking a vehicle, was about to hand Martin over to them.

"Wait," hissed Nora. "What do you mean *next*?"

Martin regarded her with his penetrating blue eyes. "Surely you do not think that this anticlimactic moment could be a suitable end to our interactions?"

The slow elegance of his diction made Nora's blood boil. Her own words tumbled out faster than ever in order to make up for his deliberateness. "What kind of end did you have in mind then?"

"The countdown began when you stumbled into my brewery," Martin said. He inhaled deeply, looking around at the cloudless sky and the softly pulsing water. After a long pause, he returned his gaze to her with a rueful smile. "Nothing remote anymore, we learned that lesson. Tick-tock."

Ben and Nora exchanged panicked looks.

"Haven't you done enough? Isn't it enough? *Call him off.*"

Martin looked at her, almost tenderly. "Oh I assure you that that is quite impossible at this point. But fear not, if you prove yourselves worthy you still might head off this final event and thwart the Fates."

Nora leaned in. "We all know that *you* are the Fates in all this. So call it off."

Martin threw back his head and laughed out loud. "Shrewd!" he said at last. "It would seem that I am indeed."

"Then register how worthy we are and call off the event yourself," Ben interjected, shaking his charge's arm ever so slightly.

"There's no drama in that, is there? No chance for heroism in a world begging for heroes." He leaned toward Nora. "Come, little negress. I'm giving you the opportunity of a lifetime. There are enough explosives in my brewery to decimate three city blocks. Think of all the precious white lives you could save. . . . It intrigued me that you sorted out the last code. This one is much harder." He tilted his head and looked at Nora, assessing her curiously. Then he said wryly, "You've been busy this week. . . ."

She regarded him with blazing eyes. "Who says *negress* anymore?"

". . . subverting my plans."

"I wasn't alone."

"Oh, believe me, this is evident. Pity we had to kill your little Indian friend. I'll admit he performed admirably, even for a homosexual. I have been watching."

"Yeah, I bet you have. Do you know we found out that you're a calculating bastard just using your little punk racist friends for your own agenda? You could care less about race war."

Martin laughed out loud. "What do I care about then?"

Nora narrowed her eyes. "Not Gabriel Baker and his agenda. Not angry laid off 'uncultured workers.' Not alt-right bullshit. You want your lifestyle and the means to keep it."

Martin laughed again. The fear in his eyes had vanished, and Nora was starting to think he was actually enjoying himself. "Maybe so. You know the old adage about fools and their money. . . ."

"You preyed on them," Ben said, tilting his head.

Martin shrugged. "They wanted to be preyed on. They thought they had finally found a leader who would raise their flag, but his own incompetence kept him from effectively keeping his promises."

"So you stepped in. All the funds they'd amassed gearing up for civil war . . ."

"Had to go somewhere. Better me than . . . well. Would it have been better to send it all to David Duke?"

"No, he'd have been far less creative," Nora spat.

Martin again laughed loudly. "See? You do understand. Life is art is performance."

"Okay, maestro. You didn't lose your nerve this time. Nice work."

Now it was he who narrowed his eyes, assessing her, realizing they knew him better than he had anticipated. "Well. Since you know my motives so well, then, you'll surely appreciate the one of redemption. A coda, if you will, to all that came before."

"This isn't a game *or* an operatic drama. You've done enough. Just tell us how to defuse it," Nora demanded.

Martin looked on placidly.

Mike Szymanowski looked at Ben and Nora, clearly unsure as to what to do. "I can leave you four officers for backup. What do you need?"

Nora didn't take her eyes off Martin. "Call Abe. Have him meet us at the brewery with his crew."

Martin's face was impassive, if slightly bemused.

Nora's frustration surged.

"You have to come with us," she demanded, bringing her face close to his. When he refused to respond, she said, "Mike, you have to just march him up this tunnel with us. He has to tell us where the trigger mechanism is and how to defuse it."

She hated the pleading sound of her voice.

Martin seemed to love it, though. A slow smile spread across his face. "Why would I do something like that? If you want the Ring, cursed as it is, you'll have to earn it. Apparently the plebeians did not deserve it enough to keep it. Then again, the mass destruction really was Baker's angle. I merely provided the packaging."

They all exchanged glances and then knew for certain that there could be no more discussion. Mike and Ben each yanked one of Martin's arms, pulling him forward. Nora trailed behind, and they started pulling him toward the tunnel.

They had not gone ten steps when they heard a crack.

Nora looked up and was stunned to see Goatee, body half hidden by the door to the tunnel. As he retreated behind the door, he dropped his weapon, which clattered onto the cement. They all drew their guns in a single breath. As Martin crumpled, the door to the tunnel swung shut once more.

Nora gasped, blinking, unsure she had seen what she'd seen. "What? No!" she shouted, crouching over Martin.

Martin had not even emitted a sound; Mike and Ben raced to the tunnel door, but the heavy lock had been slammed back into place.

Mike and Ben stepped back from the door, pelting it with bullets until the handle shattered and they could burst through.

Ben met Nora's eyes. "He's dead," she said hoarsely. "Minecart?"

He shook his head. Swiftly he picked up the discarded gun and opened the chamber. "Empty."

"That's why he didn't shoot at me. He was saving the last bullet in case Martin was caught," Nora said. She took a deep breath. "Back up the tunnel."

Ben instructed two of the pairs of officers to drive to the brewery and meet them, while the other was to accompany them on foot with Mike.

They raced along in silence for a while, Ben and Nora in the lead, the other two struggling to keep up. The small beams of light from the officers' flashlights seemed to nip at the agents' heels as they ran. Nora's desperation had left her utterly without words.

"You think a bomb could go off overhead any minute?" Ben asked Nora breathlessly.

She refused to answer that. "I'm so angry at that coward. I wanted him to go to prison so bad."

"It was never possible. Somebody like that isn't going to be caught, Nora. It's just not possible. If one of his followers hadn't killed him, and I'm sure that guy was following Martin's own instructions, he would have killed himself. There's no risotto in prison."

She felt herself running a little faster. "And yet he's left us a puzzle to solve. Maybe we can solve it. Prove ourselves worthy."

"Or maybe we'll die," Ben said.

"Maybe so."

"I really didn't want to die in *Erie*."

"Oh, come on, Benjamin," panted Nora. "Any fool can die in Philadelphia."

The EMTs had Chid on a stretcher when Ben and Nora reached the end of the tunnel. They were just attempting to wrestle him up the ramp and into the hall that ran underneath the brewing floor.

"Wait," Nora called. "We need him."

"Miss, he's lost a lot of blood," the EMT protested.

"Well, stick some back in him," Ben demanded.

Chid struggled to look at them. "What's going on? Martin?"

"Shot through the head," Ben said.

"Did you see a goateed guy pass by here?" Nora demanded.

Chid gave a gray-faced nod. "Yes. Rather huge and sweaty. I heard the minecart coming and played a very convincing corpse."

"Martin triggered the fuse before they left his office," Ben said. "Another puzzle."

The trio of EMTs suddenly looked at Nora and Ben in a distinctly less tolerant way. "We need to get out of here *now*," said the ponytailed woman.

"You'll get me some First Aid and get me upstairs," Chid said in his most commanding voice. "And *then* you can go."

The entire group began running through the dark hallways.

"It's not supposed to be remote this time so maybe that means there's no computer. We just have to find the trigger mechanism and talk it down."

"And we think there's a possibility we can do that *why*?" Chid demanded.

"Because the bad guy suggested we might be able to prove ourselves worthy and subvert the Fates," Nora called back.

"Holy Christ," Chid said. "Well that's tweaking the narrative in a radical way."

Ramp after ramp led them at last to the brewery floor once again. As the EMTs set the stretcher down, the front doors of the brewery burst open and Abe entered, panting, sweaty, half of his bomb suit on. He looked at them and called out, "Alright people, what's the story?"

"Shhh," said Ben. "You'll scare the ammonium nitrate."

"Again with this shit?" Abe demanded. "When can we get a real bomb up in here?"

"Probably when the bombers aren't angry agrarians," Chid spouted a bit weakly. Two of the EMTs had already left. One stood nervously by his stretcher. "Can't you just get me a bag of glucose? Anything?"

"You need to come to the ambulance, sir."

"Go to the ambulance, Chid; just keep your phone on speaker," Nora said.

"Oh for fuck's sake . . . I'm gonna need a laptop and someone to help me type."

Ben stared at Nora. "You go."

"No way. You."

He shook his head. "Nora, I'm serious."

"And so am I. I was there when we sorted out the last one. I can help."

"You all need to get out of here right now," Abe warned.

"No, it's a *thing*, Abe," Nora insisted. "He left us something to solve. Like last time. Only harder, he said."

"Sounds like he's fucking with you. The last one was to *trigger*. He's suggesting this one can be *defused*?"

"He's dead," Ben interjected. "But yeah, it seemed pretty clear."

Abe shook his head. "What does he gain?"

"Chance to see us sweat again. Even from down in hell," volunteered Chid as the EMT wheeled him out. "Ben, I need you now," he called weakly, making the decision for them.

Ben frowned and followed the stretcher.

Nora swallowed, then answered Abe.

"A chance at . . . what? Restitution? Redemption? In not blowing up his hometown?"

Abe looked at her askance. "Either way, sounds risky. Where's this office?"

Nora pointed up at the wobbly metal staircase.

"He's going to have hooked up a small detonator to a respectable pile of dynamite; if all the gasoline drums are down here, they will be connected to the detonator by a long wire." He began circling the wide interior of the brewery floor.

"Here," he finally called, crouching in the northwest corner. He peered at the wire snaking upward along the brick interior wall toward the office, then at Nora.

She let out a low whistle. "I can't believe we didn't see it the first time."

He brushed this off and gave her a piercing look. "I'm going up now. You need to go. I only have one suit. Go now—or wait, open videochat with Chid and leave me your phone. Then go."

"But Abe, I—"

Abe wasn't interested in discussion. He hissed something at her in Bosnian, then wrestled the phone from her hand even as she obediently punched in the commands. Nora swallowed, then gave him a small pat before running for the ambulance. Before exiting the brewery, she paused to see him leaping onto the metal staircase and making his way toward the office. Given his bomb suit, it was an awkward undertaking.

Nora dashed for the ambulance. As she entered, she was re-

lieved to see that the phone connection between Chid and Abe
was solid.

They heard Chid's voice coming through the speaker. "What's
it look like?"

Abe was saying, "It looks like the last one, only it has a small
screen attached to it and a keypad. Can you see it?" he asked,
holding up the phone to show them the small screen. "There's
eight spaces here. Eight individual lines."

"Okay, so it was just . . . six last time," Chid protested. "You
wanna argue or solve it?"

Chid cursed and then hissed something at the EMS people.

Abe's voice was over-loud: "The screen is compact. It isn't going
to take a manifesto. Just . . . yeah, it looks like short words or nu-
merical sequences, each separated by a hyphen. Two of the lines
are just one space. The rest are one space before a hyphen and
four spaces. . . ." Abe's voice trailed off.

Chid was silent, confused. "Let's do that again but in sequence,"
he said.

Abe said through gritted teeth, "Space-hyphen-four spaces.
Single space. Space-hyphen-four spaces. Three times. Single space
again. And then twice more: space-hyphen-four spaces." He
positioned it so they could see:

                         -
                        _ _ _ _ _

                         _

                         -
                        _ _ _ _ _

                         -
                        _ _ _ _ _

                         -
                        _ _ _ _ _

—

\-
— — — —

\-
— — — —

Nora watched Chid's chest rising and falling rapidly.

"Ok, so it isn't WWV numbers again," he said finally, softly, speaking swiftly to himself. "Right—it would be the opposite. The four spaces would be in the front not the back. . . . What about Götterdämmerung . . . Cast members? Scene numbers?"

Ben took to typing various searches into the laptop, opening new tabs for every topic Chid hissed at him.

Chid turned to Nora with a manic look. "What did he say to you? Tell me everything he said!"

"Ummmmm . . . He said it was a chance to be a hero. Save lives. A . . . what? A code to what came before."

"Coda," Ben corrected sharply. "He said coda."

"Coda?! Are you sure?" Chid demanded.

Nora shrugged. "What's a coda?"

"Musical afterthought—a sort of a summary to a piece of music, announcing its conclusion."

He began muttering again to himself. "Measures? No, they'd all be in the thousands. . . . Key signatures . . . ?"

Nora looked at Abe through the phone's small screen. "If we plug in something that's incorrect, will it backfire or trigger or something?"

"We won't know until we try," Abe said.

"*Nora!*" Chid's voice was even sharper now. "What else did he say?"

His voice was a tumble of rapid words. "—The coda . . . the coda . . . I need a score, call up a PDF of the score. Just type in *full orchestral score*. No, you don't need the umlauts. . . . See if you can find a numbered one," he directed Ben. Then he looked at Nora fiercely. "What else did he say? Think!"

She thought. "Something about . . . *Zift*. He said, if we wanted the Ring we'd have to earn it."

Chid nodded distractedly, frowning hard at the computer screen.

"He said we understood his motives . . . something about the motive of redemption . . ."

He whipped his head around to look at her. "What?"

"We were saying that we thought we knew what he cared about. He said we understood his motives . . . and something about redemption. Motive of redemption."

"Ben, come on, open the PDF!"

"Okay, okay!" Ben snapped. "I'm opening it. . . ."

"Scroll down, scroll down!" Chid shouted.

"Jesus, I'm scrolling down. . . . God, it's . . ."

"*Goddamn, it's long.* Yes, we all know that one." Chid didn't stop frowning at the screen.

"Okay, umm, okay, so it ends in D-flat major. Motives . . . motives . . ." Chid looked wildly around for a pen and paper and started snarling at the EMS tech. "Just—just give me the one you're using, Jesus Christ!" he cried, stretching his hand toward the ponytailed woman who had been so eager to flee the brewery.

She gave him a furious look, then handed over her pen and a notepad.

He did not immediately write anything, but instead started rubbing his head as though to extract information from his brain as he muttered "*Newman, Newman, Newman.*"

Nora and Ben stared at each other.

"Okay," he said at last, talking so rapidly and so softly that Nora could barely follow. "Newman wrote on leitmotifs, or motives— recurring musical themes—in Wagner's operas. There are a couple in the coda. Majesty of the gods, Siegfried's horn theme . . . and the theme of redemptive love that *challenges* the gods . . . and usurps their plans!"

Nora felt her breath catch. "You're telling me he might have picked *that*?"

"A coda code. Notes in a leitmotif. That theme, and it first comes in *Walküre* where Brünnhilde imperils herself to save innocent lives, is . . ." he stopped and hummed softly to himself . . . "eight notes long. And it's here then in the opera's end, see? Like . . . a palliative. The last thing we hear, the thing that Wagner leaves us with, even if he's been screwing us around for a total of sixteen hours or something."

Nora swallowed a thousand responses and contented herself with just frowning at Chid.

He himself was looking quite pleased. "Yeah. I like it. So I think Geyer would. Or Martin. Whoever."

"Because you're both evil genius types?"

A smile flickered across Chid's face as he directed Ben where to stop the cursor.

Nora pressed him. "What does he gain?"

Chid shrugged. "Well, maybe he's just doing what he was supposed to do. We're just the Rhinemaidens getting our Ring back. Power is back with the little people again. For the moment."

Nora inhaled doubtfully, holding Ben's equally doubtful gaze. "He said we'd only get it back if we prove ourselves worthy. Is you reading music what makes us worthy?"

He shrugged. "Respecting the universal language? At the least makes beauty accessible. Now, eight lines?" Chid said, his eyes riveted on the score before him.

"Eight lines," she confirmed.

"Oh . . ." He slumped onto the pillow.

"What?!" Nora and Ben chorused.

"Fuck . . . This is ten notes. . . ."

Their faces fell.

"Oh, no! Nevermind. I'm fucking right as always." He grinned at them.

"What?" Ben asked. "What just happened?"

"It's really *ten* notes. Two are *tied* though, so written, not played. We only hear eight."

In wobbly script, he wrote down the names of eight notes, then turned the paper to face the phone screen. "Can you see it? Abe?"

Abe removed his gloves and began typing on the small console. Chid read them aloud for good measure:

D-flat.

C.

D-flat.

E-flat.

D-flat.

C.

D-flat.

E-flat.

As Abe was entering them, Chid said, "That last E-flat is down an octave, but I don't see any way to designate that. . . ."

Nora thought she could see Abe's nostrils flare, but he did not comment. When he had finished, he glanced at them through the screen.

Then he looked back at the console. Nothing happened.

Nora found and held Ben's worried gaze.

Then Abe sat back on his heels and grinned at them. "Nothing happening means the world didn't just end. Nice work, kids."

With that, he detached the fuse, which sat, utterly mute, atop its small pyre of dynamite.

EPILOGUE

"**There she goes again**," **Ben said,** looking up through the ceiling. He zipped his suitcase closed and slipped into his shoes.

"She said she's got some kind of audition," Nora said.

"Got it."

"I can't believe you're going already," Nora said, staring at Ben's SUV. "You should wait around for the mayor's ceremony tomorrow."

"Nah, Chid alone deserves every moment he gets in the spotlight for all that brainiac work. Plus I used up all my vacation time for this lovely outing."

Nora pulled back from him, studying him with a confused frown. "What?"

Ben shrugged. As if for emphasis, the violin music overhead ceased and the two were left in total silence.

"What?" Nora asked again.

"I don't work in domestic terror. Or hostage rescue or any of that fun stuff. On what basis can I show up here?"

"Ummm . . . collegiality?" she ventured.

He shook his head. "Schacht and I exchanged words over it. So. You know. You know Schacht, the stickler. I said I wanted to come, he said he wasn't running a dating service or some damn thing. So we cut a deal."

He picked up his suitcase and headed out toward the street.

Nora followed, barefoot. "What kind of deal?"

"I come on my own time and on my own dime. I can volunteer my time to help out. At my own risk, of course."

Nora stared at him, dumbfounded. "I—you did that for me?"

He stopped walking and turned around to let her catch him. "Nora," he said, looking away, almost blushing, then looking back at her, his eyes clear. "Come on. It's *you*."

She leaned in and kissed him then, hard, on the lips. "I'm pretty sure I'm in love with you, Ben Calder."

"Well it's about time you caught up, Nora Khalil." He kissed her forehead, her eyelids, her nose.

"Ben . . . we're . . . in public . . ." she whispered, not fully committed to caring about that.

"Erie will survive. Erie is resilient."

Nora laughed. *"Erie will flourish again!"*

"It will indeed. Right after it comes to terms with the evil legacies of its beer tycoons."

Nora grinned. "I warned them about the perils of alcohol. After all that, Pete told me he wouldn't rest until he got me to try his fascist beer."

Ben smiled, tucking the usual loose tendril of hair behind Nora's ear. "Let me know how that battle goes."

"I'm not worried." She tilted her head, regarding him. "You'll be back at Labor Day?"

"Yes," he said, unlocking the SUV and getting in. "I promise."

He kissed her again and started the engine. She watched the car until it turned right onto State Street and headed for the Bayfront Parkway.

She sighed. With Ben's departure she felt like the last vestiges of adrenaline had left her body. She walked back to the house, her bare feet padding on the concrete walkway. She realized she had never had a walkway that needed to be swept before. Maybe she would look for a broom and sweep.

Or maybe she would sit in her sweatpants and tank top and watch Netflix.

Yes.

She turned to lock the door when it was shoved open with unbelievable force, sending her flying.

Nora's head slammed against the mirrored coat closet in the foyer. The mirror shattered as Nora sank to the ground, stunned. Her eyes wouldn't focus, no matter how hard she tried. She reached out to get her bearings but was picked up bodily and tossed face forward onto her living room floor.

She pulled herself onto all fours just in time to have her arm yanked up behind her. She cried out as she heard it snap.

"Did you really think that you could put a stop to a *movement*?" Goatee was demanding. He bent over her and picked her up, crushing the broken arm against her body and making her cry out again. Blood was dripping down the back of her neck.

"Those men are two of liberty's finest patriots!"

Nora couldn't speak. The pain in her arm was so intense that she felt faint, and her head injury had made her so dizzy. White light crowded in on her vision.

"I told him. I said no code-solving was gonna make you people deserve mercy."

She looked into his icy eyes, trying to convey her own request for mercy when suddenly a rustling sound behind Goatee gave way to a shriek as someone pounced on him from behind.

At first his massive head blocked Nora's view, but then she saw who was clinging to him. It was Rachel. *Rachel.* Rachel had a wire and she had wrapped it hard around Goatee's neck and she was holding on for dear life. Goatee was clawing at his neck, gasping. Rivulets of blood were erupting out of his neck as the wire dug deeper and deeper into his flesh.

Rachel met her eyes. As Nora sank to the floor, her eyes fighting to stay focused, she saw that tears were streaking down Rachel's face, but still she was holding on to the wire with a ferocious expression.

That look was the last thing Nora saw before losing consciousness.

"You've got to be kidding me!" she heard someone say. This was followed by a loud laugh.

She realized it was Peter. She tried to remember what she'd said that was so funny, but couldn't think of anything.

Suddenly, though, she heard another voice laughing as well. She tried hard to place it and couldn't.

She decided to open her eyes in order to see who could possibly be laughing so much. And why were they in her house?

She opened her eyes and peered around. "Oh, my God. Hamot Hospital again?"

Both Pete and Rachel immediately appeared in her line of vision.

And then everything came back to her. "Rachel! Rachel!" Nora rasped. "Pete, Rachel killed a guy in my house."

"Yeah," said Pete. "That guy broke your arm and had the hospital staff pulling glass out of your scalp for about an hour."

Nora winced. "Hence the pain I'm in right now."

He nodded. "Hence the pain you're in right now. And the concussion, so you have to take it easy for awhile. Also I think you destroyed the living room rug by bleeding on it. Don't count on getting the deposit back."

Nora smiled lopsidedly.

"I take it," Pete said, "that this guy was the guy who killed Will Martin?"

Nora was nodding, trying not to talk too much.

"Loose ends tied up, then."

"Loose ends tied up." Nora looked over at Rachel. Her normally pallid cheeks were flushed. "Rachel, are you hurt? You're okay?"

She grinned down at Nora, then held up bandaged hands. "Hands a little sliced up but I'm just fine. You think I'm not as tough as you, Nora Khalil? That you can waltz in and kill my bad guys and I can't do the same for you?"

Nora shook her head, very slowly, aware that the back of her head had been wrapped in something. "No way. I'd never underestimate you, girl. But . . . well, maybe you need a handgun or something? What did you have there?"

Rachel was laughing. "I was just about to replace the string I'd broken when I heard the commotion. And no, I will never own a handgun, although I'd agree our neighborhood is maybe a little too rough."

Nora blinked at her. "A violin string. You killed a crazed white supremacist militia guy with a violin string?"

She shrugged. "As the great Woody Guthrie said . . ." she began.

Pete joined in, ". . . *This machine kills fascists!*"

The two began laughing again, and Nora found she loved the sound of their combined laughter.

"Of course I'm probably going to need several years of therapy to recover . . ." Rachel added soberly.

Pete did not miss a beat before saying, "You know, I've had a few near-death experiences myself lately. Perhaps we could counsel each other, Miss Rachel."

"What did I say?" Nora said to Pete. "Didn't I say you'd like Rachel?"

Rachel looked from Nora to Pete, blushing furiously. "You said that about me?"

"I did," confirmed Nora.

"Well," said Rachel, averting her gaze from Peter and giving Nora a smile. "I suppose you should give me some background on Pete then . . . while he calls to tell your boyfriend you're conscious."

Nora nodded, smiling, fingertips gently brushing her friend's bandaged hand. "All you need to know is that he's a huge fan of the opera. . . ."

POSTSCRIPT

Erie, Pennsylvania, is home to more than ten thousand refugees, fully 10 percent of its population. They have come from Bhutan, Bosnia, Somalia, the Congo, Iraq, Sudan, and, yes, Syria. My students and I have had the honor of getting to meet some of them and to record their stories through Gannon's refugee oral history project. The people we have met, and the experiences we have heard about, and the lives that have been built here—out of grief, out of nothing but sheer will—bear no relationship to the discourse wielded like a blunt instrument in this most recent presidential campaign. Erie was a stop on that campaign's bitter trail, and along with so many, including the feisty Benedictine sisters, we brought our signs to protest. Ultimately we snuck in to listen firsthand. The candidate told a poisonous tale in which refugees—all refugees—were compared to a frozen, half-dead snake. The heroine in the tale took in and nursed that snake back to life. The snake then bit her and killed her.

I was grieved not so much by the tale itself but by the wild applause with which it—and the message that America needs to be purged—was met.

There are many organizations that serve refugees in our communities. I hope that you will consider becoming involved. Donations are one thing, but how much better to tutor, to mentor, to share meals, to learn someone else's story and find in it the human connections that bind us to each other? In the years that come, we will need to care for each other more, be gentler,

more patient, more alert to infringements on our human rights—
the better to weather the storm together.

The United Nations High Commission for Refugees: www.unhcr
.org/en-us

Office of Refugee Resettlement: www.acf.hhs.gov/orr

Catholic Charities: www.cccas.org/refugee-resettlement/

ACKNOWLEDGMENTS

As always, my daughters suffered the brunt of my wild-eyed, still-in-her-jammies, what-day-is-it attempt to write another book. I thank Matt Baugh, Mariana Syrotiak, and Brian Kimberling for reading early versions, but above all Laurie Hitt for reading it with ferocity and marking it all up.

I grew up in a Wagner-free household. My grandmother adored Italian opera, and my mother passed that on to me. Wagner, linked forever with Nazism, was persona non grata.

Geoff Grundy changed that. He gave me his CD of Nina Stemme and Plácido Domingo in *Tristan and Isolde*. I hadn't needed another reason to fall in love with him, but it sealed the deal. I remember sitting on a plane, my earbuds a-swell with it—and weeping, to the alarm of my seatmate. I am, for this and for so much else, in his debt.

ABOUT THE AUTHOR

Carolyn Baugh lives with her daughters at the edge of a cornfield on Lake Erie—one of the most beautiful places in the world. She received her master's and doctorate in Arabic and Islamic Studies from the University of Pennsylvania. Her book *Minor Marriage in Early Islamic Law* is forthcoming from Brill, while her translation from Arabic of Ibn Khaldun's fourteenth-century treatise on Sufism will be published by New York University Press. She teaches history and Arabic at Gannon University. At any given moment, she wishes she were home playing the piano, reading Hilary Mantel, or walking on the beach with Carmen the dog.